THE WALL IN MY HEAD

THE WALL IN MY HEAD

Words and Images from the Fall of the Iron Curtain

A Words without Borders Anthology

OPEN LETTER
LITERARY TRANSLATIONS FROM THE UNIVERSITY OF ROCHESTER

Permissions acknowledgments for all words and images
can be found in the back of this volume.

This anthology was made possible thanks to a charitable
contribution from Amazon.com

amazon.com

Library of Congress Cataloging-in-Publication Data:

The Wall in my head : words and images from the fall of the Iron Curtain :
a Words without borders anthology. — 1st ed.
p. cm.
ISBN-13: 978-1-934824-23-8 (pbk. : alk. paper)
ISBN-10: 1-934824-23-2 (pbk. : alk. paper)
1. Berlin Wall, Berlin, Germany, 1961-1989—Literary collections. 2. Post-communism—Europe—
Literary collections. 3. European literature—20th century—Translations into English. 4. European
literature—21st century—Translations into English. I. Words without borders.
PN6071.B423W36 2009
808.8'0358431552087—dc22

2009036760

Printed on acid-free paper in the United States of America.

Text set in Caslon, a family of serif typefaces based on the designs of William Caslon (1692-1766).
Layout by N. J. Furl.
Interior design template by Chris Welch.

Open Letter is the University of Rochester's nonprofit, literary translation press:
Lattimore Hall 411, Box 270082, Rochester, NY 14627

www.openletterbooks.org

ACKNOWLEDGMENTS

FROM WORDS WITHOUT BORDERS

The content and shape of this book owe a great deal to its contributors and to the well-wishers and advisers who have aided in its progress. We would like to thank the following people for their inestimable help in various quarters: Bill Martin, Philip Boehm, Susan Bernofsky, Steven Rendall, and Drenka Willen for all their advice and suggestions. Alex Zucker and Anderson Tepper for their tremendous aid in all matters relating to Czech literature and 1989; similarly, deep thanks to Paul Wilson, Viktor Stoilov, and Erik Tabery for their insight and help. Special thanks is owed to Milan Kundera and to Vera Kundera for all their gracious assistance. Our gratitude to Judith Sollosy for surveying the ground in Hungary and for identifying visual art for the book. Our deepest appreciation for all the kindnesses extended us by Katarzyna Herbert and Alissa Valles. The art, documents, and reports in the book are the result of painstaking work by art editor Gemma Bentley and could not have been collected without the help of the following people: Csaba Szilagyi at OSA Archivum in Hungary, who proved a font of inspiration and whose organization archives and actively interprets historical records, underground publications, and political ephemera from the period of the Cold War and its aftermath; Robin Randisi for her many hours in studio time spent photographing art for the book; John Cunningham at the Society for Co-operation in Russian and Soviet Studies; and most heartfelt thanks to Walter Gaudnek, István Orosz, and Brian Rose who all donated samples of their art for use in the book. Thanks to Alane Mason for the germ of this idea and for being its most ardent supporter and to Will Lippincott for backing the book so passionately and shepherding it through to its perfect home at Open Letter Books from its humble beginnings. And finally, our admiration for the incredible work of Chad W. Post, Nathan Furl, and E.J. Van Lanen at Open Letter and our thanks for their unflagging support, resourcefulness, and untiring commitment to this project.

Rohan Kamicheril   *Sal Robinson*

Introduction

BY KEITH GESSEN

n the mid-to-late 1990s, while living mostly in Moscow, I managed to travel through a good part of the former Soviet Bloc. It was a surprising experience after reading so many articles in the press about the supposedly uniform "consequences of decades of Communism." In fact, while the Russians weren't adjusting very well—or, as Dubravka Ugresic points out here, some Russians were adjusting much too well—to the new conditions, and Ukrainians were adjusting slowly, and cautiously, to not being Russian, everyone else simply went back to what they'd been doing for the past 500 years. Romanians seemed stuck in the middle ages (there were horse-drawn buggies on the road), and everyone was drunk (the horses knew where they were going), and there was a kind of elemental menace and ruin and beauty to the place. Prague really was lovely, no matter how many people came to see it, but the Czech Republic seemed hard-pressed to know what to do with its independence (except get more of it, by breaking up with Slovakia). Meanwhile Budapest, a few hours away, was already easily on its way (with the help of Hungarian native George Soros) to replacing Vienna as the intellectual capital of Central Europe. Interestingly the Poles, perhaps the most fervent and certainly the longest-serving Russia-haters in Europe, had ended up in Warsaw with the most Soviet capital city in the former

Bloc. In Tallinn, Russian teenagers roamed the streets starting fights with Estonians, but there was no question of their leaving that gem-like little Baltic town. It was, in other words, an entire multifarious universe, most of whose inhabitants were pretty sure the Soviet period was just a blip in the much longer historical process their countries were destined for.

A decade later, in these essays and stories from the post-Soviet period from all across the former Soviet Bloc, you can see that universe created all over again—though you can also see it more clearly. Some of these countries are well on their way to integrating with Europe; they write about the Communist period as something bad that happened, even something very bad, but it was something that happened *to* them and now it's over. These places—Poland, Hungary, the Czech Republic—have moved comfortably into post-history. Or so—as we see in Péter Esterházy's remarkable confession on page 136—they'd like to think.

But there are other places where everyone knows that history is not yet done. You would not get the sense, from Mircea Cărtărescu's scabrous story of a young man (though not as young as he would have liked) finally losing his virginity, that Romania has turned into a pleasant model of European normality, and you'd be right. You *might* get that sense about Russia from Vladimir Sorokin's charming essay about standing in line in Soviet times, but you'd be wrong. The account of the troubles of post-Soviet Georgia in Irakli Iosebashvili's authoritatively titled story, "The Life and Times of a Soviet Capitalist," tells you a lot about what's going on in Georgia now, when the streets are once again filled with protesters demanding the ouster of their crazy president.

∞∞∞∞

The post-Soviet period, the period covered so well in this book, is over. You can tell it's over because no one wants to hear anymore about how terrible Communism was. Russians sure don't, and not just because Communism was all their fault. For them, rather, talk of how terrible Communism was is associated with the Russian 1990s, when it was cover for abandoning millions of people to simply die. Communism was bad but starving was also bad. And so is the Putin regime bad, a mixture of Communist control of the political sphere with integration into world markets—the worst or best of both worlds, depending on where you sit.

Intellectually and politically, the post-Soviet period was about settling accounts with the Soviet past. Different countries did this in different ways: almost all of the countries in Eastern Europe (but, of the former Soviet republics, only the Baltic states) adopted limited lustration, with the Czechs and the Germans taking it the most seriously; the Russians, who couldn't possibly have done this, settled for years of anti-Communist rhetoric from their leaders, and an ironic attitude to some of the excesses of the Soviet regime, which persists even in the neo-Soviet present. But the best pieces in this book suggest how difficult settling accounts really is, in the end. There is a great moment in Mircea Cărtărescu's story where, after the trial and execution of the dictator Ceaușescu and his elderly wife (now available, like Saddam's execution, on YouTube) and the fall of the regime, an old friend comes to ask for help despite having worked for the regime—"I began to moralize like an idiot," says the narrator. "I expected her to look down, [put] her chin to her chest and weep in expiation, but suddenly she threw me a proud and ironic look . . . It was as though a great dark power remained underneath the desperation of her circumstances." We know now how thoroughly naive it was to think that the people who'd held power for so long, not out of conviction, anymore, but purely out of cynicism, would simply disappear—that the great dark power they'd wielded would not remain in their hands, to be used again when the time was right.

∞∞∞

This is a fascinating and useful book. There are some old masters working at the top of their form here, and you can spot them from approximately the first sentence, but there are also some writers who are young and unheard of outside the cities where they live. The collection is full of curious cross-border exchanges: Wladimir Kaminer is a Russian-born writer living in Germany, writing a story in German (but in the spirit of Victor Pelevin) about a fake Paris built in Kazakhstan by the Soviets; Cărtărescu is a Romanian who in "Nabokov in Brasov" has written a story that reminds me of nothing so much as Milan Kundera's great first novel, *The Joke*, about the ways in which sex and memory are more powerful than Communism (and anti-Communism)—though not at all in the way that one would like. This collection has Poles traveling to Vienna, Georgians to Moscow, East Berliners to West Berlin, capturing one of the essential novelties of the post-Soviet period: the sudden access to everywhere else, including the East. For a few years there it seemed like the entire continent was in motion, back and forth, and not just because they had a meeting at the European Parliament in Brussels—or, later, at the International Tribunal for War Crimes in The Hague.

Because there was one place you didn't go in those years, and that was the former Yugoslavia. The nasty civil wars that everyone kept claiming hadn't happened in the post-Soviet space were, in fact, happening—in Azerbaijan, Tajikistan, Georgia, Chechnya, and, of course, Afghanistan. That was something people expected. What no one expected, as Muharem Bazdulj writes in the remarkable memoir that concludes this collection, was that the most cosmopolitan, open, and least Soviet country in the entire Soviet Bloc would end up suffering the greatest amount of damage once the Bloc collapsed. "So go fuck yourselves, Nineties!" was, he tells us, the refrain from a popular Yugoslav rock song of a few years ago. That would be an alternate title for this collection. The wall, you know, wasn't entirely inside your head.

THE WALL IN MY HEAD

From *The Art of the Novel*

BY MILAN KUNDERA

(TRANSLATION BY LINDA ASHER)

Poets don't invent poems
The poem is somewhere behind
It's been there for a long long time
The poet merely discovers it.
— Jan Skacel

I.

In one of his books, my friend Josef Škvorecký tells this true story:

An engineer from Prague is invited to a professional conference in London. So he goes, takes part in the proceedings, and returns to Prague. Some hours after his return, sitting in his office, he picks up *Rude Pravo*—the official daily paper of the Party—and reads: A Czech engineer, attending a conference in London, has made a slanderous statement about his socialist homeland to the Western press and has decided to stay in the West.

Illegal emigration combined with a statement of that kind is no trifle. It would be worth twenty years in prison. Our engineer can't believe his eyes. But there's no doubt about it, the article refers to him. His secretary, coming into his office, is shocked to see him: My God, she says, you're back! I don't understand—did you see what they wrote about you?

The engineer sees fear in his secretary's eyes. What can he do? He rushes to the *Rude Pravo* office. He finds the editor responsible for the story. The editor apologizes; yes, it really is an awkward business, but he, the editor, has

3

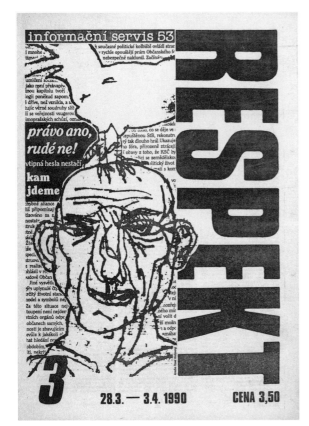

nothing to do with it, he got the text of the article direct from the Ministry of the Interior.

So the engineer goes off to the Ministry. There they say yes, of course, it's all a mistake, but they, the Ministry, have nothing to do with it, they got the report on the engineer from the intelligence people at the London embassy. The engineer asks for a retraction. No, he's told, they never retract, but nothing can happen to him, he has nothing to worry about.

But the engineer does worry. He soon realizes that all of sudden he's being closely watched, that his telephone is being tapped, and that he's being followed in the street. He sleeps poorly and has nightmares until, unable to bear the pressure any longer, he takes a lot of real risk to leave the country illegally. And so he actually becomes an émigré.

2.

The story I've just told is one that we would immediately call *Kafkan*. The term, drawn from an artist's work, determined solely by a novelist's images, stands as the only common denominator in situations (literary or real) that no other word allows us to grasp and to which neither political nor social nor psychological theory gives us any key.

But what is *Kafkan*?

Let's try to describe some of its aspects:

One:

The engineer is confronted by a power that has the character of a *boundless labyrinth*. He can never get to the end of its interminable corridors and will never succeed in finding out who issued the fateful verdict. He is therefore in the same situation as Joseph K. before the Court, or the Land-Surveyor K. before the Castle. All three are in a world that is nothing but a single, huge, labyrinthine institution they cannot escape and cannot understand.

Novelists before Kafka often exposed institutions as arenas where conflicts between different personal and public interests were played out. In Kafka the institution is a mechanism that obeys its own laws; no one knows now who programmed those laws or when; they have nothing to do with human concerns and are thus unintelligible.

Two:

In Chapter Five of *The Castle*, the village Mayor explains in detail to K. the long history of his file. Briefly: Years earlier, a proposal to engage a land-surveyor came down to the village from the Castle. The Mayor wrote a negative response (there was no need for any land-surveyor), but his reply went astray to the wrong office, and so after an intricate series of bureaucratic misunderstandings, stretching over many years, the job offer was inadvertently sent to K., at the very moment when all the offices involved were in the process of canceling the old obsolete proposal. After a long journey, K. thus arrived in the village by mistake. Still more: Given that for him there is no possible world other than the Castle and its village, his *entire* existence is a mistake.

In the *Kafkan* world, the file takes on the role of a Platonic idea. It represents true reality, whereas man's physical existence is only a shadow cast on the screen of illusion. Indeed, both the Land-Surveyor K. and the Prague engineer are but the shadows of their file cards; and they are even much less than that: they are the shadows of a *mistake* in the file, shadows without even the right to exist as shadows.

But if man's life is only a shadow and true reality lies elsewhere, in the inaccessible, in the inhuman or the suprahuman, then we suddenly enter the domain of theology. Indeed, Kafka's first commentators explained his novels as religious parables.

Such an interpretation seems to me wrong (because it sees allegory where Kafka grasped concrete situations of human life) but also revealing: wherever power deifies itself, it automatically produces its own theology; wherever it behaves like God, it awakens religious feelings toward itself; such a world can be described in theological terms.

Kafka did not write religious allegories, but the *Kafkan* (both in reality and in fiction) is inseparable from its theological (or rather: *pseudotheological*) dimension.

**"LAW YES,
RED NO!"**
Respekt, no. 3.
Informační servis, no. 53.
March 28–April 3, 1990.
(opposite page,
credit: *Respekt*)

**"10 YEARS
OF SOLIDARITY"**

Respekt, no. 25.

Aug. 29–Sept. 5, 1990.

(opposite page,

credit: *Respekt*)

Three:

Raskolnikov cannot bear the weight of his guilt, and to find peace he consents to his punishment of his own free will. It's the well-known situation where *the offense seeks the punishment.*

In Kafka, the logic is reversed. The person punished does not know the reason for the punishment. The absurdity of the punishment is so unbearable that to find peace the accused needs to find a justification for his penalty: *the punishment seeks the offense.*

The Prague engineer is punished by intensive police surveillance. This punishment demands the crime that was not committed, and the engineer accused of emigrating ends up emigrating in fact. *The punishment has finally found the offense.*

Not knowing what the charges against him are, K. decides, in Chapter Seven of *The Trial*, to examine his whole life, his entire past "down to the smallest details." The "autoculpabilization" machine goes into motion. *The accused seeks his offense.*

One day, Amalia receives an obscene letter from a Castle official. Outraged, she tears it up. The Castle doesn't even need to criticize Amalia's rash behavior. Fear (the same fear our engineer saw in his secretary's eyes) acts all by itself. With no order, no perceptible sign from the Castle, everyone avoids Amalia's family like the plague.

Amalia's father tries to defend his family. But there is a problem: Not only is the source of the verdict impossible to find, but the verdict itself does not exist! To appeal, to request a pardon, you have to be convicted first! The father begs the Castle to proclaim the crime. So it's not enough to say that the punishment seeks the offense. In this pseudotheological world, *the punished beg for recognition of their guilt!*

It often happens in Prague nowadays that someone fallen into disgrace cannot find even the most menial job. In vain he asks for certification of the fact that he has committed an offense and that his employment is forbidden. The verdict is nowhere to be found. And since in Prague work is a duty laid down by law, he ends up being charged with parasitism; that means he is guilty of avoiding work. *The punishment finds the offense.*

Four:

The tale of the Prague engineer is in the nature of a funny story, a joke: it provokes laughter.

Two gentlemen, perfectly ordinary fellows (not "inspectors," as in the French translation), surprise Joseph K. in bed one morning, tell him he is under arrest, and eat up his breakfast. K. is a well-disciplined civil servant: instead of throwing the men out of his flat, he stands in his nightshirt and gives a lengthy self-defense. When Kafka read the first chapter of *The Trial* to his friends, everyone laughed, including the author.

Philip Roth's imagined film version of *The Castle*: Groucho Marx plays the Land-Surveyor K., with Chico and Harpo as the two assistants. Yes. Roth is quite right: The comic is inseparable from the very essence of the *Kafkan*.

But it's small comfort to the engineer to know that his story is comic. He is trapped in the joke of his own life like a fish in a bowl; he doesn't find it funny. Indeed, a joke is a joke only if you're outside the bowl; by contrast the *Kafkan* takes us inside, into the guts of a joke, into the *horror of the comic*.

In the world of the *Kafkan*, the comic is not a counterpoint to the tragic (the tragi-comic) as in Shakespeare; it's not there to make the tragic more bearable by lightening the tone; it doesn't *accompany* the tragic, not at all, it *destroys it in the egg* and thus deprives the victims of the only consolation they could

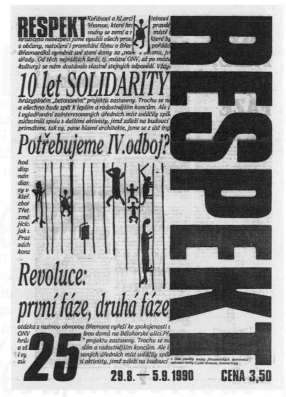

hope for: the consolation to be found in the (real or supposed) grandeur of tragedy. The engineer loses his homeland, and everyone laughs.

Paris Lost

BY WLADIMIR KAMINER
(TRANSLATION BY LIESL SCHILLINGER)

One evening [my Uncle Boris] told me about his trip to Paris. This was when his wife was still living. He was working in his business, and despite his rehabilitation, and twelve years' hard labor, he didn't dare dream of such a trip. But at the beginning of the seventies, it suddenly became a reality. Back then, every child knew that our Socialist Fatherland was beloved by all the peoples of the world, and only imperialist governments were against us. They spread lies about our daily life behind the Iron Curtain, and tried to make us look like warmongers. But we were for freedom and understanding among peoples. Besides, our government was very generous with its citizens; it couldn't be compared to an imperialist regime. And so, each year a hundred of the best proletarians were singled out—laborers, construction workers, army officers, miners or mothers with numerous offspring: they all were given a (nearly) free trip to Paris, sometimes even a trip to London, too. Naturally, on the condition that all the candidates were members of the Party.

The chosen had to agree to undergo a few routine health checks, and receive instruction from the security organs on how to conduct themselves abroad. They had to sign documents stating that they would keep to themselves everything that they saw in Paris or London. And then they could exchange two hundred rubles into foreign currency and prepare for their departure. There was only one catch. Naturally, the government could not actually send its people to France or, even worse, England. The Soviet workers would be unable to resist the temptations of the capitalist world. Besides, the evil imperialists were lying in wait just for Soviet citizens to show themselves abroad, and had different traps and provocations prepared for them, in order to be able to spread even more lies about our country. And so, such trips could exact a huge financial cost on the state treasury.

Thus, the government hit on a comparatively economical, if less exciting solution: it was to build their own "Abroad" in the Steppes of southern Russia, near Stavropol, with a real city, and many inhabitants. It served in the summer as Paris, and later, in the fall, when it began to rain and the clouds appeared, after a quick overhaul, it became London. The project had top secret status, only employees of the state security agency lived and worked there with their families. They were specially trained; in summer, they were required to speak only French among themselves and in the fall, only English.

The season began in June. The tourists would be picked up from "Orly" or "Heathrow" airport by bus and driven to hotels. In small groups, led by two travel guides, they would explore the clean-swept streets of the foreign country, buy pretty sweaters and unknown types of cheese, stare at the foreign cars that drove up and down the street, and laugh at the Eiffel Tower or Big Ben, which did not compare to Soviet monumental art. But on the whole, they found Abroad pretty neat. It was nothing special, but they weren't disappointed, either. The food in the hotel tasted strangely foreign, and the native French or English people, who were mostly unemployed, sat in their cafés all the time drinking vodka with beer, naturally not in the huge quantities we had back home, but in tiny little glasses. They greeted the Soviet tourists very kindly, and almost every one of these unemployed foreigners understood a few Russian phrases. After three or four days, the Russians flew back to their families.

My uncle really wasn't ever supposed to see this Paris because of his past, but back then there were no computers, and even the sharpest state apparatus makes a mistake every now and then. When Uncle Boris was honored a second time for his excellent work in the rubber business, he was given a three-day trip to Paris. The news spread quickly, and all the neighbors came to say goodbye. Euphorically they made up lists of presents that they wanted Uncle Boris to bring back from Paris. He himself had only one wish, which sounded very childlike: to get "drunk as a lord" on the Eiffel Tower. Everybody laughed about his dream.

Boris took a bag of Soviet canned food with him, and a Russian-French dictionary. The flight to Paris lasted six hours. The first two days, my uncle tried to get away from his group. Every time they gathered below in the Hotel lobby, Uncle Boris went to the bathroom and sat there as long as he could, in the hope that the group would go into town without him. But when he'd come out they'd all be standing by the bathroom, waiting patiently for him. After that, they drove together in the bus to the center, to go shopping.

On the third day, Uncle Boris finally lucked out. While the group was browsing in a sweatshirt shop, and the tour directors had briefly lost sight of them, a bus stopped directly in front of the store. Without pausing for long, Uncle Boris jumped on. The bus was almost empty except for a pair of crumpled Frenchmen. A bottle of vodka and a phrasebook were in my uncle's pants pocket. Now he only had to find the Eiffel Tower.

The bus driver looked at him in a friendly way. "Salut, Russo turisto!" he greeted him. My uncle thought to himself, I've seen that man once before, someplace, this plump, eyebrowless face, and this grin.

"Were you ever in Kazakhstan?" my uncle held up his phrasebook: "*D'où êtes vous? Kazakhstan?*"

"No," said the bus driver. "*Je suis de Marseille, comprenez-moi?*"

"I've seen you before," my uncle said again, but on the quick he couldn't find the words.

"*Est-ce que nous allons passer devant la Tour Eiffel?*"

"*Bien entendu,*" said the bus driver, and grinned again. The Frenchmen on the bus all began to smirk. Out the window, Uncle Boris caught a glimpse of the Eiffel Tower.

"Stop here," he called out to the bus driver. "I'm getting out here, *merci pour tout et bon voyage.*"

"Take care of yourself, Grandpa," murmured the bus driver, and put on the brakes.

My uncle jumped out of the bus. In front of him was a typical Parisian street: French coffee drinkers sat in two small bars, housewives did their shopping, a grandmother pushed a stroller in front of her. Through an open window, you could hear music. Suddenly a man stuck his head out the window and called out something in loud French. The whole street got up and started to walk quickly toward the Eiffel Tower. The first tourist buses were arriving. And a tour guide from my uncle's group was there. He ran to him, out of breath and grabbed him by the sleeve. "What shit are you pulling? Where were you trying to go?" His voice was high with agitation.

"Nowhere," Uncle Boris responded. At once, he knew where he'd seen the bus driver. It was the guy who used to drive him to work every morning, twenty years earlier, when he was still a rubber plant director, living in a dugout. The group flew back to Kazakhstan that same day, and Uncle Boris drank his vodka not on the Eiffel Tower, but in his hotel room, along with the pair of worthy workers that he had shared the room with, and a woman with numerous offspring, who had happened to drop by.

"It may be that I've missed out on a lot in my life, that I was in the wrong place at the wrong time and that I was unjustly sentenced, but all the same— I was in Paris. And that experience I'll take with me to the grave," Uncle Boris told me proudly and laughed. At the time, his story seemed absolutely unbelievable to me.

Years later, after Perestroika, as ever more unbelievable stories out of the dark past of the country came into the open, I had to change my opinion. I read the reports from eyewitnesses of people who had built "Paris" and lived there for years. Also, many novels and stories had been written about it. So I arrived at the conviction that my Uncle Boris had told me the truth after all. His Paris was a chimerical city, erected as a kind of ideological condom to protect the population from the tainted charms of Western civilization. Such methods work, but they never last; the truth comes to light sooner or later.

The Russian Paris lasted no longer than five years. During a trip through Russia at the end of the seventies, a clever Dutch journalist came across a pair of photos that a young dairymaid in a kolkhoz showed him: there she stood with her mother, a worthy dairymaid of the Soviet Union, under the Eiffel Tower, and smiled at the camera. To the Dutchman, the Eiffel Tower in the photos had a strikingly Socialist air. He put the young, naïve woman under pressure, and in the end convinced her to accept his valuable, but on a dairy farm totally useless, dictation machine, in exchange for her photos. The Dutchman vaunted the machine as a "foreign speaking machine, a true wonder of technology" and practically ripped the photos of the Eiffel Tower out of the girl's hand.

One of them turned up a few months later in the features section of a Dutch newspaper. At first nobody in the West took the story of the picture seriously, everyone thought the whole thing was a joke. But the then head of the KGB, Andropov, did not find the photo in the foreign newspaper funny at all. He ordered "Project Paris" to be torn down to the last stone in the shortest time possible. Many construction worker brigades from the congress and the Interior Ministry participated in the destruction of the French capital. It had to go down quickly, almost overnight.

According to reports of eyewitnesses, the KGB needed more money for the planning of the destruction of Paris then had been needed earlier for the building of the city. Beyond that, as a consequence of the hastiness of the demolition work, many valuable objects were lost. The whole Parisian infrastructure ended up by the roadside: among other things, more than five hundred Philips televisions, several hundred refrigerators, a few cars, and countless doors and windows. In spite of strong controls, entire houses disappeared this way: "It was stolen," was the refrain. The heads of the KGB followed the thieves, but not far; they just wanted their Paris buried and the history to be forgotten as quickly as possible.

Afterward, the fall of the city had a rather positive influence on the architecture of many villages in the southern Russian steppes. Travelers still marvel at the chic glass doors and unusually wide windows on one pigsty or another. Even ten years on, a four-meter-long broken Big Ben with its hour hands snapped off still lay in a bend in the road of the city Inosemzevo. The natives consider it one of the best sights to see in the area. They have no idea where the thing came from, but the giant clock has come to be called "Monument to Lost Time."

From *Omon Ra*

BY VICTOR PELEVIN
(TRANSLATION BY ANDREW BROMFIELD)

YURI
GAGARIN
(credit: SCR
Photo Library)

he first time in my life I drank wine was during the winter when I was fourteen. It was in a garage that Mitiok took me to—his brother, a pensive, long-haired type who had tricked his way out of army service, worked there as a watchman. The garage was on a large fenced-off lot stacked with concrete slabs, and Mitiok and I spent quite a long time clambering over them, sometimes ending up in astonishing places entirely screened off from the rest of reality that were like the compartments of a long-abandoned spaceship of which only the carcass was left, strangely resembling a heap of concrete slabs. What's more, the streetlamps beyond the crooked wooden fence burned with a mysterious and unearthly light and a few small stars hung in the pure empty sky—in short, if not for the empty bottles of cheap booze and the frozen streams of urine, we would have been surrounded by cosmic space.

Mitiok suggested going in to warm ourselves up and we set off towards the ribbed aluminum hemisphere of the garage, which also had something cosmic about it. Inside, it was dark: we could make out the dim forms of cars that smelt of petrol. In the corner was a planking hut with a glazed window, built up against the wall: there was a light on inside it. Mitiok and

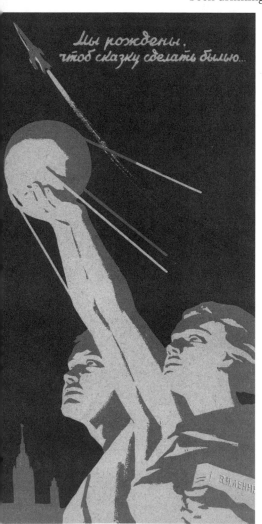

Мы рождены,
чтоб сказку сделать былью...

= В.И.ЛЕНИН

I squeezed our way inside, sat down on a narrow, uncomfortable bench, and silently drank our fill of tea from a battered tin saucepan. Mitiok's brother was smoking long hand-rolled cigarettes with cardboard roaches, and looking through an old issue of *Young Technology* magazine, and he didn't acknowledge our presence at all. Mitiok pulled a bottle out from under the bench, smacked it down onto the cement floor, and asked, "Want some?"

I nodded, although I felt uneasy about it. Mitiok filled the glass I'd just been drinking tea from right up to the brim with a dark-red liquid and held it out to me. As though I was trying to get the hang of some new procedure, I grasped the glass, raised it to my mouth, and drank, amazed at how little effort was required to do something for the first time. While Mitiok and his brother finished off the rest, I paid close attention to my own sensations, but there was nothing happening to me. I picked up the magazine that had been put down, opened it at random, and was faced with a double spread of drawings of flying machines whose names you were supposed to guess. I liked one better than the others—it was an American aeroplane with wings that could function as a rotor during takeoff—and there was a small rocket with a cabin for the pilot, but I didn't get a proper look at that, because without saying a word or even raising his eyes, Mitiok's brother grabbed the magazine out of my hands. In order not to show I was offended, I moved over and sat at the table, on which a glass jar with a water-heating element protruding from it stood among shriveling pieces of cheap salami.

I suddenly felt disgusted to think that I was sitting in this lousy little closet that smelt like a garbage dump, disgusted by the fact that I'd just drunk cheap port from a dirty glass, that the entire immense country in which I lived was made up of lots and lots of these lousy little closets where there was a smell of garbage and people had just been drinking cheap port, and most important of all—it was painful to think that these very same stinking little closets were the settings for those multi-colored arrays of light that made me catch my breath in the evenings when I happened to look out of some window set high above the twilit capital. And it all seemed particularly painful in comparison with the beautiful American flying machine in the magazine.

I lowered my eyes to the newspaper which was spread over the table—it was a mass of grease spots, holes burned by cigarette butts, and ring marks left by glasses and saucers. The headlines were strangely frightening with an inhuman cheerfulness and power: it had been a long time since anyone had stood in their way, but still they went on beating at the empty air, and if you were drunk (and I noticed that I already was, but I didn't attach any importance to it), you could easily just happen to be in the wrong place and get your loitering soul crushed under some MAJOR OBJECTIVE OF THE CURRENT PLAN or some GREETING FROM THE COTTON HARVESTERS. The room around me was suddenly totally strange; Mitiok was watching me carefully. He caught my eye, winked, and, with a tongue that moved thickly, he asked: "What about it, we gonna fly to the moon?"

I nodded, and my eyes came to rest on a small column titled NEWS FROM ORBIT! The bottom of the text had been torn off and all that was left of the column were the words "Twenty-eight days . . ." in bold type. But this was still enough—I understood immediately and closed my eyes: yes, it was true, perhaps the burrows in which our lives were spent really were dark and dirty, and perhaps we ourselves were well suited to these burrows, but in the blue sky above our heads, up above the thinly scattered stars, there were special, artificial points of gleaming light, creeping unhurriedly through the constellations, points created here in the land of the Soviets, among the vomit, empty bottles, and stench of tobacco smoke, points built here out of steel, semiconductors, and electricity, and now flying through space. And every one of us, even the blue-faced alcoholic we had passed on the way here, huddling like a toad in a snowdrift, even Mitiok's brother, and of course Mitiok and I—we all had our own little embassy up there in the cold pure blueness.

I ran outside and stood there for ages, swallowing my tears as I stared up at the blueish-yellow, improbably near orb of the moon in the transparent winter sky.

Petition

BY MIHÁLY KORNIS
(TRANSLATION BY IVAN SANDERS)

*D*ear Sirs,

With reference to your much-valued query concerning final judgment on requests respectfully submitted by the undersigned claimant (Reference No: 1909-1970, Mrs. Szalkay, clerk in charge), I hereby return the Claims Form together with a Supplementary Statement.

CLAIMS FORM
(issued in compliance with Official Decree No. 40, 1957 B.C.)

I. REQUEST

(a) I should like to be born on December 9, 1909 in Budapest.

(b) I should like my mother to be Regina Fekete (housewife) and my father to be Miksa Tábori (traveling salesman).

(In the event that you are unable to grant my request regarding the above-mentioned persons, I am open to other suggestions so long as honored parents will be recognizable as Mama and Papa.)

(c) I further request that my wife be Edit Kovács (payroll clerk) and my son, Pál Tábori (student). (See addendum to Item I (b); here the words "my wife" and "my son" are to be substituted for "Mama" and "Papa" respectively.

(d) In view of my desired date of death (see Item III), I renounce forever the joys of grandparenthood.

II. LENGTH OF STAY

I request 61 years 6 months 3 days 2 minutes and 17 seconds.
(*Note*: I have submitted similar requests to the proper authorities on a number of previous occasions—e.g. in 80 B.C., and more recently in 1241, 1514, 1526, 1711, 1849—but on each occasion, due to lack of space, my request was turned down. This is my seventh request. 61 years is not a long time; were I to succeed in gaining your favor, sirs, in this matter, I would certainly try and make the best of my brief sojourn.

III. PURPOSE

(a) I would like to complete six years of elementary school, four years of secondary school, and then take a few business courses. Afterward I wouldn't mind joining the firm of Haas & Son as a cashier, so that in 1939—with the consent of the authorities, of course—I might be able to open my own little dry goods store on Király utca, subsequently known as Mayakovsky utca. In 1940 I could realize a long-held dream and purchase a two-seat Fiat motor car.

(During the course of your deliberations please take into account that with said motor car I could take Mama to the market, though this she does not yet suspect.)

Total time used up on these activities (shop, car, provisions, cleansers, etc.): 3 years.

(b) Next I thought of a Second World War. Nazism, discrimination, persecution I will put up with; yellow star I will put on. My car and my shop I will hand over to the Hungarian Army and the Ministry of Commerce and Industry, Department of de-Judaization, respectively.

(I hereby request that if at all possible my parents will not be dispatched to the Mauthausen concentration camp. It looks as though I might be able to work out something for them at the Dohány utca ghetto.)

As for me, I would like to be drafted into a forced labor company, with all that that entails, slaps, duck walks included. I hope that in 1945 the Red Army's liberating operations will still find me alive (see Item II!); if so, I shall marry at once, start a family, and join the Hungarian Workers' Party.

(c) From 1945 to 1948 I shall be happy.

Total time spent (new shop, new car, provisions, cleansers, etc.): 3 years.

(d) In 1949 I should like to make my son's acquaintance; and it might be a good idea if that same year I was relieved for good of my automobile (I will have buried Mama by then), my business, and my Party membership.

(e) My wife should likewise be expelled from the Party.

(Should technical difficulties arise in this connection—as my wife will have no contact with the private sector other than through my own person—permit me at this point to call your attention to a

Mrs. József Csizmadia, also known as Babi, who, I believe, could be persuaded to write an anonymous letter stating that my wife attended a grammar school on Vörösmarty utca, run by a Scottish mission. In addition, it might be pointed out that she maintained, through a certain Róza Kun, ties with the United States of America that could be said to be close; she received letters from her, read them, answered them.)

(f) Because of the foregoing, my son should be denied admission to a public Kindergarten.

(g) I do not wish to participate in the 1956 counterrevolutionary upheaval; on the contrary, in protest against the disorders, my family and I will begin a fast. Four hours of guard duty nightly, on our staircase, in the company of Dr. Aurél Kovács, dental clinic resident, is not inconceivable; all the same, I would appreciate it if the above-mentioned Red Army would again come to the aid of our country.

(h) From this point on I should like to continue, or rather, conclude, my life as an assistant buyer, maybe even a buyer.

(*Note*: Aside from events enumerated above, I should like to be spared from further noteworthy historical occurrences.)

Respectfully yours,
István Tábori

ooooo

Appendix No. 1.

SUPPLEMENTARY STATEMENT

In full knowledge of my legal and civic responsibilities, I the undersigned hereby declare that it is as retail merchant, truck driver, assistant buyer and buyer that I would like to serve the Kingdom of Hungary, the Hungarian

Republic of Councils, Truncated Hungary, Greater Hungary, the Apostolic Regency, and the Hungarian People's Republic.

I will honor and respect the governments of Francis Joseph I, Count Mihály Károlyi, Béla Kun, Miklos Hórthy, Mátyas Rákosi, János Kádár, etc. and will obey their laws.

When hearing the Austrian, German, Soviet, Hungarian national anthems (as well as the "Gotterhalte," the "Giovanezza," the "Internationale"), I will stand at attention.

I will give due respect to the Austrian, German, Soviet national colors, and to the Red Flag, as well as to my nation's arms (Dual Cross, Crown of St. Stephen, hammer and sickle, wheat-sheaf, etc.).

I shall likewise respect my superiors; Edmund and Paul Haan, Endre Garzó, forced labor company commander and war hero, Kálmán Zserci, Jr., cooperative chairman, and will obey their instructions at all times. My assigned tasks, both at work and away from work (eating, sleeping, caring for progeny, visiting shelters, hospitals, polling places), I will faithfully perform. I will also help my wife with the housework (wash the dishes, clean the rooms, wring out the mop) without constant reminders.

During the course of my life I will not trouble you with special requests (e.g. flight into space, starring role in a movie, platform in Hyde Park), and regardless of whether or not I receive prior notification, I shall accept my death with equanimity; and I shall not have strange gods before me, and shall not swear false witness against my neighbor; and neither shall I covet my neighbor's wife, nor his manservant, his maidservant, his ox, his ass, nor anything that shall belong only to my neighbor.

In the hope that my request shall receive a sympathetic hearing, I remain (and shall hopefully become),

István Tábori

From *Moving House*

BY PAWEŁ HUELLE

(TRANSLATION BY MICHAEL KANDEL)

"Oh, that table!" my mother would shriek. "I just can't stand it anymore! Other people have decent furniture. We're the only ones with a thing like that." She'd point at the round table where we ate our dinner every day. "Can you really call that a table?" she'd ask, her voice faltering and her shoulders drooping.

My father wouldn't rise to her goading; he'd withdraw into himself, and the room would fill with a heavy silence. Actually the table wasn't all that bad. Its one shorter leg was propped up with a wedge, and its scarred surface could be covered with a tablecloth. My father had bought the table from Mr. Polaske of Zaspa in 1946, when Mr. Polaske packed his bags and took the last train west to Germany. In exchange, my father gave Mr. Polaske a pair of army boots a Soviet sergeant had swapped him for a secondhand watch, and since the boots were not in mint condition, my father threw in some butter from UNRAA. Moved by this gesture, Mr. Polaske gave my father, in addition to the table, a photograph from his family album. It showed two elegant men in suits, standing on Lange Brücke. I liked to look at this photograph, not out of interest in Mr. Polaske and his brother, of whom I knew very little, but because in the background stretched a view that I'd sought in vain on Long Harbor. Dozens of fishing boats moored at the Fish Market quay, the jetty was crowded with people buying and selling, and barges and steamships were sailing by on the Motława river, their funnels as tall as the masts. The place was full of bustle and life, Lange Brücke looked like a real port, and although the signs above hotels, bars, and counting houses looked foreign, it was an attractive scene anyway. In no way did it resemble Long Harbor, which indeed was rebuilt after the great fire and bombardment, but which was a wasteland of offices of no use to anyone, of red slogans hanging on walls, and the green thread of the Motława, where a militia motor boat sputtered up and down and once a day the Border Guard's ship went by.

"It's a German table," my mother would say, raising her voice. "You should have hacked it to bits years ago. When I think," she'd go on, a little calmer now, "that a Gestapo man used to sit at it and eat his eels after work, it makes me sick."

My father would shrug and hold out the photograph of Mr. Polaske.

"Look," he'd say to my mother, "is that a Gestapo man?" Then he'd tell the story of Mr. Polaske, who was a Social Democrat and spent three years in the Stutthof concentration camp because he didn't agree with Hitler. When our city was incorporated into the Reich in 1939, Mr. Polaske ostentatiously did not hang a flag out on his house, and after that they took him away.

"Well, then his brother was a Gestapo man." My mother would cut the discussion short and go into the kitchen, while my father, upset by the loss of half his audience, would tell the story of the other Mr. Polaske, who immediately after the war had gone to Warsaw with Senator Kunze to ask President Bierut to allow the Gdansk Germans to stay if they sign a declaration of loyalty.

"Then," my father's tale went on, "President Bierut twisted his moustache, and told the delegates that the German Social Democrats had never erred on the side of sound historical judgment, and that they had long since betrayed their class instinct, of which Comrade Stalin had written so wisely and comprehensively. Any kind of request—President Bierut clenched his worker's fist and hit the desk—is an anti-government act." Then Mr. Polaske's brother returned to Gdansk and hanged himself in the attic of their home in Zaspa. And why do you think he did that?" my father would ask loudly. "After all, he could have gone back to Germany like his brother."

"He hanged himself," my mother would say as she came into the room with a steaming dish, "because he was finally troubled by his conscience. If all Germans were troubled by their conscience, they'd all do the same," she'd add as she set the potatoes in jackets on the table. "They should all hang themselves, after what they've done."

"And the Soviets?" my father would exclaim, shoving potato skins to the edge of his plate. "What about the Soviets?"

I knew that a quarrel would start immediately. My mother had a great fear of Germans, and nothing could possibly cure her of that fear, whereas my father reserved his greatest grudge for the compatriots of Fyodor Dostoyevsky. An invisible border now ran across Mr. Polaske's table, splitting my parents apart, just as in 1939, when the land of their childhood, scented with apples, halva, and a wooden pencil-case with crayons rattling in it, was ripped in half like a piece of canvas, with the silver thread of the river Bug glittering down the middle.

"I saw them," my father would say, as he gulped white pieces of potato. "I saw them . . ." What he meant, of course, was the parade in the little town where the two armies met. "They raised the dust to the very heavens," my father would say, helping himself to more crackling, "and they marched abreast in step, and they sang now in German, now in Russian, but the Russian was louder, because the Soviets had sent a whole regiment to the parade—the Germans only sent two companies."

"The Germans were worse," my mother would interrupt. "They had no human feelings."

I didn't like these conversations, especially not when they got underway over dinner, and the strong flavor of broth or the fragrant aroma of horse-radish sauce was infused with the thunder of cannon-fire or the clatter of a train carrying people off to a slow or instant death. I didn't like it when they argued about such things, because they forgot about me, and there I was, stuck between them, like a used and useless object. The one to blame for it all was Mr. Polaske. And his table. That's what I used to think, as I forced down my jacket potatoes or cheese pierog. If it weren't for Mr. Polaske and his table, my parents would be chatting about a Marilyn Monroe film or this year's strawberry crop, or about the latest launching at the Lenin shipyard, which Premier Cyrankiewicz had attended. As time passed, Mr. Polaske's table became more and more like a bad tooth. Whenever the pain grew weaker and seemed to have passed, they'd be seized by an irresistible urge to touch the sore spot and start the throbbing agony again.

Was there anything I could have done? If the problem had been a chair, I'd certainly have coped. But the oak table was so large, round and heavy, with those carved legs—too massive for me to destroy without anyone's help. I began to suspect that Mr. Polaske had left it to us on purpose, that he knew about the invisible border that ran between my parents and had felt sure his piece of furniture, which he couldn't take with him to Germany, would be the cause of constant argument. My father, not liking change, stuck to his guns, and my mother burned the *bigos* or the spareribs more and more often, and continually found new shortcomings in the German table. Then, in addition to its lame leg and blistered veneer, came the woodworms, whose clandestine work, though inaudible by day, kept my mother up at night. In the morning she'd be tired and bad-tempered.

"Do something," she'd say to my father. "I can't stand it any longer! Those are German worms. Soon they'll attack the dresser and the cupboard, because they are insatiable. Like everything German," she'd whisper in his ear.

If Mr. Polaske had wanted to avenge himself, he couldn't have found a better way. Often I imagined him rubbing his hands together and laughing to himself somewhere in Hamburg or Munich. He'd have eaten the butter from UNRRA in a matter of days, and worn out the Soviet boots after a year or so, yet we were still suffering with his table. It was like a boarder who's always getting in everybody's way but is impossible to kick out. Why should he want revenge on us? I sometimes wondered. We'd done him no harm. We weren't even living in his house, which was now occupied by some high Party official. Could he have wished us ill simply because we were Polish? I could find no ready answer to that question, nor indeed to any question that concerned Mr. Polaske. For hours I'd gaze at the photograph in which Long Harbor looked like a real port; I'd count the funnels of the steamships winding their way along the Motława. Meanwhile, with each day that passed, the table seemed larger, swelling to impossible dimensions within the cramped room.

At last one day the inevitable happened. As my mother set down a tureen full of soup, the wedge came loose under the short leg and the table staggered like a wounded animal. Beet soup splashed on my father's shirt and trousers.

"Oh!" cried my mother with delight, clapping her hands together. "Didn't I tell you this would happen?"

My father said not a word. He replaced the wedge, ate his second course, and waited for the cherry blancmange in silence. It was only after dessert, that he went down to the cellar, a cigarette between his teeth, to get his saw and tape-measure. Soon he was leaning over the table, squinting with one eye, then the other, impressive as a battlefield surgeon about to operate. But what happened next was amazing. My father, so handy at repairs, couldn't fix Mr. Polaske's table, or rather, couldn't fix its uneven legs. After each cut, it would turn out that one of the legs was a little shorter than the others. Possessed by the fury of perfection, or maybe the fury of German methodicalness, my father refused to admit defeat: he shortened and shortened the legs, until at last an extraordinary sight presented itself. On the floor, beside heaps of sawn-off bits of wood and a sea of sawdust, lay the top of Mr. Polaske's table, legless, like a great brown shield. My mother's eyes glittered with emotion, my father's look was black as thunder, but nothing could stop him from finishing what he'd begun. The snarling saw began to rip into the tabletop. My father puffed and panted, and my mother held her breath, until at last she cried: "Well, finally!"

Nabokov in Brasov

BY MIRCEA CĂRTĂRESCU

(TRANSLATION BY JULIAN SEMILIAN)

A few days ago I was taking a walk, somewhere around the *New Times*, rushing ahead with my fists crammed into the pockets of my jacket. The industrial landscape was so dire it almost made you cry. Despite the fact that the sun was out it was very cold, the November morning frost hadn't melted yet. I was thinking about all sorts of literary drivel, when I heard someone call my name: "Hey Mircea, how are you, darling?"

A massive and silvery BMW had stopped by the side of the road a few steps in front of me and a completely unknown woman, sunglasses propped up on her forehead, smiled at me through the shotgun window. I walked toward the car and the woman stepped out. "Do you remember me? Do you know who I am?"

The more I looked at her, the less I knew who she was. "I don't think so," I said, smiling.

She was superbly dressed, astounding against that backdrop of miserable apartment buildings across the street, the cement factory and the crooked stands at the streetcar station.

"I am Adriana, Irina's sister. You came to see us once in Cluj."

Okay, so I'd met her, once only, many years before, it was only natural that

I didn't remember her. I mimicked the joy of recognition and we exchanged a few banal words.

"Do you still travel to Finland?" I asked in order to make sure she knew I knew her.

"Yes, I go there all the time, I work with a Finnish company. But tell me, how are you? How are things going? I keep hearing you've been coming out with new books, but you know . . . with all my work I'm way behind on my reading . . . Irina, however, buys all your books, for old times' sake, you know what I mean . . ."

I hesitated to ask, but it was inevitable. "How is Irina?"

To which this woman, completely—I mean completely—unknown broke into a kind of naïve euphoria: it was clear that her sister was the pride of the family. "Well, very, very well, for a few years now she's been in Brussels, her husband is someone very important, member of the European Parliament."

". . . because that's the way history is written," went through my head. A few more words—"Let's stay in touch" (as though we were ever in touch!), "I am very happy to see you again"—and then the man at the wheel opened the passenger side door. Then the space closed up behind the disappearing car the same way you would close a fashion magazine with impeccably photographed objects. All that remained were the apartment buildings, wet and grimy, the holes in the road and the pedestrians at the intersection, ill-looking and badly dressed.

I forgot what notary public or courthouse I was going to, what deed I had to sign, and I roamed for about a half an hour at random through those anti-utopian places. Irina at the European Parliament? Grande Dame of Brussels? The wife of a dignitary? And to think that I had hesitated to ask her sister about her out of compassion, in order not to embarrass her! All these years I had imagined Irina a total wreck, an alcoholic perhaps, haunted by a past she couldn't hide. Maybe homeless, like those who reek horribly in streetcars . . . Then I realized that it had to be like that, that life, which only a few years before had placed in my hands a kind of ready-made story, now offered me a natural ending, perhaps even an obligatory ending for her. I am not a "realist"

DECREE FROM THE ROMANIAN STATE COUNCIL regulating tools and materials necessary for the reproduction of texts, including photocopiers and typewriters. March 30, 1983. (credit. OSA Archivum)

BULETINUL OFICIAL
AL
REPUBLICII SOCIALISTE ROMÂNIA

Anul XIX — Nr. 21   PARTEA I   Miercuri, 30 martie 1983

DECRETE ALE CONSILIULUI DE STAT

DECRET AL CONSILIULUI DE STAT

privind regimul aparatelor de multiplicat, materialelor necesare reproducerii scrierilor și al mașinilor de scris

Consiliul de Stat al Republicii Socialiste România decretează:

CAPITOLUL I

Dispoziții generale

Art. 1. — Unitățile socialiste și alte organizații care funcționează potrivit legii pot deține aparate de multiplicat ca: aparate tip xerox, gheștetnere, șapirografe, heliografe și altele asemenea, materiale necesare reproducerii scrierilor, cum sînt: matrițe, litere confecționate din cauciuc, aliaje sau alte amestecuri, paste de tip poligrafic, precum și nișniri de scris.

CAPITOLUL II

Producerea, confecționarea, folosirea și evidența aparatelor de multiplicat și a materialelor necesare reproducerii scrierilor

Art. 4. — Producerea, confecționarea și folosirea aparatelor de multiplicat și a materialelor necesare reproducerii scrierilor sînt permise numai unităților socialiste și altor organizații.

writer, or a writer who chases after certain "subjects"; that's why I always hesitated to recount the three or four veritably interesting things I witnessed in my life. These days I have some peace (not peace of mind, mind you, but simply peace, solitude, in the most concrete sense—the door to my office closed, the little one asleep in his bed in another room, the older one doing something or other in the living room . . .) and I don't think about Irina, "my first woman" and a ridiculous enigma. The sorry enigma of sorry times.

I was a student at the University of Literature, an off-the-beaten-track graphomaniac, poet from head to toe (in my imagination); and yet I was colorless, short, skinny as a rail, so that the only aspect of humanity I had any interest in—girls—looked through me as if I were made of glass. I lived in a fierce solitude. Not even after I had gained a little notoriety, through the literary circles I frequented, did I succeed in attracting the attention of my female colleagues. I couldn't understand it. My most grotesque-looking friends, the most lamebrained of them, boasted of their overflowing eroticism, they bragged at parties in overwhelming detail about everything that took place on their "fucksters," as they called the couches in the tiny attic and basement rooms where they lodged. As for me, I was already twenty-three and not one woman had taken her place on my "fuckster" . . .

So, in the spring of 1979, when I went to Cluj for the Eminescu Colloquium,[1] I thought that for one moment I had finally grabbed hold of God's foot. That's where I met the first woman who gave me a vague sign of sympathy. She was four years older than I, already a graduate who had been given an assignment as a teacher in a tiny Transylvanian village. She had majored in Romanian, with a minor in English. She wasn't very pretty, looked kind of sluttish, and when she walked she seemed to be staggering with every step she took. Nothing that she wore ever fit her. From the very beginning we felt good together: two demented individuals, living inside their own fiction. I spoke only in quotes from my favorite authors, she spoke ironically and parabolically, so that at times, during our long and wise discussions on Cluj's streets, we would realize that each of us was talking about something quite different than what the other thought. Once she paused next to a street lamp and asked me: "Don't you think that Cluj is merely a state of mind? A dream from which we must awaken?"

---

1. An annual student event dedicated to Mihail Eminescu, the most important Romanian poet of the nineteenth century.

Even I realized the idiotic bookishness of her words and answered her sarcastically: "Don't you think that Borges said the same thing about Buenos Aires?"

"No, no, I really believe it. I actually believe that nothing matters, that everything is our dream or someone else's dream about us . . ."

I couldn't remove her from her reveries. At the seminar I read a piece that no one understood. Irina and I talked about it later, in a train compartment, drinking vodka from cups made from orange-peel halves. I was very surprised: she understood. I was surprised also that she let me kiss her, and more . . . but not much more.

Once home I began to receive letters from her, about once every two weeks. Purely intellectual, spare in style. What she read, what she translated . . . She really liked Nabokov and D.H. Lawrence, she read the American postmodernists in English, had developed a passion for Robert Coover. She had without a doubt a critical talent, her observations were uncommon. Only toward the end of the letters did she insinuate a kind of tenderness, of the chaste kind. She ended invariably with "Good night, sweet prince."

But I had fallen in love with a colleague from Bucharest and the story with Irina was beginning to lose its contours. But, once again, tough luck. The colleague in question was determined to remain a virgin, at least a few more years. We smooched like mad in the hallways of old houses, but my journal remained unblemished and, for God's sake, I was about to turn twenty-four! I began to write love poems, as a sort of compensation. A weak compensation. Despite my absolutely real love for my colleague, I would have slept with anyone, even an old hag. Especially considering that, at the time, an old hag for me was anyone over thirty.

Thus my hopes were reborn when I ran into Irina again the following year, this time at a poetry reading at the I Sing Romania festival.[2] I saw her in the distance, among a group of people who were waiting in line at the entrance to Arizona, the legendary restaurant (in truth, a sordid dive). She saw me and came to greet me, staggering even more than before. Her hair was now short, falling in dull stripes along her cheeks. Each time I saw her afterward, I was amazed at how ugly she was: thin dry lips, pug

---

2. National festival whose purpose was communist propaganda. Literary events took place within its framework. Many times poetry and prose were read at these events that contradicted the party dogma.

HUNGARIAN PRESS OF TRANSYLVANIA
ERDÉLYI MAGYAR HÍRÜGYNÖKSÉG

48/1985   KOLOZSVÁR, 1985 . JÚLIUS 5.

A KOLOZSVÁROTT TÖRTÉNŐ HÓDÍTÁSI ERŐSZAKSZERVEK MÓDSZEREI. A HATALMI APPARÁTUS EGÉSZE A POLITIKAI
ELNYOMÁST SZOLGÁLJA

Köztudott, hogy Kolozsvárott /Cluj-Napoca/, a Traian utcában álló és a két világháború közötti perió-
dusban épült, hivalkodó rendőrségi épületkolosszust a securitate örökölte. Az épület egy viszony-
lag tágas, betonozott udvar választja el, helyesebben egyesíti a Kerz utcára néző rendőrséggel.
A négy oldalról hermetikusan, rendíramód, ill. securitate-épületekkel zárt udvarra lehetetlen a bete-
kintés, azok, akiket kihallgatás végett behívnak vagy behoznak, időnként láthatják az udvaron
gyakorlatozó rohamosztagokat, amint állig felfegyverkezve többnyire szovjet gyártmányú támadó és
önvédelmi eszközökkel gyakorolják a gyors és hatékony beavatkozást az esetleges zavargások megaka-
dályozására. Ezek a "léthetetlen katonák" securitatés a hatékony támadás ain on csinyjára kiképzett
tisztek. A rendőrség emberei távolról sem bírnak hasonló felkészültséggel és felszereléssel, annak
ellenére, hogy őket a hatvanas évektől már háromszor is bevetették, mindháromszor az
ellátás vagy a faji diszkriminació leplezetlen megnyilvánulásai miatt lázongó külföldi /néger vagy
arab/ diákok megfékezésére. Ezek közül még egy alkalommal az osztrágus Universitatea—Dinamo fut-
ballmérkőzés után. Ekkor — mintegy három évvel ezelőtt — a világszensal kapcsolatos korrupció ellen
tiltakozó körözség és a rendőrség összecsapásának több halálos áldozata is volt. A rendőrség
mindegyik esetben csupán gumibottal volt felfegyverkezve. A securitate rohamosztagok eddig még egy
alkalommal sem kerültek bevetésre, ennek ellenére rendszeresen gyakorolnak, fegyverzetüket /pajzsok,
speciális ütőszerszámok, gázgránátok, rugósikések, stb./ sűrűn cserélik a legkorszerűbbekre.

Kevesebben tudják viszont, hogy a securitaténak távolról sem az az egyetlen bázisa, ezt legfennebb a
Központinak nevezhetnek. Megfigyelésállomásaik a város minden pontján megtalálhatóak, ezek szigorúan
titkosak és a legvilágosabban intézmények /gyárak, közpiskolák, olykor óvodik/ irodahelyiségeiben
találhatóak, ideiglenes vagy hosszútávra berendezve. Ezek közül egyik legfontosabb a főtéri, a
Szent Mihály templom bejáratával átellenes oldalon lévő un. "konspiratív bázis". Időnként látni lehet,
amint az antikváriummal utáni első, díszkeret kapubejáraton, civilbe öltözött, magasrangu tisztek és
"fényképészek" lépnek ki vagy be. Természetesen csupán egy véletlen félismerésről van pedig megismeré-
ről lehet szó, hiszen a bejárat mellett egy-egy szám sincs, nemhogy az "intézmény" megnevező felirat.
Az utcára néző négy emeleti ablak mindenképpen ide tartozik, hogy hány és miképpen berendezett iroda-
helyiség van mögöttük, az talány. Az említett bázis közvetlenül szomszédos a római katolikus parb-
kidvali; csak rom[...]

... 2

A legutóbbi időkben, átfogó reformon esett keresztül a rendőrség: a régi, jócskán korrupált, idős, sze-
szer csupán elemi képzettségből rendelkező altiszteket, erotiségizett, fiatal, általában sportklubokból
verbuválódott garnitúra váltotta föl, akiknek — nem utolsó sorban — jóval magasabb a fizetésük is.
A járőrök az eddigi egy altiszt, két tenens felállítás helyett jelenleg általában egy, vagy két tiszt,
egy altiszt, négy-öt tanonera csendületett; ez utóbbiaknál gépfegyver és több kutya teszi félelmetessé
és irreálissá ezt a vélolmat, hogy a bűzbán kirendőt őriznék. Ami pedig az egyik legfélelmetesebb
változata, és ami egyben fényt vet a romániai diktatúra cinizmusára is: immár a rendőrségnek nem az az
elsődleges hivatása, hogy a köztünfényebet felderítse, ill. fékezze, hanem hogy az elégedetlenke-
dő, esetűtán az ellenzéki hangulatúakra figyelszerzen. Az itt említett irányzatni belső, rendőrségi
gyülésaken hivatalesan is megerősítést nyert. Ilyenformán a román rendőrség gyakorla-
tilag a securitate segédszárnyává degradálódott, annak óllamával együtt, hogy rendőrségi ügyként tarol-
hatnak meg, egyértelműen nem bűnügyi eseteket is.

nose, skin dry as parchment . . . Except for the eyes: they displayed a live intelligence, a kind of romantic madness, an indifference toward everything around her. When she invited me to her place I immediately sensed the motion of the hormones in my abdominal zones: finally, good-bye childhood, this time nothing could go wrong! But something did go wrong. Because Adriana, Irina's sister, was back from Finland and we spent the entire miserable evening looking at voluminous photo albums of Finnish sunsets, Finnish firs, Finnish reindeer, Sibelius and Berzelius and Hellholelius and Fuckallius . . . Hours on end waiting for Adriana to leave and for the fun to begin, until I finally ended up leaving myself, furious and humiliated; and so, another year passed. My only consolation, a poor one at that, was that in one of the books I was reading then, *The Genius and the Goddess*, Aldous Huxley recounted how he had remained a virgin till the age of twenty-six! There you have it, it could always be worse! As for me, I swore it wouldn't take that long. Better death than dishonor.

Today I think it would have been better to remain in childhood a little longer. Because the miserable afternoon when I "became a man" is still one of the most painful and sordid memories of my life. Irina called to tell me she was in Bucharest, that she had established residence in Bucharest (how could that be? What happened to her job as a teacher in Transylvania? Had she obtained a retraction?[3] And even if she had, what was she doing in

---

3. Young university graduates were forced to work the first three years of their professional careers in villages, under dire circumstances; pressure was put on them later to establish definitive residence there. In order for graduates to avoid village duty, it was necessary to obtain proof from the Ministry of Education that they were not suited for their respective position in the village. This was called a "retraction"; it was extremely difficult to obtain, unless one had connections to the state apparatus.

Bucharest?), and wanted to meet me regarding something that was very important to her. I rode the subway until I was sick of it, all the way to the Defenders of the Nation Plaza. I found the building, went up the stairs into the hellish stink of spilled garbage, opened the door to the one-room apartment that reeked of beef stew and kissed Irina, whose cheeks and hair also reeked of stew. She was wearing a robe with little flowers. I didn't want to eat. I just wanted to solve my problem. Her face was contorted with the attitude of a femme fatale. She put a towel on the bed and stretched out with her butt on it. I myself lay next to her. The big surprise, clearly one she had planned, was that she wore no panties underneath . . . After a bit of straining I was a man, but instead of the happiness and release I had imagined, I felt nothing but intense nausea at the smell of the stew, irritation at the fact that I finished almost the moment I started, and disgust for everything about that afternoon, the ungraceful and reeking woman next to me, the one-room apartment with crooked walls, even the twilight sky sweating through the curtains over the windows. All I could think about was how to get the hell out of there and never lay eyes on Irina again. She had vanished into the bathroom for personal reasons and then returned into the room's ashen air with her large boobs, her excessive pubic hair (I had imagined women to be quite different), her muscular hips. She put on her robe and lit a cigarette.

Here the tone of my story will change from scherzo-pathetic to grave and lugubrious, something sullen, morose. But that afternoon I didn't feel any such abrupt change. Evening fell, the penumbra became dense. If something wasn't quite right, like in a movie (I thought of it like that later on), it was what she told me then, still standing, with her cigarette burning between her fingers: "Mircea, I would like you to help me with . . . something. I don't know what to do."

"What is it?" I was still in the grip of disgust. My pants were inside out—I had taken them off in a hurry—and I was digging my socks out of them.

"Look, I'm not going to beat around the bush." But instead of saying what needed to be said she balanced her cigarette on the window ledge and started to make an ashtray out of a pencil-scribbled piece of paper she tore from a notebook. When she finished it, she deposited the ashes in it until the pure incandescence of the tip was completely freed of its ashen shroud: "I was asked to join *Securitate* . . ."[4]

---

4. *Securitate* was the Romanian Secret Police during the communist regime.

SUMMARY REPORT, JULY 5, 1985, published by the Hungarian Press of Transylvania on the buildings and equipment, and surveillance, training and investigation methods of the infamous *Securitate,* the Romanian state security organ, in Kolozsvar (Cluj), a major town in Transylvania, as well as their infiltration into the ranks of the regular police. (opposite page, credit: OSA Archivum)

My mind is usually slow. I'm always thinking of something else, so I often miss the point. I lived the most important moments in my life as though they were bits and pieces of someone else's. The same in that moment, what she said wasn't getting to the depths of my heart. "And what did you say?" I asked indifferently, as though she had told me one of her dreams. Irina looked me in the eyes for the first time, with a kind of frightened defiance. After which she began a long blah blah blah, as though rehearsing a role in the mirror: rather than wasting her life as a miserable teacher in the provinces, why shouldn't she go where her qualities would be appreciated . . . young and intelligent people could change things from within . . . they could travel to other countries . . . have access to libraries . . . she could take advantage of her position to do good . . .

I wasn't listening anymore. I was slowly waking up. Oddly, thinking of *Securitate*, the most unlikely and stupid things were coming to mind: a long line to get beer at Bucur Obor, hundreds of people and a very nervous individual shouting when a few gypsies tried to cut in. "He's from *Securitate*, I know him," an old man told me with a kind of respect. "He's got power to put things *in order*." In my apartment building there were many people from *Securitate*, I played with their children. I recalled the jokes about them, Mother's warnings to be careful what I said, because *Securitate* was everywhere. Who were the people who worked for *Securitate*? What was *Securitate*? And why was it my fate, like a bad joke, to become a man with someone who worked for *Securitate*, even though she was only about to become one of them? I let her speak, I let her try her best to convince me (herself, really) that she was doing the right thing, and so she went on and on with her plea to the void, long after she realized I wasn't listening to her anymore. I could barely see her face. Through the paper-thin walls of the building you could hear everything: someone flushing the toilet, voices on the TV, music . . . After she finished she lit another cigarette and silently smoked it to the end. Then she stretched "voluptuously" next to me, kissed me "sweetly," caressed me obscenely—no quotation marks this time—and wanted to start from the top. I pushed her hand away and told her, like an automaton, without feeling the "drama" of that moment, that she was an idiot, that she would ruin not only her own life but the life of many others as well, that I didn't want to have anything to do with her if she took that step. And in fact, if she'd already accepted, what did she want from me?

"But I had no one to talk with, no one to advise me. I don't know anyone here, there is no one I'm close to. I *had* to tell somebody I could trust . . ."

I left while it was still dark and walked back home through the puddles, the mud and the gravel, staring suspiciously at the vigilant cops. Only when I lay down in my own bed did I become aware of the insanity of that evening. "Dumb bitch," I mumbled, but oddly, I was the one who felt like an idiot, like a man who had just done something very stupid . . . I fell asleep, my head feeling heavy from all the cigarette smoke, determined to forget the whole thing.

After that, things improved with my sexual journal. By the age of twenty-six, Huxley's fateful age, I had written in it, with letters of fire, four names. No longer troubled now by those matters, my poetry turned philosophical. A few months after the "evening of my becoming a man," I received, in the middle of the night, a desperate phone call from Irina. She was crying and screaming into the receiver. Was she drunk? I didn't think she was a drinker. I was trying to make sense of her very confused string of words. She was residing, for purposes of secret training, at the headquarters of the Ministry of Internal Affairs[5] in the city of Eforie. She was sharing a room with two colleagues who were "nothing but whores. They beat me all the time, Mircea! They brainwashed me, Mircea, I am forced to do awful things, Mircea, I can't take it anymore, Mircea, I can't, I can't!" She was howling with tears, repugnant as a child dripping with snot. She had barely managed to escape that evening, headed for the first public telephone. She wanted to run, she wanted to hide, it didn't matter where. "Come to my place," I shouted in the receiver, but she hung up abruptly. I waited for her in vain the entire night.

In the following few years things took a very bad turn. The weather was cold and miserable, there was no heat. *Securitate*, till then the butt of everyone's jokes, became a horrific myth. Fear spread with the inevitability of a psychosis. I was thinking often about Irina. What was she up to, that miserable creature? Was she on one of their demented missions? Had she become an instrument of terror? She, who did not believe in reality, she who was in love with Nabokov? After a very long while I began to get phone calls from her again. It was always late at night, and it was always to borrow money. Her voice sounded progressively more cracked, more insane. Most of the time she was probably drunk. I couldn't lend her any money, I was poorer than poor, but always asked her what she was up to. "I can't tell you

---

5. *Securitate* was part of the Ministry of Internal Affairs.

STATEMENT PUBLISHED

BY ZOLTÁN ZSILLE,

the Vienna-based

correspondent of Radio

Free Europe, and signed

by seventy-one others, in

which the author condemns

the Romanian state security

organs' persecution of

Hungarian intellectuals in

Transylvania, their arrests,

illegal detention, home

raids and the confiscation

of allegedly "sensitive"

documents dealing with

the political situation in

Transylvania and Hungary.

November 23, 1982.

(opposite page,

credit: OSA Archivum)

anything," she would say and hang up. Like all men experiencing insomnia, meticulously reviewing the long or the short list of their female conquests, recalling phantasmically the things they did with each of them, I couldn't forget the one who, whether I liked it or not, had been the first, was the first and would always be the first, no matter how long the list might eventually become. Despite her appalling decision, or perhaps because of it, I felt much tenderness and compassion for her. I met Irina each time she called in order to help her, despite the risks. I knew she wouldn't harm me. But around '86 the phone calls stopped. Irina disappeared—forever, I thought.

I would see her again however, in circumstances I could never have imagined. A few weeks after the revolution [6] I was hanging out with my friends Nedelciu and Hanibal in my "office," a tiny room on the second floor of the Writers' Union, where I was working. I was responsible for literary "passes," that is, assigning apartments in resort areas to writers who needed peace and quiet in order to write, but as my job lasted only a few months, from autumn to spring, I was unemployed during that time. I had even managed to set the office on fire, forgetting to turn off the stove heater one evening. The door's glass was broken, the heater was black from smoke and a few of the floor slats had turned to carbon. We were prattling on about our brand-new review, *Counterpoint,* when we heard footsteps tramping up our narrow, steep stairs. I couldn't believe it when I saw, filling the doorway, melted snow in her hair and snow on her white sheepskin coat, a woman I barely recognized as Irina. Her wide Transylvanian face was excessively covered with makeup. She wore her hair even shorter than before, in a ridiculous Beatle hairdo over her eyeliner-drowned eyes. As our heater roared at full strength once again, the snow on her jacket, a kind of down until then, turned instantaneously into rivulets of streaming water. She looked like a wet cat and during the time she spent with us she was indeed nervous as a cat. She spoke like a madwoman, nearly schizophrenic. My friends stared at her, snickering to each other.

We walked along Lilly Street all the way to the Romanian Athenaeum. The snow was falling in dense, tiny flakes. There, in the park across from the Athenaeum, with the statue of the poet Eminescu shrouded in snow, we sat down and talked. Everything around us was dazzlingly white. She told me she was scared, desperate. She felt she was being followed. "I was implicated

---

6. The Romanian revolution of December 1989, which resulted in the fall of the communist regime and the execution of the dictator Ceauşescu and his wife.

in the Brasov incident in '87."[7] That she couldn't speak with anyone except in open spaces. She appealed to our old friendship, could I find her a job, some tiny place where she would be left forgotten. "You're working at the Writers' Union now, couldn't I fit in there somehow? I could do simultaneous translations, type, proofread, anything, anything at all . . ."

I began to moralize like an idiot. "See, Irina! Didn't I tell you from the beginning you were doing something very stupid? Look at you now! What happened to your talent, what happened with everything you wanted to do?"

I expected her to look down, her chin to her chest and weep in expiation, but suddenly she threw me a proud and ironic look, as if to say: "You know what, why don't you just cut all this crap . . ." It was as though a great dark power remained underneath the desperation of her circumstances. However, she returned right away to her former whimpering: "What do you say, do you know someone who can help? Is there any hope for me?"

I explained to her I was nothing more than a miserable office worker, I'd barely been there two months, I had no connection with anyone who ran the place. It was the absolute truth. She said nothing. We walked together a few more steps, we said good-bye. I returned to my overheated little room. "Who was she?" Nedelciu asked. "Just somebody . . ."

I left my job at the Writers' Union and got another at the *Critical Review*. I didn't do very well there and was hired by the University of Literature as an assistant professor. For eleven years, during which my life became progressively busier and more complex, the times I

Zoltab Zaille Vienna   23 November 1982

Statement!

On November 6 and 7 the Romanian state security organs arrested several young Transylvanian Hungarian intellectuals. Their apartments were searched and documents dealing with political conditions in Hungary and Transylvania were confiscated. The exact number of those arrested is not yet known.
The names of the following are known: Ara-Kovacs Attila writer, Attila Kertesz actor, Geza Szocs author, Karoly Toth teacher.
Several people were questioned during the week. Those questioned included: Lorant Kertesz agricultural engineer and his wife, Eva Kertesz, Marta Jozsa, Eva Biro and Andras Keszthelyi students of philosophy and Mrs. Karoly Toth.

Some of them - like Geza Szocs, Karoly Toth and his wife - were seriously physically manhandled. Attila Ara-Kovacs and Karoly Toth were relesed after a couple of days under the condition that they will not leave their lace of residence Nagyvarad.

To this day there is no news about the whereabouts of Geza Szocs, an excellent poet well-known in the entire Hungarian speaking area. Not even his closest relatives know about his whereabouts for sure. There is a well-founded suspicion that the political police has not relesed him to this day. We call upon everybody that, whoever is able, should protest against the procedure of the Romanian authorities. We ask our Romanian friends as well to intercede on behalf of the release of Geza Szocs. We demand the release of all those who might still be imprisoned, and ask that harassment by the police be stopped.

Signed by 71 people

Magyar Szami zdat

---

7. In 1987 there was a worker's revolt in the Transylvanian city of Brasov. It was the most important revolt that took place during the communist years. The revolt was brutally crushed and thousands of workers were arrested. The revolt was infiltrated from the very beginning by *Securitate* officers, who reported its every move to the authorities.

remembered Irina were few and far between. Still, I thought of her during the nights at the University Plaza,[8] when, along with tens of thousands of others staring up at the Geology balcony, I shouted till I lost my voice: "Send *Securitate* down to the mines / Make them dig coal, WE need our lights," and remembered her each time the miners came to Bucharest in combat formations and attacked the general population. Between my nebulous projects, the thought of writing something about her never left me. Nabokov implicated in Brasov, I was thinking. Nabokov in Brasov. Robert Coover burning files at Berevoiesti.[9] D.H. Lawrence demonizing the intellectuals. And the horrific, monstrous, overwhelming *Securitate* wishing me each night before going to bed: "Good night, sweet prince . . ."

Strangely, the rare times I still recall her, Irina appears to me neither in her apartment full of landscapes from Finland, nor in her grungy one-room apartment by the Defenders of the Nation plaza; nor do I see her in the winter light of the Athenaeum. I see her as I saw her the first time, when we roamed the streets of Cluj, bantering about literary and metaphysical themes. I see her staggering in her high heels and looking as though someone had tried to obliterate her silhouette at random with an eraser. This very moment, as I write these lines, I hear her clearly saying, as we walked past the multicolored façades and gates of that Transylvanian city: "Don't you think this entire city is a figment of the imagination? You know, for me nothing counts, nothing exists for real . . ."

---

8. The University Plaza in the center of Bucharest was the meeting place, during the spring of 1990, for tens of thousands of demonstrators demanding freedom and democracy. Over time, the demonstrations took on the character of a popular festival, where people sang, derided the neo-communist regime and chanted anti-*Securitate* slogans. The demonstrations were quelled by the police and the gangs of armed miners brought to the capital by the president of Romania. The miners returned to Bucharest on several occasions, functioning as paramilitary troops in the service of the neo-communist power. Each time they terrorized the populace, committed acts of vandalism and attacked the headquarters of the opposition parties. These outbreaks came to be called "mineriads."

9. A large portion of *Securitate*'s confidential dossiers during the communist era were burned in a forest near the city of Berevoiesti. This act was uncovered and caused a gigantic scandal in the press.

From *Waltz for K*

BY DMITRI SAVITSKI

(TRANSLATION BY KINGSLEY SHORTER)

That evening distant thunder tossed and turned in its dry bed. Rolled its *r*'s. Played its skittles. Toward midnight the murk thickened ominously, writhing and swirling like milk. Shafts of lemon-yellow lightening struck at random. Windows banged. The poplar below our window shivered feverishly. Then the rain came down in torrents. It rained so hard it seemed the whole of life must be swept away. A generous, outlandish deluge.

I still have photographs from that period. One time, when I was already living in Paris, in an access of homesickness I showed one picture to a veteran of the art; he examined it at length, frowned, spilled cigar ash on the carpet, asked to see the negative. "I'll give you half the Man Ray Prize," he announced finally, "if you will explain to me how it was done." I spread my hands. What explanation could I give him? In that sundrenched room, amid a disorder immortalized by my lens—books scattered about, portraits pinned up askew, the lines with her washing and my film hung up to dry; in that room, whose dresser still played host to silver sugar bowls that had somehow not yet found their way to the pawnbroker's and icons that had escaped the depradations of the diplomatic corps—in that room, Katenka lay upon the air, her arms spread wide: wonderful, stark naked Katenka.

Her hair—she had just tossed her head—whirled like a golden comet in the suspended air of that day that was happy almost beyond bearing. There was no gimmick.

On the table lay a big packet of our Moscow photographs: Katenka in the bathroom, lying flat, like at a fakir's seance; one breast lolls to the side, nipple peeping at the lens; I stand beside her in a raincoat and hat (I had set the camera to auto-release) and hold the shower hose behind her neck—the sparkling cone of water fans down over her, time has not yet licked away the droplets on her skin. Katenka in the woods, in a little satin dress, diving head first in pursuit of a flower borne away on the wind; a bumblebee in his unseasonably luxurious fur coat provided her with a perfect bracelet, a buzzing woodland wristwatch. Or here is Katenka on a moonlit night (I was using time exposure): looking somehow already completely astral, as if drenched in the light of the full moon, in this picture she is resolved into a succession of translucent blue images—flowing turns, somersaults, silken glimmers of elbow and knee.

I cannot endure this, I don't mean describing the photographs, but calling back the days cancelled by the calendar . . . I would do better to burn the whole lot.

oooo

God, how mischievous she was! How many times did we do it in the air. The first time—the walls abandoned their right angles and rushed to intercept us, a lopsided picture broke from its cord and plunged into oblivion, a big bottle of cherries in brandy fell from the dresser with a crash (but didn't break), a scratch on my back took a week to heal—that was the window catch which, seizing its chance, gouged me between the shoulder blades. We had to learn to respect the lamp, to be mindful of nails, we had to learn prudence enough not to go crashing into the window sill, crammed with jars, cups and coffee pot. One stifling night we fell asleep in each other's arms and I awoke, after I don't know how many minutes had rustled past, feeling her all tenderly wrapped around me, warm and moist—awoke with sudden alarm. For a moment I was completely disorientated; I knew only that somewhere close by deadly brilliant drops were flaring and dying, and near my neck something was scraping and scratching. At such moments the most difficult thing is to figure out which is up and which is down. Luckily for me a sliver of moon cut through the thick midnight clouds. Then from below came a harsh grinding sound, and I saw a shower of electric sparks. I got us out of there fast, holding her tight as she began to stir—we were in the street, we had floated out the window, we were lying almost on top of the streetcar power lines.

From that night on I put a net over the window, but we soon stopped sleeping in the air: autumn came on quickly, with prolonged bouts of icy rain; no matter how tightly we wrapped the blanket round us, it would slip off. And then, at the end of an Indian summer that blazed up in russet warmth, one day the accursed telephone rang, and we learned that Kolenka had been arrested.

Rumors that there were people who could fly had begun appearing spontaneously across the land. The first time I heard about people flying was in a queue. They were selling off a few scrawny superannuated chickens. Two old girls, complete primitives bundled up in quilted coats, were shaking their heads and sending up balloons with some pretty strange bits of dialogue. Hearing ". . . and he, God forgive us, just shoots up into the sky," I moved closer. The narrator crossed herself, while her companion, a woman with permanently clenched features, nodded monotonously. "And Manya, he's flying like an angel! Everybody comes running, of course. The militia draw their revolvers, take aim, but he's already higher than the Pushkin monument. But one fellow, in civvies, shoots two-fisted—and gets him! We all run to look—but he's already gone. They carted him off, of course . . . to examine him. Maybe he wasn't one of ours. But he looked ordinary enough, I tell you Manya. Flew over people's umbrellas. Wearing trousers. Semeonovna, from the grocery, says she even saw a hole in his boot."

I got excited. But the rumors were coming in from all over. Predictably, the talk around town vested the flyers with the virtues of old-style heroes. Judging from the stories, one flew into the pawnshop opposite the Procurator's Office and before the eyes of the dumbfounded crowd carried off a hat full of gold. Of another it was told how he carried away 25,000 rubles in cash through the open window of the House of Writers on Lavrushensky. The

QUEUE AT MOSCOW TABAK STALL (opposite page, credit: SCR Photo Library)

window, they said, was on the sixth floor. The fool of a maid, they said, had opened the windows to air the place and was gabbing on the phone.

∞∞∞

Along Sadovoye Koltso the wind chased dry, swirling leaves. The puddles were frozen over. The evening crowd flowed heavily along the street, swirled in gray eddies, spitting out individuals who had lost the rhythm. A moustached militiaman stood heavily, his big boots planted wide apart. A woman climbed heavily—though still young—onto a bus. A gray wino breathed heavily on the corner, as he rested with an enormous string bag bulging with empty bottles. Even a snot-nosed urchin, though one of nature's sparrows, trudged along on elephantine feet. Oh, if only they would—just for a second—switch off the gravity generator at the center of our happy globe! If only everyone were allowed to become weightless every Friday! I envisioned the empty canyons of the streets, the sky speckled with flyers. Shame on you, I said to myself, shame on you, Okhlamonov, for this lapse into old-fashioned sentimentality. I turned off toward Nikitsky Gate. In a back alley near the School of Music, someone had scrawled in big black letters: "TO EACH HIS PLACE SOME LOW SOME HIGH."

The phone rang one dark, dank morning. Katenka was singing in the bathroom. Her little bits of washing, her ability to keep house without fuss and bother, filled me with admiration. I went over to the phone. The caller did not give his name, but I immediately realized it was one of Kolya's neighbors in the communal apartments, an old grouch, a retired jerk of an army captain. "That smart-ass friend of yours," he whined, "they've taken the scribbler and put him where he belongs!" and gave a phlegmy snigger.

It was the beginning of the end. I knew nothing as yet, but ice suddenly flowed in my veins.

∞∞∞

At the very end of the month, when the few surviving front gardens were already ablaze with lilacs, Katenka dragged me off to the country. We went a long, long way out, to our beloved Nikolsky woods. There no one could see us, but for some reason she tenderly refused to do it in the air, as we had used to, but insistently drew me down onto the grass. She hugged me fiercely, with a new ardor, wound her legs around me, her embrace almost squeezed the breath out of me, her fragrant sweat, mingled with mine, bathed her face . . . it was all more powerful than it had ever been before.

That day we definitively decided to fly away.

"Lead boots will soon be all the rage," joked Katenka. She wasn't far from the truth. Here and there "socially conscious" pensioners, not waiting for instructions from above (I suddenly realize that "from above" sounded ambiguous in those days) started putting up notices: FLYING STRICKTLY FORBIDDEN. They were already drafting new legislation against "anti-social breaking away from the collective," setting prison terms, etc., etc. It was even suggested that parents were responsible for their children, no matter if they themselves were incapable of rising above the prosaic realities of our native land.

In Tsvetnoy market the Georgians were selling tomatoes for exorbitant prices, someone had brought some plump gladioli into town, and the Prime Minister of Australia was due to arrive on an official visit, and an aphorism by the mayor of the city made the rounds of Moscow, to the effect that if anyone flew during the visit, heads would fly too—in a word, a pall of ennui and desolation had descended, and Katenka and I finally got two plane tickets to Simferopol; from there we would make our way by road to Yalta, rest a while, take a look round, and, going out to sea one night on a pleasure boat, leave the country forever.

Kolenka's warning—not to fly over large expanses of water—naturally made us a bit apprehensive, but we had no choice. The Western frontiers were now being patrolled in earnest.

Do you know what Yalta is at night? No, not Soviet Yalta, full of drunks and street brawls, reeking of cheap perfume and suntan oil! A different Yalta. Mute, dwindling, sprawled on its side like a distant dying campfire. A city from which so many have fled . . . A last memory, spiced with cheap jokes . . .

It was a close, moonless night. I had a child's compass, bought at the last minute. I was so afraid the pointer would come off the needle—

Again I go back to the photographs from those years—black and white, of course; color film from the West I got only rarely, it cost the earth. Here is Katenka bearing a tray of coffee through the air—a heavy tray from our grandmother's day. She is finding it heavy going, so her naked little form is pitched downward, her legs pointing skyward, I can see the twin hills of her buttocks, the tender confluence of her breasts. Her hair is uncombed, carelessly pinned to one side. Her downy mound still to this day gives me the shakes. Katenka under a river bridge, in one hand she is holding a rolled-up newspaper and tooting on it like an archangel. Katenka upside down in our little apartment; her hair completely covers her face, her dress too has fallen back, only her legs stick straight up like a fountain.

I have one particular photo that fills me with particular sadness—Katenka is pulling back the shade: a winter window, snow-covered branches, a sparrow, the feeble sun, wires. She is wearing an old dressing gown. Holding it at her throat with one hand, as if something were strangling her. Sometimes I think that even then she knew what was going to happen.

The most surprising thing about this picture is that Katenka is standing on the floor.

I'm reaching for the matches.

How we got ourselves to Paris is another story. We undertook no more long flights. Except Turkey, which we cut across in three hot nights alive with the incessant buzzing of cicadas. The U.S. consul in Athens issued us our first Western documents. Of course they wanted to know all about us, but we concocted a simple-minded tale involving an inflatable dinghy, supplies of drinking water, and Lady Luck. Once launched, this idyllic fiction circulated for years through all the prefectures of Europe. Pretty soon I managed to sell a dozen or so of my photos to a French agency, received an advance—it was this, incidentally, that decided our choice of a country; they had promised us the rest on arrival in Paris—and we timidly rushed out to spend what was for us an enormous amount of money. The pictures, which showed up a week later on the front covers of various thick magazines, were the sort of thing I'd been doing all my life: streets, people, mainly people. I had taken only the last few from high up—there was one of Moscow slanting away below, bristling with the sinister spires of its dwarf skyscrapers, crushed beneath the funereal weight of administrative buildings.

In Paris we lived modestly, with a sort of melancholy gaiety. Something had infused the atmosphere of our relations for good: a certain quantity of what I thought was non-lethal poison. I tried not to hear news from Russia, bought no newspapers, but whether I liked it or not the magazines that used my work slipped in commentaries on Soviet life, and I was often overcome with disgust, as in Nikakov's office—overtly or covertly, they were 99 per cent pro-Soviet.

One evening at a noisy party given by a famous art critic—every last painter was there to pay his commercial respects—Katenka and I were standing on a balcony. She was wearing a light dress and her bare hands were cupped, I'm afraid to say prayerfully, around a glass of champagne. Suddenly she started talking about Nikolai Petrovich, about his one-room library, while I looked down at the early-evening bustle of Montparnasse far below. What she was saying filled me with something heavy, and I was on the point of stopping her when I heard: "He gave it to us as a gift, and it became our salvation, and we never even try it any longer . . . not even a tiny bit . . ." Already bending, or rather pouring, over the rail of the balcony, she was slipping down. The rest happened in an instant: I saw her turn in a spiral, then plummet down, a colored ball with her gown streaming out behind; I heard the motley crowd gasp as it instantly formed itself into a perfect circle . . . Why did I rush to the stairs, to get the elevator? To this day, I don't know . . .

She was buried at Saint-Genevieve-des-Bois. There, where so many endlessly strange Russian fates have ended. There, too, visiting her grave, I once met a former Soviet engineer, now a voluntary Paris *clochard*. And the nicest possible life-loving *clochard* he was. I gave him a lift back into Paris, and when we were already sitting in a café, just about to part, he suddenly said to me: "They say those who could fly, once they get to the West they simply lose the ability."

He was a merry soul, and his smile, hanging in the dimly-lit café, reminded me of the Cheshire cat—one of ours.

Report from a Beseiged City

BY ZBIGNIEW HERBERT
(TRANSLATION BY ALISSA VALLES)

Too old to carry arms and fight like the others—

I was mercifully given the supporting role of a chronicler
I write down—not knowing for whom—a siege's history

I have to be precise but I don't know when the siege began
two centuries ago in December September dawn yesterday
we here are all suffering from the loss of a sense of time

we were left only the place and an attachment to the place
we govern ruins of temples ghosts of gardens and houses
if we lose our ruins we will be left with nothing

I write as best I can in the rhythm of these endless weeks
Monday: stores are empty a rat is now the unit of currency
Tuesday: the mayor has been killed by unknown assassins
Wednesday: cease-fire talks the enemy interned our envoys

we don't know where they are that is where they were shot
Thursday: after a stormy meeting a majority of votes rejected

the motion of the local merchants for unconditional surrender
Friday: plague broke out Saturday: N.N. a staunch defender
committed suicide Sunday: no water we resisted an assault
at the eastern gate the one called the Gate of the Covenant

I know it's all monotonous it won't move anyone to tears

I avoid comment emotion keep a tight rein write on facts
it appears only facts have value on the foreign markets
but with a kind of pride I long to bring news to the world
of the new breed of children we raised owing to the war
our children don't like fairy tales they have their fun killing
waking and sleeping they dream of soup of bread and bone
just like dogs and cats

in the evening I like to wander along the edges of the City
skirting the borders of our uncertain liberty
I watch from above an ant procession of troops their lights
I listen to the noise of drums and the barbarian shrieking
it is truly beyond me why the City is still defending itself

the siege is taking a long time our enemies have to take
nothing unites them apart from the desire for our destruction
Goths Tartars Swedes Caesar's men ranks of the Transfiguration
who can count them
the banners change their colors like a forest against the horizon
a delicate bird yellow in spring through green to winter's black

then in the evening freed from the facts I can meditate
on ancient questions remote ones for instance about our
allies across the sea I know they feel sincere compassion
they send flour sacks encouragement lard and good advice
they don't even know it was their fathers who betrayed us
they were our allies from the time of the second Apocalypse
the sons are blameless deserve gratitude so we are grateful

they have not lived through a siege as long as an eternity

they who are touched by misfortune are always alone
defenders of the Dalai Lama the Kurds and the Afghans

now as I write these words those who favor appeasement
have acquired an advantage over the party of the staunch
an ordinary mood swing the stakes are still being weighed

cemeteries are growing the number of defenders shrinking
but the defense continues it will continue to the end

and if the City falls and one man survives
he will carry the City inside him on the paths of exile
he will be the City

we look into hunger's face the face of fire face of death
the worst of all—the face of betrayal

and only our dreams have not been humiliated

1982

On Eugen Jebeleanu

BY MATTHEW ZAPRUDER

Eugen Jebeleanu is one of Romania's best known poets and public figures. Born in 1911, Jebeleanu had a literary career that spanned decades of great economic and political hardship and upheaval for Romania: the years leading up to World War II, the rule of the fascist and nationalistic Iron Guard, the postwar Stalinist Communist regime, and finally the corrupt and brutal dictatorship of Nicolae Ceauşescu.

In 1936, early in his career as a journalist, and during a time of great political ferment leading up to World War II, Jebeleanu was sent by his editors to Brasov to cover the trial of a group of Communist activists. Among them was the young Nicolae Ceauşescu, who had been beaten and jailed. Impressed by Ceauşescu's defiance, Jebeleanu wrote a provocative editorial expressing sympathy for his fate. The effect of this act—courageous, risky, and typical of Jebeleanu—would several decades later influence the course of Jebeleanu's life in ways he could not at the time have possibly predicted.

Like many artists and citizens, Jebeleanu was for a time a true believer in the values and goals of Communism. In 1959 he published an epic poem, "The Smile of Hiroshima," an impassioned critique of the nuclear bombing of Japan by the United States at the end of the war. He would become famous for this poem in the 1960s not only in Romania but throughout Europe and Latin America.

In 1965, Nicolae Ceauşescu became the leader of Romania. Flattered when reminded of Jebeleanu's early defense of his behavior in the 1930s, and aware of Jebeleanu's already considerable fame, Ceauşescu gave Jebeleanu a government sinecure, as well as wide latitude in the publication of his work. Jebeleanu took immediate advantage of this freedom, writing and publishing new poems of a startling directness. Beginning in the mid-1970s, he began to serially publish on the front pages of the major newspaper *Contemporanul* the strange, direct, emotionally blasted poems that would eventually compose *Arma Secreta* (*Secret Weapon*), his last complete collection. Jebeleanu died in 1991, less than two years after Ceauşescu was deposed and executed.

Throughout his life Jebeleanu's behavior was often oppositional, though not systematically so. When confronted with what he saw as abusive behavior on the part of the authorities, he often responded by lashing out in impassioned anger that could be almost willfully careless. While courageous, his was not the analytical resistance of dissidents such as Václav Havel. His highly personal stance of protest revealed itself sporadically in life, and in its purest and most direct form in his poems, which oscillate among strong expressions of anger, irony, self-criticism, nihilism, and joy.

The four selections from the book reprinted here are typical of Jebeleanu's sparse, direct, allegorical style. They take elemental, regular objects from the world—bread, newspapers, candles, a familiar statue of Mihai Eminescu, the father of Romanian poetry—and recast them in slightly skewed, yet very recognizable situations. These situations are designed to bring forward the landscape of Jebeleanu's hidden emotional life, which is the same as that of his fellow citizens: guilt, rage, uncertainty, anger, futility, and alienation. "Flowers at the Statue of Eminescu" is the closest Jebeleanu gets to a hopeful statement about the ability of art to survive in such circumstances, though it is also, typically, a poem of great darkness and violence that brings forward the theme of collective responsibility: "And we deserve all these things / because we have earned them."

Poems from *Secret Weapon*

BY EUGEN JEBELEANU
(TRANSLATION BY RADU IOANID & MATTHEW ZAPRUDER)

CHIMERA

A chimera is born from rain,
invisible rain.

Her hair is long,
and her face is on the back of her head.

The opaline tail of the chimera
arises from a horrible notion.
Ever since I was born
she has been hitting me with it.

Darkness and gray light.

Sometimes I try to get around the tail
to see the chimera's face.

Then the rain becomes stronger,
and I know something terrible shakes there
from rain and laughter.

Chimera is reading the news.

EARS

I have two ears from which I can be pulled
by two people at most at one time pulling.
When I sleep I usually sleep on one.
The other is a candle.

But at any time I can be awoken
in order to report
why I am sleeping—or in order to be told
to sleep in order to report.

Come closer, but not like that other time
when a few hundred came.
Pinch my ear, but only one of them.
The other is burning.

TOWN ON FIRE

Just before I would set it on fire,
I would yell, Get out of the houses!
But don't take anything with you!

And I would stay motionless—
shadow
and sign of light,
watching
how everyone would come out running,
dressed only in skins,
in their own skin.

Winged, they would leave
furniture the landscape of so many quarrels,
kitchens the site of so many shortages,
those same walls with their boredom
confronting
all those little shelves of books unread
for lack of time,
and time the color
of cold bread.

Now fly! I would shout,
blowing in order to lift them,
and they would fly, all of them,
without ever looking
over their shoulders.

FLOWERS AT THE STATUE OF EMINESCU

Why you would find this useful, nobody knows.
Meaning it isn't useful at all.
The poetry of poverty
is getting stronger everywhere.
The only strong ones
are those who can mount.
The horses get weaker and weaker,
and the horsemen more and more bestial.
And the ribs of the horses
are solar jewels
in the prison of dead visions.
And we deserve all these things
because we have earned them.
Now you are bronze,
and you don't care about anything.
Or, maybe, I don't know . . .
Because, last night
it seemed to me that
cautiously rotating
your infinite
oceanic
eyes
you pulled one carnation
from the wreath caressing your back
and swallowed it
secretly.

From *Imperium*

BY RYSZARD KAPUŚCIŃSKI
(TRANSLATION BY KLARA GLOWCZEWSKA)

THE THIRD ROME

When in the fall of 1989 I began the cycle of my travels over the territories of the Imperium, my contacts with this power, although sporadic and individually brief, already had their long history. I thought that they would now be of great help to me. I was mistaken. This last series of journeys was for me a great revelation for two reasons. First, I had never taken a close interest in this country; I was not a specialist; I was not a Russicist, a Sovietologist, Kremlinologist, and so on. The Third World absorbed me, the colorful continents of Asia, Africa and Latin America—it was to these that I had almost exclusively devoted myself. My actual familiarity with the Imperium was therefore negligible, haphazard, superficial. Second, as the epoch of Stalin and Brezhnev recedes more and more, a knowledge about this system and country grows geometrically. Not only does each year and each month bring new materials and information, but each week and each day! Someone newly interested in communism as an ideology and in the Imperium as its worldly political incarnation might not realize that ninety percent, if not more, of the materials now available to him had still not seen the light of day just a few years ago!

Just as Columbus lived in the epoch of great geographic discoveries, when every sailing expedition altered the picture of the world, so we live today in the epoch of great political discoveries, in which ever newer and newer revelations continuously change the picture of our contemporaneity.

In the spring of 1989, reading the news arriving from Moscow, I thought: It would be worth going there. It was a time when everyone felt a sense of curiosity about and anticipation of something extraordinary. It seemed then, at the end of the eighties, that the world was entering a period of great metamorphosis, of a transformation so profound and fundamental that it would not bypass anyone, no country or state, and so certainly not the last imperium on earth—the Soviet Union.

The climate conducive to democracy and freedom prevailed increasingly across the world. On every continent, dictatorships fell one after the other: Obote's in Uganda, Marcos's in the Philippines, Pinochet's in Chile. In Latin America, despotic military regimes lost power in favor of more moderate civilian ones, and in Africa the one-party systems that had been nearly ubiquitous (and as a rule, grotesque and thoroughly corrupt) were disintegrating and exiting the political stage.

Against this new and promising global panorama, the Stalinist-Brezhnevian system of the USSR looked more and more anachronistic, like a decaying and ineffectual relic. But it was an anachronism with a still-powerful and dangerous force. The crisis that the Imperium was undergoing was followed throughout the world with attention, but with anxious attention—everyone was aware that this was a power equipped with weapons of mass destruction that could blow up our planet. Yet the possibility of this gloomy and alarming scenario nevertheless did not mask the satisfaction and universal relief that communism was ending and that there was in this fact some sort of irreversible finality.

Germans say Zeitgeist, the spirit of the times. It is a fascinating moment, fraught with promise, when the spirit of the times, dozing, pitifully and apathetically, like a huge wet bird on a branch, suddenly and without a clear reason (or at any rate without a reason allowing of an entirely rational explanation) unexpectedly takes off in bold and joyful flight. We all hear the *shush* of this flight. It stirs our imagination and gives us energy: we begin to act.

If I could—I am planning in the year 1989—I would like to traverse the entire Soviet Union, its fifteen federal republics. (I am not thinking, however, of making my way to all the forty-four republics, districts and autonomous regions, for I would simply not live long enough to do that.) The most far-flung points of my itinerary would be:

In the west—Brest (the border with Poland)
In the east—the Pacific (Vladivostok, Kamchatka or Magadan)
In the north—Vorkuta or Novaya Zemlya
In the south—Astara (the border with Iran) or Termez (the border with Afghanistan)

A huge area of the world. But then the surface of the Imperium measures more than twenty-two million square kilometers, and its continental borders are longer than the equator and stretch for forty-two thousand kilometers.

Keeping in mind that wherever it is technically possible, these borders were and are marked with thick coils of barbed wire. (I saw such barriers on the border with Poland, China, and Iran) and that this wire, because of the dreadful climate, quickly deteriorates and therefore must often be replaced across hundreds, no, thousand, of kilometers, one can assume that a significant portion of the Soviet metallurgical industry is devoted to producing barbed wire.

For the matter does not end with the wiring of borders! How many thousands of kilometers of wire were used to fence in the gulag archipelago? Those hundreds of camps, staging points, prisons scattered throughout the territory of the entire Imperium! How many thousands more kilometers were swallowed up for the wiring of artillery, tank, and atomic ranges? And the wiring of barracks? And various warehouses?

If one were to multiply all this by the number of years the Soviet government has been in existence, it would be easy to see why, in the shops of Smolensk or Omsk, one can buy neither a hoe nor a hammer, never mind a knife or a spoon: such thing could simply not be produced, since the necessary raw materials were used up in the manufacture of barbed wire and that is still not the end of it! After all, tons of this wire had to be transported by ships, railroad, helicopters, camels, dog teams, to the farthest, most inaccessible corners of the Imperium, and then it all had to be unloaded, uncoiled, cut, fastened. It is easy to imagine those unending telephone, telegraphic, and postal reminders issued by the commanders of the border guards, the commanders of the gulag camps, and prison directors following up on their requisitions for more tons of barbed wire, the pains they would take to build up a reserve supply of this wire in case of a shortage in the central warehouses. And it is equally easy to imagine those thousands of commissions and control teams dispatched across the entire territory of the

Imperium to make certain everything is properly enclosed, that the fences are high and thick enough, so meticulously entangled and woven that even a mouse cannot squeeze through. It is also easy to imagine telephone calls from officials in Moscow to their subordinates in the field, telephone calls characterized by a constant and vigilant concern expressed in the question "Are you all really properly wired in?" And so instead of building themselves houses and hospitals, instead of repairing the continually failing sewage and electrical systems, people were for years occupied (although fortunately not everyone!) with the internal and external, local and national, wiring of their Imperium.

The idea of a great journey was born in the course of reading the news about perestroika. Almost all of it originated from Moscow. Even if it concerned events in a place as distant as Chabarovsk, it was still datelined "Moscow." My reporter's soul would rebel, In such moments I was drawn to Chabarovsk; I wanted to see for myself what was going on there. It was a temptation all the stronger because, even with my slight knowledge of the Imperium, I was aware how much Moscow differs from the rest of the country (although not in everything), and that enormous areas of this superpower are an immeasurable terra incognita (even for the inhabitants of Moscow).

But doubts at once assailed me—was I really right to search for perestroika outside Moscow? I had just read a new book, published in early 1989, by the eminent historian Natan Eydelman, *Revolution from the Top in Russia*. The author regards perestroika as just one more in a series of turning points in Russian history and reminds us that all such turning points, revolutions, convulsions, and breakthroughs in this country came about because they were the will of the czar, the will of the secretary-general, or the will of the Kremlin (or of Petersburg). The energy of the Russian nation, says Eydelman, has always been spent not on independent grassroots initiatives, but on carrying out the will of the ruling elite.

The message between the lines: perestroika will last as long as the Kremlin will allow it to.

So, if one wished to know the direction and strength of the wind, perhaps it would be better to be in Moscow, near the Kremlin, and to observe the seismographs, thermometers, barometers, and weather vanes that are situated around its walls? For Kremlinology more often reminded me of meteorology than of knowledge such as one gathers at the crossroads of history and philosophy.

It is Autumn 1989. My first encounter with the Imperium in years. I was last here more than twenty years ago, at the start of the Brezhnev era. The era of Stalin, the era of Krushchev. And before that: the era of Peter I, Catherine II, Alexander III. In what other country does the persona of the ruler, his character traits, his manias and phobias, leave such a profound stamp on the national history, its course, its accents and downfalls? Hence the rapt attention with which the moods, depressions, and caprices of successive czars and secretaries-general were always followed in Russia and around the world—how much depended on this! (Mickiewicz on Nicholas I: The Czar is surprised—the inhabitants of Petersburg tremble with fear, / The Czar is angry—his courtiers die of fear; armies are marching, whose God and faith / is the Czar. The Czar is angry: let us die, we will cheer up the Czar!")

∞∞∞

To fly into Moscow at the end of 1989 is to enter a world dominated by the proliferating, unbridled word. After years of the gag, of silence, and of censorship, the dams are bursting, and stormy, powerful, ubiquitous torrents of words are flooding over everything. The Russian intelligentsia is once again (or, rather, for the first time) in its element—endless, indefatigable, fierce, frantic discussion. How they love this, how good this makes them feel! Wherever someone announces some discussion, immeasurable crowds immediately gather. The subject of the discussion can be anything, but of course the preferred theme is the past. So, what about Lenin, what about Trotsky, what about Bucharin? And the poets are as important as the politicians. Did Mandelshtam die in the camps of hunger or as a result of an epidemic? Who is responsible for the suicide of Tsvetaeva? These matters are debated for hours on end, till dawn.

But even more time is spent in front of television sets, watching broadcasts of the sessions of the Supreme Soviet that go on night and day. Several factors contributed simultaneously to this explosion of political passions. First, politics at the highest rungs of power was surrounded here for centuries by an airtight, almost mystical secrecy. The rulers decided about the life or death of people, and yet these people were never able to see the rulers with their own eyes. And then, suddenly, here they are, the rulers, getting angry, their ties askew waving their arms around, picking their ears. Second, as they follow the deliberations of their highest popular assembly, Russians for the first time have the sense of participating in something important.

And finally—perestroika coincided with the explosion of television in this country. Television gave to perestroika a dimension that no other event in the history of the Imperium had ever had.

From *The Tower*

BY UWE TELLKAMP

(TRANSLATION BY ANNIE JANUSCH)

THE RIDE HOME

The strand of lights that decorated the tree had a defect, its lemon-shaped bulbs flickering on and then off, erasing Dresden's silhouette along the Elbe River. Christian pulled off his wet mittens, which had become beaded with ice on the woolen insides and rubbed his fingers, nearly numb from the cold, briskly against each other. He breathed on them, his breath drifting like a patch of fog in front of the dark, hewn stone entrance to the Buchensteig leading up to the Arbogasts Institute. The houses on Schillerstraße tapered off in the dark; a power line ran from the nearest, a half-timbered house with latched shutters, into the branches of one of the beech trees above the stone path, where an Advent star blazed, bright and motionless. Christian, who had come over the Loschwitzer Bridge—the Blue Wonder—and across Körnerplatz, walked further away from the city and towards the main road, soon reaching the funicular. The roll gates were down over the windows of the businesses that he walked by—a bakery, a creamery, a fish market. The houses lay half in the shadows, drab with ashy contours. It seemed as though they were huddling together, seeking protection in one another from something vague and unfathomable that might float up out of the darkness—just as the icy moon had slid up over the Elbe a short while ago when Christian had stood on the empty bridge, looking at the river, and pulling the thick wool scarf his mother had knitted over his ears and cheeks in the biting wind. The moon had climbed slowly, breaking free of the river's cold, sluggish, fluid mass to stand alone above the countryside with its pastures wrapped in a cocoon of fog, above the boat house that lay to the Old Town side of the Elbe, above the mountains that trailed off toward Pillnitz. A church bell in the distance struck four, taking Christian by surprise.

He walked toward the train, placed his bag on the weather-beaten bench in front of the gate that closed off the platform, and waited, his gloved hands in the pockets of his green military parka. The hand of the station's clock seemed to advance very slowly. Besides him no one was waiting for the train, and to bide the time he studied the notice board. It hadn't been cleared in a long time. There was still an ad for Café Toscana on the Old Town side of the Elbe, one for the Nähter that lay closer to Schillerplatz, and another for the Sibyllenhof, the restaurant in the end-station at the funicular's top. Christian began to go over in his mind the fingerings and melody of the Italian piece he was supposed to play for his father's birthday. Then, he looked into the darkness of the tunnel. A faint light grew, gradually filling the tunnel cavity like water rising from a fountain; at the same time the sound grew: a distorted creak and groan, the guiding cable of steel wires under the weight. The train jolted closer, a capsule filled with oceanic light; two headlights illuminated the track. You could see the hazy outlines of the individual passengers in the train car, and between the passing shadows, the gray-bearded conductor who'd driven the route for years: back and forth, back and forth, always alternating. Maybe he closed his eyes in order to escape the all too familiar route, or to see it inwardly while blocking it out, or to ward off ghosts. He probably saw by hearing, though, every jolt during the ride must have been familiar to him. Christian took a coin out of his bag and studied it—the oak leaf next to the crudely cut *10*, the tiny worn-down year with the *A* beneath, the flipside with the hammer, compass, spiked wreath—and thought how often they, the kids on Heinrichstraße and Wolfsleiten, had rubbed the stamped face of such a coin onto a piece of paper with a pencil. Ezzo and Ina were more skilled at it, more eager, too, than he'd been at the time, back when they dreamed of great counterfeiters, robbers, and adventurers, like the heroes in the films, running in the play of light streaming through the fir trees, or in the Karl May and Jules Verne books. The train came, softly braking to a halt. The graduated doors opened, letting the passengers out. The conductor got out and opened the gate and a narrow aisle beside it, for those getting on. A fare box had been installed there. Christian threw his fare into it and pulled down the lever on the side; the coin slid from the turntable and fell to the bottom with the others. Sometimes, instead of coins, the children in the neighborhood threw in smoothly polished pebbles from the Elbe that they called bread-and-butter, or buttons—much to the consternation of their mothers, since the small aluminum coins you could get easily, whereas buttons were hard to come by. The funicular's doors were closed. You had to pull on a cable to open them in the winter, and they closed as soon as you let go. The conductor went into the station, poured himself a cup of coffee, and watched the bustling passengers disappear like shadows, heading around corners, to Körnerplatz or Pillnitz. After a few minutes a tired voice sounded from the loudspeaker, something Saxon that Christian didn't understand, but the conductor got up and carefully closed the station door behind him. Slowly, the round leather coin purse swung over his scuffed uniform, and he went into the conductor's compartment with the control panel, whose many buttons seemed point-less to Christian since the funicular was steered by cables and pulleys, and even if the cable should snap, its ingenious mechanism braked automatically. Maybe there was some other reason for the buttons, maybe they served some function of communication or psychology: buttons that existed also had to mean something, fulfill some function, require some knowledge, prevent some monotony or work fatigue, apart from maneuvering around the other train at the halfway point along the route. The door slammed shut behind the conductor. "All aboard" said the voice from the loudspeaker. The train stood still another moment, then set calmly into motion, gliding out and upward from the station. Christian turned around and saw how the path and waiting area diminished in perspective until only the oval remained of the tunnel cavity giving way to the firestone-green sky. Gradually it got smaller, a backdrop of darkness pushing itself forward slowly from the side, and for a little while, before the exit came into view, only the tunnel lamps and the headlights issued sparse light. Christian took from his bag a book that his uncle Meno had given him. In the past week he'd barely gotten around to reading: the Christmas spirit had been unmistakable in Waldbrunn with classes not as strict as usual, but the preparations for his father's birthday party and the daily bus rides home in order to be able to practice the Italian piece with the others had cost him time. Christian wanted to read the book thoroughly during Christmas vacation. Bound in coarse linen, it was quite thick and printed on fibrous paper; the portrait on the cover he recognized from a facsimile edition of the Manesse Codex that he'd seen in his uncle's library, and at his cousins Niklas, Ezzos, and Reglinde's house, too, there was an especially beautiful and well-preserved copy that their father often read aloud from. The painting portrayed Tannhäuser, the Minnesinger of lore, a red-haired man in a blue robe with a white cape, a black cross on the breast; stylized vines climbing beneath a black and yellow coat of arms and the plumed helmet beside it. Tannhäuser's—or "Tanhuser" as his name was inscribed—left hand was raised in warning, or perhaps, cautious greeting, his right hand gathering the cape. Christian opened the volume and read: "Old High German Poems, Selected and With Remarks by Meno Rhode." Then, he opened the book back up to an old legend he'd already been reading on the trip from Waldbrunn to Dresden. The light in the ceiling above him began quivering, giving the open pages a grainy, ashen appearance, and the letters blurred before his eyes from the train's gentle vibrations. He couldn't concentrate on the tale of the knight with the gold spurs who'd sailed out with seventy-two ships to free the princess bride. The light went out. He put the book back in his bag and felt around for the barometer, a gift for his father that he'd picked up from the former skipper's clubhouse on the Elbe. It was well-packed and cushioned in the ball of dirty laundry filing his bag.

The train continued its slow and steady ascent, occasionally shuddering with a jolt from an uneven shift in grade. When it reached the altitude of the beech trees that ran alongside the track, the train sailed for a while just a few meters above the ground. You could see into the lit windows—an outstretched hand could have touched the train car without any effort. Up by the second tunnel the Sibyllenhof Restaurant came into view. Closed years ago, its terraces jutted out like writing slates forgotten there by giant school children. The train would head toward it, and just before the lowest terrace, swerve into the tunnel to the end-station. Christian sometimes dreamed of bygone feasts in those halls that now lay dark and unwelcoming, of dapper gentlemen in starched shirts with jet-black buttons, watch chains dripping from their vest pockets; flower peddlers in page uniforms, summoned to the table with a mere snap of the fingers, to present a rose to ladies whose jewelry was set alight by the crystal pendants of the chandelier; a band playing dance music, the pale violinist with pomaded hair and a chrysanthemum in his lapel . . . The icy glow of the moon skated over the gleaming rooftops of houses, descending dramatically down to the main road, giving their snow-covered gardens a powdery brightness, accented here and there by snowcapped wood piles and sheds that fused together with the shadows cast by shrubs and trees.

Christian noticed that they were just above Vogelstrom's house, that gray manor belonging to the painter and illustrator, which Meno had named "the spider web house." Christian thought of this now as he looked out the window, his face close to the cold pane, the day's austerity playing out behind inaccessible windows and beneath tall trees. The main road was only partially visible now, a pale ribbon swinging into the depths, and just beyond it, the dormant mass of the Loschwitz hillside where the moonlight vanished into a needle-thin thread before the Ostrom watchtowers, fading at the bridge where the soldiers at the checkpoint aspired to some higher purpose. The garden of the spider web house lay dark, shielded from events and glances; Christian could barely recognize the snow-dusted crowns of the pear and beech trees, whose fine branches hung like cobwebs of smoke; the contours of the narrow cleft between the beech trees and the rooftops, like light in the hatchings of old unfinished drawings. He saw the well, the nearly overgrown path that led up over mossy steps and formed an arc around the weathered stonework that depicted a catfish spouting water. The opening lines of a poem were chiseled into the tablet above, the washed-out letters nearly half erased. As much as he tried, Christian couldn't think of the wording, but he could see clearly before him the crumbling baleen of the fish, the blinded eyes and the dark gown of moss; he recalled his superstitious fear of the creature and of the well, too, silently breathing its crypt-like coldness whenever he and Meno had visited Vogelstrom. The peculiar conversations that Meno and that gaunt painter in the spider web house had had only fed his childish fear more. It was less the words and themes themselves that seemed strange than the atmosphere of the house. With a childlike non-, or at most, half or three-quarter's sense, as a young boy of eleven or twelve, he had found the little that was to be understood to be correct and appropriate for the grown-up world. Words like "Merigarto" or "Magelone," he recalled having seemed more like incantations than terms that meant something in the real world. These two words struck him profoundly and he hadn't forgotten them since, although they'd seemed less mysterious to him than the paintings in

Vogelstrom's somber hallway: idyllic landscapes, garden scenes in pale blue light with flute-playing fawns and water nymphs; a line of ancestors, serious-looking men and women holding a flower, a nettle, or—what he would gaze at most in amazement—a golden snail in their hands. Vogelstrom, and even Meno, only rarely cast a glance as they passed by these paintings, dawning in the hallway and conjuring those two words: the island of Merigarto, and Magelone, the maiden who rose from the depths of time only to vanish into them again. He'd memorized these words and tasted their forgotten melodiousness over and over again in murmuring conversations with himself. It was sound, too, that clung to him from his uncle's conversations with Volgelstrom, a streaming whisper from Vogelstrom's atelier when it was so cold in winter that the frost nipped at the easels and the diamond-patterned wallpaper, both men moving about the room with smoking breath—Meno with Vogelstrom's coat over his shoulders, Vogelstrom himself in several sweaters and shirts—their voices barely decipherable when they were in the library. Christian would eavesdrop from the hallway, pretending to study one of the ancestral faces; occasionally cautious laughter, turning into a rebuke or praise of one or the other's tobacco. Sometimes Meno would call him over to show him something, the painter leafing carefully through steel and copper engravings in musty-smelling folios, and at those times it seemed that words might lapse—words that lingered in the ear as something strange and never before heard, words like those two magical names.

The light trembled back on. Out of the darkness below the tunnel and the Sibyllenhof, the descending train crept towards them, reaching the loop at the same time as they did, where the lane split and one train could make way for the other. You could see the driver, a motionless phantom in an empty capsule gliding past. He returned the greeting of the gray- bearded conductor with a slight nod of the head, then the train sank down and disappeared from sight. Christian remembered having first heard something by Poe in the spider web house. Meno and Vogelstrom had been looking at illustrations of a story. In particular he remembered the piece of paper on which Vogelstrom's artful etching needle had portrayed the castellated abbey in the sinister night; Prince Prospero with his court of a thousand knights and dames in the abbey with its chambers welded shut. Under Vogelstrom's thin, fine-jointed hand, it had looked to him as if they were promenading and chattering, as though society were playing its hale and lighthearted games, while outside the pestilence devastated the country; as though Prospero were walking through the chambers in the euphoria of the great masquerade. Melodies streamed, people danced, and the chiming of the ebony clock that stood in the chamber of tapestries echoed to the abbey's furthest reaches. Since Prince Prospero suffered no sadness, the howling of the dogs outside at the gates and the cries of the wretched were not to be heard over the laughter, the gaiety, and song. The train slowed down, coasting the last few meters. Sunken in memory and thought, Christian had barely noticed that the train was pulling into the top tunnel, which seemed lighter here through the whitewashed walls than below. He cast a habitual glance, but without taking anything in, at the bright and friendly whitewashed building, its gracefully vaulted roof, the brick construction with the neon sign "Funicular," the engine room adjoining the vestibule, where you could wait and look at photos displayed in a vitrine depicting earlier models and technical details. The train came lightly bouncing to a stop. The doors rattled open. Christian threw his bag over his shoulder and walked, still buried in thought, down the flat steps of the station and toward the exit gate. The conductor shuffled toward the vestibule, felt for the button hidden in the wall that buzzed the doors closed, and Christian stepped outside. He was home, in the tower.

My Grandmother the Censor

BY MASHA GESSEN

"**H**ungarian! Who invented it? My brain couldn't retain a single word—not 'thank you,' not 'hello,' not 'one,' 'two,' or 'three.' I've never felt so much like a foreigner."

I am complaining. I have just come to Moscow after reporting a story in the Balkans. It is 1993. I am an American journalist, but for the previous couple of years I have been spending more and more time in Moscow, the city of my birth, I am getting to know my two grandmothers, who were left behind when my family left for the United States in 1981, when I was fourteen.

"Ah, Hungarian," says my grandmother as we step off the bus into the sleeting greyness of a Moscow spring. "Never could wrap my mind around it either: Italian, Czech, Romanian, Polish—none of those were a problem. German, French, English, of course, I knew. But Hungarian—no matter how much I struggled, I could not get past the dictionary."

I stare down at my grandmother in surprise. I know she translates books from English and German, and that she also knows French. But Czech, Romanian, Polish? "What's with all the languages?" I ask. "I never knew you translated from those."

Or did I? Let me recall what I knew before we stepped off the bus.

I knew that my grandmother Rozalia, Baba Ruzya to me, was a member of the Communist Party. When I was about ten and torn between the nauseating (but appealing) aesthetic fed to me at school and the compelling dissident sympathies of my parents, my mother told me that Baba Ruzya belonged to the Party. Reared in a closed circle of Jewish intellectual types I was not aware of anyone else I knew being a member.

"Baba," I asked one day, "why did you join the party?"

"Because I believed in the goals and ideals of the Party," my grandmother said slowly and carefully.

I didn't pay much attention to the past tense or the care in her reply and walked away feeling frustrated with an answer that sounded as if it came out of a school book. What I really wanted to know had nothing to do with this story. I wanted to know why the day I got my red Young Pioneer kerchief was the happiest day of my life. Why, if I had already been reading Solzhenitsyn? But that was a question about belonging and my grandmother's stories are about anything but that.

I also knew something else. Sometime in the late 1970s my mother got her hands on a copy of George Orwell's *Nineteen Eighty-Four*. She quoted it endlessly; she told stories from it as though they were real-life anecdotes. At the kitchen table one day, she talked, with a high-pitched laugh, about the Ministry of Truth—imagine that! Imagine a place where news is routinely rewritten to fit the ideological line!

"And what do you think I did at Glavlit?" Baba Ruzya asked, slowly and carefully again.

Glavlit. *Glav* as in *glavny*, or head, the chief. *Lit*, as in *literature*. Meaning the Head Directorate of Literature. Baba Ruzya tells me what she did there as we walk from the bus. At first, for three years, she worked in a department known as the Department of Control over Foreign Media. The control was exercised as soon as the foreign media—books, magazines, anything in print—crossed the border. The post office forwarded all such parcels to Glavlit, where an army of readers, known then as "political editors," but, later, in their retirement documents, simply called "censors," examined printed matter for signs of anti-Soviet prejudice.

"Sometimes we stamped them 'Permitted,' and then they were allowed into libraries or shops," my grandmother says. "But this hardly ever happened.

For the most part, we stamped things 'For internal use.' I mean, sometimes you could rip a few pages out and clear it, but mostly you just had to ban it. Because there was hardly a magazine or a book where the Soviet Union was not somehow maligned. It's not like people were sending Shakespeare and Dickens across the border. They were sending contemporary literature. All it had to contain was a phrase like 'even such an undemocratic society as the Soviet Union . . .'—and it would be condemned to a classified library."

There was one man in Paris who kept sending large quantities of books and magazines to another man in some tiny village in the far north of Russia. Soon after she came to work there one of the more experienced staff explained that the man in the far north was a member of the pre-revolutionary nobility, a scholar, perhaps a biologist, who had long ago decided not to emigrate. His brother, an artist, had moved to Paris. The scholar was arrested and exiled to the far north. On learning of his brother's fate, the artist decided to try to improve the quality of his life by sending him reading materials. Most of these ended up in classified libraries in Moscow. "This biologist got tiny crumbs out of those parcels." Neither, of course, would ever know that more was sent or that less was received: no one was meant to know about the existence of the Department of Control over Foreign Media.

Why was my Baba Ruzya working at Glavlit? She had wanted to be a history teacher. She attended a remarkable school in the center of Moscow, the enclave of the educated if not always privileged. They adored their teachers there. But one was especially inspirational. She punctuated her history course with a particular expression: "And this is no mere coincidence." Ruzya envisioned a career in which she could also tell her pupils: "And this is no mere coincidence."

"The first, the biggest, mistake I ever made was attending the history department at the university. I knew I could never teach school. I couldn't lie to the children." And there was another thing. Teachers got paid very little, and Ruzya needed money.

By 1943 she was a twenty-three-year-old war widow with a one-year-old daughter. She had a bed in one of the two rooms that belonged to her parents-in-law in a communal flat in Moscow. She had no milk; it vanished on the day she got the news that her husband had been killed. But she had a friend who said she could get her a job.

The problem with that job was Ruzya's father: "He was a man who was honest beyond reproach. He never tried to convince me to quit; he just expressed his surprise tenderly." When he first found out about Glavlit, he said, "But you are doing a policeman's work." Otherwise it was better than school: "Here I was lying only to myself. As a teacher, I would have had to lie to forty children. Here I lied with a clear conscience, so to speak, because if I hadn't been doing that job, someone else would have. But to lie while looking children in the eye—that would have been terrible."

In 1946 she had been working at Glavlit for three years. She had passed the annual exams, and she was known to have an aptitude for languages. So when the Soviet government, in a fit of post-war politesse, divorced censorship from diplomacy—transferring the responsibility for censoring foreign correspondents from the Ministry of Foreign Affairs to Glavlit—my grandmother was chosen to work in the new department. It comprised three people who came from Foreign Affairs, three people from the Ministry of State Security (which would later become part of the KGB), and my grandmother.

There were advantages. Unlike the department that controlled foreign media—words coming into the Soviet Union—the department that controlled foreign journalists—words going out—did not lead a secret existence. Its staff had a separate entrance at the Central Telegraph office, where they worked, but that was to prevent the censors from meeting the people they were censoring. The foreign journalists knew that they were there: the conditions of accreditation for foreign correspondents were that all dispatches be filed from the Central Telegraph building, where they would be cleared by the censor.

I have loved the Central Telegraph building since I was a child—for its rotating multicoloured globe, its digital clock and its catholic architectural aspirations. My grandmother's office had a door through which the clerk brought the dispatches, an electric bell she rang when she was done with a piece, and two telephones. She used one for routine calls, and the other when in doubt, to telephone her translation of a text directly to Stalin's secretariat.

NEWS ITEM FROM RADIO FREE EUROPE'S CENTRAL NEWSROOM reporting on continued persecution of Hungarian dissident intellectuals, as well as home raids conducted at their apartments in search of unauthorized literature and samizdat publications. January 27, 1984. (opposite page, credit: OSA Archivum)

SCREEN ON WOOD FRAME AND ROLLER USED IN SCREEN-PRINTING.

This particular piece was used by the Hungarian democratic opposition to produce various samizdat publications, including periodicals, political posters and other ephemera. 1980s. (credit: OSA Archivum)

Every time a correspondent from a new country was accredited, she was crash-taught his language. German, French and English she knew already. Italian, Czech, Romanian, Polish—none of these were a problem. But Hungarian—no matter how much she struggled, she could not get past the dictionary.

There are two things I ought to make clear. First, almost as soon as she starts telling me about her career (as we wade through the sleet from the bus stop to the market), my grandmother declares that the head of the department, Alexei Lukich Zorin, was a good, decent man.

Second, as I listen to the story, I am surprised but not horrified, even though my Baba Ruzya has told me that for eleven key post-war years she censored what the rest of the world could learn about the Soviet Union.

There are certain things she remembers very well. Certain journalists. Walter Cronkite from UPI—he filed a lot of stories, but it was your regular wire copy stuff, dry and dull, "amazingly boring." But Harrison Salisbury from the *New York Times*—there was a writer to be savored. "He had his own point of view, you see, and he just expressed it how he wanted, so bravely." She translated his articles in their entirety and sent them by messenger to Stalin's secretary. Hours later, Salisbury's "corrected" copy would go over the wire to New York. Every day at the end of her shift—generally it ended in the morning, since most dispatches went out overnight—she prepared a summary of the day's news for Stalin's office, mainly a circular exercise of translating back into Russian what foreign correspondents had culled from foreign newspapers—a re-spinning of Soviet stories was pretty much all that was allowed out. "Altogether I worked at Glavlit for fifteen years, and never in that time did I make a mistake in translation." She would have known if she had. Mistakes were lethal.

Certain episodes she remembers very well. The Doctors' Plot episode. The Stalin death episode. The Fellini episode.

The Doctors' Plot began in 1952. She heard of it originally from a typist in the office. But first you have to know how frightened Ruzya was by then of losing her job. The Anti-Cosmopolitan Campaign was entering its fifth year, the fifth year of rabid official ant-Semitism, the fifth year that Jews could not find work or hold on to university places. Without her job, Ruzya and her child would have faced destitution. And you have to know that she was the only Jew in the department that controlled foreign correspondents, and that she was the only staff member who did not belong to the Party. By this time she was so afraid of losing her job that she would have joined—but she no longer could, because she was Jewish. And the typist said: "You know, they are going to exile the Jews to Siberia."

And then the correspondents began to write stories saying the same thing. It was obvious, really; Stalin had exiled other ethnic groups in their entirety: he had moved the Chechens and the Ingush from the Caucasus to Siberian Kazakhstan; he had moved the Tartars from the Crimea, and the Germans from the Volga; and now that the Jews were the scapegoats of the nation, he would surely move them too. The Anti-Cosmopolitan drama was clearly drawing to a climax, with every Soviet newspaper hot on the heels of the Doctors' Plot, the chilling story of a conspiracy by Jewish doctors to kill innocent Soviet citizens. They were called the "killers in white coats." As the story went, there would be show trials, executions in Red Square and pogroms throughout the country. Then, in a show of saving the Jews, the magnanimous Soviet government would exile them to northern Siberia.

Salisbury kept writing about this likely sequence of events, and she kept crossing it out. It was obvious to her that the stories were true, and it was obvious that she could not let them through, because every day that she did her job well enough to keep it was another day when she might not be deported. In effect, Salisbury was writing for her; reminding her of her future nearly every night.

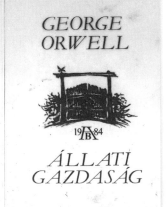

In the day, when she slept, she had a recurring nightmare. She is in a cattle car, cradling her ten-year-old daughter, who is asking for a drink of water. But she has no water.

When important events happened on one of Ruzya's nights off, a messenger would appear at the door. In 1953, she was living with her parents. In the

BACKGROUND
REPORT FROM
RADIO FREE EUROPE
on Romania's Law of the
Press adopted on March
28, 1974, which, among
other things, calls for the
establishment of the Press
and Printing Committee,
a *de facto* censorship
body to control publishing
activities. April 22, 1974.
(opposite page,
credit: OSA Archivum)

early hours of March 4 that year, the messenger said, "Comrade Stalin has died, and Comrade Solodnikov is summoned to work." Her mother started wailing. Ruzya thought: "I have a moron for a mother."

That is how my grandmother remembers it. My own mother had a different memory. She woke up to see her mother dressing for work at four in the morning. "Mama, what happened?" she said.

"Nothing important, dear. Stalin died. Go back to sleep."

Here is an episode they both remembered. There would be no classes, the teacher announced on March 4, because Comrade Stalin had died. The other children wailed. My mother drew a thick black frame, signifying death, around Stalin's portrait in her textbook, and wrote HOLIDAY, signifying no school. Happening to glance at the page, the teacher ripped the textbook out of the girl's hands and summoned her mother to the school.

"Buy your child a new textbook and explain some things to her," the teacher said. We were lucky to have happened upon a teacher like that, family legend concludes: a teacher who concealed instead of informing.

After Stalin died, there were the days of carnage and fear. Gorky Street, the avenue that led past the Central Telegraph to Red Square, was closed to all vehicles and people. Parallel streets teemed with human traffic, hundreds of thousands who had walked for days to view the body of the Father of the Nation. Those who worked or lived on Gorky Street were issued special passes that enabled them to pass through the barricades of military trucks. My grandmother was one of those let through. "On my way to work I stopped by the stores and it was delightful. I was able to buy things I could never have had. I bought calf tongue—imagine, calf tongue!—it cost pennies back then, it's just that you could never get it, but there I was practically the only customer." But it was frightening. It was still cold, and the truck drivers kept gunning their engines, and the roar of the crowds on the other streets mixed with the roar of the engines and filled the streets with dread.

She and her child shared a room in a giant communal flat in a basement off Trubnaya Ploshad, a square at the bottom of two hills, just below the streets that led to the Body. People fell over and got trampled in the crush. Bodies rolled down the streets on to Trubnaya Ploshad. They were carried past their basement windows—endlessly, it seemed.

"People said, 'He lived in blood and died in blood.' But you know, others, the idiots, they cried and cried. It was frightening. And then the happy day came when the newspapers announced that the doctors had been released and the investigation was stopped." That was on April 4, 1953, a month after Stalin died.

The censors were not allowed to have any contact with the foreign correspondents, though they had all seen my grandmother many times. As the only young woman in the department—pretty at that—she was the one designated to attend all the press conferences, posing as a Soviet correspondent.

A couple of years after Stalin's death, the clerk came in with a dispatch and a small envelope: "The Italian correspondents sent this for you." The envelope contained a ticket to the morning show of the Italian film festival. "It was the first foreign film festival, you understand? It wasn't international, it was Italian, but it was the first Western film festival here in the USSR. I was dying to go, but there was no way to get tickets. The cinemas were swamped. You see, we had no televisions in the Soviet Union then, no refrigerators even—these came much later—we had never seen . . . And there was a ticket, just a ticket with a seat number, for the morning show right after I finished work, and there was no note. It was my signal to act."

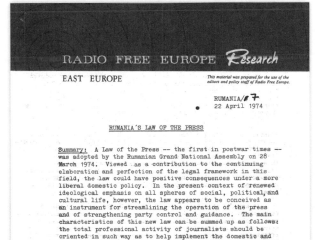

She risked her job for a film. Of course, after Stalin's death, she was risking only her job and nothing else, and after twelve years she was willing to give it up for a movie. She took precautions. She arrived at the theater at the last minute, walked into the hall when the lights had already dimmed, and slipped out in the dark just before the end credits came up. "I never looked to either side of me, I was so frightened. But of course they saw me."

She can still recount Fellini's *La Strada* in detail. She has seen it twice since and cried every time. She says it's a great film.

From *The Wall Jumper*

BY PETER SCHNEIDER

(TRANSLATION BY LEIGH HAFREY)

Pommerer listens carefully, thinks a while, orders a second round of vodka and beer, and then asks, without wasting another second on Kabe: "Do you know the story of the three moviegoers?"

∞∞∞

The house where the group met has supposedly been torn down since. Even now the neighbors are afraid their whole dead-end street will be declared off limits because of the disgrace brought on it by the people who lived at the very end.

It was the zigzag course of the border that put the house in an exposed position. Like a pipeline whose direction people couldn't agree on until the last minute, the Wall headed straight for the house and then veered to the right just short of it. So the building nearly abutted on the concrete mass which, overnight, turned its front door into the back.

At that time two families occupied the house, and two of the three future wall jumpers were just learning to walk. The Wacholt family had the ground floor; the Walz family lived upstairs. Both families owed the survival of their residence to their Party cards and to the fact that they had been among the first to welcome the "anti-fascist bulwark." Since they generally showed a consciousness in keeping with their front-line living conditions, they could be expected to teach their children the difference between a state boundary and a garden wall.

The two sons, who were almost the same age, coincidentally answered to the same name. They knew for sure which Willy was wanted only when one called for the other. This may have contributed to the fact that the two otherwise unremarkable boys developed the habit of listening more closely to each other than their parents. Besides—as their defense attorney pointed out later—the children's danger naturally increased when Mr. Walz died and Mr. Wacholt moved away to live with his mistress. From then on the Party could not have been adequately represented in the house. But since the two Willys behaved like other children, learned how to jump rope and play soccer, didn't mourn for a paper airplane that flew too far, didn't stand out in political indoctrination classes or in high jumping, their mothers saw no reason to forbid their jumping in the courtyard, the hall, and on the stairs.

Mrs. Walz later reproached herself for not carrying out a plan made by her late husband. He had intended, once the two Willys reached the rebellious stage, to nail down a dormer window in the attic. This window gave access to the roof of a veranda-like porch that served as a tool shed. From the roof, the already short distance between house and state boundary was so abbreviated that a leap from the edge would carry even a middling jumper to the top of the Wall. What's more—as Mrs. Walz might have noticed, had she not been overly trusting—the border guards in the nearby watchtower weren't always strict in their duty. During years of observation the two teenagers discovered loopholes in the surveillance system; in any case, they were reaching the age where they saw only the shortcomings of adults—for example, the fact that a pair of human eyes can't look in two directions at once.

The two Willys learned that guards develop habits on duty. At first the boys only noticed that a man was often alone in the tower and that he shifted his line of sight according to a definite rhythm. They could predict almost to the second when he would show them the back of his head. Then they began to suspect that he didn't notice them even when he was looking in their direction. Experiments on the roof of the porch, starting with a wave of the hand and culminating in a brandished red flag, proved that the roof and the stretch of Wall close to it lay in a blind angle of the view from the tower.

The two Willys might never have made use of their knowledge if the older one hadn't confided in a friend from Prenzlauer Berg. This was Lutz, who spent his life at the movies instead of at work, and who immediately gave the Willys' discovery a practical turn. He screwed a sturdy hook into the ridge of the porch roof, knotted a rope around it, and threw the other end over the Wall. Lutz was the first to leap the narrow chasm between East and West, after which he anchored the descent of the whole rope team from the other side of the Wall.

Once on Western soil, the trio asked for the nearest U-Bahn station and stole a ride to Kurfürstendamm. At the movie house there, they had a choice of *The Schoolgirl Report, Part III* or *Once upon a Time in the West*. Lutz made a successful case for the Italo-Western.

They ran into their first major obstacle at the box office, where the cashier disdainfully hefted their light-weight DDR money. Lutz demanded to see the manager and pointed out that he'd come all the way from Prenzlauer Berg over the Wall to Kurfürstendamm just to watch Charles Bronson. Now, Lutz complained, the cashier wanted to discuss the difference between East marks and West marks. How would he explain that kind of reception to his friends back in the poor part of town?

At first the manager didn't believe the boys' story about their trip from the house behind the Wall to his theater. But when they showed him their identity cards, he accepted them as admission tickets. The six o'clock show had already begun; Lutz knew roughly how the story went, and filled the other two in on what they had missed.

(credit: Winfried Hammann)

After the show the boys checked the date of the next film—not a real western, Lutz said, but worth seeing because the stars were Brigitte Bardot and Jeanne Moreau. Then they headed home. Barely four hours after their first trip to the movies in the West, the two Willys lay in their beds, and Lutz was racing back to Prenzlauer Berg on his motorcycle.

∞∞∞

At this point I have to interrupt my story, because the three moviegoers can't possibly have crossed the border in the way I just described.

The border between the two German states, and especially between the two halves of Berlin, is considered the world's most closely guarded and the most difficult to cross. The ring around West Berlin is 102.5 miles in length. Of this, 65.8 miles consist of concrete slabs topped with pipe; another 34 miles is constructed of stamped metal fencing. Two hundred and sixty watchtowers stand along the border ring, manned day and night by twice that many border guards. The towers are linked by a tarred military road, which runs within the border strip. To the right and the left of the road, a carefully raked stretch of sand conceals trip wires; flares go off if anything touches them. Should this happen, jeeps stand ready for the border troops, and dogs are stationed at 267 dog runs along the way. Access to the strip from the East is further prevented by an inner wall, which runs parallel to the outer Wall at an irregular distance.

Nail-studded boards randomly scattered at the foot of the inner wall can literally nail a jumper to the ground, spiking him on their 5-inch prongs. It

is true that long stretches of the inner wall still consist of the facades of houses situated along the border, but their doors and windows have been bricked up. Underground in the sewers, the border is secured by electrified fences, which grant free passage only to the excretions of both parts of the city.

These facts also struck the experts when the court addressed the matter of the three boys' jumps. Even granting that they could jump the distance from porch to Wall, how did the defendants keep their footing on a surface where even cats slip off? A border crossing seemed conceivable only if a rope had been anchored ahead of time on the Western side—and that presupposed Western accomplices. Lastly, how could the three defendants be sure that they would find this rig still in place on their return? Any passerby with a pocket knife could have severed the umbilical cord linking them to socialist life.

But as the defense attorney pointed out, everyone knows that even the

WALL-FRIEZE

by Kiddy Citny and

Thierry Noir

Waldemarstraße.

Kreuzberg, Berlin.

(opposite page,

credit: Kiddy Citny)

outer Wall stands within DDR territory, in order to leave room for painting and repair work. Even if a rope had hung down on the west side, Western citizens would have considered it untouchable. In addition, the defendants had made their jumps when the "modern border"—as it is called to distinguish it from the old, single Wall—wasn't complete. The inner wall still had weak points, while the outer Wall was often a brick structure flat on top instead of round.

These arguments did not allay skepticism about the boys' improbably aerial route; the suspicion was that they had found some underground passageway to the West which might still be serving a band of successors. The means that Lutz and the other two Willys did in fact use to make it over and back have vanished in the wilderness of oral transmission. Technical difficulties that seemed insurmountable were resolved in the imagination of those who spread the story. The remarkable thing about it, after all, was not that the trio found a way to the West, but that they traveled the route in both directions.

As casually as other DDR citizens drive out to Müggelsee on a Sunday, Lutz and the two Willys went to the movies on Kurfürstendamm every Friday. Moreover, they always went to the same theater at the same time. Though they soon knew their way in the dark, they preferred to go in the afternoon rather than risk finding a sell-out at the evening show. Sometimes they took a break when the film went into its fifth or eighth week and wasn't worth seeing again. And so, within half a year, they gained a complete overview of programming at the last Cinemascope theater on Kurfürstendam.

In all, the trio jumped twelve times. Their achievement first came to light in a story by a West Berlin journalist. On the day they crossed over to see Marlon Brando in *Queinada!* they were stopped by a West Berlin patrol. Lutz denied that they were refugees; he presented himself and the two Willys as fans of westerns. That, and the fact that the three refused point-blank to stay on in the West, struck the policemen as so incredible that they phoned the city desk of their favorite newspaper. A reporter caught the trio that day as they were leaving the theater and loosened their tongues with curried sausage and whisky.

The newspaper story put the State Security Service on the boys' trail. The two Willys were arrested at their desks in school and brought to court for repeated violation of the passport law and illegal border crossing. The defense based its case on the unquestionable patriotism of the defendants.

After all, they had had a dozen opportunities to leave the DDR and hadn't taken them—a proof of royalty hat few DDR citizens could match.

This defense was rejected and the boys were found guilty. The older Willy was taken out of school and thrown into the army; the younger one was sent to a youth work camp. Lutz—who had turned eighteen and was subject to the full weight of the law—escaped imprisonment owing to his passion for movies. On the evening of the trio's last excursion, Lutz had returned promptly to his favorite neighborhood movie house in Prenzlauer Berg for a showing of *High Noon*. He had been standing in line a quarter of an hour when the projectionist announced that the show was canceled—the film was torn. At that moment Lutz felt that something inside him had torn too. "You run your heels off from Kurfürstendam to Prenzlauer Berg to be on time . . . and then the film is torn," he snarled at his neighbor. "That does it!"

Lutz stepped on his motorcycle's starter, raced at top speed back to the Wall, and hurried through the darkness into the West, in order to at least be able to catch the late show of *The Big Country*. It was his last transit. In the West he became what he had always wanted to be in the East: a lumberjack. But since he knew the West only from American and Italian westerns, he was poorly prepared for logging in Western woods. To this day he can't understand why a lumberjack should have to buy his own ax and saw.

Farewell to the Queue

BY VLADIMIR SOROKIN
(TRANSLATION BY JAMEY GAMBRELL)

n era can be judged by street conversations.

"Look, there's a line."

"What're they giving out?"

"Just get on it, then we'll find out."

"How much should I get?"

"As much as they'll give you."

This touching dialogue from the Brezhnev era should be etched on the stern granite of Lenin's mausoleum—in memory of the great era of socialist paradise. And if anyone were to think seriously about a monument to that period, I would suggest that the empty mausoleum (should Lenin's body ever be finally consigned to the earth) be filled with those deficit, prestige items for which Soviet citizens suffered such torments standing in line. American Lee and Levi Strauss jeans, Camel and Marlboro cigarettes, "spike" heel and platform shoes, "stocking" boots, cervelat sausage and salami, Sony and Grundig tape recorders, French perfume, Turkish sheepskin coats, muskrat hats, and Bohemian crystal—I can just see it all, under glass like the eidos of real socialism, lying in the triumphant half dark of the mausoleum. Every year, the number of people wanting to catch a glimpse of Lenin's stand-in would increase, so that decades later the line would be a unique, living relic of bygone days . . . But enough about bygone days. Here we are—in the new, post-Communist era:

"Look, there's beef. And no line."

"I haven't got enough money. Let's buy potatoes instead."

Not all that long ago, Soviet people couldn't even have imagined such a scene, and it proved tremendously difficult to come to terms with it. The ordeal of the free market turned out to be more frightening than the Gulag, and more burdensome than the bloody war years, because it forced people to part with the oneiric space of collective slumber, forced them to leave the ideally balanced Stalinist cosmos behind. The steel hands of the world's first proletarian government, which carried us from cradle to grave, cracked and fell off. Along with them went all the familiar socialist ways: free education and medical care, the absence of unemployment, the irrelevance of money, and finally, an entire system of distribution. It turned out to be particularly agonizing to part with the latter. It was the living flesh that inhabited the rigid ideological armature of the government, it lubricated and cushioned people from the Party nomenclature *apparatchiks*, and it stimulated the black market, which brought Soviet people all sorts of small pleasures. Then, suddenly, everything, everything turned to dust. And the queue? That fantastic, many-headed monster, the hallmark of socialism? Where has it gone, the monstrous Leviathan that wound entire cities in its motley coils? Where are the long hours of standing, the stirring shouts, the dramatic confrontations, the joyous trembling of the person at the head of the line?

In a catastrophically short time—just a couple of years—the line was dispersed and reborn as a crowd. It's probable that the queue is gone for good. Like everything epic that has plunged into the Lethe, it arouses interest. Not merely socio-ethnographic interest. One composer I know is seriously considering writing an opera titled *The Queue* in the style of a Russian epic: with mass scenes, choruses, a complex plot. Perhaps at the opening, many of the viewers, despite their own rich personal experience of standing in line, will ask the question: What was this thing after all, the queue?

Paradoxical as it may seem, the line was a purely Soviet phenomenon. Until the Bolsheviks came to power no such phenomenon had been observed in Russia. There are three events in Russian history that allow us to understand the phenomenon of the queue more fully. The first took place on May

18, 1896, on Khodynskoe Field near Moscow. In honor of the coronation of Nicholas II a public celebration was announced and it was promised that bags of gifts from the Tsar would be distributed. Each of these bags contained an enamel mug, a cloth, a link of sausage, a bottle of beer, some sugar, and spice cookies. Newspaper advertisements and word of mouth carried the news of the Tsar's gifts far beyond Moscow. The field was filled with people more than a day before the celebration. Night fell, and people kept arriving.

At dawn, according to the well-known writer and journalist Vladimir Giliarovsky, who witnessed the scene: "Khodynskoe Field resembled a huge

barrel packed with herring, stretching all the way to the horizon, over which there hung a thick cloud of human breath." Whether by some sinister irony of fate or the stupidity of the organizers, the field was surrounded by ditches and fences that transformed it into an enormous trap: you could get in, but you couldn't get out. The booths where the gifts were to be distributed were clustered in one area. About six o'clock in the morning someone waved a hat. This was taken as a signal that the gifts were being handed out. The crowd moved toward the booths. A terrible crush ensued: people fell, they were trampled, they tumbled into the ditches, were crushed against fences. Giliarovsky, a man of extraordinary physical strength, known to bend horseshoes and coins with his bare hands, only just managed to break free of this hell, and fell into a deep faint. Altogether, more than two thousand people died on Khodynskoe Field.

The event itself is extraordinarily metaphorical and significant: a huge crowd accumulates in an enclosed space, consumes food in a frenzy, and crushes itself before the eyes of the young Tsar! It should be noted that the mass revolutionary movement began in Russia after the Khodynskoe tragedy. It is no exaggeration to say that a new type of object or metaphorical subject was born into Russian history that morning on Khodynskoe Field: the collective body. This body grew with each year, acquiring energy. Its actions against the Tsarist regime became more and more aggressive and decisive. The authorities tried to conduct negotiations with this body; they bribed it, surrounded it with troops, and finally shot at it, as happened on Bloody Sunday, January 9, 1905, when an enormous crowd in St. Petersburg set out toward the Winter Palace with a petition for the Tsar. In 1914 those same authorities tried to use its energy for military purposes, directing it against an external enemy. But the collective body's response was rather sluggish; in foreign fields, far away from the Motherland, it lost its energy, entropied. Having dissolved into molecules by 1917, it overran the capital only to gather itself into a raging fist and strike a crippling blow to the powers that be. The last two years of the Civil War didn't stop it, and by 1920 the collective body had come to power for good, inaugurating the era of the "Uprising Masses," which displayed to the world at large its astonishing ethics and aesthetics.

It was after the victory of the collective body that the phenomenon of the queue appeared in Russia with all its classic attributes. numeration (the person's number in line was usually written on the hand); the periodic roll call and ruthless elimination of anyone who stepped away for a moment; a strict hierarchy (those standing behind were supposed to obey those standing in front); the quantity of goods allotted per person (this was also decided collectively), etc.

The time of interminable lines began. People stood in line for everything—for bread, sugar, nails, news of an arrested husband, tickets to *Swan Lake*, furniture, Komsomol vacation tours. In communal apartments people waited in line for the toilet. In overcrowded prisons people queued up for a turn to lie down and sleep. According to statistics, Soviet citizens spent a third of each day standing in lines.

"We go to the lines like we go to our jobs!" my grandmother used to joke. The Russian word *sluzhba*, job or service, implies not only work (in an office, a factory, or, before the Revolution, for the gentry) but a church service. And in the Russian Orthodox Church there are no pews, people stand during the service.

"I stood through an all-nighter."[1]

"I stood three hours for butter."

The ambiguity of such dialogues is obvious. No, it was not only for butter and nails that people stood in endless lines. The queue was a quasi-surrogate for church. Through the act of standing up, standing up for, through, and

---

1. The same sentence could be translated as "I stayed through the all-night mass," or "I stood in line all night."

IN THE GROCERY SHOP of the village of Priber, Irshansky district. The shop had an average monthly turnover of 70–80,000 rubles. (opposite page, credit: SCR Photo Library)

in and on lines regularly for several hours, people participated in a sort of ritual, after which, instead of the Eucharist and absolution of their sins, they received foodstuffs and manufactured goods.

The collective body was steadily ritualized by queues. It was taught order and obedience, and rendered maximally governable. At mass demonstrations, show trials, Party congresses, and soccer games the collective body was allowed to express the orgiastic side of its nature: it applauded stormily and raged, it shuddered with countless orgasms. But on ordinary workdays the line awaited it. Gray and boring, but inescapable, the line dissected the body into pieces, pacified and disciplined it, gave people time to think about the advantages of socialism and about the class struggle; and in the end they were rewarded with food and goods.

In essence, during the Stalin years the populace engaged in a daily rehearsal for the Line of all Lines, in which virtually the entire collective body would stretch itself out and in so doing mark the end of the stormy era of the "Uprising Masses." The occasion for such a line arose on March 5, 1953, when the heart of the People's Father and Great Empiricist of the Masses stopped beating.

For three days, Stalin's body lay on view in its coffin in the House of Unions in central Moscow so the people could say farewell. The enormous line to see Stalin stretched through half of the capital. Muscovites and pilgrims from cities and villages all over the country came in an endless stream. Russia had never seen such a queue.

Once again, as on Khodynskoe Field, the collective body was surrounded, this time by army trucks. On the last night a stampede began. Tears pouring from their eyes as they mourned their Leader, the crowd flattened people against the trucks, trampled them underfoot. No one knows exactly how many people perished that night, but corpses were taken away by the truckload.

The goal of the Stalinist era was achieved—the collective body organized itself into the Line of Lines, stood through it, and, having made a traditional sacrifice to the deceased leader, dissolved into obedient molecules. Stalin tranquilized the Russian people. The period of the "Tranquil Masses" began.

During the motley era of Khrushchev's Thaw, the ritual of standing in lines acquired definitive features, having cleansed itself of arbitrary individualism and non-canonic collective movements. During the reign of Brezhnev—the northern Buddha, as some called him—the line had already become a genuine trademark of developed socialism and occupied an honored place next to such profoundly symbolic phenomena as St. Basil's Cathedral, Russian caviar, the Russian soul, Lenin's mausoleum, and the Soviet military threat.

Like semiprecious stones polished by time, ritual phrases shone in all their sacred purity. No line could do without them:

"Comrades, who's last in line?"

"What are they giving out?"

"How much a head?"

"You weren't standing here!"

"I've been standing since five this morning!"

In the 1970s, the carefree days of "stagnation," people no longer stood for butter and sugar, which were in adequate supply thanks to the wise policies of détente and cheap Soviet oil. Instead, they waited in line for "imports": American jeans, German shoes, Italian knitwear. They waited happily, with humor, in a familial atmosphere that was even rather cozy. After an hour of togetherness waiting in line, the man in front of you in a leather cap with a tanned, friendly face might tell you stories of his dangerous work as a geologist in the far north, about a bear hunt that almost turned tragic, about the ecological problems of the northern rivers, about fantastical sunsets in the taiga and songs around the campfire with a guitar. The woman standing behind you, dressed in a colorful sweater, her eyes slightly swollen from tears, would begin with the standard phrase: "All men are the same," and then tell you about her divorce (which finally went through the day before yesterday) from her alcoholic husband, who shamelessly drank up her mother's life savings (an invalid of labor!) and her father's too (a hero of the battle of Stalingrad!). All of this seamlessly flowed into the roll call carried out by some decently dressed, slightly nervous pensioner, most likely a former lieutenant-colonel. An hour later, having paid the government a trivial sum, you joyfully hid the desired foreign-label item in your briefcase . . .

But, unfortunately, *Tempora mutantur, et nos mutamur in illis.*

The twilight eighties arrived. The empire crawled slowly toward collapse. Every year, the provision of the collective body with essential goods worsened. The many-headed caterpillar no longer wound its way waiting for Levi Strauss and Salamander shoes but for sausage and butter.

The hysterical era of perestroika began. The jokes and soulful confessions once heard in line dwindled. A morose readiness for new hardship appeared on faces. People expected endless queues, four-figure numbers on their hands, days and days of standing. Old people recalled the war years, the siege of Leningrad and its daily 125-gram bread ration, they shared their survival experiences. But what came crashing down on the collective body in the beginning of the 1990s turned out to be scarier than the Leningrad blockade.

It was the atom bomb of a market economy.

After its raucous explosion, people standing in lines discovered three terrible truths:

1) Money is real. 2) The people standing next to you in line have different abilities. 3) There are not three kinds of sausage, but thirty-three. Or even 333. The queue shuddered and began to waver. Entrepreneurial citizens who wanted to open their own stores and sell sausage, rather than stand in line for it, immediately left its ranks. They were followed by those active citizens who wanted to make money in the stores of the new sausage entrepreneurs.

Those who remained continued to wait heroically. When the new stores opened, not with 333, but only ten types of sausage, the line split up into ten small lines. It turned out that people could choose their sausage. The Soviet line couldn't handle the ordeal of choice. When another novelty like Snickers or Bounty appeared on store shelves, queues rapidly shortened. The massive influx of German beer, Royal liquor, and women's stockings simply did it in, and the line caved.

The collapse of the line was much more painful for the collective Soviet body than the collapse of the Soviet Union. With the loss of the queue people lost an important therapeutic ritual of self-acknowledgment which had been honed and polished over the course of decades and had become a daily necessity, like drugs for an addict. Then, suddenly, there were no drugs. The collective body experienced a terrible withdrawal: furious demonstrations under red flags began, evolving into desperate clashes with the police, the ridiculous attempt at the first coup, newspapers shrieking about an "American occupation of Russia," the mass conversion of former communists to Russian Orthodoxy, and the creation of Committees for National Salvation from the Antichrist to Coca-Cola, etc. But all of this could not compensate for the loss of the line—the absinthian agony was too painful. The collective body grew smaller every day and, like some living Blob in a horror film, it frantically tried to figure out what else to transform itself into.

Its last incarnation was the Supreme Soviet of Russia. On September 21,

1993, Yeltsin dissolved the Collective Body. Hollywood-style convulsions began: red-brown goo oozed over the white marble of Moscow's White House, crowd scenes sprang up, the area of the film shoot was solidly cordoned off. Soon, as the genre requires to terrify the viewer, the blob broke through the cordon. It dribbled into trucks and set off to capture the television station, probably wanting to burble to the whole world: Give us back our Queue!

On October 4, the third and last signal event in the life of the Collective Body took place. Several tank salvos put an end to its history. The wounded blob/monster was evacuated from the burned White House; the evacuation took the form of that very same queue. Not a small one either. Watching the holdout members of the Supreme Soviet file out of the White House, one's heart sank. The era of the "Great Standing Masses" was departing, departing forever. Every departure, especially under the barrel of a gun and with hands raised, provokes

nostalgia. You start remembering things. But not the number on your hand, not the elbows in your ribs, not the hysterical cries: "Only three per person!" You remember other things. Pleasant things.

1971. The beginning of summer. Moscow is awash in poplar down. I'm fifteen years old. There's an extraordinary event near our apartment on Lenin Prospect: the neighborhood store, Fish, has black caviar. There's a small line, about a two-hour wait. I'm standing in it. My parents are away, on the Black Sea. I have a ton of money—forty rubles. For half this sum I can buy a kilo of caviar and treat my girlfriend Masha. About an hour and a half later I reach the counter, but some corpulent caviarphiles push me out of the line. One more minute and the death sentence will sound: "Boy," someone will say, "you weren't standing here." But I'm saved by our neighbor, nicknamed Pear for the extraordinary shape of her body, which widens down below. With two swerves of her enormous ass she shoves the people at the head of the line and pushes me back to the counter.

"One kilo!" I exhale, thrusting forward my fist with the crumpled twenty rubles.

"Our norm is half a kilo!" the sweaty salesgirl brays at my face.

"Give him a fucking kilo, goddammit!" Pear shouts for the whole store to hear; turning to the line, she adds for appearance sake, a placating explanation: "They've got a regular infirmary at home! Everyone's sick!" The salesgirl belligerently tosses two greasy paper packages at my chest. Each contains half a kilo of black caviar. Hugging them, I make my way out of the store and on to the street, turn the corner, and go up to Masha's window. It's open. A breeze flutters the curtain.

"Masha," I call.

Masha appears. She's wearing a sleeveless dress of light, silvery silk. I show her my trophies. Smiling, she taps a finger to her temple.

Soon we are sitting on the windowsill. Between us in a porcelain soup bowl is a mountain of black caviar. We eat it by the spoonful, wash it down with warm lemon soda, and kiss with salty lips . . .

Where is it all?

Where is the poplar down? Where is Masha? Where is the caviar?

Farewell to the Line.

Comrades, who's last in the queue?

Tower of Song:
How the Plastic People of the Universe Helped Shape the Velvet Revolution

BY PAUL WILSON

When modes of music change, the fundamental laws of the State always change with them.—Plato, *The Republic*

> *When the mode of the music changes;*
> *When the mode of the music is changed*
> *When the mode of the music changes*
> *The walls of the city shake.*
> —Tuli Kupferberg, The Fugs

Washington, D.C., May 2005. We're in a night club called The Black Cat—a long, low basement room with a bar running along one side and a stage at the far end where a band is playing very loud, eccentric music. To all appearances, it's a conventional rock ensemble: two guitars, bass, sax, viola, keyboards, and an electric cello, but what they're playing is definitely not mainstream rock. It's a gloomy, rhythmic, throbbing, repetitive kind of music punctuated by wild, free-form solos, or by lyrics, half spoken, half sung in a strange, dissonant language, something perhaps best described as "rock noir." Some of the musicians seem grizzled and old—at least as old as Bob Dylan or the Rolling Stones, without the benefit of fitness programs.

There's a cluster of tables at the back of the room and around one of them is an odd collection of people—let's call them The Formers. There's a former U.S. Secretary of State; a former Canadian diplomat, once stationed in

Prague; a former Czech dissident who is now the Czech ambassador to the United States; a former Czech president, Václav Havel, nursing a Manhattan and trying to explain to a couple of guys in tuxedos, who work for the National Endowment for the Arts, what the band on the stage is all about. And there is one final "former," me, a former member of the band.

The band is the Plastic People of the Universe, and it's been around for almost thirty years, which automatically makes it a bona fide rock-and-roll cliché: the "living legend." They still rehearse every week, and regularly tour the Czech Republic, Europe, and occasionally, North America, and Asia. They still have a large following at home, though some of the followers are the children of the band's original fans. You can buy their complete works on CD at discount stores in Prague for the equivalent of about twenty bucks. Apart from improvements in musicianship, some new blood, and vastly improved technology, the music they play sounds pretty much the way it did back in their heyday in the 1970s and '80s, when the Communist regime treated the band as a public enemy and they recorded their music clandestinely, on two-track, reel-to-reel machines. For the most part, their repertoire is the same too.

This fidelity to their roots moved a long-time fan, now living in New York, to dub their current appearances "musical archaeology," though with equal truth he could have said that their music still had the power to rise above its totalitarian origins. The fact is that different people see different

things in The Plastic People. Before this concert in Washington, the *New Yorker* called them "a symbol of Eastern European dissidence." A blogger referred to them as "the greatest obscure rock band of all time." Most extravagantly of all, the publicity material for Joe's Pub in New York, where they played for a couple of nights before coming to Washington, said: "Their music demands that we re-examine the way we live our lives."

That night in the Black Cat, former president Havel was trying to explain The Plastic People's enduring appeal to the two NEA men in tuxedos, but it was hard over the din of the band, especially given his limited English and the frail state of his health. I could see him flagging, and knew what

was coming next. In a pause between numbers, he turned to me and said: "But here is
Paul. He can tell you how it was."

∞∞

Like many rock 'n' roll sagas, the story of the
Plastic People began in the 'burbs, in this
case a residential neighborhood on the edge
of Prague called Brevnov, where a young man
had a dream. Milan "Mejla" Hlavsa, who died
of cancer in 2001, was a teenager in 1968 when

the Soviet tanks rumbled into Prague and put an end to the Prague Spring,
but his head was so filled with visions of rock stardom that he barely noticed the invasion. He had already played in bands with names like "Glow-
Worms," "Black Stockings," and "The Undertakers" when, sometime in the
fall of 1968, someone lent him a copy of the Velvet Underground's first
record. He took it home, and listened to it all night. From then on, his
ambition was to put together a band that would play that kind of music and
present it with a proper "psychedelic" flare.

He got together with two schoolmates, Jiří Števich and Michal Jernek,
and formed a band. They tried out several names before settling on "Plastic
People," a name they'd taken straight from one of Frank Zappa's early songs,
but without really being aware of Zappa's withering sarcasm. But the name
felt too short, so they added "of the Universe," and then set out to conquer
Prague.

The reigning psychedelic band in Prague at the time was an art-rock
ensemble called "The Primitives Group," who had a team of artists manag-
ing the visual side of their show. One of this team was a young art critic
called Ivan Jirous. One night, Jirous saw the Plastic People perform, and,
as rough as they were, he saw their potential to take the music further, so
he left the Primitives—which were about to break up anyway—and joined
forces with the new band.

Jirous was from a country town in the middle of Bohemia. He was a
rebel in school, but despite his grades and his "bourgeois" background, he
managed to get into university to study art history. His main passion at the
time was renaissance music, but when he saw the first Beatles movie, *A Hard*

HRADECEK, HAVEL'S
COUNTRY COTTAGE,

during the "Third Festival

of the Second Culture."

From left, Vratislav

Brabenec, Jiří Kabeš, Ivan

Jirous, Václav Havel.

(credit: Ondrej Nemec)

Day's Night, he was an instant convert. He let his hair grow long, sought out like-minded souls in Prague's music and art scene, and began looking for ways to make a contribution to the city's growing music scene, though he could scarcely carry a tune.

Many of Jirous's peers at university and in the art scene thought he was mad, or just plain wrong, to embrace "Big Beat," especially with the country now under military occupation. Sometime in June 1969, almost a year after the Soviets had invaded, Jirous and Hlavsa were walking through Prague, distributing tickets to an upcoming Plastic People concert when they ran into an acquaintance and tried to sell him a set. The acquaintance was aghast: "You can't be serious!" he said. "The whole nation is on its knees and you guys are going around strumming your guitars?"

"The nation may be on its knees," Jirous retorted, "but we're not."

At that time, the Plastic People of the Universe were a professional band with an official sponsor, but that was not about to last much longer. After the invasion, the new regime moved quickly to defuse the hopes aroused by the Prague Spring. They devised a strategy they called "normalization." To the outside world, it was an almost invisible process, which was exactly the point. There were no spectacular repressions, and only a couple of small show trials. Censorship was reintroduced gradually, almost unobtrusively at first, and the rest was accomplished by a fiendishly simple but effective device: every student and working adult in the country was vetted by a tribunal of their peers and asked point-blank about their attitude toward the Soviet invasion. Most people, out of fear for their jobs, lied about their real feelings. Resistance seemed futile.

Eventually, musical ensembles were subject to the same kind of screening process. Groups had to agree to perform only in Czech, to go by Czech names, wear their hair short, and submit their lyrics to censorship. The Plastic People refused and, as a result, lost their professional status. Their instruments were confiscated and they had to go back to work or face arrest for "parasitism." But rather than give up playing, they decided, instead, to regroup as an amateur ensemble.

I first met Ivan Jirous in the fall of 1969, when I'd been living in Czechoslovakia for over two years and the band was still legal. The following year, as the band was rebuilding, he asked me to join. My role was to help with the general strategy, which was to develop a repertoire of cover songs, mainly by the Velvet Underground and the Fugs (another New York band) interspersed with original songs written by the band, but translated by me and sung in English. That way, Jirous believed, we could test the limits of the possible.

And that's how I became a rock'n'roller—a fate I had never quite imagined for myself. For the next two years, we practiced and played in the most primitive conditions (it's hard for a rock band to be secretive) though probably by most rock'n'roll standards, they weren't too bad. In the two years I played with them, I think we performed about fifteen times in public. Inevitably, the Plastic People—and Jirous in particular—started attracting the attention of the authorities. And thus a third player entered the game— the State Security Police, or StB, whose job it was to protect the country from "subversion" from within. From about 1972 on, they were a looming presence in the life of the band and its expanding circle of fans.

By 1973, it was clear to just about everyone that the Russian troops were here to stay, and that it was no longer just a matter of hanging on until they left, but of surviving for the long haul. That year marked the beginning of a more serious cultural resistance, signalled by the organized appearance of *samizdat*—self-published books by banned authors. For the Plastic People, it was the year they finally found their true voice. They began performing in Czech, with a full repertoire of their own songs, setting the music of underground poets to music. My usefulness to the band was over, so I stepped aside and took part in other ways. Along with this, a wonderful thing happened: new bands started appearing on the scene. Some of them, like DG 307, were spawned from the inner circle of the Plastics; others came out of smaller music scenes in towns outside of Prague. Commune-like settlements were set up in old abandoned farm houses in the countryside, often gathering around a band, or a samizdat venture. Connections were made with

Ellonzék (demokr.)

FF150   B-WIRE   24-MAY-84 22:54

EAST -- HUNGARIAN PUNKS LOSE PRISON APPEAL

BUDAPEST, MAY 24, REUTER - FOUR HUNGARIAN PUNK MUSICIANS, THE COITUS PUNK GROUP (CPG), HAVE LOST THEIR APPEAL AGAINST TWO-YEAR PRISON SENTENCES FOR SINGING SONGS ATTACKING COMMUNISM AND THE SOVIET UNION, DISSIDENT SOURCES SAID TODAY.
TWO OF THE MUSICIANS, SINGER BELA HASKA, 20, AND DRUMMER ZOLTAN NAGYZ, 20, ARE ALREADY IN PRISON, BUT LEAD GUITARIST AND LYRICS WRITER ZOLTAN BENKOE, 21, IS STILL AWAITING A SUMMONS TO SERVE HIS TERM, THE SOURCES SAID. THE SENTENCE OF AN UNDERAGED MEMBER OF THE GROUP, BASS GUITARIST ZOLTAN VARGA, WAS SUSPENDED.
THE FOUR PUNKS FOUNDED CPG IN THE SOUTHERN CITY OF SZEGED IN 1981, BUT MOVED TO BUDAPEST AFTER BEING EXPELLED FROM SCHOOL. THEY WERE ARRESTED LAST JUNE, SENTENCED IN FEBRUARY, AND THEIR APPEAL AT THE BUDAPEST METROPOLITAN COURT WAS HEARD YESTERDAY.
ONE SONG, A WELL-KNOWN RUSSIAN FOLK TUNE WHICH THEY PERFORMED ONLY A FEW TIMES, POKED FUN AT COMMUNIST WORK ETHICS, AND THEN ADDED THE CHORUS: "YOU BLOODY STINKING COMMUNIST GANG, WHEN WILL YOU ALL BE HANGED?"
ANOTHER SONG, ENTITLED "SS 20", COMPLAINED ABOUT NUCLEAR WEAPONS IN BOTH EAST AND WEST, AND OF TOTALITARIANISM AND POLICE HARASSMENT.
TW

FEATURE FILE FROM RADIO FREE EUROPE reporting on the appeal case of musicians from the Hungarian Coitus Punk Group (CPG), whose members were standing trial for performing songs with anti-communist lyrics. May 24, 1984. (credit: OSA Archivum)

underground writers and artists of older generations, most notably Egon Bondy, whose poems the Plastic People set to music.

By this time, the only way to organize a concert was to do it privately, under the guise of wedding celebrations, where traditionally restaurants were reserved and bands brought in to provide music. Suddenly, in the relatively free-living Czech underground scene, there was a rash of weddings. It didn't take the police long to figure out what was going on, but each time they did, it was usually too late to stop it. But a storm was gathering, and one sign was an ugly incident in the town of České Budějovice. A rock festival at which the Plastic People were to have played was brutally broken up by the combined forces of the police and the army. Hundreds were beaten and hundreds more taken into custody.

In early 1975 Ivan Jirous, just released after a year in prison for a minor offense, wrote an essay innocently entitled "A Report on the Third Czech Musical Revival." It was a history of the "underground" music scene that he had helped to create, but it was also a manifesto. "One of the highest aims of art," Jirous wrote, "has been the creation of unrest. The aim of the underground here in Bohemia is the creation of a second culture, a culture that will not be dependent on the official channels of communication, social recognition, and the hierarchy of values laid down by the establishment, a culture that cannot have the destruction of the establishment as its aim because in doing so, it would drive itself into the establishment's embrace . . . This is the only way to live on in dignity through the years that are left to us."

Note that Jirous was not calling for the overthrow of the regime. He was simply saying: this is where we and the regime part company. The term "second culture" became part of the lexicon of resistance.

About the same time, Václav Havel was writing his own manifesto: an open letter to Dr. Gustáv Husák, the Communist Party's General Secretary who had just been appointed president of Czechoslovakia. Havel's letter was an eloquent description of the utter wasteland the regime had created through its policies of repression. The miserable state of the republic, Havel suggested, had nothing to do with the poor economy, but with the state of culture, in the broadest sense. By banning all but the most servile of plays, books, magazines and ideas, the regime was starving society of the vital trace elements and vitamins it needed to survive. Invisibly at first, but inevitably, Czechoslovak society was already well on the way to a serious breakdown, he warned.

But Havel went further. Society also had something like a secret life, one that could not be stopped by any earthly force. A regime may curb this life force for a while, but it can't suppress it altogether. Sooner or later, those hidden impulses will break through and society will come alive again.

These two essays, both widely distributed in samizdat, fit together like a lock and key. The "second culture" that Jirous had described—the birth, against all the odds, of a genuine music scene—was a manifestation of Havel's "secret life of society." Alone, each essay was powerful as an idea, but together, they provided a blueprint for the future.

In hindsight, it seems inevitable that Jirous and Havel would eventually get together. Sometime in early 1976, a mutual friend arranged for them to meet in his studio. They talked; Jirous played Havel some of the Plastic People's music and showed him his essays; they moved from the studio into a bar where the bartender was a mutual friend who closed the place and let them go on drinking; they drank and talked all night long, and went home as the sun was coming up and people were going to work. Havel agreed to come to the next underground festival of music, planned for a couple of weeks later.

Before that happened, though, on March 16, 1976, the StB started arresting people in the musical underground—eighteen altogether, including Jirous, all of the Plastic People, and some members of other bands. There was a huge investigation; there were house raids and countless tapes and manuscripts were confiscated. Hundreds of people were interrogated, and eventually charges were laid. In early July, the musicians were formally charged with "disturbing the peace" by "publicly and repeatedly committing crude indecencies by performing lyrics and songs the contents of which are

APPENDIX A

Charter 77 – Declaration,
1 January 1977

In the Czechoslovak Collection of Laws, no. 120 of 13 October 1976, texts were published of the International Covenant on Civil and Political Rights, and of the International Covenant on Economic, Social and Cultural Rights, which were signed on behalf of our Republic in 1968, were confirmed at Helsinki in 1975 and came into force in our country on 23 March 1976. From that date our citizens have the right, and our state the duty, to abide by them.

The human rights and freedoms underwritten by these covenants constitute important assets of civilised life for which many progressive movements have striven throughout history and whose codification could greatly contribute to the development of a humane society.

We accordingly welcome the Czechoslovak Socialist Republic's accession to those agreements.

Their publication, however, serves as an urgent reminder of the extent to which basic human rights in our country exist, regrettably, on paper only.

The right to freedom of expression, for example, guaranteed by article 19 of the first-mentioned covenant, is in our case purely illusory. Tens of thousands of our citizens are prevented from working in their own fields for the sole reason that they hold views differing from official ones, and are discriminated against and harassed in all kinds of ways by the authorities and public organisations. Deprived as they are of any means to defend themselves, they become victims of a virtual apartheid.

Hundreds of thousands of other citizens are denied that 'freedom from fear' mentioned in the preamble to the first covenant, being condemned to live in constant danger of unemployment or other penalties if they voice their own opinions.

In violation of article 13 of the second-mentioned covenant, guaranteeing everyone the right to education, countless young people are prevented from studying because of their own views or even their parents'. Innumerable citizens live in fear that their own or their children's right to education may be withdrawn if they should ever speak up in accordance with their convictions. Any exercise of the right to 'seek, receive and impart information and ideas of all kinds, regardless of frontiers, either orally, in writing or in print' or 'in the form of art', specified in article 19, para. 2 of the first covenant, is punished by extrajudicial or even judicial sanctions, often in the form of criminal charges as in the recent trial of young musicians.

Freedom of public expression is repressed by the centralised control of all the communications media and of publishing and cultural institutions. No philosophical, political or scientific view or artistic expression that departs ever so slightly from the narrow bounds of official ideology or aesthetics is allowed to be published; no open criticism can be made of abnormal social phenomena; no public defence is possible against false and insulting charges made in official propaganda; the legal protection against 'attacks on honour and reputation' clearly guaranteed by article 17 of the first covenant is in practice non-existent; false accusations cannot be rebutted and any attempt to secure compensation or correction through the courts is futile; no open debate is allowed in the domain of thought and art. Many scholars, writers, artists and others are penalised for having legally published or expressed, years ago, opinions which are condemned by those who hold political power today.

47

THE FIRST PAGE

OF CHARTER 77

utterly incompatible with the legal and social principles of our citizens."

Once the charges had been laid, Havel and his friends went into action, writing letters to the authorities, and to their friends abroad. The most interesting letter, sent to the German novelist Heinrich Böll, contained a watershed observation: the writers who signed the letter, including Havel and the poet Jaroslav Seifert, who went on to win the Nobel Prize for literature a decade later, said that they were renouncing their status as a "protected species." Until that point, their renown in the outside world had protected them from the harsher aspects of police repression. Now they were throwing in their lot, come what may, with those who had no protection whatever.

I won't go into the story of how Charter 77, the Czech human rights movement, was created a few months later by Havel and his friends. It was a petition asking the government simply to honor the commitment it had signed onto in Helsinki—commitments to respect their citizens' basic human rights. Many young people from the musical underground signed the petition as well. It was a commitment the regime could not honor, and instead, Charter 77 brought down persecution on the heads of everyone who had signed it. Rather than back down, the signatories became even more active. When the Plastic People and their colleagues were finally released in 1977, they went on playing, though the days of holding concerts disguised as weddings were long over. Havel made his country retreat available for gatherings and recordings. Other friends opened up their country communes to them as well, but each time that happened, the communes were mysteriously destroyed. By the 1980s, there was nowhere the Plastic People could play, even in private.

Havel was also put under extreme pressure. In 1979, he went to prison, along with five of his fellow activists. He was offered a rear exit: the regime gave him the chance to go to the United States—just to get rid of him—but he refused and did hard time instead. He was released in 1983 with serious health problems that plague him to this day. Jirous, all in all, spent well over nine years in prison—and was only released from his final sentence in 1989, just as the Velvet Revolution was getting underway.

We know now, because the police archives are available for scholarly research, that all during the late 1970s and the 1980s, a vast contingent of state secret police was assigned to deal with the "problem" of "wayward youth." We know, too, that the police mounted "Operation Guitarist" aimed at pressuring the founder of the Plastic People, Milan Hlavsa, to turn informer. The internal tensions created by these tactics took their toll, and in 1988, the Plastic People disbanded, to cries of treason from their hard-core fans, regrouping as Půlnoc (Midnight.)

And so the Plastic People of the Universe remained silent for the next ten years, until President Havel brought them together again in 1997 to play in the Prague Castle at a celebration of the twentieth anniversary of Charter 77. In the meantime, the members of the band all went on to do other things in music, and Milan Hlavsa, with a group of his own called Fiction, became the rock star he had always dreamed of being. His death in January, 2001, made headlines across the country and obituaries appeared in major newspapers across Europe and North America, including the *New York Times*.

MILAN HLAVSA,

1970s

(credit: Abbe Libansky)

∞∞∞

The claim is sometimes made that the Plastic People helped to bring down the Communist regime, that the example of the Plastic People proves that music has a revolutionary power that demonstrates the truth of Plato's thesis, that there are certain kinds of music that can rock a society to its foundations. But how true are such claims?

I'm not sure any of this can be proven, or even how important it is to do so. What's undeniable is that at a crucial time in their history, the Plastic People of the Universe had the good fortune to be led by Ivan Jirous, a man of vision and courage who was eloquent enough to persuade them to be true to themselves despite the risks. They had the good fortune, when trouble came, to gain the unequivocal support of Václav Havel, who in turn drew inspiration from them and then took his struggle to another, more universal, level. I would even venture to say that Havel could never have written his best essay, "The Power of the Powerless," with the same conviction without the living example of the Plastic People of the Universe and of Jirous's notion of the "second culture." The message of that essay is that the simple act of living in truth, that is, living and behaving in harmony with your conscience, confers power on those who take the risk. The Plastic People of the Universe embodied that truth before Havel articulated it. In that sense, they were a catalyst for change almost in spite of themselves.

But there's another sense, also inadvertent, in which they were influential. In the 1980s, when the Plastic People were being so viciously harassed, a whole new music scene grew up under the noses of the secret police. I believe a careful study of the StB archives will show that by wasting so many of their resources in a futile effort to shut down the Plastic People and the underground music scene, the police were unable to control the much larger groudswell of unofficial popular music that happened in the 1980s. Thus the Plastic People served as a kind of lightning rod for police harassment, and because they were the focus of police attention, other bands, singers, and songwriters could more easily slip under the radar. Likewise, because Havel and the dissidents spent time in jail, or under constant surveillance or house arrest, others who were less in the public eye were freer to organize, to prepare for the future.

In December 1989, two key events signalled that the old regime was dead. One of them you know about: the remarkable election of Václav Havel as president of his country. The other remarkable event you've probably never heard of. It was a huge two-day music festival, held in mid-December, called A Concert for All Decent People. Dozens and dozens of musical groups, rock bands, choruses, folk singers, gypsy bands, jazz ensembles, played almost non-stop in the largest indoor sports arena in the country. The concert was a glorious celebration of a musical culture that had grown up right under the noses of the regime—a true tower of song that the regime had desperately tried, and failed, to topple.

In Pictures

**"SHOT WHILE JUMPING
THE BERLIN WALL"**

Black and white acrylic on
canvas, 28" x 30", Walter
Gaudnek, 1988. (credit:
Walter Gaudnek)

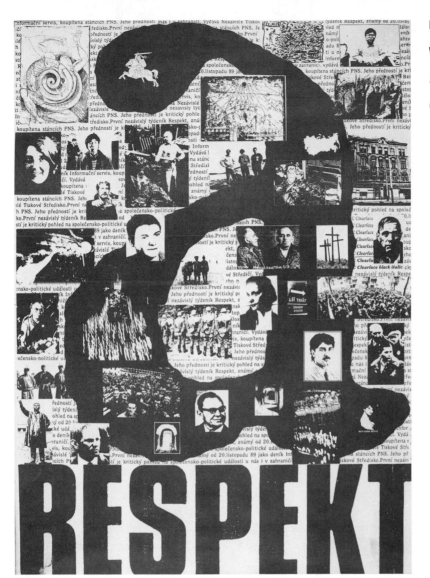

POSTER FOR THE
WEEKLY NEWSPAPER
RESPEKT, 1990/91.

(credit: *Respekt*)

BLANKENBURG, 1987.
The border followed the middle of the Werra River. Many bridges, like this one, were dismantled. One border fence runs along the east side of the river while another can be seen high up on the ridge. (credit: Brian Rose)

EBERTSTRAßE, 1989.

The last two weeks of 1989 it seemed the world had come to Berlin. People crossed back and forth through the newly opened checkpoints. Here, near the Brandenburg Gate, people stepped through a large hole in the wall for the benefit of a film crew. Shortly afterwards, the East German guards ushered everyone back over to the West. (credit: Brian Rose)

HEINERSDORF, 1987.

Next to larger towns and
other built-up areas, a
concrete wall was used
instead of the more
common fences.
(credit: Brian Rose)

OFFLEBEN, 1987.

A guard tower and the border fences lie just behind a neighborhood in West Germany.
(credit: Brian Rose)

PALAST DER REPUBLIK, 2004.

The East German Palace of
the People stripped and vacant
awaiting demolition. In the
foreground are excavations of
the former Berlin City Palace
(Stadtschloss) foundations.
(credit: Brian Rose)

**THE GROUNDS AT THE
ANA ASLAN GERIATRIC AND
GERONTOLOGY INSTITUTE**

in Bucharest, Romania.

(credit: Oana Sanziana Marian)

SOVIET MEMORIAL, 1990.

WWII Soviet memorial and burial

ground in Treptower Park in Berlin.

(credit: Brian Rose)

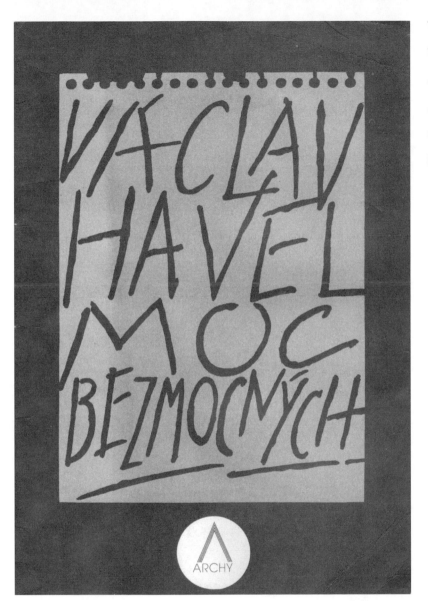

The Revenge

BY ANNETT GRÖSCHNER
(TRANSLATION BY INGRID LANSFORD)

In the summer of 1989, the Baltic beaches were infested with a plague of ladybugs. At first it wasn't obvious. The first specimens were welcomed, especially by the children, who caught them, had them crawl along their arms, and counted the dots on their wings for good luck; the more the merrier. Before long there was too much of a good thing. The red and black bugs spread across the beaches in dense swarms, settling everywhere, crawling into every crevice, and as soon as they ran short of food, began to attack people with tiny, painful bites. No one had seen that many ladybugs at one time. Families left the beach one by one, until only the ladybugs remained, apart from a few dyed-in-the-wool individualists, who took to the water and dove themselves senseless, refusing to let their vacation be ruined, and who preferred to share the beach with biting ladybugs rather than hordes of tourists.

A few days later there was a storm tide that washed away ten thousand beach chairs and several places to stay. This caused many people to leave. Double trouble was too much, even for citizens of the German Democratic Republic.

In retrospect, the vacationers traveling to Hungary had apparently been the last straw; they had crawled though an opening in the barbed wire and simply run off without looking back. No one talked about the vacationers on the Baltic. Baltic tourists only occurred in the stories about the night twenty-eight years earlier, when blissful and sunburned, they slept in their crowded vacation cabins while other people, who had either been ordered back from their vacations or had been commandeered, barricaded the borders to the various occupied sectors in the deserted city of Berlin. Later it was said that only the absence of crowds had given East German authorities the courage to stage this surprise coup.

(credit: Winfried Hammann)

∞∞∞∞

The ladybugs were not on my mind when, on November 10, 1989, I stood on the Oberbaum Bridge among thousands of people. I had never seen the structure from this angle, because, seen from the east, the bridge was beyond the hinterland wall and was part of the border area. It ended at Kreuzberg, where I stood, as did the other people beside, in front, behind, and, as I worried, perhaps even under me—I was, after all, constantly stepping on something soft without having a chance to bend down between the bodies pressing against my own. I was surrounded by Narva's early shift. It was a group excursion, and all had come along. They had just completed their eight hours at the assembly line producing light bulbs, and now they meant to enter the West. Have a look and then go home, or maybe make a day of it until the next early-morning shift, but in any case, get their *Begrüßungsgeld* [welcome money]. Amazing! Fantastic! Shopping along the Ku'damm! That's what they said.

For the time being we were in no man's land. After racing through the weeks following summer at tremendous speed, we suddenly stood still, because we had to pass through the eye of the needle, a little door in the Wall that was so narrow it would only admit one person at a time. If they even let us. They might easily have closed it again long ago.

Gradually the scene was enveloped in dusk. If we were to reach the West this day, it would be steeped in darkness. I was seized by panic. I tried to focus my eyes on a point outside the Wall.

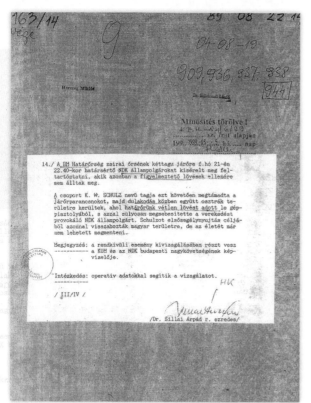

For the first time ever, I saw the covered red brick walk on the east side of the bridge which had once been reserved for pedestrians, and noticed a second story, which must have carried traffic at some point, perhaps a suburban train or subway. Indeed, when I turned, I saw that the rail line continued up to a building on the eastern side, which I had never identified as a railroad station. I had thought it to be a shop belonging to the lightbulb factory.

A few meters below me flowed the Spree, an utterly lazy river, which to my mind, accustomed to the Elbe, deserved the name "river" only in this section between the Oberbaum Bridge and the Plänter Forest. Now I was afraid of it. Thousands of people marching in step could cause a bridge to collapse. Here there were thousands, most of them stomping their feet in place because it was cold. Could the bridge carry that much weight? Had it not been blown up in 1945 like the other Spree bridges, and after the war, just been jerry-rigged together? And didn't I stand exactly in the middle? There had been no automobile traffic in twenty-eight years; it had been a pedestrian border crossing. When my friends from West Berlin walked back to Kreuzberg at night, generally one minute before their visa ran out, or five minutes late, I had sometimes accompanied them to the end of Warschauer Straße. Every time before they vanished into the West through the little gate, there would be the half-joking, half-serious exchange: "Come with us." "Maybe some other time."

I was searching for something which I suspected I wouldn't find in the West either. I vacillated between rebellion and helplessness, as did many for whom the West offered no alternative, though the agony of the East was unbearable.

This was similar to my situation when the baby arrived. I had neither wished for a child nor tried to prevent it. Suddenly, on a cold January day in 1989, there it was, two months early. Neither of us was happy. I felt rooted within my circumstances, and the baby had a bellyache. His father had married a woman from the West unknown to him and was waiting for his day of departure. A few weeks later he would be nothing but a return address on letters from West Berlin.

By the beginning of summer I was exhausted. Night after night I had walked the bawling child through my part of town. I knew every bulge in the pavement, every bullet hole in the housefronts, every lowered shutter, every broken bulb in the fixtures above the street doors. The baby howled its way through Luchener, Schliemann, and Dunker Streets and back along Dimitroff, Senefelder, Raumer Streets, and Prenzlauer Avenue. Under the streetlight at the church in Senefelder Street he finally fell asleep with exhaustion. To this day, almost twenty years later, I remember the child's frustrated features passing into unconsciousness and looking very peaceful in the beam of light.

Those were the nights when I thought the baby and I were completely alone in the world.

Early that summer, students lay dead in the Square of Heavenly Peace in Beijing, shot by the People's Army, and the East German authorities applauded: finally something had happened toward restoring order. Gradually, their State was falling into disarray as well. Monday after Monday people were taking to the streets in Leipzig. Everyone had an inkling that something would happen, but there was a fear that perhaps they wouldn't survive this. Many in my street didn't come back from their vacations. They had left their old lives behind, which gathered more and more dust until someone else took over their apartments. But then the whole thing simply collapsed and a breathtaking month began, during which we experienced several years simultaneously. It lasted from October 7 through November 9. All borders were suddenly open except for the Wall, but the Wall at that moment was only a problem of marginal interest.

That was the first time I approved.

Why I was so furious the night the Wall came down is almost beyond me today. I kept hearing the same announcement on the radio, the same sentence from the press conference was repeated over and over: The Council of Ministers had decided, "er, to issue a provision, rule, that would allow every citizen, er, to leave via DDR border check points . . . immediately, without delay." The man who said

HUNGARIAN SECRET POLICE REPORT

on the shooting to death of Karl Werner Schulz, the only casualty among the thousands of East German refugees who illegally crossed into Austria just days before the Hungarian government decided to open its borders. August 22, 1989. (opposite page, credit: OSA Archivum)

(credit: Winfried Hammann)

COUNTRY: HUNGARY
SUBJ: TAKE 1 OF 2 -- MTI CARRIES NOTE TO GDR

REF: LD1409174889 BUDAPEST DOMESTIC SERVICE IN HUNGARIAN 141630
          -- GOVERNMENT REJECTS GDR ACCUSATION OVER BORDER

SOURCE: BUDAPEST MTI IN ENGLISH 1849 GMT 14 SEP 89
TEXT: NOK

    //((+NOTE BY HUNGARIAN FOREIGN MINISTRY+ -- MTI HEADLINE))

    ((TEXT)) BUDAPEST, SEPTEMBER 14 (MTI) -- THE HUNGARIAN FOREIGN
MINISTRY ISSUED A NOTE IN REPLY TO THE SEPTEMBER 12, 1989 NOTE OF
THE FOREIGN MINISTRY OF THE GDR, WHICH PROTESTED AGAINST THE
HUNGARIAN DECISION MAKING IT POSSIBLE FOR THE GDR CITIZENS STAYING
IN HUNGARY TO TRAVEL TO THIRD COUNTRIES. THE REPLY NOTE WAS HANDED
OVER TO GERD VEHRES, AMBASSADOR OF THE GERMAN DEMOCRATIC REPUBLIC TO
HUNGARY, BY STATE SECRETARY LASZLO KOVACS AT THE FOREIGN MINISTRY ON
THURSDAY.
                  XXX ((SUBHEAD))

         THE GOVERNMENT OF THE HUNGARIAN PEOPLES REPUBLIC NOTED WITH
    REGRET THAT THE GOVERNMENT OF THE GERMAN DEMOCRATIC REPUBLIC MET
    WITH INDIGNATION THE DECISION AIMED AT SOLVING THE UNTENABLE
    SITUATION CAUSED BY AN INCREASE IN THE NUMBER OF GDR CITIZENS
    STAYING IN THE HUNGARIAN PEOPLES REPUBLIC WHO WERE UNWILLING TO
    RETURN HOME. THE GOVERNMENT OF THE HUNGARIAN PEOPLES REPUBLIC
    INDICATED IN DUE TIME THAT THIS STEP WOULD BECOME UNAVOIDABLE IF THE
    TALKS BETWEEN THE GERMAN DEMOCRATIC REPUBLIC AND THE FEDERAL
    REPUBLIC OF GERMANY, WHICH ARE PRIMARILY CONCERNED IN THE AFFAIR,
    AND THE EFFORTS OF THE GERMAN DEMOCRATIC REPUBLIC SERVING THE RETURN
    OF THEIR CITIZENS, END IN A FAILURE. THE GOVERNMENT OF THE
    HUNGARIAN PEOPLES REPUBLIC PASSED DECISION ONLY AFTER IT WAS
    CONVINCED OF THE FAILURE OF THE SAID TALKS AND EFFORTS. IT BECME
    CLEAR THAT THE GDR LEADERSHIP WAS NOT IN A POSITION TO MAKE A
    PROPOSAL THAT WOULD SETTLE THE ISSUE WHICH CONCERNED A LARGE NUMBER
    OF GDR CITIZENS. THE DECISION IS A CONSEQUENCE OF A SITUATION WHICH
    EMERGED INDEPENDENTLY FROM THE INTENTION AND POSSIBILITIES OF ACTION
    OF THE HUNGARIAN PEOPLES REPUBLIC. THE ALLEGATION THAT THE
    HUNGARIAN SIDE CAN BE REPROACHED FOR THE STEP THEREFORE LACKS ALL
    FOUNDATION.
         THE GOVERNMENT OF THE HUNGARIAN PEOPLES REPUBLIC DID NOT VIOLATE
    INTERNATIONAL LAW BY TEMPORARILY SUSPENDING THE APPLICATION OF SOME
    PARAGRAPHS OF THE AGREEMENT ON VISA-FREE TRAVEL AND THE RELATED
    PROTOCOL.
         THE 1969 VIENNA CONVENTION ON THE LAW OF TREATIES, WHICH THE GDR
    NOTE REFERRED TO, STIPULATES IN PARAGRAPH 62 THAT FUNDAMENTAL
    CHANGES IN CONDITIONS MAY SERVE AS A CAUSE FOR ABROGATING OR
    DISREGARDING A TREATY IF THE CHANGE CONSIDERABLY MODIFIES THE EXTENT
    OF OBLIGATIONS TO BE MET.
         FUNDAMENTAL CHANGES IN CONDITIONS FORCED THE HUNGARIAN GOVERNMENT
    TEMPORARILY TO SUSPEND THE APPLICATION OF SOME PARAGRAPHS OF THE
    SAID BILATERAL AGREEMENT AND RELATED PROTOCOL.
         ON PASSING DECISION, THE GOVERNMENT OF THE HUNGARIAN PEOPLES
    REPUBLIC CONSIDERED THE NORMS CONCERNING THE FREEDOM OF LEAVING
    COUNTRIES INCLUDING ONES OWN, LAID DOWN IN THE INTERNATIONAL
    COVENANT ON CIVIL AND POLITICAL RIGHTS AND THE CHAPTERS DEALING
    WITHG HUMANITARIAN COOPERATION IN THE FINAL DOCUMENT OF THE VIENNA
    FOLLOW-UP MEETING OF THE CONFERENCE ON SECURITY AND COOPERATION IN
    EUROPE.
         THE APPLICATION OF THE STIPULATIONS OF THE PROTOCOL RELATED TO
    THE AGREEMENT ON VISA-FREE TRAVEL IS INCOMPATIBLE WITH THE
    OBLIGATIONS STEMMING FROM THE COVENANT, PARTICULARLY FROM ARTICLES
    NOS 12 AND 13, AND CONCERNING BOTH THE HUNGARIAN PEOPLES REPUBLIC
    AND THE GERMAN DEMOCRATIC REPUBLIC. ACCORDING TO PARAGRAPH 3 OF
    ARTICLE 30 OF THE VIENNA CONVENTION, THE TREATIES CONCLUDED EARLIER
    SHOULD BE APPLIED ONLY TO SUCH AN EXTENT UNTIL THEIR STIPULATIONS
    ARE COMPATIBLE WITH THE STIPULATIONS OF OTHER TREATIES CONCLUDED ON
    THE TOPIC AT A LATER TIME. FROM THIS ASPECT IT IS AN IMPORTANT
    CONDITION THAT BOTH THE GERMAN DEMOCRATIC REPUBLIC AND THE HUNGARIAN
    PEOPLES REPUBLIC BECAME PARTIES TO THE COVENANT AND THE VIENNA
    FINAL DOCUMENT AFTER THE CONCLUSION OF THEIR AGREEMENT ON VISA-FREE
    TRAVEL.
         AS EVIDENCED, THE GOVERNMENT OF THE HUNGARIAN PEOPLES REPUBLIC
    ACTED IN COMPLIANCE WITH INTERNATIONAL LAW.
         THE HUNGARIAN PEOPLES REPUBLIC CONFIRMS THAT IT RESPECTS THE
    SOVEREIGNTY OF THE GERMAN DEMOCRATIC REPUBLIC. THE COUNTRY DOES NOT
    RECOGNIZE IN ANY FORM THE OBLIGATION OF THE FEDERAL REPUBLIC OF
    GERMANY TO CARE FOR ALL GERMANS, AS EVIDENCED BY THE FACT THAT THE
    AUTHORITIES OF THE HUNGARIAN PEOPLES REPUBLIC DO NOT RECOGNIZE THE
    PASSPORT ISSUED TO GDR CITIZENS BY THE BUDAPEST EMBASSY OF THE FRG

this had been in China a short time before, so why should he be trusted? Particularly since he pretended not to know anything, as though he were only reading an announcement someone else had just handed him. The people at once took him at his word. I heard the doors in my house slam as they walked out, taking nothing but house keys and IDs. I listened to the rapidly developing news with my ear pressed to the radio. When the gate at the Bornholm Bridge opened up, the voices cracked, shouted, wept, and stammered messages for the world. They were speechless with happiness.

I knew that this moment spelled the end of anarchy. Opening the Wall was the ultimate revenge of those whose power had long dwindled. And it was their most effective revenge. No more discussions. They simply let go. Like a sphincter yielding and letting everything out.

The man who opened the gate without an explicit order in view of the shoving multitude, later ran a newspaper kiosk in my street for years. He could never remember the price for the *Frankfurter Allgemeine Zeitung*. Very likely, he didn't want to remember. He stood behind his counter eating lunchmeat sandwiches and reading the *Berliner Kurier* while taking in money from his customers. He was an amiable man, and at first glance it wouldn't have occurred to anyone that he had been a colonel with the border guards. Yet, in spite of his lethargy, if you met on a daily basis, he couldn't conceal the smartness of his movements. He moved like a person who many times had abruptly and swiftly turned 45° on his heel.

I felt myself being pulled in two directions. I would have liked to leave too to take part and watch the people being happy. But should I take the sleeping baby from his cozy crib just because the Wall was opening up? What would he get out of it—he would not be able to remember and might even be squashed by the crowds. And who knows, a soldier might lose his cool after all and start shooting. Or should I leave the baby asleep and walk off by myself? What if they closed the Wall again with me on the other side? And the baby alone in the apartment with no one to hear him.

As far as I can remember, I was alone with my child that night. My sister, on the other hand, claims she was in my apartment. She claims that she was the one who dissuaded me from going. She allegedly said, Lie down and sleep; they aren't going to close the Wall again. If indeed she was with us that night—and I must believe her, for my sister remembers everything much better, and in startling detail—then she was right. The next day the Wall was still open, even if by a mere crack. I left the baby with my sister and rode to the Oberbaum Bridge. According to friends who had come back, things had looked just as bleak behind the Bornholm Bridge as in front of it, and even the house numbers continued.

The shift workers got their lunch boxes out of the carrier bags almost all of them had on their wrists; only few had briefcases. They were metal lunch boxes which made scratching and scraping sounds as they were opened. They took out their breakfast sandwiches, saved because in contrast to me, these workers were practical-minded. I smelled liver sausage. I smelled blood sausage. I smelled the strong odor of Harz cheese. No sliced cheese, though, because sliced cheese was odorless and tasteless. The workers were joking, The welcome money will let you buy far better things.

I became nauseated, I felt claustrophobic and short of breath. I wanted to go back to East Germany. But the crowd stood like a living wall. A joking, blood sausage sandwich-consuming wall.

For a while I dug in my heels, but gradually was shoved backward into the West. There was no going back. The crowd was right. It was good that way, even though I sometimes ask myself what would have happened if the Wall had not been opened abruptly, but had been dismantled inch-by-inch. But that would have been a different story.

OFFICIAL NOTE FROM THE HUNGARIAN MINISTRY OF FOREIGN AFFAIRS

sent in response to a note by the Foreign Ministry of the German Democratic Republic (GDR), which protested against the decision of the Hungarian government to allow GDR citizens on its territory to leave for a third country. September 14, 1989. (opposite page & below, credit: OSA Archivum)

```
COUNTRY: HUNGARY
SUBJ:     TAKE 2 OF 2 -- MTI CARRIES NOTE TO GDR

REF:      LD1409212589 BUDAPEST MTI ENGLISH 141849///FRG AS VALID.

TEXT:

    ((TEXT)) TAKING INTO ACCOUNT THAT THE CAUSES OF THE DECISION OF
THE GOVERNMENT OF THE HUNGARIAN PEOPLES REPUBLIC ARE STILL
EXISTENT, THE HUNGARIAN SIDE DOES NOT HOLD POSSIBLE TO REVOKE THE
DECISION.  IT CONFIRMS ITS POSITION THAT THE COMPREHENSIVE
SETTLEMENT OF THE ISSUE HAS TO BE AGREED ON BY THE TWO GERMAN



STATES.  AT THE SAME TIME, IT EXPRESSES READINESS TO HOLD TALKS WITH
GDR AUTHORITIES AND CONTRIBUTE TO AN ACCEPTABLE SOLUTION OF THE
PROBLEM.
    WELCOMING THE SIMILAR INTENTION OF THE GERMAN DEMOCRATIC
REPUBLIC, THE HUNGARIAN PEOPLES REPUBLIC RECONFIRMS ITS
PREPAREDNESS TO FURTHER STRENGTHEN FRIENDLY RELATIONS WITH THE
GERMAN DEMOCRATIC REPUBLIC IN THE SPIRIT OF THE AGREEMENT ON
FRIENDSHIP, COOPERATION AND MUTUAL ASSISTANCE.
(ENDALL) 141849 MIDDLETON/AG 14/2201Z SEP
BT
7879
```

The Souvenirs of Communism

BY DUBRAVKA UGRESIC

(TRANSLATION BY ELLEN ELIAS-BURSAĆ)

I.

A year or so after the Wall came down, I paid a brief visit to Moscow. The first thing I noticed was that the taxi cab drivers in Moscow, always masters of small talk, were repeating themselves.

"Where are you from?" a driver would ask.

"From Yugoslavia."

"Has communism bit the dust there?"

"It's still holding on . . ."

"Well, here it's dead and gone!" the driver would boast.

While the drivers of taxis tried to convince me that communism had bitten the dust, in the Hotel Belgrad cafeteria I waited patiently in a long "communist" line for my first morning coffee. Some guy spoke up behind me, hoarsely . . .

"Devushka, let me buy you an eklerchik . . ."

"A what?" I asked.

"A mini-ekler for you, a mini-cognac for me . . ."

The man waiting in line had kindly offered to buy me a Soviet version of the eclair, a sad little pastry, a product of the communist conveyer belt. The display case, of course, had nothing else to offer. Touched by the sight of the squished little pastry behind the glass, nostalgic in advance for the vanishing of the landscapes of everyday communist life long before they actually disappeared, and softened by the use of the Russian diminutive, I agreed to share the table with the stranger. I sipped at my weak coffee. The man nursed his 250 grams.

"Devushka, who are you, anyway?" asked the fellow.

"Me? A . . . writer."

"Will you look at that? I have run into all kinds of babes in my life, whores and drunks, but I've never met a woman writer!"

"And you, who are you?"

"Me!? I am a lush," the fellow said courteously.

The alcoholic told me how he had sworn many years ago that he would live until he'd seen communism dead.

"Only then will I be able to go peacefully to my grave . . ."

"Well? Isn't it dead, now?" I said rudely.

"I'll be sticking around another year or so . . . Just to make sure . . ." said the self-ordained forensics expert.

2.

The threat of communism no longer hovers over Europe. No one, however, can say precisely when it was that communism gave up the ghost: some claim one thing, others something else. Some claim they personally dealt it its final blows (it is usually former party members who say that), while others say that it collapsed in on itself. The third group, the skeptics, still have their doubts and are seeking the dead heart of communism, so that they can pierce it, just in case, with a hawthorn stake.

It took a while for the communist corpse to be moved from the formaldehyde basin to the academic autopsy hall. Today universities are embarking on anticipational (and, we hope, emancipational) post-communist studies, post-socialist studies, and the study of comparative communism—all in places that experienced nothing of communism. An American Slavic department advertises its intellectual services on the web with the cheery communist-sounding slogan: *Uchites' post-komunizmu!* (Learn the Ways of Post-Communism!). As far as anthropological, sociological, historical, and political research into the subject is concerned, it's not as if there hadn't been any before. Indeed, to the contrary. But as the subject itself—a massive

A COMMEMORATIVE
POSTER FROM
ISTVÁN OROSZ

from 2005: "A strange
paradox: the light balloon
and the weighty brick wall,
symbol of a divided Europe,
which has been a thing of
the past for the last twenty
years, yet its weight—who
knows for how long—will
haunt us." (opposite page,
credit: István Orosz)

ideological system with its supporters and its opponents—was read for years either from the position of the supporters or the opponents, even those who researched communism couldn't be, nor were they, held to a scientifically scrupulous standard. In that sense, in terms of research, even the Bushmen fared better.

As far as the citizens of former communist countries go, they have failed. While communism was alive and well, its inhabitants were a witty people. As soon as communism breathed its last, and bananas, previously a rare commodity, appeared in the shops, humor suddenly became the rare commodity. Today in Moscow, Bucharest, and Prague they can buy Prada shoes, but the jokes—are gone. As long as Lenin was lounging, dead, in the mausoleum, everyday Soviet life bristled with jokes at his expense.[1] When communism drew its icons, including Lenin, with it into the tomb, the tiresome, belabored debates began: what to do with the mausoleum? Should Lenin be left there or buried elsewhere? There was no one who dared propose that a Kentucky Fried Chicken be opened inside the Lenin mausoleum once it had finally become a possibility.

3.

The culture of the Russian avant-garde which marked the twentieth century—Bulgakov, Babel, Pilnyak, Olesha, Zoshchenko, Platonov, and many, many more—produced exciting, powerful, dark, and witty literary texts about the fantastic everyday life of communism. The novel *The Golden Calf* by Ilf & Petrov is one of the most comic and politically subversive novels written under communism. "Smooth operator" Ostap Bender—whose sole goal in life was to become a millionaire and move to Rio de Janeiro—is one of the great classic heroes, standing shoulder to shoulder with Cervantes' Don Quixote or Hašek's Švejk. The novel appeared in 1931, five years before the Kharkov conference and the imposition of socialist realism, and nothing finer has been written in that genre to this day. Hungary, Czechoslovakia, and Poland all spawned top political thinkers, writers, and film and theatre

---

1. I remember an amusing alternative project from the communist period designed to avoid those kilometer-long lines at the entrance to Lenin's tomb on Red Square. The idea was to re-make the mausoleum as a cuckoo clock. Lenin would pop out of the tomb every hour on the hour so that interested visitors could see him without the wait.

directors, and created great, artistically interesting and subversive culture during the time of communist rule.

Russian soc-art—a neo-avant-garde artistic movement which subverted the culture of the Socialist regime with an unusual anticipatory nostalgia—penetrated to the heart of Soviet communist everyday life and interpreted its language and symbols, ending its "commemorative" work before the death of communism. Artists such as Ilya Kabakov, Komar & Melamid, and many others moved to the West only when their artistic "mission" was done. The cult figure of Russian samizdat, Yuz Aleshkovsky, who made the Soviet reading public laugh with his absurdist literary texts, emigrated, and, though his books have been translated, he has not been a success in the West. Western readers did not have the feel for communist everyday life, the author's humor was not understood, the linguistic subversion left readers cold, and the absurd and grotesque aspects of the totalitarian world remained opaque to them.

That is why those writers who came after the demise of communism—the people selling damaged goods and seconds, the "translators" (those, who "translated" the complex everyday life of communism into a simpler language within the grasp of the Western reader), the writers of confessions of personal suffering during communism, the producers of cheap communist "souvenirs," all those who told of everyday communist life second-hand—enjoyed success on the West European and American markets. The market was flooded after the Wall came down, when the Cold War was over, with works that repeated the repertoire of Cold War themes and its narrative strategies.

The authors of these works revisited East European toilets that had no toilet paper; rude waiters; humiliating lines; bad dental hygiene; repression of sexual, gender, religious, and ethnic identity; people who ate dog food instead of steak; unsightly architecture; ridiculous communist statues; the fat, drunk, and incompatible people; and the supermarkets in which there was nothing on the shelves but tea and cheap canned fish. The literature of the post-communist showdown with communism was just as clichéd in its ideological strategies and artistic achievements as the literature of Stalinism had been. And for that very reason, all the more penetrating. The authors of these works managed to find the pressure points in the imagination of the Western reader. It turned out that the pressure points are not the inconceivable absurdities of communism, but simple, understandable things: poor dental hygiene and empty shops. The second switch that flicked on Western fantasies and found pressure points was the opening of the borders and the moment when the European Easties poured into the West. There were nightmarish "urban myths" about the Russian and Ukrainian mafias; about Russians who sent their children to schools in Switzerland and bought diamonds like popcorn; about a "tsunami" of Russians flooding the Côte d'Azur; Russians who bought luxurious villas in the finest places in Europe and the United States; East Europeans strolling around New York, Berlin, London; about the "new Russians," a post-communist mafia; about the former communist Gotham City, Moscow, which no longer swims in tears but in cash. These stories have set in motion a complex morass of feelings: from open anticommunism to a hidden chauvinism, from an insulted Western ego to the collapse of a Western self-confidence that has been sustained for years by the notion that Westerners deserve to live far better than the commies beyond the Wall. The instantaneous post-communist mastery of the rules of capitalism—and the Russians have shown genuine talent—was the greatest blow for the typical West European citizen. Perhaps this is the reason for the absence of sympathy for the post-communist Romanian panhandlers playing the "Gypsy" accordion in European cities, for the Bulgarians who scrub European toilets, and for the former Moldavian and Ukrainian teachers, who are now working as prostitutes on the streets of West European cities.

4.

Soon after its demise, communism moved onto the stands of cheap souvenir vendors: they were the first to sniff out the profitability of nostalgia for the material relics of a culture which had vanished. After the fall of the Berlin wall, petty merchants in Berlin dealt in Soviet rabbit-fur hats, hats with earflaps called *ushankas*, old communist medals, military uniforms and chips of the Berlin Wall. A park of communist statuary was opened in Budapest, which looked as if it had been designed according to plans drawn up by some anti-communist from the McCarthy era. A visitor to the park has the impression that the museum was opened only to eradicate the idea in every tourist that there was anything to communism besides unsightly monumental statues. The only souvenir one can buy at the museum is an expensive empty can, in which crouches the spirit of communism.

And the only living detail I saw when I visited the museum was a Hungarian radio from the 1950s, situated in the booth where the ticket seller sat, which was playing the "Internationale," the communist hymn, in Hungarian.[2] Out of all this—from the post-communist damaged goods and instant literature (which only reinforced the stereotypes about communism that had been set for years), and the souvenir trash—came nothing but boredom. If by some chance America had been a communist country, American mass media souvenirs would have flooded the global market. The American comic book character Superman is your typical positive "communist" hero: a replica of Prometheus, a communist icon, a superman who does good and brings people the light. There are striking similarities between the two opposing systems: an obsession with the sky and flight, a powerful scientific imagination, a focus on the future, the desire to control the world, and maniacal, mega repair projects. It turns out that communism fell into the hands of a part of the world that did not have a healthy market imagination, in a word: to people who didn't deserve it.

---

2. Before I visited the Museum of Communist Sculpture I visited a large exhibit of the anti-communist dissident movement, mostly Hungarian, Czechoslovak, and Polish, in Budapest. It was as if things were being brought into balance despite the good intentions of the authors of both the museum and the exhibition. The exhibition was every bit as boring and unimaginative as the museum of soc-realist sculpture.

The Road to Bornholm

BY DURS GRÜNBEIN
(TRANSLATION BY INGRID LANSFORD)

On the evening of November 9, 1989, Rufus Rebhuhn, ex-student now turned freelancer, sat in his darkened old apartment in the East Berlin district of Prenzlauer Berg watching what may well have been the most momentous newscast of his life. He was alone and still somewhat numb from just having regained his bachelorhood after cutting loose from his girlfriend. He'd had it with relationships for the time being; this late fall, he was preoccupied with history. Like many of his fellow countrymen, he could no longer concentrate on anything else.

It had all happened at once in the last few months. First there were those distressing local elections with their ridiculous record of nearly 99% approval for the policies of the sole governing party, almost lending a North Korean aura to the concept of democracy. Then the Hungarians opened up the Iron Curtain (theirs was only a type of chicken wire, easy to cut through), with the result that fresh air penetrated to the farthest corners of the Eastern Bloc—giving some a chill, while others felt a pull. Thus, during the height of the vacation season, a particularly mobile part of the population, the young and those wishing to leave for years, had defected. Entire families disappeared into the West across the Hungarian border, or sought asylum in Prague's and Warsaw's West German embassies. This led to the first, fascinating TV pictures and to the snowballing of escapes in the midst of summer. Then the legendary Workers' and Peasants' Republic celebrated its fortieth anniversary with grim pomp and a particularly lugubrious type of the usual military parades. It was a funeral march with rocket vehicles, all kinds of road-building equipment, and dashing tank commandants saluting, proper to the occasion, in black coveralls. This government-run circus was the last straw.

All of a sudden, in the larger cities, whose nights had been distinguished by their solid deathly quiet, street incidents and demonstrations soon became the rule, as did collisions between malcontents and police or security forces. The reason for the upsurge was a bundle of unsolvable contradictions, from the miserable future prospects for most citizens (despite their undiminished historical mission), to the stagnation of an entire society (which knew prog ress only as an ideology) due to the erosion of all their members' self-confidence (lauded as the development of a mature socialist personality), down to lifelong imprisonment (in order to protect the people from themselves and their misguided wants). Of all these, it was mainly the problem with free travel that sparked the turmoil. Apparently, most people had only now grown aware, through a sudden review of their years so far, of the prospect of permanent lock-up. For those who had nothing to lose but their lives, this had led to last-minute panic.

Rufus R. had never been able to reconcile himself to this issue either. By the time his mother was pregnant with him, the Berlin Wall had been fully completed, a somewhat oversized christening gift for the unbaptized child, yet one he'd have to live with from then on. The official reason for its construction had also served as the lie about its birth. In order to stop mole activity by the West, they were plugging up all the holes for the population in the East. The entire thing didn't make much sense; the causal connections had become somewhat muddled. The government forgot to explain where the moles might be, inside or outside—at any rate, the long escape tunnels were all being dug from inside. The Wall therefore was the silliest contradiction set in concrete, a monument to nonsense and a grandiose aberration. The sickness hidden behind it, a deep identity crisis, was initially masked and later, denied. Since that time, a deceptively schizoid jargon, DDR language, had been escaping through the cracks in their rigid, inbred logic. The Socialist idea was so attractive that only prison architecture could preserve it. One day Rufus stumbled on two lines by Robert Frost, which to him summed up the whole paradox of the Wall in a nutshell: *Before I built a wall I'd ask to know / What I was walling in or walling out . . .*

Meanwhile the situation had become intolerable. The pressure was increasing every day. The government had its back to the wall, the very Wall it had built. It was no great help that, at the last minute, a few chessmen were traded at the top. Even deposing the General Secretary and the Head of the Stasi was only a sacrifice of pawns that made no real impression on anyone. Some comrades had gone into shock at the sight of the rising tide, while others' eyes had glazed over, but no one had shed any tears.

Rufus R. had no complaints. The crisis had cheered him up, for he knew that the end was coming. A sense of satisfaction spread within him, a calm inner fire comparable to the effect of Scotch whiskey smoothly overflowing the rim of a glass. Government organs regarded the likes of him as hooligans. To the bigwigs he was *a hostile negative element*. That assessment was quite correct: he had taken part in the first riotous assembly, back when things first got rolling on the Alexanderplatz in Berlin below the World Time Clock. He had been a protester from Day One. Once, with friends, he had run into a road block and in birthday party high jinks, had mocked the police. The trap had snapped shut. Everyone had been arrested and been loaded on trucks, swaying at each bend in the road on their trip across town. They had finally been dragged to police headquarters for interrogation and stand-up torture until the early morning hours. He had run the gauntlet, had police yell in his face under

(credit: Winfried Hammann)

floodlights in a parking lot, and had been harassed by yapping guard dogs. The older cops had been the worst. Angry old men, police colonels with guns dangling from their belts, had beaten him with nightsticks, calling him a counterrevolutionary bastard. One had slapped Rufus's ID on the table like a greasy playing card, so that it landed on the floor at the officer's boots: "Pick it up" They were punched in the hollow of their knees if they dozed on their feet. Their mascara smeared from crying, the girls looked like punk ghosts. Red Prussia had staged a farewell performance for him. God knows he was sick and tired of this. *How embarrassing, how discomfiting*, he had rhymed during the long, dull wait in the hallway at the Weissensee police station, *the awkward didactics of strong-arm tactics.*

They had ordered him into their booking room. A stocky little man in a blue uniform, who reminded him of his industrial arts teacher, had fingerprinted him, and another civilian had taken his picture from three angles: front, left profile, right profile, That's how he entered the political criminal database and became a candidate for the planned internment camps he later, to his mild surprise, found out about on a newscast. They had fined him 500 marks and with delicate cynicism, had again informed him of his lack of future prospects before dismissing him.

Instead of simply trotting home, Rufus first sought asylum in a church, with idealists he trusted, levelheaded people in parkas and wool sweat-

ers, who meticulously listed every perversion of justice, including his case. A few feet from the altar, which was draped in a sheet to symbolize the vigil for the wrongly incarcerated, he bowed down in gratitude, signed his name by flickering candlelight, and was back in the streets the next day for further demonstrations. The water cannon, the ballet of police intervention—in sum, the inscrutable choreography of events—had a magical attraction for him.

They had failed to take folks like him out of circulation. Now it was too late. His kind of people turned disillusionment into opposition, turned griping and bellyaching into a new gravitational force in current affairs, though Rufus Rebhuhn, budding author, was thoroughly apolitical. Like every other writer, he at first only wanted a place in the sun—the sun of Remembrance.

∞∞∞

He was sitting at a crooked trestle table by the dim light of a rice paper globe, pecking away at his electric typewriter in the large, spartan room of his student digs in Berlin, when the background noise beneath his window markedly changed. During those days he had always kept one ear tuned to the street sounds, ever since the street had turned into a stage. Of late, illegal performances with crowd scenes and sudden nocturnal protest chants had been performed on this stage, and any moment could bring surprises. His internal barometer would register the minutest atmospheric change, every pedestrian eddy and every reduction in traffic flow. But what he now heard was quite new. It worried him. He stared into space for a while, listening to the hubbub brewing below, which had something rousingly cheerful, almost festive about it like a block party, a socialist carnival. Then he turned on his TV set.

This TV set was nearly the only object of value in his household, as well as a memento. An artist friend had left it behind, before he, too, had made off toward Hungary with his wife and child. Now Rufus R. watched the *Tagesthemen*—the daily news topics—on the little Sony color screen, where East German television was broadcasting a news conference, after some chatter, about the last session of the Central Committee of the United Party regarding new regulations for travel, permanent emigration, and private travel abroad—still more chatter—until politburo member Günter Schabowski, apparently a comedian among party bigwigs, pulled out that absolutely ridiculous, soon-to-be-famous note, smoothed it, read it in haste, began to stammer, and awkwardly rummaged through his papers, all on camera. And then it happened: a slip of the tongue, a lapse, the most incredible verbal blunder by government authorities in the history of the East German State, a colossal joke for all future textbooks. Rufus heard how the newscaster, a robust North German, announced, rolling his R's: "The DDRrr is opening its borrrders!" Only a few little words, but so plain that, of course, the audience couldn't grasp them, couldn't believe their ears.

Rufus R. walked out on his balcony. By this time a human stream, fed by every neighboring side street, was passing two floors below him. The stream didn't surge toward downtown East Berlin as usual, attracted by the TV tower's Sputnik sphere hovering above everything else, but was headed out of town, in a northerly direction. It was a cold November evening with temperatures down to freezing and the air was moist and misty. An anemic moon stood above the transformer station on the opposite side of the street, a red brick industrial building from the Weimar period detached from its gray background like a Feininger drawing. Somewhere back there, beyond the big transformer station humming like a beehive at night, was West Berlin, a dream city so near, and yet as unattainable as Honolulu or Xanadu.

Though the sight sent shivers down Rufus's spine, he couldn't keep from chuckling. There had been something heartwarming about the Western reporter's naïve question, "Mr. Schabowski, what's going to happen to the Berlin Wall now?" He had intended to spend the evening by himself, writing uninterruptedly, munching bologna sandwiches, his legs propped on the table, reading Flaubert (who was his idol in those days). Now this had become unthinkable. He was already late when he climbed the stairs to his only friends inside this classical Old-Berlin tenement building, a married couple, both physicists, with whom he enjoyed exchanging views now and then. The fear of all sensation-seekers, that of missing out on the best part, drove him on. But he was one of a crowd that night. He could have rung any doorbell to find almost everybody eager to come along, except for military personnel, hard-boiled party secretaries, or personnel in the large Stasi network. But there didn't seem to be many of those in the neighborhood.

"Did you watch the news?" the friends asked one another. "It can't be true. They must be putting us on, don't you think?"

"But he said, *immediately, without delay.*"

"Did you notice him rolling his eyes? I wonder if he'd had too much vodka. Absolutely crazy, the whole thing."

"It can't be true." His neighbors were born skeptics like all scientists. But by this time, Rufus R. believed anything possible. He had arrived at the gleefully desperate state where the breakdown, the total collapse of power and principle, or whatever was taking place, made him pleasantly giddy and curious. He was dying to see something he would never forget in a lifetime.

Less than five minutes later the three of them were in the street. The procession they joined resembled the train of cheerfully waddling figures following the golden goose of fairytale fame. They made up several hundred when, at the end of Sonnenburger Straße, they crossed the suburban train bridge (all in this ridiculous single file), and then several thousands when, after a zigzag walk along the grid squares of city blocks, they reached the Bornholmer Straße checkpoint. Here every other front door released instant pilgrims, some well bundled up with their hands in their coat pockets, eager to explore, as though prepared for a lunar eclipse or a passing comet. Several hikers did indeed look at the sky as if searching for portents of great things to come. All night long there were figures like that, spontaneous mystics, their heads tilted back. Bars emptied at the shout of a watchword from the door, gatherings broke up, school groups, at least the more intelligent among the girls, seemed to have arranged to get together. Hardly anyone came with a bag or a backpack, a dachshund, or even a camera. Almost everyone walked unencumbered, some looking as if they had valiantly jumped out of bed and just thrown on their winter clothes over their pajamas. In tune with the general dress code, calling for muted colors, Rufus R. and his companions quickly vanished within the crowd. All the young men wore windbreakers, faded blue jeans and sneakers, the older gents more often plastic and polyester, including padded, hooded coats in beige, metallic gray or dirty white.

Jammed up before the crossing point with its red and white barrier and the incredible bottleneck in the distance was a population made up of all ages and social strata: retirees in peaked caps, unshaven construction worker types, academics, students, a few resolute old ladies in ankle boots, and not one person unemployed, because unemployment had been eliminated by decree. As drained and overtired as most people seemed, particularly by the dim street lighting, at this point everyone was high, and their eyes were blazing with a sense of history.

When Rufus and his friends joined the procession, the scene before them was that of a siege in an advanced stage. Several squad cars sat tight within the crowd at angles, their rotating blue lights turning bystanders' faces into carnival masks. Shouts urging people to desist, to be reasonable, came over the megaphones, but went unheeded. Those in front had either engaged the border guards, identifiable from afar by their conductor's caps, in tough negotiations, or were being processed in small batches, while a column of motor vehicles over a half-mile long had lined up on Bornholmerstraße. Rufus R. got irritated at these low-brows in their *Wartburgs* too lazy to walk. Suddenly, he was fed up with the stinking, rattling little two-stroke *Trabants*, whose noise drowned out the choruses. There were, after all, loud calls in front, single, untrained, chickenhearted voices trying to yell a slogan. After a while the throng agreed on two versions, the somewhat fastidious "Open up your gate," which felt oddly Christmassy to him, and the brusquer, very plain "Let us out!" Though this was not a roaring crowd, it was, nevertheless, no longer totally harmless. Until the last moment, the prison system had staunchly ignored the fact that here stood a thoroughly well-behaved, disciplined population, self-denying stoics only wanting to look across their neighbor's fence, the same as all villagers since time began. But by this time, even without rioters, without provocateurs, the critical mass had long been exceeded, and there was no turning back. A huge wave had piled up and neutrality was over once and for all.

∞∞∞

By the time a few days had passed, Rufus R. remembered only fragments of the hours that followed. As long as twenty years later, he recalled the moment of hesitation, including the unclear chain of command and general uncertainty before the great surrender, as the finest passage in this requiem. He remembered having regretfully said good-bye to his physicist friends. They had to return for the sake of their two little children, who had stayed at home in their grandmother's care. The matter had become too risky for them, for it took on an air of irrevocability as soon as things really got underway. No one could predict if they might have problems coming back. The term *expatriation* made the rounds. There were rumors that this was an operation to separate the wheat from the chaff. And yet men and women impatiently waved their IDs, begged like children, and joyfully danced around the few people in uniform with their frozen expressions. *The people in uniform, the people in uniform . . .*

(credit: Winfried Hammann)

Until the last moment there had been excited telephone conversations with some kind of headquarters, and corks were heard popping, the only shots fired that night. Some of the redundant customs officers discreetly drew back behind a crowd barrier. Then the dike burst and the checkpoint was flooded, having at last become indefensible.

Rufus R. was swept along. Suddenly wide awake, he saw the barrier rise and watched the crowd rush past the check-in stations, leaving the control tower behind. The people seemed to forcibly tear themselves loose. Because the first bottles had shattered on the ground in the crush, Rufus stepped on broken glass as he pushed on. A few officers stood in the human surge, gritting their teeth, their fists on their hips, watching the rush in a state of shock. They looked like silent movie actors who had just had the rug pulled from under them. Since there was no point any longer to guardians of the status quo, the term *livelihood* suddenly loomed large. All of these sergeant types, the well-trained guard soldiers and people-controlling police, the whole close-knit corps of Wall security guards, including loutish little Secretary Mielke—the night of November 9 was the first time Rufus felt sorry for them. Obviously their day was over. Soon their ridiculous berets, military caps and leather belts, as well as the less amusing riding breeches of the staunch elite troops, who were never able shake off the acrid horse barn smell of their Prussian pedigrees, would be consigned to oblivion.

Shortly before midnight the city had gone into a freeze. Inhospitable and chilly as its cellars, Berlin retreated into the icy corridors of its wide streets and black canals, prowled around the skeletons of leafless chestnut trees, entrenched itself behind cemetery walls and overbuilt lots once covered with rubble, and crept into railroad platforms and tracks. For this time only, its inhabitants were exempt from the icy cold. This was the night when the robust nickel-steel structure of the Bornholm Bridge carried several thousands of excited people sharing a spontaneous New Year's Eve high. Actually, this bridge, with its mighty arches extending lengthwise and crosswise, and with its sawtooth struts—didn't it look like jaws of the kind you gleefully entered when boarding a carnival ghost train? Fairytale and legend had also touched the name the bridge officially bore since post-war times. The road to freedom led across the Böse Brücke—literally "Wicked Bridge"—named for a hero of the Communist revolution.

The last time Rufus R. looked back, he noticed the breath of the border guards in the amber glow of the whip-pole streetlights. As he walked on, he found the time to observe the endless row of fortifications, which reminded him of Siberian vastnesses and aerial photos of German concentration camps. He glanced at the neatly leveled, grimly glittering death strip and wondered what kind of perverted exercises had been performed there for the sake of deterrence and military fitness. The Wall had been the most secure national border in the world. Now all that lay behind him. He was surprised to read "Bornholmer Straße" on a sign on the Western side. He had never considered that, on a city map, the connecting routes might continue uninterrupted, that the names might simply go on as before the Wall was built. How full of promise the name had rung across time, he only now realized, painfully late. As a child, from a cliff on a narrow Baltic island in the summer, he made out something blurry and gray in the mist behind the horizon once—a tip of Denmark far beyond the Sea. But it hadn't been Bornholm.

He now sought to get away from the area near the border, eerie enough even on the Western side, as fast as he could. Like all other East Berliners, he took the subway to the center of town, and in the early morning hours, after a long, aimless hike, stood on the Kurfürstendamm. Brightly lit, the West was dancing around him. Then he remembered the mocking line from one of the poems of Reiner Müller (the gloomiest bard of the sinking Republic): "That the corpse should be so colorful!"

The change in lighting was in fact the most radical experience. Everything else came later. He glided past long lines of West Berliners, who regaled him with applause and pats on the shoulder as in a triumphal procession. But he didn't know anyone on this side, and no one knew him. Double-decker buses revolved around him, and so did sycamore trees speckled as with the reflected stroboscope light of many disco balls. News supplements were passed out. Rufus caught the large headline of one of them, "The Gates Are Wide Open!"

Was he angry, sad, euphoric? He felt as though he'd returned from a deep, mind-numbing absence, as though healed from a severe illness. Destiny never granted him to participate more intensely in an historic event, either before or after. What really happened that night is buried deep in his memory. He was not one to look back after everything had been decided.

ooooo

After spending a year in the Middle East, after sailing down the Nile, climbing the pyramids, and visiting the holy places, Gustave Flaubert writes to a friend, "Among the first studies I shall undertake after my return certainly will be that of all the miserable utopias troubling our society and threatening to cover it with ruins." And he soberly adds, "Any attempt to draw conclusions would be foolish."

Regardless of the Cost
Reflections on Péter Esterházy's *Revised Edition*

BY JUDITH SOLLOSY

Wouldn't it be great if the whole thing turned out to be no more than a bad joke?— Péter Esterházy, *Production Novel*

"Regardless of the cost, human or otherwise, we will continue as long as we have raw material," this is how Péter Esterházy's *Revised Edition* (*Javított kiadás*, 2002) begins, a quote from fellow writer Miklós Mészöly. And the raw material of *Revised Edition* shocked a nation, especially affecting those who had read the author's previous book, *Celestial Harmonies,* an elaborate prose tribute to his father Mátyás, though it is far wider in scope, adroitly blurring the lines between fact and fiction, claiming *everything* as its field of play. However, when the manuscript of *Celestial Harmonies* was at the typist, the author decided to take a break from work ("I had reached the limits of my . . . capacities. It feels good, reaching your limits, except you're just a wee bit helpless") and have a look at the recently declassified secret police files on himself in the Historical Archives, and while he was at it, to glance at his father's dossiers as well. Perhaps they'd been wiretapped. ("Around here, everybody thinks that half of the secret police were set on their trail.") But when a well-meaning official hesitantly pushed some brown dossiers towards him ("a slight motion, but alarming just the same") and he opened them, what he saw were not reports *on* his father, but reports *by* him. From March 2, 1957 to March 12, 1979, Mátyás Esterházy, who had always shown a staunch refusal to have anything to do with the Communist regime that was stifling his country, had been informing on friends, relatives, and acquaintances for the notorious "Section III/III" of State Security. That's twenty-two years. His pseudonym: Csanádi. We have that sickening moment of discovery on the part of the son about the double life of the father to thank for the existence of *Revised Edition*, which is aptly subtitled "Appendix to *Celestial Harmonies*."

The question begs to be asked: What is being appended to the previous "book of the resurrected father"? For one thing, the personal drama of a well-known son confronting the new, darker history of his well-known father, and for another, the drama that gradually unfolds in our own heads as we read and begin to ask our own questions about the implications of *Revised Edition*.

As some have recognized, the writing of *Revised Edition* is an exemplary moral act. In a country that will not come to terms with its recent past, where—to the satisfaction of many—everything has been swept under the great national carpet (and *remains* swept), thereby creating the illusion that except for the usual suspects (Stalin, Rákosi, Kádár) everyone was as innocent in a corrupt regime as a newborn babe, Péter Esterházy not only goes public with his father's shame, but even takes some of the blame upon himself. "I was not the one to commit the atrocity," he reflects, "but neither was it someone else! There was an 'us' inside me, I internalized everything, my father, too." He also writes that when he met people before *Revised Edition* was published, he couldn't help thinking to himself, "You have no idea who I really am!" In short, the moral gesture of *Revised Edition* is diametrically opposed to the comfortable communal silence about the past that still holds sway in post-Communist Hungary and contributes to a complicity of silence and an appearance of innocence.

When reading *Revised Edition*, readers are naturally curious: Why did Mátyás Esterházy become an informer? What coercion was used (if any)? Who did he inform on? How did he feel about his double life? And indeed, how could such a thing happen in the first place? How could it happen to Mátyás, to Péter, to the Esterházy family, to the country?

One of the best things about this book—for me, certainly—is the lack of answers and the lack of judgment on the part of the author. Little of essence is forthcoming, yet much is revealed. We do not know and will probably never know how or why Mátyás Esterházy, the former count, became an informer. We will also probably never know how he felt about it, though his growing alcoholism during those years is telling. (Under the circumstances, he would not have been alone in his drinking; how could a man of principle, for he was, I venture, an honorable man who committed dishonorable acts, go on with his betrayal from day to day without dulling his senses?) And though we are curious to learn who he may have informed upon, even this is withheld from us, since his son—whose shock, dismay, anger, and self-pity are also at the center of the book—made the authorial decision to supply only initials to indicate the characters in his father's accounts. Again, the question is: why? And the answer may well be that Péter Esterházy's *Revised Edition* functions—and may have been meant—as a communal public meditation on the absurdity of life under Communism.

As we read *Revised Edition*, we ask along with the author and son: Why did Mátyás Esterházy succumb? We don't know. What else did he include in his reports that is not in the book? We don't know. We only know that what happened seemed—and continues to seem—inconceivable, both to his son and to the public. We also know now that our knowledge has been pitifully limited, and will probably continue to be limited. The perplexity of the son is the perplexity of the public. Why, one wonders, was it necessary for the secret police to break in an Esterházy, when he, as we learn from the holding officers' marginal notes, was reluctant to "deliver the goods"? The only logical answer is that an aristocrat, and an Esterházy at that, must have been quite a feather in their caps. See? Even a former aristocrat has sided with us! It is not the truth that counts, as the adherents of socialist realism had been preaching since the 1910s, but the truth as we, Communists, will it into existence.

Communist dictatorship, the subject of the book suggests, had its own rationality and motives, its own aims and purposes, except that these had nothing in common with normalcy, logic as we know it, or everyday life. At first we wonder, when, in his life or reports, was Mátyás Esterházy Mátyás Esterházy, and when was he Csanádi? But as we read along, the question loses relevance, because we realize that in a Communist world, the whole idea was the blurring of the lines.

This was one of the supreme triumphs of Communism, this general state of existential uncertainty in which whole nations were kept. In a Communist dictatorship we don't know what the limits are or *where* the limits are, so we play it safe—where our borders are we knew only too well, witness the Berlin Wall. We don't know the degree or quantity of an informer's freedom of choice—or our own, for that matter. We don't know how "they" (because there was "us" and there was "them") think, not because it is a secret, but because by any rational measure, it is absurd, surreal, irrational, and therefore inconceivable. The fact that *Revised Edition* can only raise questions, or at best imply but not provide answers, is not a fault but a virtue, a carefully elaborated plan on the part of the author. Its lack of answers when faced with the workings of Communism is its answer about the nature of Communism.

Péter Esterházy's *Celestial Harmonies*, to which *Revised Edition* is the Appendix—the last chapter, if you will—ends with these words: "When we enter the apartment, my father is already sitting by the Hermes Baby which is clattering steadily, like an automatic machine gun, he's pounding it, striking, it, and the words come pouring out, going pit-a-pat on the white sheet, one in wake of the other, words that are not his own, nor were they ever, nor will they ever be." What was Mátyás's family and what is the reader witnessing: a man finishing a translation deadline or firing off yet another secret agent's report? It was not only Péter Esterházy's personal tragedy that he cannot know, it is a national tragedy as well. "I didn't want," he writes, "I didn't want it in the least that the family, my father as victim, should be put on a pedestal. I wanted to show that history really devoured everything but everything." When all is said and done, a wall raised from the stuff of well-orchestrated confusion, senselessness and irrationality can be as destructive as the toughest wall of brick and cement.

Preface to *Revised Edition*

BY PÉTER ESTERHÁZY

(TRANSLATION BY JUDITH SOLLOSY)

Regardless of the cost, human or otherwise, we will continue as long as we have raw material. This is the sentence I'm hearing over the radio now (at 2 P.M. something on the afternoon of January 23, 2001, I failed to note down the minute), a sentence from Miklós Mészöly's *Film*[1] that—after putting it off again and again—I have finally launched into this piece. It's as if my old colleague were prodding me on, giving me strength, yet slightly disappointed, too, that I need this prodding, that I can't manage on my own.

I could use all the help there is now, just when I am left to my own devices like never before. (I will try to avoid self-pity, though I can tell already that it's no use.)

If I had my way, I would like only those people who have read *Celestial Harmonies* to read this book. Of course, the reader does whatever he wants, and as for begging, forget it, although as you will see, during this writing, or better still, the *happening* that follows I would have often been willing to

---

1. A novel by Miklós Mészöly written in 1976 that uses the technique of very close, minute observation of people, as in a series of closeups, never taking his eye from them.

do anything, begging being the least of it.

I wouldn't mind beating about the bush some more, but it is time.

Just like anything else, this, too, is work.

∞∞∞∞

In the fall of 1999 I asked K.'s help, because I wanted to take a look at my files, if any, in the Historical Archives to see whether they were having me watched or wiretapped *back then*. Around here, everybody thinks that half the secret police were set on their trail. But not me. On the contrary. I could've sworn that this was not the case. Still, I needed tangible proof. Besides, I somehow felt it my duty both as a citizen and a democrat not so much to clarify the past but rather, by having a look at the files, if any, to show a certain attentiveness towards it.

K. is a professional, he knows the ropes, and he also knows how to go about these things. Typical. My first reaction was to find a privileged way in. It never crossed my mind that I could just walk into the archives, whose doors were now open to the public. But as it turned out, K. explained that if I say that I wanted to research the "subject," I could get my hands on more material than I could as a private citizen.

What do I want? To see if they've got anything on me. In which case I might as well have a look at the family's files as well. Maybe they had wiretapped my father. (For a time K. had worked with him at the now defunct *Budapester Rundschau*, and I had planned earlier to have him "talk" for *Celestial Harmonies*, but nothing came of it. I also interviewed my aunts and uncles, the legendary, cosmic *tantes*, sometimes taping the conversation, and though these meetings proved to be extremely interesting, it was soon apparent—it was apparent because I saw what I saw—that I couldn't get off just by talking to them, because, yes, I was hoping to be spared something, specifically, work; I was hoping that I wouldn't have to do everything myself. But I was mistaken. And so, as far as that earlier novel was concerned, I didn't mind in the least that nothing had

"COMRADES FAREWELL."
The poster that famously celebrated the beginning of the withdrawal of Soviet troops from Hungary in March, 1990, just before the free elections that made József Antall the country's first democratically elected Prime Minister. (credit: István Orosz)

REPORT BY HUNGARIAN
SECRET AGENT
ON THE LITERARY
MAGAZINE *TISZATÁJ*

In paragraph 3, it describes
how the problematic
parts of an article from its
October issue, discussing
the population exchange
between Hungary and
Czechoslovakia, was to be
removed from the 3,000
copies already in print and
replaced with the corrected
version. October 26, 1982.
(opposite page, credit:
László Péter)

come of the interview with K.; later, I thought, there will be plenty of time to find out this and that about my father; for the time being, what I have is enough, enough already!)

I still have the slip on which I made notes while I was on the phone with K. Like a child, I was noting down my chores. That I should write to the Customer Service Department of the Archives, request an official form, what? An official form to conduct research. I had him repeat it twice. And the '56 Institute would give me a recommendation. And what should I say was the subject of my research? My role in Hungarian literature since the 1970s. (At first it was "PE and his Times," I think, but I flat refused to put that down.) And I think later I had to change this to the E. family, but I'm not sure any more.—That's the problem, the problem that keeps rearing its ugly head like never before, to wit, that I must accommodate myself to reality. Before, it was words.

∞∞

But I didn't pay much attention to all this because I was finishing *Celestial Harmonies*, working in a daze from morning to night. I finished it several times, meaning that I thought I had finished it several times, meaning that what was left was mere formality, whereas I should have known, from experience as well as the dictates of common sense, that there's no such thing, there is no mere formality, there's no "it's just a technical problem now." Until it is *really* finished anything is possible, everything is left wide open. If something is almost finished, it is not finished.

I had to stop work for three days, coitus interruptus, basically for the sake of another coitus (considering what is to follow, this is stylistically more than objectionable, it's off, but then I'm off, too; after all, I'm living as if the thing I must now describe didn't even exist); this was when I was awarded a state prize in Vienna. It turned out to be a pleasant three days, elegant hotel, first-class restaurants, leisurely walks, a ceremony at the *Bundeskanzleramt*,[2] an easy golden glory. And as I was listening to Dés[3] playing the saxophone for my benefit, I wasn't even fidgety, since this was a big, leisurely intake of breath before the last days of work. I had no idea that this was also the

---

2. Office of the Chancellor.

3. László Dés, the Hungarian saxophone virtuoso.

last time in my life that I would be as happy as I know how, because I'm really good at it, it's my nature; I have the gift of good cheer, this is my gift from the Heavens above (and the Lord said: Be cheerful, damn you!, and so it came to pass, a way of singing His praises); I had no idea that this would soon end and a great big shadow would settle inside me . . . okay, not so big, no bigger than myself; I had no idea that this was the last time my heart would be light, and then never again.

I first finished *Celestial Harmonies* on December 16, 1999, and to show the seriousness of my purpose, self-satisfied, I wrote in my notebook, *11 P M , 7 minutes,* and also, *FINISHED.* In caps. The beginning of Part One was not quite right, I had meant to fix it during the summer, but didn't (I needed the time to write my speech for the Buchmesse in Frankfurt[4]), I didn't attribute any importance to it, so much technical nitpicking; I need to fix the order of the first ten sentences, one pleasant workday.

And so I began the pleasant workday, which had a nightmarish end because, to make a long story short, when the first ten were in place, yes, let's make this the first: "It is deucedly difficult to tell a lie when you don't know the truth," and so on, and here I need a new one, and so on, and I was reaching for the eleventh, when I couldn't help seeing that that's not where it belongs but that the former sentence, number eighty-seven, belongs there (let's say). And the twelfth is not the twelfth, but the hundred and first. In short, I would have to rethink the whole thing again, and prepare thematic lists, and keep everything in mind again, but that's the easy part, because I would also have to make lists of the lists, but first and foremost, I would have to concentrate very hard and pull together and reshape the entire first part, something I had not foreseen at all.

I passed the holidays in a daze, and then began perhaps the roughest workweek of my life; I didn't get dressed, ate sporadically, didn't shave, and

---

4. In 1999 Hungary was the official guest of the Frankfurt Bookfair.

fell into bed at midnight so that before I knew it, it was seven in the morning already, and I ambled around in my room, no one and nothing existed except for the text and the numbers—in short, the order of the sentences. Sometimes I'd take a short nap in the afternoon, something I do at other times as well, except now I slept like a dead man, death-like in my immobility (like my father, *cf.*, *CH*, p. 809).

I had reached the limits of my physical, intellectual, and moral capacities. It feels good, reaching your limits, except you're just a wee bit helpless. I felt that if anyone were to so much as look at me now, I would burst into tears. Or punch the individual in the nose. It must have been some picnic, living with me.

But only Miklós (13) bristled. Or he's the only one I noticed. A father's not like this. A proper father. Well, then, what?, I asked apathetically sitting in the kitchen. A proper father has time for his son. A proper father plays ping-pong with his son. His son! Understand? A proper father goes hiking with his son to the surrounding hills! But, but . . . I know, I know! The novel! See? Forget the see. The family comes first!, he shouted like a severe wife past all hope. Which jolted me back to life. This is a subject I know something about, and like a husband with a bad conscience, I responded with force. He knows perfectly well how important the family is to me. Very. But work comes first! At which he, still the offended wife, dashed out of the kitchen. I shrugged. Go on, dash around all you want. It is out of my hands, there is nothing more I can do. And he must have understood this helplessness, too, because fifteen minutes later, when he came back for his pizza, he didn't say anything as far as that goes—for there was nothing to be said—but as he was leaving he stroked my shoulder as if he were the calm grownup and I the child, alright, so you're the way you are. From now on, this is what we'll call a proper father.

I finished on January 8, and again I wrote down *FINISHED*; it was at noon on Saturday (I didn't write down the minute), then I took the notebooks to Gizella, the typist. I'm not surprised at Dostoyevsky, who fell in love with his secretary. He kept dictating to her until . . . Gizella is the first stranger to read my novels, and as such her situation is delicate, because mine is delicate. She is a fine, cultured lady, and though she is a severe soul (unless, of course, she is lying), her behavior in my defenseless state (the text I hand her is still warm, it's still steaming, it's that fresh) is faultless, and for this I am eternally in her debt. She doesn't offend me, but she doesn't spare me either. As for me, I want to wring quick praise from her (basically, I'd like her to swoon because my work is so brilliant, and I'd slap her face ever so gently, come, come, Gizella my dear, do get a grip on yourself, don't do this, don't exaggerate, though I know exactly what you mean); I repeatedly give her a chance to praise me, so then, this is perhaps all right, more or less, don't you think?, but she'll speak only when she wants to, not when I'd like her to. She's tactfully severe, maybe that's the best way of putting it. She doesn't like so-called four-letter words (she doesn't have it easy, she also types for Nádas), for which she chides me now and then, a game, no more, but her question is serious, why?, what's the use?, what's the purpose?, is it really *necessary*?

I'm rambling on, playing for time, which is a mistake, and pointless, too, seeing how time does not exist. What was has had its day. Everything is in the present tense.

The following day, on January 9, I lay in bed with a headache brought on by overexertion, but in the afternoon I set about ironing out Part Two just the same, which promised to be a pleasant, uncomplicated business, shifting through the remaining slips and inserting them if there was space, and generally reading and nursing the text some more. But my body wouldn't let me. On Monday morning it got up at six in the morning, by six-thirty it was in my room, without bothering to dress, covered in a simple dressing gown, like some distinguished English culture-vulture, plus woolen socks. I got up at six on Saturday the 15th as well, and at four in the afternoon I wrote in my notebook: *now it's FINISHED!*, and I underlined it twice. And I was really finished. I rushed off to Gizella with this heap of notebooks, too, tried to pry something out of her about the previous batch, but in vain. Then I opened a bottle of champagne at dinner and afterwards watched *Pulp Fiction* on television again.

ooooo

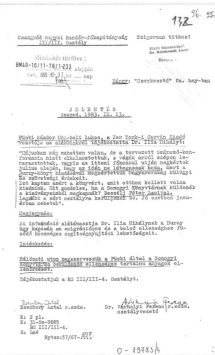

REPORT ON HUNGARIAN ÉMIGRÉ PUBLISHER SÁNDOR PÜSKI, owner of the Corvin Publishing House and bookstore in New York, who planned to go to Hungary, but because of a controversial book he published, is advised to postpone his visit. September 13, 1983. (credit: László Péter)

Back in the fall I decided that once I was finished, I would go with my wife (my baby) to the end of the world, somewhere warm, the sea, the Maldives, anywhere. In the end it's the last option that materialized, the anywhere, *Dichtung und Wahrheit,* we spent four days at the writers' retreat at Szigliget. It was very nice. We left on Sunday the 23rd and came back on Thursday the 27th. We walked, we slept, my back hurt a bit (it pained me). Before we left for Szigliget, though, a message was waiting for me on Friday evening that M. had called from the Historical Archives and would I return the call. Which I did from Szigliget, and we agreed to meet on Friday the 28th, at 1 P.M.

I am trying to remember that Thursday, which in a certain sense was also the last of its kind but I can't. In the evening I attended the usual end-of-the-month *ÉS*[5] dinner, it's the only regular social life I have. I enjoy going to this open dinner between editors and readers, even when I'd been working and I'm tired it makes me think that there is a country, a city, an editorial office, colleagues, friends, male and female—and even the food is acceptable. The last old-time Thursday of my life ended in good cheer.

Cheer was getting the better of me anyway, more than cheer, less than happiness, because I thought I could see the good fate of my book. On Tuesday the 25th, Paul's Day, Zs. called and said she's read the manuscript and—and? and? . . . I was standing in the office of the writers' retreat, R., who had made me a gift of beautiful, rare words six months previously that helped me render the resettlement scenes more authentic was sitting across from me at her desk, tactfully not looking at me, while I was listening to Zs. beaming like an elated, absurd schoolboy in response to—and maybe it's no exaggeration—her awed tones; I heard how the book had enchanted her, and how my father had enchanted her. This, plus G.'s enthusiasm from the publishing house gave me the most pure joy regarding the novel, because all the good things that happened after its publication were overshadowed by the events of the following day, the 28th, under whose weight I have been living ever since and shall continue to live forever.

On the 28th I immediately began to write a diary of sorts, which I will make public below. But I made no notes about this particular day, which I now regret, because as we will see, I can't use my power of imagination here, humble enough to begin with. Károly and Karola's day, I could check

---

5. Short for *Élet és Irodalom,* the popular weekly to which Péter Esterházy is a regular contributor.

when the sun came up and when it set, and I can safely say that it did come up and it did set (I've checked: 7:16 A.M. and 4:38 P.M. respectively), *1h, Eötvös 7,* it says in my notebook, *chores, ill humor,* with reference to the morning. Then *1:!!!!,* four exclamation marks, and: *numb → book store, Mora, Goethe 7:30.* In short, that Terézia Mora was giving a reading that night at the Goethe Institute.

It goes without saying that I wasn't expecting anything out of the ordinary and yet as I climbed the wide stairs to M.'s office, I felt anxious. Ah, those Kádár-regime knots in the stomach! M. must have been some sort of policeman prior to 1990, I thought. He greeted me warmly, even cordially. We had coffee, an important person visiting another important person. He seemed ill at ease, which I thought was excessive because my vanity made me think that he's ill at ease because he's a snob. Three brown folders lay in front of him. Well, well, so the boys have been busy after all, I thought smugly. Hemming and hawing, at last M. launched into what he had to say, that they received my

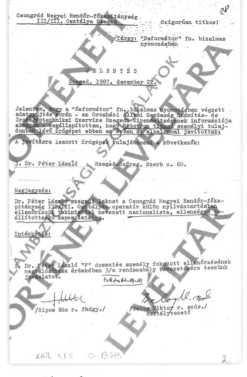

research request, and that there wasn't much they could come up with, and that anything from after 1980 first had to be cleared by the Interior Ministry, and that takes time, he's sorry.

I listened to this self-important display with annoyance. He kept touching his fingers to the folders. And that he's got something else to tell me, but I mustn't be anxious, I turned down the corner of my lip in scorn, still, he felt duty-bound to show me these, and well . . . how should he put it, I'm not going to like it, and well . . . he's at a loss for words, maybe I should just have a look and then I'll see what this is, what he means is, what it's all about, and he pushed the folders toward me. A slight motion, but alarming just the same. This is a work dossier, an agent's dossier, an agent's . . . and he heaved a deep sigh that confused me, as if the existence of agents pained him personally, an agent's reports.

Why all the fuss, I thought, I'm so tired of these grown men all tied up in knots, why can't he talk like a normal human being?, and I opened the dossier.

I saw what he meant right away.

There was no believing what I saw. I quickly placed my hand on the desk,

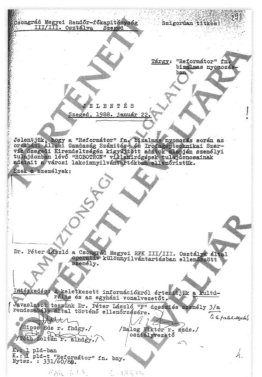

because it started to shake. What am I to do now? It seemed like a dream. I think I'll faint, that should take care of the problem. Or jump out the closed window and make my escape. I immediately began to act a part (like so many times since), I thanked him for his confidence, and said that I'd like to read what he'd handed me. At which he said something like he'd already had a look, and I shouldn't worry, they're among the best. Something like that. I walked along Andrássy út, glancing up at the houses to see if they'd come tumbling down. But no.

This is no crime story where I should or where I even could make sure that the identity of the killer, if any, will come to light only at the end (while there is nothing I would like better than to play for time), for as soon as I opened the dossier, I recognized my father's handwriting.

∞∞∞

In what follows, I will make public the agent's reports, i.e., the parts that I copied from them, including the notes I made as I was working. I don't (I didn't) want to do too much editing, while all the time I knew full well that I must give shape to this, too.

I watched myself, like an animal, curious to see how I would conduct myself in this situation, how I would react to things, and how things would act on me.

From *Mandarins*

BY STANISLAV KOMÁREK

(TRANSLATION BY MELVYN CLARKE)

The main character of Mandarins—*the sinologist Jindřich Krottenbacher, Ph.D.—lives out the epoch-making year 1989 (the fall of Communism in Bohemia) and the post-revolutionary era up to 2001. This excerpt takes place in the spring of 1990 (after the Velvet Revolution), and describes the foundation of a new department (the Faculty of General and Special Studies—FGSS) of the fictive Ferdinand University (FU) in Prague. Jindřich Krottenbacher works (together with his friend Slíža) at the Institute of East-West Comparative Studies (IEWCS) of the new faculty.* Mandarins *describes the development of the new institution and the other ventures of the main character in Prague, China, and Russia. Against the backdrop of this unsettled period, Komárek sets his thrilling—and in patches fanciful and ambiguous—plot, in which make-believe is extremely difficult to distinguish from reality. As with Komárek's earlier work,* Mandarins *is about the nature of fate, and the fragility of human plans and life's ambitions. With symptomatic irony it portrays the "life and institutions" of its place and time. Jindřich Krottenbacher, too, fails to win the game of chess he has been playing with his destiny.*

In January and then through to April, there followed a whirlwind of legislation aimed at transforming the country into a traditional European state with all its political and economic apparatus. This was no easy task, somewhat reminiscent of Baron Münchhausen's efforts to drag himself and his horse out of a swamp by his hair. There has been ample experience throughout Europe of nationalizing and smothering pluralism, but how this entire process is to be put into reverse while still in motion . . . ?

It is rather difficult to slowly transform, say, a crab into a cat while it's on the move: both the cat and the crab are animals that are functional in their own way, although the numerical ratio of cats to crabs kept as pets clearly shows where people's affections lie—crab cannot be used dry or frozen, but then again you don't have to feed it every day and it doesn't miaow. Still, turning its external skeleton into an internal one and radically rearranging all its organs, without the creature actually pegging out on you, is a problem on the borderline of solvability. The only transformation of this kind that *has* ever been carried out was the denazification of Germany, but that too had broken down and was under the all-powerful administration of a foreign occupying force. This country was intact, even though it had suffered an attack from a very chronic disorder when a more or less malignant growth had swept all before it.

A "third way" may well have still been under consideration in various forms, but it was becoming obvious that the "construction of capitalism" was underway, along with all that entailed. Those who still remembered the horrors of the "construction of socialism" erroneously imagined that the entire process would be something rather heroic accomplished on rations of three hundred grams of bread a day—in that brief interval between the two periods of profligacy they did start talking for a short time about the need for austerity and economizing. Negotiations were already under way over the withdrawal of the occupying forces, even though it would take almost two years to repair what was done in a single night. After all, as an oriental proverb has it: *It took a fool no time to drop a stone down a well, but seven wise men could not draw it out.*

Sometime in the middle of the month Slíža phoned to tell Jindřich that the following afternoon a preliminary meeting was to take place in a Nové Město apartment to create the new faculty. When he arrived on the fourth floor of the Secession-style tenement block, the largest room in a four-room apartment was already bursting at the seams.

As blue smoke from the many cigarettes rose towards the crystal chandeliers, our protagonist surveyed with interest the faces, clothes and behaviour of this, the dissident intelligentsia. Not that there weren't a few individuals amongst them from the Academy, but the predominant type here was quite different.

Jindřich was struck by the number of full beards and half beards of various lengths, and contrary to his normal habit he even lit up and puffed on a cigarette guardedly, so as not to stand out like a sore thumb. Everybody was sipping coffee or tea and debating with everybody else. The extent of Slíža's social contacts, which Jindřich had never guessed at, was now evident. Slíža did not pay him any attention at all, having clearly discharged his obligations by inviting him. Next to him the son of Marxist reformist thinker Pospíšek was talking about how the StB had urged him to denounce his father, who had fallen into disfavor. "He's an old Bolshevik, gentlemen, that he is, but he's still my dad," he'd answered them and evidently they never came back. Suddenly everyone fell silent. A huge, bearded man aged about sixty, whom Jindřich had never seen before, started speaking about the basic idea of a Faculty of General and Special Studies. "That's Marhold," Slíža whispered by way of explanation. Jindřich was perhaps one of the few people present who did not know Dr. Marhold, a close friend of the president's, or who did not know his remarkable story. He was the son of First Republic General Marhold, a Russian legionnaire, who may not have held any really prominent position in the army, but who at the time of the Siberian anabasis knew not only Masaryk, but also Emanuel Moravec.[1] This unusually sociable general's friends also included Alberto Vojtěch Frič,[2] who was a frequent guest at Marhold's villa in Ořechovka. This association ultimately proved fateful to him in a rather bizarre manner. After the Germans arrived, Marhold Senior was pensioned off and as he only flirted with the resistance from a great distance it seemed he would see out the war in good health. But it was not to be. Marhold shared not only a passion for gardening with Frič, but also a hatred for his fellow general Moravec, then Minister of Education and National Enlightenment. So he was jubilant when Frič wrought his vengeance on Moravec by breeding some tomatoes with the Japanese-sounding name of *Ritsushima*, a joke from the Czech "*řiť s ušima*" meaning "buttocks with ears," a nickname for the bald-headed Moravec. He told all his friends and acquaintances this hilarious story and in August 1943 he even handed round some ripe ritsushimas. The Minister, who had had it in for Marhold since before the war, fumed with rage, but he knew that by accusing the famous traveler of breeding a tomato to caricature him, he would at best make himself look rather foolish in the eyes of K. H.

---

1. Emanuel Moravec—famous Czech quisling and collaborator with the Nazis, former a general of the Czechoslovak Army.

2. Alberto Vojtěch Frič—famous Czech traveller and explorer in South America.

Frank.[3] All he could do was inform Frank of his serious suspicions regarding Marhold's anti-Reich activities. Nothing specific was investigated, but just to be sure, the general was placed in protective custody until the end of the war and sent to Buchenwald. Thanks to his resilient nature he survived in good health until April 1945, when the front lines were closing in on Thuringia from all sides. The Americans, who were about to liberate the camp, dropped a large number of leaflets in several languages on it to announce their imminent arrival. As even the SS had now correctly guessed that the end was nigh, discipline in the camp broke down and a number of prisoners, including General Marhold, ran out into the area between the barracks, enthusiastically waving at the American planes. He alone was hit on the head with full force by a package of leaflets that had failed to open in the air, and broke his neck. Frič was dead too by then, having been infected with tetanus from a rusty nail, and shortly afterwards Moravec committed suicide just as his Gestapo driver, while trying to save him from the Prague Uprising, ran out of petrol on the hill below Hradčany and was about to refill the tank. For some reason the Grim Reaper wanted them all right away. Marhold's son, who was at first treated as the child of a national martyr, eventually managed with difficulty to complete his studies in the 1950s, but only in engineering, with a doctorate in practical aerodynamics. Even as a boy he took a liking to Jan Smuts, the South African general, statesman, and biological and social theorist, and he later took up Chelčický and converted to the Moravian Church accordingly. In 1967 he managed to get to a Smuts Conference in Sapporo, Japan (is there anything at all that these Japanese aren't involved in?), and in 1968 went to Britain for six months, returning with much gnashing of teeth. Having signed the Charter, he joined the Building Engineering Department as a digger which, thanks to his stature—even greater than his father's—he coped with easily, apparently without ever taking a single day off, wielding his pickaxe even when he had the flu and a thermometer under his armpit. Naturally, at apartment seminars he was tired-out and dozed off, but the opportunity to become a night porter a year before the events of November enabled him to get more involved again. With his submissive wife entirely devoted to his family, like a cutout from a macho fantasy, he was still living in his inherited villa, albeit with one wing occupied by tenants forced on him by the mother party.

---

3. Karl Herrmann Frank—Nazi *Reichsprotektor* in Bohemia.

They had the blessed number of seven offspring, all girls except one, and from the eldest an entire gaggle of grandchildren. Their only boy was not so much involved in intellectual pursuits as in arranging hard rock concerts, often on the fringes of old-regime legality. In other ways too, Marhold's life became the stuff of popular legend—not only that his villa housed a collection of statuettes and portrayals of St. George, that Christian transformation of the Thracian horseman, but also that three key items supposedly came from the collection of Archduke Franz Ferdinand: during his proletarian period he had swapped them for two bottles of rum from a fellow digger, formerly the caretaker at Konopiště Castle[4] and subsequently a down-and-out alcoholic, who had "appropriated" them and kept them in a hut. One quite unbelievable story, which was apparently true, was about Marhold's grandmother, a small factory owner in Počátky, Vysočina. Although her factory manufactured stockings, she had evidently not had enough of knitting, even on Sundays, so there she sat in a rocking chair in Počátky Square, in her old-world fashion, knitting away. Imagine her dismay when the half-wit hydrocephalic son of Jebavý the cobbler from next door ran into one of her needles in his oligophrenic raving, and it pierced his still-soft head. Panic erupted and the dismayed entrepreneur did not know what to do when she saw his oversized head leaking some bloody effusion. However, a couple of gold florins pressed into their palms dissuaded his parents from suing, as did the fact that the boy didn't die, but actually made a full mental recovery following this crude and unintended tapping of the brain ventricles. He then went to school as normal and grew up to be the poet Otokar Březina. If you don't believe it, go and see for yourself.

After a short introductory speech Marhold began to explain the idea behind the planned school: it was to be divided into three "Sections": Formal Natural Sciences, which would involve the mathematical modeling of various processes, particularly physical-chemical ones; Economics, also with an emphasis on mathematical applications; and the Life Sciences Section, which was, surprisingly, also to include Slíža and Krottenbacher, as it was here that Marhold's school classified people and their cultures. This section included the Institute for Bioethics, the Institute for Inter-Gender Studies and also the Institute for East-West Comparative Studies (IEWCS

---

4. Konopiště Castle—the seat of the Archduke Franz Ferdinand with plenty of souvenirs of him.

FGSS FU). Clearly, thanks to Marhold's contact with friends in the West, going back to his visits during the sixties, he had a good idea of what was in demand at universities there, and at that time economics *was* the science of sciences: veneration of the Invisible Hand of the Market might not have got through to the working masses yet, but "up there" it was now being progressively adopted.

A long and highly detailed discussion broke out, during which Jindřich had the opportunity to closely observe the dissident intelligentsia in action. Apart from their appearance, complete with sweaters that were frequently stretched out of shape, and corduroy jackets, he was particularly struck by many individuals' pronunciation, sentence stresses and vocalization; a number of them had peculiarities and defects in their pronunciation, at least from the standpoint of the speech therapists of the day, as well as a common intonation which differed from that of the majority of the population. Casual observers might have associated the entire phenomenon with foreignness and an inadequate command of the phonetics of a new language. But these were not foreigners, as would have suited the former regime, but people who would be described in German not as *Ausländer*, but as *Ausweltler*, people who do not feel at home in a rather grubby everyday reality. Moving into dissent (from *dis-sedere*, to move away) also correlated strongly with an imperceptible feature of many of those present—rather poor motor coordination, which made activities such as dancing, volleyball and driving a car unpleasant or impossible. It seemed as if those who found that many things did not come naturally to them, showed an inclination to think not only of themselves, but also of society as a whole. In comparison with the respectable Western intelligentsia, where even non-conformity is stereotyped and calculated to achieve an effect, they looked like handmade pottery in contrast to factory-made pots: each item was an original, every one was different, though of course some pieces might have been suddenly called upon to decorate the display cases of illustrious museums, whereas others would have been hard to move at a Ghanaian market. For the most part they had only seen the rear end of their fate so far: bureaucratic bullying and the need to bow to chance and the high-and-mighty in order to earn a living, a lack of literature and critical thinking in their own ranks and the inability to publish except in typewritten samizdats or by riskily smuggling texts abroad. The fact that they had enough time for their not-exactly-numerous books and that they could read and think them all through, that they did not have to pour out articles just to get one in a list, that making a living out of their favorite subject maybe was in many respects close to the thrill of having an amorous experience and then getting into prostitution, and that criticism also has its competitive and aggressive side—of all this few of them were yet aware. Krottenbacher had already seen this in Munich, if only out of the corner of his eye. Besides, in contrast to the oppressive stuffiness at the Academy, here the atmosphere was relaxed, even homely, and everyone knew everybody else. Never had the power of money been so small and the power of human ties so great as at that time, although the phenomenon was now beginning to wane. Both in the party and among the opposition, one only trusted those within one's own "extended family," with whom, for the sake of self-preservation, one had to be in cahoots, sometimes more happily than at others. Fortunately, the times had long passed when you risked execution or years in prison by just being friends with somebody. Besides society was now full of alternative families, from "hikers," setting out in droves on Saturday mornings for the Brdy Forest, to emigrants.

Eventually it was agreed to make a proper announcement in the newspapers, to conduct interviews for the new positions in April and to start teaching proper from October—even with all the goodwill in the world they would not make it for the summer semester. The building itself was coming together, not far from the Rudolfinum, and had previously been used as an auxiliary office building by the Socialist Youth Organization municipal board. Alarmed by the sudden developments, the "Youth" had agreed to hand over the building in the near future. That autumn the faculty would arrange a conference for its foreign supporters and intellectual sympathizers entitled Overcoming Borders—The Intellectual Dimensions of Europe Today.

Krottenbacher was all in a trance as he left Slíža after numerous goodbyes, but then Slíža put on a meaningful expression and invited our protagonist to the pub. There he pulled out two cigarettes of an odd shape and told him they were from his Western sources and contained the highest quality hashish, evidently smuggled from Afghanistan via Islamabad and Karachi. At that time hemp products had not yet assumed the dimensions that they eventually would in Czech urban folklore, but the first swallows had already arrived. Jindřich had not carried out any experiments of this kind in Munich. When he was a student he had bought some peyote, *Lophophora williamsi*, for five crowns at the Young Cactus Growers shop and consumed it, but without result. All the more to look forward to now. On Slíža's advice he kept the smoke in his lungs for as long as possible, despite a huge urge to cough, and he began to see something like arabesques. When his tempter produced another couple of joints he just nodded avidly. He then observed with interest and dismay as the grammatical structure of his language fell apart, objects assumed a very odd "neoclature" and his speech took on absurd new forms. Overcome by curiosity, he began to draw a picture on the reverse side of the check, which undulated oddly in front of him. Although he had depicted all the parts correctly, the whole was exceptionally bizarre because the overall meaning of the drawing had been sacrificed to local associations and nothing remained but to call it a "raverie." As if from behind a veil he perceived the uncouth waiter throwing them out, yelling that they would not put up with junkies there, and Slíža paying up and disappearing. Only with difficulty did Jindřich find his bearings on the street and although it would have been more sensible to walk the short distance home, he decided to take the metro. The rattling carriages themselves appeared monstrous and alien to him and he only got in with the greatest effort. He remained standing by the doors, where the usual "*Do not lean on the doors*" sign had peeled away to reveal: *n e o d o r.* The doors had slammed shut by the time he grasped all the associations and realized just how naïvely he had been caught in this trap. With all his strength he tried to open them and get out of the departing train, paying no heed to those standing round. All of a sudden he saw the awful grimacing face, indescribably monstrous behind the window. The Neodor! He let out a ghastly yell as he leapt at the doors with all his strength and crashed onto the floor. He had hardly got up again when, shortly before the next stop, he saw on the wall a face that was even more dreadful . . . the Paleodor! Ignoring the alarmed passengers, some of whom were even trying to seize him, he rushed out onto the platform and went off home.

Brother and Sister

BY CHRISTHARD LÄPPLE
(TRANSLATION BY STEVEN RENDALL)

Hans and Helen Heller are brother and sister, now in their sixties. When she was young, Helen escaped from East Berlin to the West; Hans stayed behind to help build the socialist utopia. In 1985, Hans is recruited by the Stasi to spy on his sister and her boyfriend, a West Berlin television reporter. Hans invites them to have dinner with him, his wife, and their parents at the Ganymede, a posh East Berlin restaurant:

THE CHECK

Eating a meal together is a good way to start the evening. The wine, a rare *chasselas* from Meißen, loosens their tongues. They all talk about their lives. Difference has its attractions. There's no lack of things to talk about. Brother and sister reminisce about their childhood, their narrow-minded teachers, their shared adventures in summer camps. The mood is relaxed.

"We had a pleasant evening in the Ganymede. Moreover, we talked about the GDR in a very friendly way. We spoke mainly about old times. Politics didn't come up. You could say the atmosphere was agreeable. I remember that I gave my brother a sweater."

Helen is surprised by her brother, who for such a long time has refused any contact with her and is now so open. She has still not forgotten the dinner at the Ganymede.

"The five of us spent an evening together. We felt like a family. We celebrated without bitterness or discord. Life can be so beautiful."

The TV reporter is taken with the GDR. Here no minders, no busybodies, or officials sit at the table. Here he learns what people really think, what makes them laugh, what annoys them. He tells them about meeting Heiner Müller, the famous playwright at the nearby Berliner Ensemble theater. When he comes to the important part, the well-traveled man speaks more softly. No one must hear. They lean toward each other conspiratorially.

The TV reporter tells one story after another. Heller's head is spinning; he has been assigned to observe as much as he can.

The other customers have long since left when the bill is brought to Heller on a small silver tray. He conceals a double take when he sees what is written on the slip of paper: 248.30 marks and "We hope you enjoyed your meal." The bill is as much as his weekly salary. He pays and for an instant isn't sure

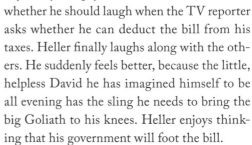

whether he should laugh when the TV reporter asks whether he can deduct the bill from his taxes. Heller finally laughs along with the others. He suddenly feels better, because the little, helpless David he has imagined himself to be all evening has the sling he needs to bring the big Goliath to his knees. Heller enjoys thinking that his government will foot the bill.

Before leaving, they drink to the generous birthday boy, and then the TV reporter tells a final story he's recently heard. "One evening the composers Hanns Eisler and Paul Dessau met here in the Ganymede. Eisler was grumpy, Dessau in high spirits. Eisler complained that it was forbidden to perform his works in the GDR. The subversive Dessau leapt to his feet, hurried over to the two musicians, asked for a violin, and played one of Eisler's original works, the GDR national anthem. For a moment the guests in the restaurant, many of whom were well-known actors or high officials, were unsure what to do: should they stand up during the anthem, or not?"

Heller rises and says he has to go, he has to work the next day. Relieved, he embraces his birthday guests and thanks them for a pleasant evening. It is precisely nine minutes past midnight when the TV reporter leaves East

Berlin with Heller's sister. The exit stamp from the nearby Friedrichstraße border crossing, which divides the city into two worlds, indicates the time. The document is among Heller's spy papers in the Stasi archive, filed under the date of his birthday.

The papers do not say what Helen asks her television reporter friend on the way back to West Berlin. She wants to know what he thought of her brother. Without much hesitation, he says he likes him a lot, particularly his openness. He's sure Brother Hans is a very decent guy.

OVERTIME

The apartment building's intercom clicks. Heller gives the password: "Greetings from Workmate Fichtel." The door buzzes open. Heller flits like a shadow to the elevator, hoping he doesn't meet anyone. He hates this sneaking around for months, using passwords, meeting in empty new apartment buildings, and constantly being on his guard. Neither his daughter nor his new companion is to know anything about his second life. He says he's working overtime. Work for the collective, desk work, whatever's still lying around, somebody has to do it. His companion accepts this explanation, doesn't ask further questions. Heller is considered very dutiful, reliable, somebody who doesn't have stupid ideas.

He pushes the button. The elevator door groans shut. He's alone, thank God. Nonetheless, beads of sweat run down his forehead. Sometimes he just wants to stop. This cat-and-mouse game has been going on for two years. Constant fear of making a blunder. Constant worry about being caught. Why is he doing this to himself, he wonders. He's mulled that question over, but arrived at no clear answer. He has never said no. But he hasn't said everything; he's concealed some things from the officials. These little acts of resistance are good for his inner health. He doesn't want to be someone who rats on others, informs on them or gets them in trouble. He doesn't consider himself a traitor. One time he resists when the officials demand a written commitment he doesn't want to make. But they keep at him, they pressure him and appeal to his sense of duty. Finally he signs a promise to keep silent. It's a compromise he can live with. The three lines come from the comrades, the hand is his.

The elevator door opens. Heller glances left, then right. His eyes sweep the floor. It's quiet. Nobody about this evening. Someone's TV is on, the

noise comes through the thin apartment door. He slinks along the walls like a cat, always ready to leap. What has become of him? The remarkable transformation of Hans Heller into a secret agent for the Party.

"I felt like a remote-controlled robot," he now says. Again and again, he forces himself to put on a suit and tie, mind his table manners, and play the interested, understanding brother, as best he can. He gets himself invited to high society gatherings with talkative but remarkably stiff people. He hangs out in expensive bars and meets prominent people at parties. He becomes another person, if only for a few hours. Strange that he succeeds at this mummery; otherwise he has no acting talent. He's amazed that Helen hasn't long since seen through all this. Is she naïve or maybe blinded by love? Or has the whole business simply gone to her head?

Heller is surprised by her innocence. His handlers aren't. They press him for results. He's supposed to finally make something out of his contacts with all these prominent people.

THE ASSIGNMENT

Heller is sitting with his colleague Fichtel. Whether that's his real name, Heller doesn't know. And he doesn't care, either. Fichtel pesters him with questions about a radio program. A station in the West has reported problems in agriculture, precisely in his collective. Where did this information come from? Another time Fichtel shows him photos taken during a party for television people. They're portrait shots. They show relaxed, cheerful, self-confident people. In the middle, clearly recognizable, the TV reporter, usually with Heller's sister at his side. Heller finds himself in only a few photos, mostly standing stiffly in the background, like a foreign body. He notices that he is never smiling.

On this evening the official is particularly meticulous. Who is this, who is that? What does he know? What contacts with Western journalists does he have? How did this person get invited? "I was supposed to identify someone.

But I didn't recognize anyone." The official wants a personality profile, he's interested in distinctive features, strengths, weaknesses, alcohol consumption, affairs. The conversation is becoming almost an interrogation. Heller feels he's being held accountable. He finds it reassuring to recall that dangerous opponents are playing their dirty game here. The Westerners' superiority and arrogance annoy him. This feeling helps him calm growing pangs of conscience. He looks at a photo in which his sister is happily flirting with the camera. She's obviously ready to do a great deal in exchange for a little power. Is she even his sister anymore? Heller is very tired, he feels drained, he wants to leave.

But the man from the "Firm" says that they still have one more thing for him to do. Heller says he wants to go home, his day begins at five A.M., he has to get up with the hens and do his work.

The man replies that he's working, too; his job is protecting the country. The ministry sees to it that workers and farmers can get up in the morning without capitalistic exploiters.

In the fall of 1988, the comrades plan to send Heller to the front, over the wall into the "operations area" in West Berlin. The story will be that he's going to visit the "Green Week"; they can tell people, especially Heller's distrustful colleagues in his own company, that it's for educational purposes. "The unofficial agent was assigned to see what legal opportunities he could use to intensify the relationship with his sister," a document in Heller's Stasi file says, and thus he is authorized "to make an official trip to WB." WB stands for West Berlin. This time he won't be handing out fliers or putting up posters in West Berlin: he's supposed to get as much information as he can from a representative of a "hostile television station" at the very heart of the enemy camp. On February 9, 1989, a report on another meeting notes that Heller was "assigned" to draw a "floor plan of the apartment," list the names of the neighbors, and get a copy of the key. Agent "Rudolf" (name changed)—that's the name that appears in the Stasi archives—is supposed to finally produce valuable results.

AN UNDERCOVER PHOTO DURING A STASI RAID on the apartment of Kerstin Starke, who was later sentenced to a seven-year jail sentence on a charge of "agitation against the state." (credit: BSTU)

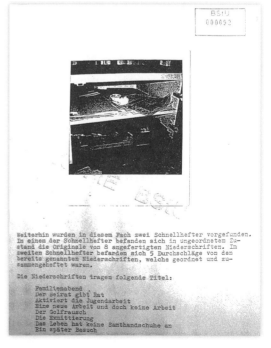

EVERYTHING TURNS OUT DIFFERENTLY

Today, Heller vehemently denies ever hearing of any such assignment or even any plans for a secret operation in the West. In fact, the documents show that in this phase collaboration became increasingly complicated. Because no one in Heller's Agricultural Production Collective is supposed to know about his connections with Western television, he has to be constantly on his guard. Conscious of his duty, Heller keeps his distance from his coworkers. He avoids coffee breaks with them. At this time he's attentive to everything he hears. Despite all his doubts, he continues and does not try to break off his agreement with the Stasi.

Is it his damned sense of duty? Does he see collaboration as patriotic action undertaken to defend his country? What would his father say? How did he get into all this? How can he get out? At night, Heller tosses and turns, looking for answers. His sister herself is to blame, he tells himself, she was the one who "took off" for the West. On the other hand these people from the Stasi are constantly meddling in his private life. Just recently one of them criticized him for not having developed "an emotional bond" with his sister. What business is that of his?

Then for months all is quiet on the Stasi front. The "Green Week" in Berlin comes and slips away like a Fata Morgana on the horizon. Spring brings new work; on the screen, the TV man smiles as he reads the news. Everyday life returns. Heller receives no further word from the men at the Firm. Did his doubts have an effect? Did they decide to spare him the risky mission in West Berlin? Do the comrades have more important things to do?

Heller goes back to the small and large concerns of ordinary life, recalcitrant apprentices and production quotas that are far too high. One day he finds a message in his mailbox: "Greetings from Workmate Fichtel. Meeting tomorrow evening on the Panke."

They're at it again, Heller thinks, and begins to sweat, but he can't do anything to stop them. The powerful man has had enough. He decides to terminate his collaboration the very next day, definitively, finally, and forever. He has only one remaining thought: Why don't they leave me alone?

The next day the official is curiously reserved, far less talkative than usual. Abruptly, he declares that the collaboration is over, at least for the time being. The TV reporter has turned elsewhere, probably has a new girlfriend. At first, Heller's sister didn't know he had another woman; the blow-up came a few months ago. At some point the reporter separated from Heller's sister. She no longer comes to the capital, no longer sits on the throne, no longer reigns as queen. Consequently his job is done, the man from the ministry says.

Heller waves all this aside and asks how his sister is getting along. The official says he's not sure, but he's obviously not telling all he knows.

From this we can glean that Stasi officials were well informed about many details at that time. Informants hinted that Helen was pretty confused after the separation. One spy even claimed that she had tried to commit suicide. These rumors circulated in the documents.

The sister's relationship with the journalist ended in a document full of foggy conjecture and speculation.

At the end of October 1989, when people in the GDR were marching in the streets, a final notation was made in Heller's file. It says that in 1989 "contacts [with Heller were] significantly reduced because he can no longer be used against 'Leopard' (name changed)." In conclusion, the document notes that the matter is being "considered" to determine whether the informant "can be used in other ways."

Nothing ever came of this. The Change made such sand-castle games pointless. After the Wall came down, Comrade "Fichtel" never called again. Heller confirmed this: "I never heard from him again. He vanished as quickly as he had appeared."

A STASI OBSERVATION OFFICE.

(credit: BSTU)

Faraway, So Gross

BY DOROTA MASŁOWSKA
(TRANSLATION BY BENJAMIN PALOFF)

A year before I was born my folks got a place in a high-rise by the woods. Since then I've been abroad about a thousand times and given about as many interviews, and it always pops up, the same question, cleverly calculated from my date of birth, about Communism, whether I remember the food lines, the vinegar on store shelves, the fall of the Wall and all the other bloodcurdling stuff they didn't have over on its other side. Of course I do, I say with a mix of triumph and pain, as if I were just then supposed to pull up my sleeve to reveal something like scars from the kiddie internment camp or the marks from when the police beat me during an interrogation and wave them before the eyes of my interlocutor like a wad of photos from some exotic trip. Yes, my dears, I was there, back when you had no idea about anything: while you were scarfing down those dainties in little tissue-paper cups, I was fighting on the front lines of childhood! Here are my scars from drinking vinegar straight from the shelf! Say what you want, you may have every other kind of scar there is, but you don't have these.

Do I remember Communism? But I have to remember something, right? Drag some nugget out of the swirling muck of memory, strip it of superfluous detail, snap a shot of the heroes' faces and let them march across the table, funny or forlorn, in rain slickers and stupid old boots that say "Relax" on their tags, with mesh shopping bags hanging low from the greenish, budding potatoes rumbling around inside. So this is the country they call Poland, these boxy buildings scattered by the woods are a small town, those two little people trudging through the snow over there are my grandma and me, and that dark spot up there—that's daybreak. That thing inching along the street, bloated and undulating, tightly linked, no gaps, that's a line for hot dogs, and that thing inching along even less mercifully is time. The little bundle in wet, white paper is a couple of hot dogs, one for me, one for my brother. After many hours of standing I am so hungry that I scarf down both on the way home. Yes, that steely winter morning and the absolute futility of human endeavors—which from that moment on I have tasted as the flavor of that cold, pale hot dog, which I didn't even taste out of hunger—will draw forth dread and disbelief on the face of the Western reader. And we all know that this image of those years is multidimensional with that same special tourist's multidimensionality as the Arafat rag on the teenager's pimple-bespattered neck, carton-pasteurized country-style milk, as well as lacquered Dutch clogs with paintings of windmills and little houses. A manufactured postcard believed by neither the sender, nor the recipient, but which is nevertheless nice to give and no less interesting to receive.

(Recently I had this conversation when I went out to smoke a cigarette in front of a London hotel and was approached by the hotel gardener. He was slim, older, and had black fingernails and clear eyes, like someone who had only just recently been born. "Where are you from?" "Poland." "What's Poland like?" "Pretty ugly. Everything was destroyed during the war, and then the Communists destroyed everything else." "That's awful," he said, deeply moved, shaking his head with sympathy and disbelief. "That's really terrible." "Yeah." Speaking in languages you don't know is a godsend. Everything is suddenly so incredibly simple!)

In fact, I don't remember anything in particular from that time, barely any event at all, barely any feeling, just this sort of grayness and nausea raised to the highest degree, such that it was almost the idea of grayness. I was about five years old, I knew a few indispensable numbers, a couple of basic letters, my Catholicism was enjoying its heyday, after which one could speak of it only in terms of regression. Yes, I think that my perception of the reality of those years was in some sense perfect! Grayness. Nausea. Water from the tap. In this, as in some brownish galantine or rolls of recycled toilet paper, linger those knickknacks that bring tears to the eye: Donald Duck bubble gum, cans left over from Coke and deodorant lined up like trophies on a shelf, pseudochocolate: a sort of brownish, semisweet plastic in tablet form. That's all that is definite. As though time flowed within objects, as though they themselves were a unit of time. The clothes I wore, the peeling wallpaper and the furniture losing its luster, the food and the dishes we ate it on, buildings, shoes, sidewalks. Memory is slush, a muddy puddle in which the little ships of things now sink, now surface triumphantly. I remember Communism exclusively as a style and an aesthetic category.

So then there was this apartment high-rise. It stood not far from several others, similar, sticking straight up out of the bald, brownish sand. How many times I stared upward at the clouds gliding along the industrial tape of the sky, and the high-rise started to sway, to break apart, and any moment it would come crashing down like a ton of bricks.

Everywhere else was the plump forest, a kind of world unto itself. Only we stuck out in the air, in some absurd wilderness paved over here and there. Among its paving stones, carelessly scattered over the surface, some preposterous mutant nature sprouted: dandelions, grass, thistles. There were black puddles in the potholes with a delicate, rainbow-colored film of gasoline. The basements were seething with cats. Always that stink of urine by the stairs, nervous little eyes glaring from behind the banister and the dirty, shattered panes of glass. And then there were the ants. Which was good for the kids, kids need something to torture, to watch die, or at least to look at when already dead, to learn that horror, that life depends on blood flowing forward, and that death starts to spread out to the sides and then all over along the sidewalk.

A balding, moist willow reeking of urine grew on the bald lawn in front of the door to our building. There was also a parking lot. My grandma liked to sit at the kitchen window with a pillow, melancholically smacking her lips. A dwarfish aide-de-camp stood at either elbow, me on the left, my brother on the right, ascribing some exceptional order to that melancholic lip-smacking and struggling from time to time to reproduce it through his own gapped teeth. Thus we tried to cheat time until lunch, though it was time that cheated us and dragged on and squiggled like a pale and shapeless noodle between the arrival of one car and the departure of another. That's how we spent our time. From time to time our childhood milieu was racked by a wave of gravitational enchantment. Shattered projectiles of egg and other such revelations dried on the sidewalk. There was a little boy, too, who one day fell out from one of those floors up top and it seems just laid there among the clothespins and cigarette butts.

None of this was really bad or particularly sad. It was just grayness, heinous—even the sunlight passing through the drapes had the color of urine. Even the food was gray. Gray bread, pale margarine, dyed yellow. Stringy ham and filmy milk. And every so often I still remember the poster paints packed in sixes and their enigmatic names—burnt sienna, ultramarine, cinnabar—which concealed in their euphemistic, incomprehensible shrouds the biodegradable hue of mud, beets, sickly yellow bile, liver spots, hardening mustard. Even the black wasn't black, but dark gray, which was logical, cohesive, and consistent, for only these paints allowed for a realistic treatment and conscientious response to such themes as My City, My Courtyard, My School, My Country during daycare art classes, while I was waiting for my mom to come back from the factory and the hospital. It was this very world that had produced these very means, deadly well-suited to its reproduction.

The clothes I wore, the toys. Pieces of brick, chestnuts, shattered glass buried in the ground as a sign of undying friendship. You know, there were these teddy bears, dolls, all of them in these shitty wine-colored dresses, their cold, unbending legs the color of the peaches that grew down by the gas station. These unfortunate, cross-eyed, sexless creatures, made from poorly shaped plastic and now moldering somewhere in basements or biodegrading against their will in garbage dumps, were nasty to perfection.

Once, in a designer store in New York, I saw this matchbox car, the kind that over here rot in basements and cubbies. Could it be that in a couple years there won't be anything that *doesn't* make it into the glossiest superposh catalogues of design, fashion, and beauty?! Kate Moss à la East Germany 1985, head of hair like straw, her hydrochloric acid perm held for an hour, preferably done by her sister. While one Moss sister is carefully winding another's hair around wooden rollers doused in ammonia, her children, in stylish tights pulled up to their armpits and slippers from H&M with the big toe worn out at the factory, are throwing that delicate tissue paper that they wrap around hair rollers out their apartment window. How beautifully it flies! How beautifully it gets tangled in the branches of the willow, floats into the parking lot or flies high, up and over the forest. Over the entire high-rise, in which, from floor to floor, the same life goes on in identically arranged apartments, with their identical plywood furniture in the ultraviolet of the television standing in the very same middle of the house, where, like in some aquarium, Blake Carrington is buying more oil wells, this time in Denver. The sky stops right here over his head, the wooden body of the Neptune-brand television, and has a crocheted napkin pinned to it for decorative purposes, as well as something especially ugly in its worthlessness, this chipped, porcelain, nausea-colored ballerina thing. He wouldn't be so bold if he could see how his horizon ended.

And I'm flipping through this magazine with glossy pictures, flying to New York in the strange teleporter of the airplane, my stomach full of foiled, rainbow-colored food, the stewardesses with their dental-ad smiles, and I know that I'm bringing all that with me, my whole head tattooed with and marinated in grayness, the entire collection of postcards with a view of emptiness, a brownish expanse, an overflowing desert of piss-colored sand, and the road from the airport is like slowly tearing away the paper from some remarkably complicated, unbelievably multimedia, demonic toy that has been terribly slow to arrive. And only the hermetic character of the skin on my skull keeps it from blowing up!

Then came the demonic nineties, the landscape changed on a daily basis, pretty much out of control, as if the dumpster had flipped over in the desert. No one believed yet in the singularity of anything, least of all in anything so beautiful as plastic. This durable, water-resistant, and shatterproof material was the very opposite of glass, string, and soggy cardboard, so that before its value later dropped, people washed grocery bags and yogurt containers. From the age of two we would spend every evening in front of the television watching *Wheel of Fortune*. It was a game show. A rainbow-colored disk spun around before the antsy contestants, totally freezing the blood in their veins, and infecting the television audience with the poisonous seed of impossible possession, opening the Pandora's Box of one's wildest dreams. A television! A Sony! A waterbed! Three and a half million zloties in value! And, of course, the grand prize: a Polonez, a car that was long and flat like a trampled worm, preferably a heavy pistachio color, dirty rose, ultraviolet, savage fuchsia! Every evening all the windows of the housing project spasmed simultaneously with the blue light of televisions, as if playing to the cosmos in Morse code. A water bed! Or an inflatable one, for guests, the kind that are nowadays scattered around the basest depths of the cheapest discount stores, coming back by a roundabout path as a consolation prize for those who, in all these years, haven't won jack.

Now for the triumphant return of the colors. A crusade of colors, their revenge for this purgatory! They still recalled nothing of nature. Thank you very much, but we've already had these. Now we have the colors of hard candy, orangeade, and burning light bulbs. Ultraviolets! Glazed greens! Day-Glo orange! In keeping with the expression that haste makes waste, things got even uglier. Outside the window, the playground hardened in the sun and rain. Corroding scrap metal, what had once been a swingset, protruded from the sand like the most perverse art installation on the subject of what children should play with, a rusty padlock set in place to drive the point home. Besides that, the tar-smeared reinforced concrete slabs of the apartment blocks were then covered in canary-yellow Styrofoam and pealed from the paint of a window replaced with PVC.

You'll see all this yet, and more, in the most perverse lifestyle magazines! Right in the middle of New York there'll be this high-rise apartment block spray-painted up to its bottom half with the name of some football team, designed by some subversive artist. And I, in search of lost time, will buy myself an apartment there with a view of a parking lot, and in my acid-wash cotton jumpsuit, from a glass shaped to look like a yogurt container, I'll be sipping my vinegar.

From *Urbancholia*

BY DAN SOCIU

(TRANSLATION BY OANA SANZIANA MARIAN)

Obligatory chapter of memories from Communism.

Dear Pascal, you must know that I was also once a part of the word PEACE.

Sweating inside a chalk-circle, I shook a piece of poster-board above my head, proud that, somewhere up there, someone was reading us. COMRADE was reading us. My pals in COMRADE claimed that they had it made. Their instructors couldn't be bothered. Back over in PEACE, they were screaming their heads off. There was one, the shop teacher, an analphabetic head case who kept us with our arms raised in the air for hours on end, to make dead sure that her letters came out best. Then there was "Little Miss Headmistress," as we'd dubbed her, making a fuss about how *she'd* been in Ceaușescu's nostril. In fact, at one August 23 demonstration, she'd been right in his left eye. She was a Troop Commander and maybe that's why.

Ranks were important in those days, and the highest rank I ever made was Group Commander. And after a week, they demoted me and took back my red cord because I had pushed over a barrel of chlorine in the school bathroom. I really thought I'd get it from my old man, but instead he called bragging to my uncle, "Hello, Eagle? Hawk, here. Over." And my uncle, "Hawk, what's the status? Over." And the whole game always ended, inevitably, with the same question: "Ioane, you think *he's* going to keep on living much longer?" Sometimes, when he was bored, my father would pick up the phone and, without dialing any number, say "Vasile, let's go to the Rhapsody Bar tonight, a cognac on me." Some of their games I only understood much later.

Once I accidentally brought my father's entire salary to school, to the Recycling. He'd put the money inside an older notebook for safekeeping. I brought everything to the Recycling that seemed worthy of bringing, paper and cardboard. I was a very zealous child. For hours my father rummaged frantically through piles of cellulose in the storage of School No. 11, while I stuffed copies of *The Brave Ones*, the Pioneer's magazine (that's what we the Communist youth were called), into my coat. When we got home, the first thing he did was pick up the telephone.

Something I never did and even now regret not having done during Communism is eat Pork and Beans from the jar. Those jars with the brown labels were about the only kind of food you could find in the grocery store, as far as I can remember. I could have died with craving every time I saw them. Because behind our block there were some garages and workmen, and that's the only thing those guys would ever eat.

A real manly kind of food, I used to think. But my mother would never buy it. She'd hedge by saying that we had beans at home—I actually hated beans—and pork—I hated pork, and generally anything with lard, even though, or maybe specifically *because* my grandfather was a butcher and we never lacked for meat. But those jars with the babyshit brown labels left my mouth watering. My mother would serve up the same excuses when we went to the bakery, too. When the display case was full she'd say "Dutzu, it means the pastries aren't good. Because, you see? No one's buying them." And when there were a just a few left, it meant they'd been there awhile and they were probably stale.

And so why did we sacrifice ourselves during the Revolution, my neighbor Cipi and I? Why did we go out in front of Town Hall with a red flag, on which we had written WE WANT FREEDOM, in toothpaste, instead of going to the go-cart park, the way we'd planned the day before?

Why did we go to Bookshop No. 8 and take out all the books about/

with/by Nicolae Ceauşescu and make a great big fire with them and dance the "Unification Round" until 10 in the evening, and then head home, dirty, hungry and victorious, screaming in our pre-pubescent voices down the alleys DOWN WITH CEAUŞESCU! DOWN WITH COMMUNISM!?

And Comrade Revolutionary Teacher Mr. Curca (that means "turkey hen," and it really *was* his name) was addressing a throng from a balcony, while some people were throwing giant metal letters, painted in red, off the roof of the Town Hall (in those days, every institutional building was scripted with a propagandist over-title). First they threw down the words LONG LIVE, and the words fell with a clamorous thud at the feet of the crowd below.

And the crowd: "Yeeeeee!"

And then they hurled COMRADE NICOLAE CEAUŞESCU—all at once, they were soldered together—and the crowd: "Heeeeee!"

But then, just as we were winding up for the fall of THE PARTY, Comrade Teacher Mr. Curca yelled, "No, No! Leave those alone, Communism is a good thing, it's just *those traitors* who ruined it!"

To which, the crowd, displeased: "Hooooo!"

And Comrade Teacher, frightened: "Take them down! Down with Communism!"

Cipi and I had stolen the flag at an August 23 demonstration. We climbed down into his cellar, which was our headquarters. Some demonstrators were lying passed out along the wall of the apartment complex, and one of them had left his flag right by the ventilation duct. Cipi pulled it inside and we hid it under a pile of wood.

The same day, we climbed to the roof of an apartment building. We wanted to see the Helicopter, and the Secret Service wouldn't let people look out their windows. We couldn't give a rat's ass; we wanted to see the Helicopter, and so we took provisions, a watermelon, a knife, a loaf of bread. It was a great day. We crawled around on our elbows, we whispered and made signs to each other, just like in the movies. Then Cipi realized that right on the edge of the building there was a giant, red manifesto placard on which it said LONG LIVE COMRADE NICOLAE CEAUŞESCU in large, white letters made of polystyrene.

Cipi kicked some of them so it said ONG IVE COM ADE, in the way little kids talk.

Miss Headmistress said that at the entrance into the stadium, their little bags with sandwiches and juice bottles were confiscated. She asked her parents why, and they said it was a security measure. As in, they don't want the little pioneers throwing Quik-Cola (our version of Coca-Cola) and bread with jam at Comrade Ceaușescu. Such a precaution seemed to her a great offense. An injustice, really. She even started misting over.

I told her that it was too bad she hadn't kept that black, pleated skirt, the white knee-socks, the white blouse, the red scarf, the belt . . .

I would have liked to see her dressed up like that.

Whenever I see Romanian films from the seventies, when my folks were young, I feel like crying. An insufferable nostalgia hits me, as if it were *my* youth they recalled. That time and those people seem purer to me somehow. I know it's a trick; I am aware that an ideology requires the directors to idealize, and the actors to infantilize, but I still see that time as an Age of Angels.

I have the hot water schedule to thank for one of my most vivid memories of my father.

Since there was only hot water for a few hours a week, we would take baths about once a month, two or three of us at a time. One evening, it was my father and I. I was about ten or eleven years old, it was right before the Revolution, and my father was a formidable man with a lot of hair "down there." I'd never seen him so naked, and I was a little intimidated. While we were soaping up, the old man told a joke (actually, he wasn't old at all, only thirty-five, but he would be dead in two years).

The joke was that one day George, who was a shepherd, lost his sheep. He starts to look for them, he looks and looks and can't find them. He sees John leaning on a fence, up to nothing useful. He says to himself, "Let me just go over and ask John, maybe he's seen my sheep." And he goes to John and says, "John my friend you haven't seen my sheep grazing around here, have you?" And John thinks to himself, "If I tell him that I've seen them he'll start asking about this black one and that other one and which way did they go and will just drive me nuts. And if I say, no, I haven't seen them he'll start telling me that I'm just pissing in the wind and ask me just what I'm doing guarding the gate anyway and so on and so on . . . better to give him an evasive answer . . ." And he says, "Listen, George, how 'bout you just fuck yourself!"

And my father, who was also a few sheets to the wind (as he was more often than not during those days) exploded in laughter, looking at me with complicit expectation, waiting for me to bust my sides, too, so we could take it to the hilt, like men.

You remember, Pascal, that night in Iasi, at that club Black Out, I had started to tell you this story, and you asked, "And why didn't you laugh?" And just as I was about to answer you, Viviana motioned to me to go outside.

It's strange how every time I get attached to any kind of father figure, I always find my way to this story, but I never get to finish it.

Fuck it, Pascal, I don't even know what I'm trying to say, exactly. I'm on my eleventh beer, so don't be surprised if I'm becoming less and less coherent. And the less coherent I get, the more coherent I am, like any drunk trying to walk straighter than needed. It's hotter than hell, and I am dreading the moment when I will have finished this endless email full of shit and will effectively need to unstick this laptop from my genitals. Ouch.

There's nothing we can do; as the writers of *The Young and the Restless* would say, "Every character's story should be long and slowly drawn out . . ."

Even my tongue hurts. I have some kind of sore on my tongue, I think from some toothpaste gone off. When Viviana was here, she'd get on me for leaving the tube open. Shit, Pascal, I'm not the fragile sort, I'm really not; all this is just the pathetic whining of someone who lived with his mother until the age of thirty suddenly having to fend for himself. This is something that you have to understand.

Still, I suppose I ought to finish the obligatory chapter of memories from Communism.

First of all, because I was stunned by the expletive. My father's face had turned blood red, the veins along his neck were swollen, and he kept repeating the punch line, in a rage. I was trying to let out a squeak at the very least, to show some engaged amusement; my father was slapping the water with his palms, his face strained. I was thinking he might drown me, so finally I managed a cackle close to what he had been waiting for, accompanied by tears and sprays of spittle, and my father calmed down.

I'd had no clue what the word "evasive" meant.

I can't stay longer than fifteen minutes in the bath. I bring magazines, rubber duckies and boats. I dump relaxing bath salts in the water, get drunk beforehand; it's no use. After fifteen minutes and generally even before fifteen minutes are up, a kind of anxiety hits me, I feel guilty, ashamed, I have to get out.

How do I know that I love her? That night, at the Moldova Hotel, we slipped, without talking, into the bath. We splashed around for a good few hours and I never felt any panic. To the contrary, everything seemed as if it would always be all right.

It was the first time anything like that had happened to me.

There was no music, but I think "Lullaby," by the Cure, would have been right.

By around 11 in the evening, my folks had already had enough of the Revolution and its MVP's, Caramitru, Dinescu, Iliescu, and so my father said, "Let's see what the Russians are up to." On the Russian channel there was a band of Bessarabians playing ukuleles, and these guys took our minds off things somewhat. In short, they cheered us up. My mother, who taught Russian back then, started to hum along. My old man always liked it when his wife read him Dostoyevsky in the original. Dostoyevsky in the original is something else altogether. Now, my father disappoints me the most in June of 1990, when students thronged the University Square. He'd said then, "Those kids are just a bunch of losers who grill sausages over manhole covers . . . the last time Senator Dumitriu met Mr. Iiliescu, you know what Iliescu said? He said, 'If you only knew how tired I am,' and then he braced his head against the senator's shoulder."

Now I consider my old man a dead man, in every sense of the word. Because—and this is what gets me the most—in December of '89, instead of going to the Eminescu Theater to say a few words the way Mr. Curca did, my father got soused, to celebrate the fall of Ceaușescu. And it wouldn't have been difficult. My father was a well-respected mathematics professor in Botosani, people would have listened to what he had to say, and he wasn't even a member of the Party. He didn't need to be, my grandfather had killed a collectivization propagandist, he'd even worked on the Canal, which made him kind of like a family hero. Although, less for my mother, who was convinced that her husband was dead as a result of some residue of the curse thrown by the propagandist's widow, even though they'd left that county a long time since, maybe even before the Repartization.

ROMA CHILDREN

(opposite page, credit:

Oana Sanziana Marian)

If my father had moved his ass off the barstool at the Rhapsody (then the seat of the "Nomenklatura,") where, although the son of a criminal, he sucked his cognac every night, I would have been a made man: four thousand meters squared of land, within and beyond the pale, tax exemptions, free rides on just about any means of transportation, and all sorts of other benefits. And even these perks were just for the most modest of the revolutionaries, the least active. The real advantage was, after all, the connections that this kind of activism would have created. I would have entered sooner into the world that, thanks to Derrin and Miss H, I entered anyway.

Since moonshining was illegal, and I knew it, anytime my grandfather would pick on me, I'd go yelling through the yard, "I'll tell police officer Ciotoi that you're making booze!" My grandmother would threaten to throw me to the same Ciotoi if I refused to take my afternoon nap.

I found out online that our boogeyman died a few months ago. He died in his sleep, without suffering, the way a Backgammon-playing old man had every right to die. God bless him, I'd like to say; he'd held our family together.

You're not even three years old and they give you your first taste of booze. *Go on, give him a drop, what harm can it do?* That is, if they're not already in the habit of sending you off to sleep as a baby by letting you suck on a rag dipped in moonshine. But only the really far-gone families do this.

The rest of them teach you to drink socially, ritualistically. During the holidays, at christenings, weddings, funerals, Sundays and simple family gatherings. When they butcher the pig, when they make the moonshine, or just sitting around chatting about this that and the other.

You're five years old and your grandfather has set up the alembic and has gone to work. It's winter, and it's so great to be sitting by the stove stoking the embers with a poker. The booze drips into a bowl, you lean down to the mouth of the tube to lick a drop or two. You peel a baked potato and it burns your fingers. You smother it with butter and salt. You lean down and suck a little more from the copper piping.

It's the first batch, the really potent kind, which, if you light, burns on the table with a blue flame.

You see, Pascal, in Ceaușescu's Romania we had this system that sent college graduates to work across hell's half acre in some isolated village, away from their families. The Repartization, as it was called, was an apparently brilliant idea trying to bring light to the far reaches of the country. This happened to my parents, too, and so I was sent to live with my grandparents until I was about six years old. I am sure that they loved me; it's just that Romanian peasants are not the kind to say it.

None of us says I love you. Terms of endearment are trifles; the best way to show someone you love him is give him food. Put things in his mouth.

There was a TV serial, *The Freckled Kid*, about a kid who helped the outlawed Communists fight the fascists.

For a long time after my father died, I lived the following fantasy: I was the Freckled Kid and I was supposed to hand over an underground press to a man carrying the paper the *Universe* in his jacket pocket. The Kid would enter the post-office, wait a few minutes, scrutinizing all of the men's pockets, when all of a sudden my father would lay his heavy hand on my shoulder.

"What are you doing here?"

"Aw, nuthin'." I'd shuffle my feet, straining for an excuse, "Just came here with someone and he asked me to wait for him."

"You have any idea what time it is? Your ma's waiting for you, you little rascal!"

And I could see just a corner of the *Universe* peeking out of his coat pocket. *He* was the contact, the guy who printed the manifestos! My dad was a Communist activist, too, just as I was!

That Fear

BY ANDRZEJ STASIUK

(TRANSLATION BY MICHAEL KANDEL)

Yes, it's only that fear, those searchings, tracings, tellings whose purpose is to hide the unreachable horizon. It's night again, and everything departs, disappears, shrouded in black sky. I am alone and must remember events, because the terror of the unending is upon me. The soul dissolves in space like a drop in the sea, and I am too much a coward to have faith in it, too old to accept its loss; I believe it is only through the visible that we can know relief, only in the body of the world that my body can find shelter. Would that I could be buried in all those places where I was and have yet to be. My head among the green hills of Zemplén, my heart somewhere in Siedmiogród, Siebenbürgen, Seven Towns, Transylvania, my right hand in Czarnohora, my left in Spišská Belá, my sight in Bukovina, my sense of smell in Rășinari, my thoughts perhaps in this neighborhood . . . Thus I imagine the night when the current roars in the dark and the thaw wipes away the white stain of snow. I recall those days when I took to the road so often, pronouncing the names of far cities like spells, Paris, London, Berlin, New York, Sydney . . . places on the map for me, red or black points lost in the green and sky-blue expanse. I never asked for a pure sound. The histories that went with the cities, they were all fictions. They filled the hours and helped the boredom. In those distant times, every trip resembled flight. Stank of panic, desperation.

One day in the summer of eighty-three or -four, I reached Słubice by foot and saw Frankfurt across the river. It was late afternoon. Humid blue-gray air hung over the water. East German high-rises and factory stacks looked dismal and unreal. The sun: a dull smudge, a flame about to gutter. The other side was completely dead, still, as if after a great fire. Only the river smell had something human in it—decay, fish slime—but I was sure that over there the smell would be cut off. In any case I turned, and that same evening I headed back, eastward. Like a dog I had sniffed an unfamiliar locale and continued on my way.

I had no passport then, of course, but it never entered my head to obtain one. The connection between those two words, *freedom* and *passport*, sounded nice but failed to convince. The nuts and bolts of *passport* didn't fit *freedom* at all. It's possible that in Gorzów my mind had fixed on the formula: There's freedom or there isn't, period. My country suited me fine, because its borders didn't concern me. I lived inside it, in the center, and that center went where I went. I made no demands on spatial dimension and expected nothing from it. I left before dawn, to catch the yellow-and-blue train to Żyrardów. It pulled out of East Station, crossed Downtown, gold and silver ribbons of light unfolding in the windows. The train filled with men in worn coats. Most got off at Ursus and walked toward the frozen light of a factory. Dozens, hundreds barely visible in the dark; only at the gate did the mercury light hit them, as if they were entering a huge cathedral. I was practically alone. The next passengers got on somewhere in Milanówka, in Grodzisko, more women in the group, because Żyrardów was textiles, fabrics, tailoring, that sort of thing. Black tobacco, the sour smell of plastic lunch bags mixed with the reek of cheap perfume and soap. The night came free of the ground, and in the growing crack of the day you could see the huts of the track walkers, who held orange caution flags; cows standing belly-deep in mist; the last, forgotten lights in houses. Żyrardów was red, all brick. I got off with everyone else. I was the shiftless one here, but whatever I did was in tribute to all those who had to get up before the sun, because without them the world would have been merely a play of color and meteorological drama. I drank strong tea in a station bar and took the train back, to go north in a day or two, or east, without apparent purpose. One summer, I was on the road seventy-two hours nonstop. I spoke with truck drivers. In the cabins, their words flowed in ponderous monologue from a vast place—the effect of fatigue and lack of sleep. Scenery in the window drew close, pulled away, to freeze at last, as if time had given up. Dawn at a roadside somewhere in Puck, and thin clouds stretching over the Gulf. Out from under the clouds slipped the bright knife edge of the rising day, and the cold smell of the sea came woven with the screech of gulls. Quite possibly I reached the beach itself then, quite possibly after a couple of hours of sleep somewhere by the road a delivery van stopped and a guy said he was driving through the country, north to south, which was a hundred times more appealing than the tedium of tide in, tide out, so I jumped on the crate and, wrapped in a blanket, dozed beneath the fluttering tarp, and my doze was visited by landscapes of the past mixed with fantasy, as if I were looking at things seen by an outsider. Warsaw went by as a foreign city, and I felt no tug at my heart. Grit in my teeth: the dust raised from the floorboards. I crossed the country as one crosses an unmapped continent. Between Radom and Sandomierz, a terra incognita. The sky, trees, houses, earth—all could be found elsewhere. I moved through a space that had no history, no experience worth preserving. I was the first man to reach the foot of the Pepper Mountains, and with my presence everything began. Time began; objects and scenes started their aging only from the moment my eye fell on them. At Tarnobrzeg I rapped on the tin wall of the driver's cabin: impressed by the size of a sulfur outcrop, I wanted to stop. Giant power shovels stood at the bottom of the pit. It didn't matter to me where they came from. From the sky, if you like, to bite into the land, to chew their way down through the planet and let an ocean surge through the shaft to drown everything here and turn the other side to desert. The stink of the inferno ascended, and I could not tear my gaze from the monstrous hole whose lifelessness spoke of the grave, piled corpses, the chill of hell. Nothing moved. It could have been a Sunday, assuming there was a calendar in such a place.

In other words, no Poland here: this sequence of images was not a country, it was a pretext. Perhaps we become aware of our existence only when we feel on our skin the touch of a space that has no name, that connects us to the earliest time, to all the dead, prehistory, when the mind first stood apart from the world and did not yet realize it was orphaned. A hand stretches from the window of a truck, and through its fingers flows the most ancient. Yes, this was not Poland; it was the first loneliness. I could have been in Timbuktu or Cape Cod. On my right, Barany, "the pearl of the Renaissance," I must have passed it a dozen times in those days, but it never occurred to me to stop a moment and look. Every place was good, because I could leave it without regret. It didn't even need a name. Endless expense, constant loss, waste such as the world has never seen, prodigality, shortage, no gain, no profit whatever. The morning by the sea, the evening in a forest outside Sano; men over their steins like ghosts in a village bar, apparitions frozen in mid-gesture as I watch. I remember them that way, but it could have been near Legnica, or forty kilometers northeast of Siedlce and a year before that or later in some village or other. We lit an evening fire, and in the flickering light, village kids; probably the first time in their life they were seeing a stranger. We were not real to them, nor they to us. They stood and stared, their enormous belt buckles gleaming in the dark: a bull's head, or crossed Colts. Finally they sat near, but the conversation smacked of hallucination. Even the wine they brought couldn't bring us down to earth. At dawn they got up and left. It's possible that a day or two later I stood for ten hours in Złoczów and no one gave me a lift. I remember a hedgerow and a small stone bridge, but I'm not sure about the hedgerow, it could have been elsewhere, like most of what lies in memory, because, when I put memories there, I tear them from their landscape, making my own map of them, my own imaginary geography.

One day I went to Poznań and took a pickup truck. The driver shouted, "Hop on. Just watch the fish!" I lay among enormous plastic bags filled with water. Inside swam fish, no larger than a fingernail. Hundreds, thousands of fish. The water was ice-cold, so I had to wrap myself in a blanket. In Wrzesien the fish turned toward Gniezno, so at dawn I was alone again on the empty road. The sun had not risen yet, and it was cold. It's possible that from Poznań I went on to Wrocław. Most likely heading for Wybrzeże a day or two later, or Bieszczady. If toward Bieszczady, around Osława, in the middle of a forest, I saw a naked man. He was standing in a river and washing himself. Seeing me, he simply turned his back. But if it was Wybrzeże, then I was at Hawk Mountain and it was evening, a forsaken beach, and I walked barefoot in the direction of Karwia and saw, against the red sky, the black megaliths of Stonehenge. I had nowhere to sleep, and these ruins as if they fell out of the blue. Fashioned from planks, plywood, burlap. Such things happened in those days. Someone built it and left it, no doubt a television crew. I crawled through a hole into one of the vertical pillars of rock and fell asleep.

Speech at the Opening Session of the 13th German *Bundestag*

BY STEFAN HEYM

(TRANSLATION BY JOHN K. COX)

November 1994

our years ago, in this place, Willy Brandt inaugurated the work of the first *Bundestag*[1] of reunified Germany. I recently read his speech again in preparation for making my own, and I observed with regret that not everything he envisioned has come true. Willy Brandt has left us, but we remain, I maintain, in his service.

In the perilous year 1932, Clara Zetkin also stood in this place and opened the newly elected *Reichstag*. We know what became of the parliament after that noble-minded woman set its work in motion: Hermann Goering was elected speaker, and the chancellor soon to be named was Adolf Hitler, and almost two hundred of the members of parliament ended up in prison and concentration camps—with over half of them meeting a violent death—and the *Reichstag* building itself, in which we find ourselves today, burned.

---

1. "*Bundestag*": This word is commonly used today to mean the German parliament. It is actually the "lower house" of the country's bicameral legislature (the other being the *Bundesrat*, but it is the more active and important of the two houses. In addition the word has a long history. It was used colloquially for the relatively weak main national assembly of the various German federal and confederal bodies between 1815 and 1871, and it also denoted the chief West German legislative body after World War II. The East German parliament after World War II was known as the *Volkskammer*.

I saw that fire myself. Shortly thereafter I had to leave Germany, and, the next time I saw it, I was in an American army uniform. I was a survivor, and years later I returned to the eastern part of the country, to the German Democratic Republic, where I soon got into conflicts with the authorities; and when someone such as I, possessed of this personal history, addresses you from this spot and is allowed to open the thirteenth session of the Bundestag, the second of post-unification Germany, then it gives nourishment to my hopes that our contemporary democracy may rest on more solid foundations than that of Weimar, and that this assembly, like every one of them to come, might be spared a fate like that of the last Reichstag of the Weimar Republic.

In the next four years we will not have an easy time of it. I can imagine that the issues that are going to come our way are things that precious few of us are ready for, things that cannot be papered over. What was it that the great American president, Abraham Lincoln, said? "You can fool some of the people all of the time, and all of the people some of the time, but you cannot fool all of the people all of the time."

The crisis to which this Bundestag has been elected is not merely something cyclical that comes and goes. Rather it is structural and enduring, and it is global. True enough, most of the peoples affected by Stalinism and post-Stalinism have liberated themselves from those constrictions, but the crisis of which I am speaking, which has become a crisis of industrialized society as a whole, has thereby only come even more sharply into focus. How long will the planet Earth—the only one that we have—put up with the way this human race of ours makes and consumes its thousands upon thousands of products? And how long will humanity acquiesce in the way these goods are distributed? The 13th Bundestag will not be able to solve the problems created by these two issues, but it can set to work on a solution. It can accept the challenge.

Germany, and more particularly unified Germany, has acquired a significance in the world to which we must prove ourselves equal. Because the point is not to throw our weight around chiefly for our own short-term benefit, but to ensure the survival of future generations.

As Brecht wrote:

> Grace spare not and spare no labour
> Passion nor intelligence

That a decent German nation
Flourish as do other lands.

That the people give up flinching
At the crimes which we evoke
And hold out their hand in friendship
As they do to other folk.

Neither over nor yet under
Other peoples will we be
From the Oder to the Rhineland
From the Alps to the North Sea.

And because we'll make it better
Let us guard and love our home
Love it as our dearest country
As the others love their own.

Unemployment and homelessness, disease and hunger, war and violence, natural catastrophes of a magnitude hitherto unseen—these are our daily companions. The finest armies are impotent against such things. Here it is civic solutions that are required: political, economic, social, and cultural solutions.

Let us not only talk about debt relief for the poorest of the poor—let us relieve their debt. And it is not the refugees thronging towards us that are our enemies, but the people who put them to flight. Tolerance for and regard of every individual, and contradiction and diversity of opinion—these are what we require. A political culture through which our country, the united country, can introduce its finest traditions into a united, free, and peaceful Europe.

And let us use the power we have—above all, financial power—wisely, and with sensitivity; power, as we know, corrupts and absolute power corrupts absolutely.

Humanity can only survive through solidarity. But, first off, solidarity inside one's home country is needed. West. East. Up. Down. Rich. Poor. I have asked myself constantly why the euphoria over German unity dissipated so swiftly. Maybe it's because each of us kept an eye out first of all to see what material advantage the process would bring to him or her. For some it is markets, real estate, a cheaper workforce; more modestly, for others, it is hard currency and a boundless assortment of trips and goods. We spent too little time thinking about the possibilities that could have emerged—and, I hope, still might be able to emerge—through the unification of differing experiences, both positive and negative, for coexistence and the development of our new, old nation.

It will be incumbent upon this Bundestag to see to it that issues relating to our unity no longer fall primarily under the purview of the Ministry of Finance. The nonviolent revolution of the fall of 1989 brought people in the "old states" opportunities for economic expansion, and to the people of the former GDR it brought rights and freedoms that no one now wants to do without and which—and I underscore this emphatically—they struggled for and won for themselves.

And those citizens of the GDR who held the weapons that were meant for the preservation of the unloved system had enough restraint to renounce their use; and in my opinion this fact should at least be taken into consideration in future judgments on them.

The *Vergangenheitsbewältigung,*[2] so much discussed today in the interest of justice, should be an undertaking of the entire German people, so that further injustices are avoided. But let's not forget that, seen historically, the decades of the Cold War, which brought us the partition of Germany along with the Wall and its consequences, were the result of the Nazi regime and the Second World War that originated with that regime.

The efficiency of the West, its democratic frameworks, and other aspects of the quality of life there that would be to the benefit of the East Germans to adopt—these are plain to see. And aren't there also experiences from life in the erstwhile GDR that it would be worth our while to appropriate for the joint future of Germany? Job security, perhaps? Guaranteed career paths? The right to have a roof over one's head? The protests of countless

---

2. *Vergangenheitsbewältigung*: This term refers to the post-World War II effort among Germans to come to terms with the country's recent (especially but not exclusively Nazi) history. The word literally means "overcoming the past." The processes it connotes were educational, cultural, and political, and its goals fall somewhere between truth and reconciliation, on the one hand, and investigation and judgment on the other. At any rate, illuminating one's past and "owning" it are fundamental to the process.

citizens of the ex-GDR are not gratuitous: their life accomplishments and contributions are little valued. They are barely acknowledged or even turned to account.

Please do not underestimate a human life in which, despite all the caveats, money is not the all-deciding factor, where men and women have equal claim to the workplace, where rent is affordable, and the most important part of the body is not the elbow. I know all too well how difficult it will be to amalgamate the positive from the East and West. We have, however, lived—and survived!—for so long in different systems and with different maxims about life that we ought now to be capable of closing the gap between our differing ideas through tolerance and understanding on both sides.

Of course that assumes that people's fears will be dispelled: the West Germans' fear that the East will cost them their savings and their jobs, and the East Germans' fears that the West might rob them of their houses and apartments and little parcels of land and their jobs, to boot, or for some reason refuse to recognize their training qualifications or slash their pensions. Fears? So often these are actually sad realities! Let us amend such realities, then.

And such a convergence of thinking presupposes that the government of a country that is as rich as this now unified Federal Republic will commit to taking earnest and above all effective steps to create new jobs, even when no investors will turn additional profit from such efforts. Mass unemployment, ladies and gentlemen—your parents went through it many years ago—decimates society and drives our country over the cliff.

People expect those of us here in this room to seek ways and means to defeat unemployment, to create affordable housing, to take the edge off poverty, and in conjunction with those steps, to guarantee our safety in the streets and squares of our cities and in the schools of our children, and to provide every man and woman with access to education and culture. In other words, people expect us to occupy ourselves first and foremost with the creation of acceptable, socially just living conditions and with the protection of our environment. It may be that the views in this building on how to do these things will diverge tremendously. It is all right if we argue over them. But, hopefully, in one thing we will be agreed: chauvinism, racism, anti-Semitism, and Stalinist methods should forever be banned from our country. This Bundestag will not be able to prevent such things altogether, but it can have a hand in creating a climate in which people who embrace such mistaken mindsets meet with ostracism. But this cannot be the concern of one party or parliamentary faction alone. It is also not even simply the affair of a legislature. It is the affair of all citizens, men and women, West and East alike. And if we are expecting moral behavior from these citizens, and generosity and tolerance in their interactions with one another, then surely we, as their elected representatives, must proffer a good example.

And for precisely that reason I urge that the debate over the necessary changes in our society must become a matter for a large coalition, one such as has never existed: a coalition of reason that presupposes a coalition of the reasonable. With this in mind I open the 13th German Bundestag and wish us all luck in our common tasks.

The Life and Times of a Soviet Capitalist

BY IRAKLI IOSEBASHVILI

When he was a growing up, my father-in-law was known as one of the best football players in his neighborhood, if not in all of Tbilisi. He was a skinny kid with curly black hair like a ram's and big soulful eyes, and everyone was sure he would play for the legendary *Dinamo* club in a few years. Then the Red Army took him and made him a paratrooper, all but ending his football career, since jumping out of Soviet airplanes is murder on the knees and ankles. Nevertheless, all of the attention he received in the football days soaked into him, and for the rest of his life he retained the broad-smiling, backslapping charm of the well-loved athlete.

His father was dead and his family was poor, so he began looking for ways to make money as soon as he left the army. Eventually, he would make incredible amounts of it. What was an incredible amount of money in the Soviet Union? A good paycheck in those days, the Soviet 1970s, was about two hundred rubles per month. This was the province of the privileged few, usually generals and professors, two professions that remained dear to the Communists throughout their seven decades in power. Two hundred a month put meat on the table three times a week, bought a dress or two a year for your wife, took your family on a Black Sea cruise in September and even gave you enough left over to make a small deposit in Sberbank, the country's one and only savings bank. It was a magical number, more than most citizens could aspire to, yet enough within the realm of possibility for anyone to imagine what spending that money would feel like.

My father-in-law didn't make two hundred rubles a month. In a good month, he pulled in about two *thousand* rubles. In a really good month, three times that amount. He owned a car at a time when there were so few cars in Tbilisi, people would identify him as "Misha, you know, the one with the car." His wife, a few years after they were married, developed the habit of standing shoeless and dumping all of the gold he had given her around her bare feet to see if it would cover them, and it usually did. He wore fedoras from Turkey and sheepskin coats bought in the Baltics, bell bottoms and shiny boots with big heels. His little girls wore sundresses from China and shoes from Yugoslavia, home to the best shoe manufacturers behind the Iron Curtain, and each one had a full set of magic markers from Italy. At home, there were always guests, and so much food that nobody except his mother-in-law, who set the table, remembered what color the tablecloth was.

And that was all you could spend your money on in the Soviet Union— food, whatever clothes the smugglers brought in, and a single car. Only one, because otherwise somebody might take an interest in where a man who is registered as a—let's see here, comrade—a *factory worker*, with nary a general or academician in the family, was getting it all. And then nothing would help you, not your cousin in the Party, not your gangster friends or the cops you paid off on a monthly basis.

Because of this, there was often the very un-Soviet problem of *having too much money*. But there was a solution. At weddings, my father-in-law and his friends—who, in a Soviet court, would be reviled as smugglers, speculators and currency traders, and in the West would simply have been called capitalists—would show up with their suit pockets stuffed with rubles. They danced with the bride and sent showers of bills cascading over her head. They tossed handfuls at the band and the band played like madmen. And deep in the night, when half of the guests had already passed out, they sat around a table and, with smiles of pure enjoyment on their face, set fistfuls of money on fire.

The bad times came with the deceptively lazy speed that is the hallmark of destructive storms—one minute you're watching some funny clouds inching closer, not really thinking about what they could mean, and the next the sky is a sickly yellow, the electric smell of ozone is thick in the air and fat drops of rain are spattering on the pavement.

The Soviet Union began to shiver and howl like some great poisoned beast, then went off to its noisy, drawn-out death. In 1991, for the first time in seventy years, Georgia held presidential elections, bringing a man named Zviad Gamsakhurdia to power. It must have seemed a logical choice—during the Soviet years, Gamsakhurdia had been a dissident, Georgia's first member of Amnesty International, a sculptor and poet who had spent his entire life upholding Georgian culture and traditions. Within months of taking office, however, he became, by all accounts, a rabid nationalist and dictator whose slogan was "Georgia for the Georgians."

Some claim that it was this nationalism that caused Abkhazia and South Ossetia, where significant portions of the population were non-Georgian, to break away. Others say that the bad blood had been around for years, a consequence of Stalin's habit of redrawing borders and relocating populations. In any event, one thing was clear: in less than half a year, Georgia had gone from crown jewel of the USSR to international basket case. Armed men roamed the streets of Tbilisi, commandeering vehicles, breaking into houses. Anybody suspected of having money was kidnapped and ransomed to family members, then kidnapped again and again until they went broke, got themselves killed or left the country. Overnight, millions of rubles in Soviet currency lying under mattresses became worthless; those who spent their entire lives outfoxing the Soviet system in order to enjoy a comfortable retirement found themselves penniless.

Misha, himself suddenly bereft of 100,000 rubles, decided that this was no place for a businessman to be. He left his family enough money to survive on for the next six months and set off for Moscow, where he had heard big things were happening.

ooooo

There was a man in Moscow that he knew, a Georgian Jew named Roland who used to drive a trolley in Tbilisi and now, if rumor was to be believed, was making millions selling shoes.

Moscow in 1993 was not the glittery Babylon it is today. It was still the monolithic, gray Moscow of the Soviets, but the order that the Soviets had once kept was now replaced by a barely controlled chaos. Freedom had hit Russia like a great slap, and people were still reeling from the shock. Almost every day, somebody took to the streets—Communists, ultranationalists, unhappy miners, cavorting paratroopers. Pyramid schemes, faith healers and nationalist movements, each stranger than the next, sprang up on a daily basis. Gangsters were everywhere, partying or dying like flies. Still, there was electricity and heat, the garbage was picked up regularly and you usually didn't get shot unless you deserved it. After what Misha had seen for the last six months in Georgia, the place must have seemed like Switzerland.

Everyone liked Misha, and Roland was no exception. When times were good, Misha had set him up with work, introduced him to people, spoken for him. Now Roland wanted to return the favor. A car—a Mercedes—came to pick Misha up at his hotel, and an hour later, he was walking through a dank warehouse that smelled of rubber, shoe leather, and decades of cigarettes. Behind a desk, in a shabby little office was Roland, looking exactly like he had in Tbilisi—bald, thin and sporting a bushy moustache—and not at all like a man who had been busy making millions. He came out with his hand outstretched, kissed Misha and called him *genatsvale*, that untranslatable Georgian term of endearment. They drank a glass of cognac, asked about each other's families, then sat down to talk business.

People here have money, Roland explained. Nobody has a lot, but many have a little, and everybody is trying to make just a little more. And when they make their money, they spend it on things they couldn't buy during Soviet times. Little things, mostly. And shoes were the one little thing that everyone needed.

Misha took a pair of mid-length ladies boots out of a shoebox and examined them, bending them in his hand, peeling open the zipper to read the labels with a dubious eye. Imitation leather, made in China. And right at that moment, a pair of massive Russians dressed in black berets and Special Forces camouflage came into the room, deposited what looked like a mail sack on Roland's desk, and left without a word.

Roland picked up the sack and turned it over, and Misha could smell the magical odor of dollars even before the first stack came tumbling out.

"There's half a million in there," Roland said.

He held up a brick-sized bundle of hundreds.

"You have to understand, my friend, that we're living in special times. Very special times."

∞∞∞

While Misha toiled in Moscow, trying to establish a beachhead for his family, things in Georgia went from bad to surrealistically bad, the kind of hard times that people once imagined happening only in Third World countries. Gamsakhurdia, surrounded on all sides by enemies, imprisoned his right-hand man, a gangster and bank robber named Jaba Ioseliani, who proved that he was precisely the wrong man to imprison. He broke out and, with the help of a 10,000-strong paramilitary force, chased the president out of his own country, replacing him with former Soviet foreign minister Eduard Shevardnadze. Gamsakhurdia would form a government-in-exile in Chechnya, then mount a final, ultimately unsuccessful offensive before dying, perhaps by his own hand, in a desolate village on the Russian border. The long-simmering ethnic conflicts in Abkhazia and South Ossetia erupted into full-fledged wars; Russia stood behind the breakaway republics, sending mercenaries and equipment, and Georgia lost ground with each passing day. Abkhazia's quarter of a million Georgians were driven out of their homes. Only a small percentage were airlifted to safety; the rest had to walk through mountain passes where they froze, starved and were robbed by brigands. In Tbilisi, the fighting had been causing electricity shortages for months; now, with winter coming, there was no heat either. People began taking their furniture out into the street, chopping it up for firewood and congregating around the fire, the way they once gathered in their living rooms.

Misha's two daughters went to school haphazardly, if at all. Every morning, the family flipped on the television and listened to news of battles around the city like they once listened to the weather report—if the fighting was particularly heavy, the girls stayed home.

My wife remembers her fifteenth birthday. Amazingly, every one of the dozen friends she invited braved the city streets and came. Since there was nothing to buy, the presents were a potpourri of things that had been salvaged from the depths of closets and armoires. One girl brought a set of pillowcases and a wool blanket, another a small picture of Old Tbilisi that had been hanging in their kitchen for years. Somebody brought a pair of brand new ballet slippers, which everyone oohed over for a few minutes even though my wife had never taken a single ballet class. They ate beans and *khachapuri* and cheered when dessert—a bottle of Coca-Cola that had been obtained for the occasion a week in advance—was brought out. Everyone agreed it was one of the best birthdays they had been to in a long time.

As the war dragged on, food became even scarcer, until the entire city was eating nothing but beans. The boys my wife went to school with all became gangsters, or drug addicts, or went up north to fight the war. Before long, breadlines sprang up, and traditional Georgian values—chivalry, respect for the elderly—went right out the window. If you were too weak to get to the front of the line, that was too bad for you.

Misha finally moved the family to Moscow. On the way home from the airport, he pointed out the warehouse that he was renting, told them he had five more like it all around the city. When they got home, he showed his wife the money he'd been making—he's been storing it in shoeboxes, and the shoeboxes now filled an entire closet.

His wife nodded, took his arm and pulled him aside.

"That store downstairs," she whispered. "Did you know they have *bread?*"

ooooo

There's a story that Nino, my mother-in-law, tells about their first year in Moscow. She's riding the metro with her youngest daughter when they notice a skinhead looking at them from the other end of the train car. He doesn't look happy.

Moscow does not welcome foreigners with open arms. There is no Statue of Liberty offering shelter to the storm-tossed, no respected archetype of the industrious immigrant trying to build a better life. At best, you are told that you're a guest, and that you better not forget it. At worst . . .

"Goddamn blackasses," the skinhead says, getting up.

For Nino, it's like looking up at a block of stone that's about to fall on top of her. There it is, getting bigger and bigger, yet she's frozen. Then she remembers that her daughter is with her and all at once, everything un-locks. She stands, pulling her daughter up by the arm just as the skinhead approaches—and walks right past them.

He comes to a stop in front of a man sitting a few seats away, a birdlike little Azerbaijani with white hair and mahogany skin. He's oblivious to it all, reading a newspaper with the help of a pair of owlish eyeglasses. The skinhead looms over him.

"You dirty blackass fuck," he says. "Why did you come here?"

The old man looks up, blinking. He doesn't get it.

"What did you come here for, you old goat?"

"But," the old man says with genuine surprise, "*you* just came *here.*"

Somebody, some idiot watching all of this, actually titters. The skinhead turns a deep red. He snatches the paper away. The glasses fall from the old man's head and are smashed by a booted foot.

"They think they can come over here and run the fucking place," says the skin. "Well I'll show them."

He rolls up the paper and brings it down with a *thwock* on the old man's head. The old man covers up, says something, pleads for help but no one is helping, not a single one of the two dozen people watching it all. The newspaper comes down again, then a third time, and then Nino yells:

"Is it possible that there's not one real man in this goddamn train car?"

A short, serious-looking Russian kid, dressed in a red sweat suit, gets up.

"He looked tough," said Nino, who saw her brothers fight nearly every day growing up. "One of those tough small guys."

The kid in the sweat suit walks over to the skinhead, grabs him by the collar, and pulls him down to his level. He whispers something in his ear. And the skinhead turns pale.

"The doors were opening, and he just turned around and left. He started cursing and yelling again, but only when he was out of the train and the doors were about to close."

This is the story Nino has at the ready when she wants to make a point about Russian xenophobia.

"The Russians are like anyone else," she says. "You have your idiots, but you have your good people too."

∞∞∞

For three years, Misha worked fifteen hour days, leaving the house at five in the morning to do a circuit of his warehouses, then manning a counter along with his ten-dollar-a-day salesgirls to hawk shoes till dark. Most of the money he makes goes back into his business, and month by month, the business grows. And then he decides that the family has lived modestly long enough, and throws open the floodgates to reap the fruits of his labor.

Right after New Year's, the family left their apartment on the edge of Moscow, in a building that reeked of cat piss and ground-out cigarettes, and moved to the city center. The new place had four bedrooms and ten-foot-high ceilings, and soon the quaint Soviet-era wallpaper was stripped and the rotting floors ripped out, to be replaced by parquet and marble and a chrome Siemens refrigerator and pretty white doors ordered especially from Vienna. Downstairs, there was a BMW, parked in a private garage several blocks away. That year, the family vacationed in Greece, the oldest daughter was sent to study in Barcelona. Misha sent tens of thousands of dollars to Georgia, where a

hundred dollars could feed a large family for a month. While a good part of the country was living in stupefied poverty, his relatives strutted around in designer clothes and bragged about their cousin Misha in Moscow.

"That's probably where things started going wrong," Misha later recounted. "People talk too much, and you start attracting the wrong kind of attention."

Then again, he's not sure. So many things went wrong so quickly, it was hard to pin down a single cause. But he does know that 1997, when the family moved into their new apartment, marked the last of the good years. After that, there would be an almost uninterrupted black streak of loss and treachery and theft. But '97, six years after he first came to Moscow, would always be his year, the one where everything went right.

∞∞∞

The first time they got him was on the night of his thirtieth wedding anniversary. He had dropped the women off and gone to park the car, and now he was coming back, staggering just a bit because he had been drinking hard that night. There had been a dozen relatives and a great band playing the folksy old Tbilisi music that he liked, and as he entered the lobby he remembered everything that had been good about that evening, all of the toasts that had been said, how the table had looked with all of the food and booze laid out. He was almost definitely smiling. He might have even had his eyes closed. And that's probably why he didn't see them until the last second.

Five men, waiting for him by the elevator. Dressed in black. Georgians. Robbers.

Their boss, potbellied and graying around the temples, opened his jacket to show the gun in his belt.

"We were planning on kidnapping you and ransoming you off," he said. "But if you take us upstairs and give us what you've got, we can avoid all that."

Misha wondered why he wasn't scared. Was it the booze, or was it his luck, pulsing through him, making sure that everything turned out okay?

"My wife and daughter are up there," he said. "If you can give me your word that nobody gets hurt, you can have it all."

The boss promised, and into the elevator they all went. When they came into the apartment, Nino, who was in the kitchen, heard Georgian being spoken and figured that Misha met some friends on his way from the garage and brought them upstairs, something he had been known to do. She sighed and began laying plates and leftovers out on the kitchen table. When they got to the kitchen after surveying the rest of the apartment, there was a good meal waiting.

"We have some company, Nino," Misha said. "Just take it easy, and we'll be fine."

Nino's eyes went to the men, then to her husband's face.

"There's food," she said in a half whisper.

They all looked at the table. There was a plate of cucumbers and gigantic, deep-red tomatoes, the most expensive ones you could get. There were boiled eggs and red caviar, several different types of sausage, a chicken Nino broiled that morning and three different cheeses, a pitcher of apple juice and a bottle of vodka from the freezer, still covered with frost.

Misha couldn't help but chuckle.

"In my house, even the thieves eat well," he said. "Go ahead, guys, go ahead. Have a bite, do what you have to do, then get out."

He sat down and began pouring shots of vodka. He offered one to the boss, who became instantly conflicted. On the one hand, he was robbing a house. On the other, there was the automatic politeness that any Georgian man of a certain age displayed when being asked to the table. In the end, the politeness won out.

"Thank you," he said. "I'll just have a bit."

The thieves all sat down, one by one. The irony of the situation did not escape anybody.

"I've been on a lot of jobs, but this . . ." said one of them to no one in particular, shaking his head.

They proceeded to have a quick, quiet meal, and followed it with a quick, quiet robbery. Misha never really believed in banks, and kept his money, literally, under his mattress. There was also gold, silverware, fur coats, jewels, a coin collection and several worthless but expensive-looking family heirlooms. The robbers took it all. But when one of the men asked Nino to take off a heavy gold chain she had on, the boss stopped him.

"Don't touch the lady, or anything she's wearing," he said, and thanked Nino for the meal.

Nino says that it proved he was a professional, knowing people could get out of hand when their personal space is violated and things are taken off their bodies. Misha said that it proved that the son of a bitch, may he rot in hell, was nonetheless a gentleman thief of the old Tbilisi variety. In any case, the necklace stayed.

But most everything else they had was gone.

∞∞∞

The next time the robbers came, they were not so nice. It was six months later, and a different set of robbers, and when Misha saw them standing in front of his door he could tell that this lot, who he described as "a bunch of scumbag killers from various parts of the Caucasus," would not be gentlemen. Without even thinking about it, he knew there was no way he was letting them into the apartment with his wife and daughter.

"No way," Misha said. "Go fuck yourselves."

After all these years, he could still move. When they tried to grab him, he stepped aside, whirled around, slipped through their fingers, shoved, swung, was almost past them and at the staircase, where he could make a dash downstairs. But there were five of them. Someone caught him by the collar, and before he could shrug his jacket off and run they had his arms and were pulling him to the door.

"Nino!" he yelled. "Get my gun!"

Nobody knows why he said that. He didn't have a gun. But the robbers did.

A shot rang out. Wild with adrenaline, Misha fought. He would die today, he decided, but the door to the house was staying closed, the family safe. And then, incredibly, the robbers fell back, then turned and ran down the stairs.

Misha looked around. Yes, it was the hallway outside his apartment, but everything felt unreal. He wondered if he was dreaming. Then the door flew open and his wife and daughter rushed out, and Misha realized he was on the floor only when he saw their faces bending over him.

∞∞∞

Later, they found a bullet hole in the door, inches away from where Misha's head had been. His luck had held, but not completely; while the bullet missed, they'd gotten him with a knife, deep enough that his spleen had to be taken out.

Misha healed in body, but his mind remained deeply troubled, and his finances only grew worse. He put what little money he had into opening a currency exchange booth on the edge of Moscow, but the business required long hours and its profits barely stocked the refrigerator. Everything else he tried failed almost immediately. The worst part of it was that everyone around him was making money—the ruble had rebounded, oil was soaring and real estate prices were doubling every year. But Misha, who had never found out who put the robbers onto him in the first place (and the robbers never just found you, someone—a former business partner, a competitor, a jealous relative—always sold you out), was now suspicious of everyone. Most of all, he became suspicious of other fellow immigrants from the Caucasus, especially other Georgians.

His mistrust drove his old business partners away and kept him from attracting new ones. Connections withered, and fresh opportunities appeared less and less frequently. As the money dried up, the once-grand apartment began to come apart, seeming to peel, crack and leak everywhere at once. He crashed his BMW and could not afford to repair it. He began suffering from strange, hard-to-diagnose ailments. The doctors told him they were all in his head, and he told the doctors they were all a bunch of assholes.

Always, looming over every word and action, were the robbers. For hours on end, he thought about who could have sent them, and why, and whether they were coming back. The family was plagued with mysterious phone calls, men with Georgian accents inquiring about Misha's well-being.

"It was after *they* came that all of this started," Nino often said, as if the robbers had left some small, radioactive piece of themselves that was slowly poisoning the family's good fortune.

∞∞∞

They say that if something happens once, it might never happen again, but if it has happened twice, it will surely happen a third time. On an autumn night in 2003, a black Volga pulled up to Misha as he was walking home from the parking garage.

"We have to talk, Misha," said a young man with an Armenian accent. "We have your daughter."

My wife was at home with Nino and me—Misha had just talked to her a minute ago. His other daughter was in Tbilisi, with her husband, and Misha felt there was a pretty good chance she was safe as well.

"You don't have shit," Misha said. "Now leave me alone."

Misha turned around and walked away. The Volga did not follow.

"We'll deal with you later," someone called out as the car pulled away.

∞∞∞

"They were amateurs," Misha later said. "Flunkies."

We were having a war council of sorts; Misha, my wife's uncle Anzor, who had flown in from Tbilisi to look for a job, and me, the new son-in-law. It was the autumn of 2004, a mere six months since I'd left New York to get married and move to Moscow.

"Nice family you married into, eh?" Misha said, giving me a wink. "In any case, you can relax. There's nothing to worry about."

Nobody believed that, least of all me. I'd been the one who had seen his face, ashen with fear, when he came home. These particular robbers might have been bumblers, but that didn't mean they weren't dangerous.

Life took on a surreal quality in the weeks that followed. Every time Misha left the house, Anzor and I went with him, armed with a motley assortment of items culled from around the house, like a band of deadly carpenters—Misha usually carried a short axe, Anzor had a carving knife and I packed a hammer.

Misha, for his part, was strangely upbeat. When I asked him why, he said it was because of the Rose Revolution, which that autumn had swept Georgia's corrupt president out of power and replaced him with the fiery, hopeful Mikheil Saakashvili.

"Georgia turned things around," he said. "Things will turn for us too."

I wondered if that was it, or if Misha was once again feeling his luck.

A few days later, Misha told us that he had met an old friend who was coming over tonight to help solve our problems. When Misha said the friend's name, Nino shook her head in dismay.

"That's exactly what we need," she said. "More gangsters."

∞∞∞

The gangster in question was G.R., who grew up together with Misha on the same twisted, crumbling street in Kharpukhi, one of Tbilisi's oldest and poorest neighborhoods.

"He had a bad leg and couldn't run," Misha recalled. "He liked to watch me play football. I felt sorry for him, and we became friends."

G.R. was small for his age, and quiet. He liked the way Misha's mother made *lobio*, a traditional bean stew, and came over whenever she served it. He rarely went to school, but neither did anyone else in the neighborhood. This is the sum of what Misha could tell me about the childhood of G.R., who had once been one of Georgia's most notorious gangsters.

They saw each other less often as they grew older. Then G.R. disappeared completely, and Misha heard that he was doing time for robbing a bank in Rostov. When G.R. got out of jail a decade later, it was widely known that he was now a *vor v zakone*, a term from the Russian underworld that can be roughly equated with a "made guy" on *The Sopranos*. Whenever he and Misha ran into each other, G.R. was reserved but friendly, always asking about Misha's mother and her *lobio*. Then, after many years, he happened to walk into Misha's currency exchange booth to change a fifty-dollar bill, and Misha asked him to come over.

He arrived exactly at eight, after calling in advance to say that he wouldn't be staying long, wouldn't be eating and couldn't drink because he was on blood pressure medication. When I opened the door, there stood a short, potbellied man with salt-and-pepper hair, leaning on a cane. He wore a black sweater, dusted with dandruff around the shoulders, and shapeless black pants. His handshake was limp, his voice, tired. And yet . . . there was something about him, a kind of crackling, unfocused menace—similar to the unsettling vibration you feel when standing next to a power station—that warned you away.

We sat down at the table. Nino informed G.R. that despite his request to withhold dinner, she had made *lobio*, and he shrugged his shoulders and said well, he was just going to have to eat it. After dinner and some halting conversation, we sat drinking coffee and watching the evening news.

Putin came on, and G.R. grunted his approval.

"My type of guy," G.R. said. "He forces people to respect him."

Then they went live to Tbilisi, where a hundred thousand people were joyously celebrating the Rose Revolution in the streets of the city. They carried flags and crosses and of course, roses, danced traditional Georgian dances and honked their car horns.

I asked G.R. what he thought of Saakashvili.

"An idiot," he said. "What does he need America for, when Russia is right next door?"

Maybe Russia hadn't been such a good neighbor over the years, I started to say, but G.R. cut me off.

"Let me tell you something," he said. "In all of its history, Georgia never lived as well as it did during Soviet times. Everyone had their piece of bread, and some people got wealthy. Culture, art, sports, all the best of everything came from Georgia. Everybody was friends, and nobody got in each others face. You can thank the Russians for that."

Was living in the Soviet Union, a country that was once called "The World's Biggest Prison," really that good? I asked.

G.R. lit a cigarette, took a long pull and exhaled an enormous cloud of smoke. He stared into it for a long time.

"I hated the Communists," he said. "But look at what people have to go through now. You think what they have in Georgia is freedom? Being able to eat, that's freedom. They ruined a great thing, those bastards."

I looked at Nino and Misha. They had moved closer together and were both wearing that dreamy, contemplative look they often got when thinking about the old days. G.R., too, was looking at some place near the ceiling, a slight smile on his face. I sipped my coffee and looked for some football on television.

∞∞∞

The next day, G.R. accompanied Misha to work. Misha had his currency exchange booth in a kind of open-air market in northern Moscow, a bustling place occupied mostly by foreigners. First G.R. sat with him at an outdoor café, drinking tea out of a plastic cup. Then they had *khachapuri* at a tiny restaurant filled with Georgian migrants. After that, they took a long, slow walk through the winding lanes and alleys of the market. G.R. made sure that enough people saw that Misha was with him, that Misha was a friend. Then they shook hands and G.R. went home, and in the following weeks, everything—the robberies, the phone calls—stopped, as if a faucet had been shut off.

In the next few months, Misha's luck slowly began to turn. He started selling Georgian pastries—baked at home, by Nino—to cafés around the city, and customers couldn't get enough. Pretty soon he expanded the menu, and before he knew it, he had a catering business on his hands. It's a thriving operation, but small, and that's the way he likes it. A big business attracts the wrong kind of attention, which is the last thing he wants. And sometimes, usually after we've had a few shots of cognac, he'll settle back and tell about the old Georgia, the mythical Soviet Shangri-la where they burned money just for the hell of it.

The War Within

BY MAXIM TRUDOLUBOV

(TRANSLATION BY ALEXEI BAYER)

The 1980s left the heaviest and dustiest traces in my folks' home; stacks, piles and bundles of magazines, journals and newspapers. No other period in my memory is associated with so much paper. The 1970s are remembered for their china and crystal, the 1990s left no recollections while the 2000s brought new furniture and a flat-screen TV set. Those bundles of paper lingered for a long time. My parents moved them from under the table to the closet, and then from the closet up to the attic. Then they went through the papers and tore out and saved only the most important stuff. Then the most important stuff had to be thinned out, too. By now little remains of those clippings.

Today, when nothing is important any longer, a circulation of 100,000 copies per week for a quality publication is a major commercial success. But back in the late 1980s, *Novy Mir*, the monthly literary journal for the intelligentsia, which serialized quality novels and published poems and polemical essays 5,000-8,000 words in length, boasted a circulation of 2.5 million. The weekly *Ogonek* sold 4 million copies every week. (The readership of each issue was even greater, with at least one family reading each copy.) Not only were there such enormous circulation figures, but all those publications were being read. They were read so much because never before had there been so much of importance happening and so many new names. The new names reached us from beyond the country's borders and from the underground.

Those people were underground or abroad largely thanks to Yuri Andropov, the chief of the KGB in the 1970s and briefly the Secretary General of the Communist Party from 1983 to 1984.

In 1973, he wrote in a report to the Central Committee of the CPSU (the Communist Party of the Soviet Union): "A wall has been created separating the people and the most progressive representatives of the intelligentsia, Sakharov and Solzhenitsyn, which is no shorter and no less secure than the Berlin Wall." Those were not Andropov's own words. Instead, he quoted writer Lydia Chukovskaya. There was clearly no need to quote a dissident in a document of this kind, but Andropov, a dogged crusader against dissent, apparently liked the metaphor.

The comparison to the Berlin Wall worked both for the dissident Chukovskaya and her persecutor Andropov. If dissidents themselves acknowledged that a wall existed, then the secret police had done its job well. There was no need for physical walls or new arrests. It was enough to keep troublemakers from being published, to move them out of big cities, to subject them to compulsory psychiatric treatment or, in extreme cases, expel them from the country. A year after Andropov reported on his success in separating the people from the troublemakers, Alexander Solzhenitsyn and Alexander Galich, an author and performer of "anti-Soviet" songs, were sent out of the country. That same year, 1973, Andrey Sakharov became the target of a campaign of harassment which began with a nasty open letter about him published in *Pravda* and signed by forty members of the Soviet Academy of Sciences. It was also the year when I started preschool. My parents had not read *The Gulag Archipelago* and I do not recall hearing Galich's songs at home.

That was how we were separated by a wall from those who knew and understood more than we did. For us, on this side of the wall, they simply didn't exist. "When someone attempts to climb over the Berlin Wall, which separates one part of a nation from another, shots ring out," Andropov went on, quoting Chukovskaya. "Every shot is heard around the world and resonates in every German soul. In our country, the struggle for the soul of the 'common man,' for the right to communicate with him by getting around the censorship, is conducted in silence."

Indeed, it was carried out very quietly. Most people disappeared not into prisons (only the most dangerous ones were given jail terms), but into silence instead. More people were frightened of saying anything openly than had been arrested. Stalin used to make independent minds into enemies. Andropov made them into the marginalized dregs of society.

A BREACH IN THE WALL

It was an era when a long-hidden part of our life began to return, and the first major return—as well as the first significant breach in the wall—occurred in early 1986, when Mikhail Gorbachev telephoned Sakharov, who had been under house arrest in Nizhny Novgorod for six years. The Secretary-General of the Party gave the Academician permission to return to Moscow. "You have an apartment there," said Gorbachev without uttering a single word of apology. "Go back to your patriotic work."

It is an old tradition that the new Czar frees those who were in prison under his predecessor. This was precisely that kind of gesture, but the words Gorbachev used were important. To criticize the Soviet system was no longer a form of antisocial behavior but patriotic work. When Sakharov returned, it turned out that very few people shared his views. He was well ahead of the rest of the country. Nevertheless, he was universally accepted as a moral authority. He set a humane tone for the second half of the 1980s in Russia.

The basis for his moral authority had been laid earlier, of course, when Sakharov was known in the country as a semi-mystical privileged academician who for unknown reasons rebelled against the system. "I've heard it dozens of times: 'I'm going to write to Academician Sakharov.' Or 'I'm going to Moscow, to Academician Sakharov.' Even though the man who says this may not even know his address. Even if he knew it, he probably would not have gone. The important thing was that it seemed like there was an alternative authority to which you could appeal," wrote Sergey Dovlatov in *March of the Lonely Ones*. That alternative authority suddenly became an almost official one—albeit only for a short time.

All of a sudden, telling jokes about the CPSU, hiding behind irony and placing the responsibility for Soviet reality on the old fools in the leadership was no longer the only way. Now everything that was outrageous and irritating, that was opaque or absurd could be openly called by its name. It was not much perhaps. But judging by what my parents said at the time it felt like a major change. To pass from denying reality to evaluating it and to admitting the disease was indeed a major step.

It was a time of reading, discovery and reflection. Reflection on a nation-wide scale. It should be noted that it was a time of sobering up, literally, as well. People started to drink less. In the second half of the 1980s the authorities began their widely despised anti-drinking campaign. Those who came up with the "measures to overcome drunkenness and alcoholism" rightly believed that one of the most important causes of stagnation in the economy was widespread laxity, or as it was called then a "careless attitude to work."

UPON SOBER REFLECTION

Gorbachev got a lot of criticism for his campaign against vodka drinking, and it was considered a failure, but mortality in the country did go down. Daniel Treisman in his work "Alcohol and Russia's Mortality Crisis: Policy, Prices, and Self-Destructive Drinking" notes a correlation between availability of vodka and mortality. If in 1990 the average monthly wage was enough to purchase ten liters of vodka, by 1994 that amount had increased to forty-six liters. Vodka was considered a "social medicine" and in the early 1990s increases in vodka prices were deliberately held in check. Street kiosks began to sell grain alcohol in one-liter bottles. Unlike food, clothing and goods for kids, for example, strong liquor of the lowest possible quality became more and more affordable. All restrictions on the sale of liquor were removed. The result is well-known: The period between 1990 and 1994 saw the first post-Soviet spike in mortality rates.

It was not just drinking, of course. In the 1980s, people not only drank less but they also read and thought more. During that spell of sobriety, they read books that had never been published before. Émigré memoirs, collected works of previously banned writers, books by mystics, Christian philosophers, and yoga gurus were published, purchased and read. People began to go to the theater, to visit churches and libraries.

This new environment created a desire to get down to work. But the period of moral sobriety was short-lived, partly because of economic difficulties and cheap vodka. Reading and thinking stopped and messianic aspirations returned. The 2000s have been an age of new drunkenness. People have been drunk not so much on alcohol, but on rising incomes and conspicuous consumption. However alcohol consumption increased as well, and another spike in mortality occurred in 1998-2004, in part due to the increased availability of and low prices for vodka.

This period has now come to an end, too. It will be interesting to see what kind of awakening follows. Will it be another era of sobering up or will there be another war as we try to prove something to the rest of the world? It should be recalled that in the 1980s the sobering up was accompanied by rising circulation figures for newspapers and magazines and larger print runs for books. Today's version of this jump would be a spike in the use of the internet. Nothing like that has been seen yet, but it may be too early to tell. It is important to understand what happened in Russia at that time and how it made it possible for a national awakening to take place at all.

CORRECT OR WRONG

The early years of the new, non-Soviet and non-imperial Russia were marked by an intense search for a new identity. All that remained of the totalitarian state was a stage set. Not only was the system no longer scary, it had become ridiculous. That was obvious even to high school students. The old curricula in history, social studies and literature had become obsolete, but there were no new ones. A new party line had not been developed.

Our teachers were divided into those who had a sense of humor (usually, the ones who taught math and physics) and those who did not (the ones who taught history and literature). The former, perhaps because their field was natural sciences, could acknowledge reality, whereas the latter, steeped as they were in the history of Party Congresses and the literature of Socialist Realism, stubbornly refused to do so. They fought to preserve their rapidly disappearing world in every way they could. "Why were the decisions of the 27th Congress of the CPSU so important not only to the Party but to the entire Soviet people?" asked Raisa Vladimorovna staring me hard in the eye. "Could it be because we only have one party?" "Wrong. Zakharov, you?" "Because it is the leading and directing force in our society." "Correct."

But judging by the tense look on her face, Raisa Vladimirovna was no longer entirely sure what the leading force now really was, or what was correct. She had not been told anything except to follow standard Ministry of Education instructions, but instruction booklets were hopelessly behind the times. A similar situation prevailed in the country at large.

No one really knew what was correct any more. Glasnost had been declared, but it was not decreed what could be openly discussed. Common sense suggested that certain flaws had to be criticized. The idea proposed by the most progressive people of the time—which I learned about from my father, who read everything and recounted to me the most important things—was as follows: We should recognize the mistakes of the recent past and go back to that pure, immaculate layer after which things began to go wrong. It was a Slavophile-like idea of searching for an ideal in the past. But while the Slavophiles believed that the Russians had been a godly nation in pre-Petrine Muscovy, the Communists, once the scales had fallen from their eyes, began to dream of a pre-Stalinist Soviet Russia.

The official Soviet picture of the world had no room for admitting that history can take wrong turns. The very admission that layers of the recent past could be removed because they were flawed was revolutionary. Arguments raged over how far the edifice of the state would have to be demolished in order to reach the solid foundations on which to build anew. The most cautious proposed to touch up the roof and fill in the cracks through heroic, self-abnegating labor, just like those who had toiled on the construction sites of the early Five-Year Plans. But how to motivate people to work if the production facilities of the Gulag had been long ago dismantled, and the KGB was so busy combating dissent that it had lost its ability to force citizens to work?

In 1987, in a highly influential article, "Advances and Debts," economist Nikolai Shmelev proposed to rewind the tape sixty years, to Lenin's New Economic Policy. Shmelev's main idea, to shift from a command economic structure back to economic incentives, seemed logical and attractive. But NEP was a particularly unhappy choice as an ideal from the past. It was a temporary policy of market half-measures, which Lenin adopted only when he realized that he was about to lose power. To hold on to power in an impoverished nation seething with anger toward the Bolsheviks, he agreed to loosen controls over the economy. However, he never abandoned the goal of returning full control to the state at some point in the future, at a moment known only to himself. Such circumstances did not seem to provide a solid foundation on which anything worthwhile could be built.

The dream of finding a starting point some time before Stalin's great turn persisted until 1989. But the First Congress of USSR People's Deputies forced the nation to look further back. During the Congress, which the entire nation watched like a soap opera on Channel One, a previously inconceivable thought was uttered, that the October Revolution itself might have been a mistake. What we needed to do was return to pre-Bolshevik Russia. At the end of 1989, the Inter-Regional Group of Deputies called for Article 6 of the Constitution, which proclaimed the leading role of the CPSU, to be struck down, a proposal which was heard without any burst of indignation.

A TRUCE IN A CIVIL WAR

The most important thing that happened then, thanks to all those publications and television broadcasts of the Congress, was that the wall between the people and "the most progressive representatives of the intelligentsia," which Party ideologists and their henchmen from the KGB had created by means of murders, censorship and exile, began to dissolve and nearly disappeared, at least for a time.

Did the masses temporarily become the intelligentsia? Or was it the other way around? It may be that in place of the "Soviet people" the early shoots of new society began to emerge, aspiring to become a nation. The wall disappeared because the Soviet people wanted to go beyond themselves and take a look at themselves from the outside, in order to understand where Russians came from and who they were. That was the reason for Russians' unprecedented interest in their origins. "Genesis has become the present. It is no longer some old stuff, but the latest thing. The question has become *where from?* and without finding an answer to it we won't be able to find an answer to the question *where to?*" This quote comes from another important article of the time, an interview by historian Mikhail Gefter with journalist Gleb Pavlovsky, titled "Stalin Died Yesterday."

Gefter meant that Stalin's legacy was still fresh and it had not yet been completely understood, to say nothing of its being overcome. He identified the state of permanent civil war as the main feature of Stalinism. After the victory of 1945, Stalin saw that returning front-line soldiers, who came home from the war believing in themselves and in their unity as a nation, were a danger to him. To break up this new unity and prevent a thinking nation from emerging, he started a new wave of repression. Man was set against man once again, enemies were once more discovered who were bent on causing trouble and the country was declared to be swarming with "traitors." Alongside the Cold War fought between the USSR and the West there was an internal Cold War inside the USSR, in which a distinction was made between "us" and "them," or between those who accepted the rules of the game and those who did not. Both wars ended with the fall of the Berlin Wall, but on the home front the peace that was achieved in the late 1980s proved to be more like a short-lived truce.

A CONFUSION IN THE HEAD

Back then, life for me seemed like happy chaos. For all practical purposes, the past had been abolished, if not officially at least morally, but nothing new had taken its place as yet. There were no rules, no new textbooks and no notion of how they would be written. We laughed at the lecturer who tried to teach our college freshman class the old history of the CPSU. But what could he have taught us instead? Back then, in the heat of the argument, I would have proposed the history of the Gulag and the history of the church. But most people were not ready for anything like that. Nor were there any professors who could have put together and taught such courses.

Looking back, I realize that the confusion of those times was not such a joyride, after all. Rather, dismay and confusion were a tragedy, especially since time to reflect on the fate of Russia and the world was actually very short. The country was about to plunge into an economic abyss, but nothing was forthcoming except more abstract reflections.

Where to seek the truth in such uncertain times? Publishers began to issue books by émigré writers and philosophers. But they could not offer much, either. Their readers could argue about Vladimir Solovyev's metaphysics of total unity or Nikolai Berdyaev's views on the tragedy of creativity and the sin of ownership. Ivan Ilyin—who is, incidentally, much admired by Prime Minister Vladimir Putin—wrote that the Western concept of the law merely creates a framework for individual self-realization and includes the freedom to sin. It is probably no surprise that this point of view is often taken by those at the highest levels of the Russian Orthodox Church who are close to Putin.

Émigré philosophers in Europe and the United States bitterly debated each other over their conflicting visions of "Russia as it should be," an ideal country of the future. Each had his own distinct concept of religion and society and whether the law or spirituality had to be paramount. None of them, either liberal or conservative, knew economics. As a college student, I found their arguments extremely interesting, but perhaps they were not the first thing that a poor, confused nation needed, especially since its economic and social system had just crumbled.

Nor were the intellectuals living in Russia at the time of much help. Most had no practical experience, but were human rights activists who stood up for high-minded moral values. No team of specialists existed who could be enlisted to produce a realistic reform program for the economy.

This became clear only later, after 1989. At the time, it seemed that there was plenty of time to think about how to organize Russia and fill in the shortages in most professional fields. Then the dam had broken and our stagnant pond had been flooded with everything that had not been accessible to generations of Russians. Men and women who had stewed in their own juices for seventy years, getting only censor-vetted snippets of foreign culture, had to digest quickly what their contemporaries abroad had spent years assimilating at an unhurried pace; everything from concepts of economics and the free market to modern clothes and the basics of personal hygiene.

The tragedy was that so much time had elapsed in the big world on the other side of the wall. The world which the first generation of Russian émigrés inhabited had long disappeared. They were convinced that the Soviet regime would collapse at any moment and they were getting ready, to the best of their ability, to go back. Subsequent waves of emigration had stopped hoping for "Russia as it should be." Those who stayed in Russia were not ready for profound change. There was no real understanding of the way the modern world worked, and no way it could have been attained.

THE MUSIC OF RETURN

This lack of knowledge, too, became clear later. Back then, in the late 1980s, life was beautiful and rich in events. For me, the most important ones were connected to our former compatriots and their return. I almost physically felt that every new visit, show or concert changed us a little. It still didn't seem like the Soviet Union would ever come to an end. The thought of seeing the world beyond the wall with one's own eyes still seemed a wild dream. The reality was still quite Soviet, poor and gray, but an inner content was already changing.

When Marc Chagall died, I remember reading his obituary in the *Literary Gazette*, which was illustrated with his self-portrait. It was a simple pen drawing. I had never seen anything like that in a newspaper. It was not really avant-garde, just a spur-of-the-moment, bold sketch. All of that taken together—the article, the drawing, the half-remembered, strange name—seemed to come from a different world.

When pianist Vladimir Horowitz came to perform in 1986, there was no way to get tickets to his concert. I watched it on TV unable to take my eyes off the screen. He played the way no one did here, holding his hands "flat" on the keys and not making use of sheet music. He looked like a foreigner, but he spoke Russian and smiled a non-Soviet smile.

Émigrés were particularly fascinating, perhaps because they looked like foreigners. Foreigners were foreigners, but Russians were a different story. If a Russian could have a non-Soviet appearance, smile, and speak a foreign language—I thought at the time—then we weren't intrinsically different. We in Russia merely didn't have the same clothes and weren't in a good mood. All was not lost yet.

When Mstislav Rostropovich performed at the Berlin Wall, I already knew that there were different kinds of Russians. Still, it was amazing. Not only because the Wall was coming down. Yes, it was coming down, but the point was that he sat there in a chair with the graffiti-covered Wall behind his back. The juxtaposition of Bach and graffiti didn't seem to bother anyone. Everybody liked it that a major musician played serious music in an inappropriate setting. It may be hard to explain, but the fact that it was possible, that it could be done that way, struck me even more than the event itself.

I hoped so much that one day it could be that way in my country, too. There seemed to be more than enough time to do what needed to be done. To buy foreign clothes, learn everything, understand everything and then decide what this country should look like and how to get there. And yes, to learn to smile that non-Soviet smile.

Any Beach but This

BY DAVID ZÁBRANSKÝ

(TRANSLATION BY ROBERT RUSSELL)

Democracy on the loose!—Here I am in the café of the Museo Nacional del Prado, thinking of Vienna.

Bartlett (the guy I flew to Madrid to see) warned me about Vienna. He said that's where Hitler learned to hate the Jews. "He was born in Austria, but to get his show on the road he had to move to Munich. Vienna couldn't stomach his paintings—those amateur daubs of his—or his Nazism. Vienna's way is different: in-depth destruction. Instead of attacking from the outside, it destroys from within."

Why go to a town where waltzes sound like marches and marches sound like waltzes? Why go to Vienna at all?

ooooo

The moment I landed at Schwechat I realized Bartlett had got it wrong. I was surprised at how fresh the Viennese air was. If Vienna were Lagos or Delhi there would be two Viennas—the tourist one and the real one—and being a tourist I would naturally have seen only the former. But Vienna is not Lagos or Delhi. What I saw was Vienna.

Italians strolled around in shorts, with bits of clothing round their waists and cameras round their necks. Austrians stepped out of cars and walked past palaces, past the unchanging backdrop of the democratic West that is everywhere the same.

Of course you are surrounded by history (this is Vienna, after all!)—so much history it can be quite daunting. All those pictures in the galleries, all those plays in the *Burgtheater*, all that music in the concert halls—it can get quite scary. But here in Vienna they lay that vast weight of history and culture on you so gently you hardly feel a thing.

Waiting, credit card in hand, in the queue at the Albertina ticket desk (my pockets full of fliers of every description, behind me a group of Italians in shorts and sandals arguing about their flight home, all around me modern art and architecture, the laid-back lightness of the West), I recalled Bartlett's words and had to laugh out loud—then apologize to the Italians. Neither in Vienna, nor in Italy, could anyone learn to hate the Jews: Freud's house is now a museum, and so is Mussolini's birthplace in Predappio.

(As we stroll through Vienna or Madrid or an Italian village, do we ever pass houses and apartments that will one day be museums? Sure we do. But won't they be the houses and apartments of movie stars destined to play Mussolini or Freud in some yet-to-be-made film?) I ordered a fresh orange juice.

Madrid is awash with oranges—picked in Andalusia by Moroccans, Poles, Romanians, Ukrainians, etc. The Moroccans stay on after the harvest, but the Poles, Romanians, Ukrainians, etc. return home. So Madrid is more and more awash with oranges picked by Poles, Romanians and Ukrainians, etc. and less and less with oranges picked by Moroccans. The Ukrainians pick oranges and go. The Moroccans pick oranges and want to stay. But what Spain wants is picked oranges, not Ukrainians, Moroccans, etc. Spain doesn't want any of them; it just wants the oranges they pick.

Da-da-da!
Dum-da-da-daa!

ooooo

A couple of tables away I spot a young couple—honeymooners, lovers? I'm not sure about him, but she is certainly not Spanish. Her hair is too fair, her skin is too fair, her features too Slavic. Her manner lacks a certain type of femininity natural to women born under a scorching sun. Her body is incapable of that rapidity, that severity and simplicity that seems to relax every muscle under their skins. Unlike Spanish women she has no vestige of the animal about her, of the beast that seeks out the shade. Her cheekbones are not prominent, her lips are not half-parted in a constant sucking-in of air, nor does her body remind you of a sculpted wooden torso. Unlike Spanish women she does not look like an animal tormented by sun and thirst. Nothing about her suggests primal suffering or physical thirst or physical fatigue. Or, for that matter, physical passion.

Unlike Spanish women she seems fluid, washed-out—in fact she reminds me of a watercolor, an artist's attempt to express disillusionment with the present, nostalgia, or at any rate some feeling that feeds on the past, not like the feeling I get when I look at those boldly striding Spanish women, confident in their bodies and clothes and gestures.

She gets up and goes to look at a poster for an exhibition in the Prado. Then, left foot turned out, hips relaxed, she starts fiddling with the end of the scarf draped casually round her neck, first winding it onto her finger, then unwinding it until the scarf hangs once more against her blouse.

She does this several times, until the scarf slips off her shoulder and drops to the floor. Quickly, glancing around in furtive embarrassment, she stoops to pick it up.

She's out of place here—she'd be out of place even in Vienna. Here years of democracy have eliminated embarrassment from public life without a trace. Maybe it survives as an endangered species in private life, in intimate situations. Maybe there is still a place for embarrassment and coyness in the bedroom (possibly as the most effective form of titillation, since it's the only place you'll find it). But on the street, in cafés and museums, in planes, trains and offices, it has become extinct.

Just as History in the West entered its last lap after the Second World War (since History now only affected those on the other side of the Wall) and came to a final halt (waving cheerfully as it crossed the finishing line on the last stroke of historical time) when the Wall collapsed and the East ceased to exist—so, too, embarrassment has become a thing of the past. Instead we have absolute naturalness. Man is the measure of all things. In the postwar era Western man blossomed at an unthinkable pace. No democratic or humanist system in history has ever borne such luscious human fruits, so unselfconscious, so self-possessed, so natural. It was the naturalness of the

Viennese, and of the tourists in Vienna, that transmuted the vast weight of culture and history into—*dadada!*—a bland amusement for tourists.

Watching her—she's still looking at the poster for a Tiepolo exhibition—I feel increasingly sure she's not from Madrid, she's not from the West, and she definitely doesn't belong in the West.

Where does she belong? In the Eastern reservation. On the other side of the fence that still separates the West from the East (although historically speaking the East has collapsed and the West is helping itself to more and more of it). She belongs on the other side of the fence, in that place where occasionally they bark, but otherwise just gaze in envy, at the West.

"Hey, there's Polina!" says Bartlett, reaching over the table with one hand to shake mine while waving to her with the other.

"Sam's a teacher. Where was he born? Bradford. And Polina's from Ukraine. She was born in Ukraine and most likely she'll die in Sam's arms in Madrid. What a wonderful fate, eh Polina?"

Again she's embarrassed. She says "they" don't want to disturb us.

"They met in Ukraine. She talked him into leaving Ukraine and taking her with him. Good-bye and good riddance! Said she couldn't lead a decent life in her native land, same as me in fact. Good-bye to all that. Grappa?"

∞∞∞∞

"She's not very natural," I say, as he returns with two glasses. "I was watching her. She kept twiddling her scarf round her finger. Then she dropped it and looked awfully embarrassed. She's out of place here. She doesn't belong in the West."

"She doesn't belong in the West because she's not natural? Nonsense! She doesn't belong in the West because she's not original. Her main aim in life is to look the same as everyone else, but in her attempts to be the same she's never had to deal with the terrifying need to be different—which has now become absolutely suffocating, even here."

"But fancy making such a fuss about a scarf! I wonder what she'd do if she were naked? Imagine: her blouse falls apart at the seams, her skirt drops round her ankles, she steps out of it; maybe she's still holding her glass; maybe it slips out of her hand and shatters on the floor, but she pretends not to notice and carries on walking round the room. She's just the same as before, except now she's naked. Then and only then will nobody doubt she belongs here."

"Very original! Any crazy streaker who runs onto a football pitch gets his picture in *El Mundo* the next day. Nudity is the preferred political weapon of those who have no political power. Imagine you want to cycle from Lavapies to Sol. You don't work in City Hall so you can't issue an order banning traffic from the Lavapies-Sol road. What do you do? You find someone who also wants to cycle from Lavapies to Sol, you strip off, and you cycle from Lavapies to Sol. 'Why strip off?,' people ask. You tell them you want to draw attention to the deplorable lack of cycle paths and the deplorable behavior of motorists. You talk gravely about a grave problem and pretend not to notice you're naked. You point a finger at the scandalous behavior of drivers, and the next morning you'll be all over the papers and half of Madrid will be pointing at *you*. Scandalized cyclists will argue with scandalized motorists and scandalized councilors—but you, unlike them, will be naked, because being naked is the only way you can say something with any hope of being heard. Nudity is the price you pay for not being a politician."

"But nudity stopped being original years ago! Most people are perfectly happy to undress anywhere, anytime. Being naked doesn't make you a star, it just makes you ridiculous."

"To be original you'd need some physical defect. Maybe Polina's got only four toes on one foot?"

"Somehow I doubt it. No, if she really wanted to be what you call original she'd first have to do something about her clothes. She could start by going round this café borrowing stuff from people. The room would fall silent; there'd be expectant looks, catcalls, applause—depending on what she happened to pick. But none of that interests me. What I really want is for her to take her clothes off. I'd like to see her natural charm—after all, when we say 'personal charm' don't we simply mean naturalness? That's how I'd like to see her—naked, silent, natural."

"Naked and dead."

"So she couldn't talk about her originality."

"As it is she wears so much lipstick she never dares shut her mouth."

∞∞∞

They met in Ukraine, where Sam worked in a language school. In those days he wore rings in his ears and nose. Now, when he shows you a photo of himself from back then, Polina dismisses it with a wave of her hand and an indulgent smile: "Oh, that was ages ago." But behind the wave and the smile there's a sense of revulsion, as if she felt like adding: "That's not how it was!"

Revulsion, because those two loops of metal, which in those days represented freedom (piercing for an Englishmen meant you were somebody, while for a Ukrainian it meant you were nobody), she now found frightening, as if the beast that could be tied up by them—tethered so it couldn't move—was not him, but her.

ooooo

He was twenty-seven. At twenty-five he'd realized he didn't like living in England, and decided there and then to go to Eastern Europe. But after barely a year in a small Polish mining town full of vodka and "lurid tumors" (as he called the new forms of advertising and dress, the new television programs and shopping malls) he was convinced there was no such thing as Eastern Europe—only varying degrees of that quality known as "East." After barely a year he realized he needed more East, so he left Poland and went to Ukraine. The brochures they sent him about Charkov described Charkov as an ordinary Ukrainian town. Which is precisely why he moved to Charkov.

Ukraine was more bearable than Poland. One of his students was Polina, with her beautiful eyes and poor English. She was secretive, passionate, forever taking refuge behind the slowly crumbling barrier of language. For two years she'd been going out with an ex-schoolmate, who listened every night as she told him, in her mother tongue, about the foreigner who for some weird reason had ended up in Charkov. But gradually the mother tongue was replaced by motherly feelings. Ukrainian became the language they used to misunderstand each other, and before long their life together was so dull it had to come to an end.

She and Sam both longed for something different: she didn't want to speak Ukrainian with a boy she'd known since she was ten; and he was looking for something deeper—something he could only find in another culture and another language.

They rented an apartment together. He pampered her and spoke English to her for hours on end. Sam took his stay in Ukraine seriously, because Ukraine was different from England. He took Polina seriously, because she was different from his mother. She listened to him and didn't contradict.

Laughing with those wide-open eyes of hers, she timidly repeated the English words she'd learnt—though her pronunciation was far from English. She had no inhibitions about crying, or about making love. He would stroke her neck and ask her if she knew the English word for what he was doing.

She was a part of all that was new and unknown and unfathomed. In her he saw the headscarf worn by every Ukrainian woman, the dollars sent home by every Ukrainian abroad, the Ukrainian delight in little things, all the thrift and impulsive generosity, all the poetry and half-empty shops, all the absurd old cars on all the absurd Ukrainian streets. She had a big soul, and into it he packed everything he saw around him. In falling in love with Polina he fell in love with Ukraine—and vice-versa.

He was patient. He learnt Ukrainian and drank her relatives' vodka. He was faithful and thought about the future. He knew his place was not in Ukraine, he knew he was and would remain a foreigner, he knew he'd always have difficulty understanding and making himself understood. He talked openly about everything he thought, but there was one thought he never spoke out loud. If he had, it would have been: "We outsiders have to admire these people. They have no idea how beautiful their lives are compared with ours—or how quickly they'll ruin them if they keep copying us!" But it remained unspoken. Besides, Ukraine had no wish to hear such thoughts. Quite the reverse—Ukrainians and Polina loved the West. And Sam loved Polina! So what else could he do but start learning to love the West too—or at least stop hating it?

What else could he do but discard a thought that anyway remained unspoken and yield to Polina's admiration for everything he had turned his back on? Wasn't Polina's soul big enough to contain not just Ukraine but the whole world? And wasn't Sam the loving parent, incapable of taking away from his beloved child the toy she cuddles at bedtime? Doesn't there come a point when the loving parent starts to see the once detested toy quite differently, through the eyes of the child? Is not the power of love so great it can sweep aside common sense and replace it with all-embracing acceptance?!

For that is what their love was: all-embracing acceptance—all, that is, except Ukraine. At first their love songs were addressed to different corners of the world—Polina's to the West, Sam's to the East—but gradually their voices merged in a single deafening unison. Together they criticized Ukraine: the corruption, the squalor, the shabby people and politics. Polina spoke for both of them when she announced she wanted to get out. To Italy, or France. Anywhere but Ukraine. Yes, Ukraine was beautiful, but who'd want to live there if they didn't have to?

There's no future for us here! There's no future for me here! And you can teach English anywhere.

∞∞∞

Did he go back to the West with her? Yes. Because he loved her? No. He went back with her because he still had that vision of something he longed for.

He said he longed for something deeper, which he could only find in another culture and another language. But that wasn't strictly true.

What he really longed for was the need to make an effort, to be forced to avoid simplifications. He longed for *problems*. Ukraine had been his challenge. Now his challenge would be the West. For her sake, he told her, he would sacrifice himself.

He told her he would sacrifice himself (meaning that all of a sudden *he would have no more problems*), but in fact it was no sacrifice. He didn't care what sort of burden he shouldered; he only cared how heavy it was. He didn't care if it was a kilo of feathers or a kilo of iron.

If he was to leave, he would leave with Polina, and he could be quite sure that in the West *he would have plenty of problems*, since Polina was a Ukrainian and Sam was her lover. A relationship with a Ukrainian changed everything: going back to the West with a Ukrainian girlfriend did not mean going back to an old world of terrifying simplicity, but arriving in a new world of exciting complexity. Suddenly the feathers on the western side of the scales were heavier.

He sent letters to London inquiring about other places. "No, Ukraine is wonderful" (he wrote in reply to the questions that came back). "We just need a change. I met a girl here" (he explained). "Her whole family live here, but they all agree she should get out." He took the rings off his face and before long he told her they were going to Madrid.

∞∞∞

For the first week they lived in the school, then they stayed in a hotel for a few months. Polina spent her days strolling down the wide streets looking at shop windows; Sam went to the language school to teach Spanish children, and in the evenings explored the city on his bike.

He got by with English, but Polina spent hours on end studying Spanish. At first she shed secret tears over her Ukrainian songs, but after a while Flamenco and Spanish folk songs took their place. She bought her first Spanish newspaper, *El Mundo*, which she painstakingly attempted to translate—at first word by word with a dictionary (a paragraph over her breakfast coffee, a whole page after lunch); then without a dictionary, trying to work out the new words from their context and writing them down on a piece of paper, and only later looking them up and copying them into a little notebook, with which she then sat on the hotel balcony, committing them to memory.

They looked for an apartment in the city center—Polina had fallen in love with Madrid and wanted to live *in it*. Every time they turned up at precisely the appointed hour, and every time the queue of applicants stretched halfway down the stairs. They started turning up an hour early, but the apartments (all of which they liked) always went to someone else.

On Sundays they went to the Prado. Polina studied all the leaflets carefully before sliding them unfolded into her bag, over which she then placed a protective hand.

At first they were just worthless handouts. Later, at her request, they began buying ever more expensive booklets and catalogs. Her idea was to cover the walls with posters of famous exhibitions, reproductions of well-known paintings—but she said she wouldn't put them up until they had a place of their own. Meanwhile she stored them under the bed in the hotel.

The only thing she put up on the hotel wall was a photo of them both in Ukraine, arm in arm in front of an Orthodox church—not only to remind her of Ukraine, but most of all to remind her that the hotel they were living in was not yet Madrid, just a more bearable Ukraine. Her purpose was less nostalgic than cautionary.

ooooo

She fell in love not only with the Prado but with art *tout court*. After a few weeks in Madrid she was no longer tempted by rock concerts, preferring more intimate music like the *Goldberg Variations*. How much more sensitive this music was, how much better suited to those lonely hours she spent poring over the dictionary! It contained all the tears in the world, all the one-way tickets out of Ukraine!

That was when she wrote her first poem.

LIKE A PINCH OF SALT

Fingers linking hand and ring

Following your every move
Above the white plate
And the clink of cutlery

When she and Sam listened together to the *Goldberg Variations*, only she knew what the music meant. At such moments she thought about *real* beauty—a beauty beyond the notes of the piano, a beauty which, unlike that of Bach's music, only she could hear. She became convinced that beauty dwelt in secret things, in things she could not discuss with Sam, in her poem that only made sense in connection with Bach. That was it—her poem could only be understood when accompanied by Bach. (Conversely, Bach could only be understood in connection with the poem, written on the back page of her now almost full notebook.)

She felt like a mother who pretends to her child that the world is simple, while bearing alone the whole inexpressible weight of its complexity.

But just as a mother knows she can't keep up the pretence of simplicity forever, Polina also knew that in time others would come to see—would *have* to see—her hidden depths, just as she would come to see the depths of her own poem, however much that might hurt.

Deep down she felt that only poetry could raise her to the level of Madrid—and to other, far more exalted places.

ooooo

She soon learnt where to find *bargains*, and was amazed to discover that for fifteen minutes' worth of Sam's salary she could buy a candlestick, or for twenty a dish-rack. It was all packed away in their hotel room ready for the move, the boxes carefully stacked and marked: bathroom, kitchen, living-room (décor), bedroom (décor)

Sam's new friend and colleague from school (Bartlett) decided to move out of his place in Calle Calvario near the city center and persuaded the owner to let it to them.

Bartlett became a constant visitor—in fact their only one. Polina, though grateful, had imagined their first "family" friend somewhat differently. Without so much as a glance at her posters, or even her first attempts at painting that now covered every wall (she'd started painting just for fun, to make her feel good), he would take them off to his favorite bar just round the corner.

At Domingo's she talked about looking for work and the fantastic atmosphere of the Calle Calvario. She wore a floral skirt and short leather ankle-boots that felt wonderfully light and seemed to her just right for Madrid. She now dressed quite differently—back home she'd never really "dressed." Madrid was so much more interesting. Polina felt sure that one day she'd be walking down these streets rid at last of all her nagging thoughts and cares.

Though she put up with Bartlett, she longed for the day when, having made new and better friends, she'd be able to drop him. His shabby suit, his sarcasm, his cigarettes, his divorce—it all reminded her only too painfully of something she would rather forget. Yes, somehow it reminded her of that sense of revulsion she'd had at the sight of Sam's ring-pierced face, that sense that he was not a human being, but an animal.

∞∞∞

Soon her Spanish was better than his. When they haggled over something in a shop, it was always she who had the right expression to hand. And now it was she who stroked his hair and asked him: what's Polina doing?

One day she underlined an ad in *El Mundo* (Western Union seeks staff from Eastern Europe), and the next day she went to a tenth-floor office in central Madrid and got the job. Her desk would be like a little piece of home. Ukraine is a strategic market for Western Union—and who better to handle it than Polina? She stuck the company's advertising slogan on the fridge: *If you can't be there, your money can!* In her lunch break she sat on a bench in the park and gazed at a statue of Don Quixote and Rocinante as she munched a ham baguette.

Canaletto! Manet! Tiepolo!—Caravaggio! Prada! Prado!

∞∞∞

The first summer they went back to Ukraine for a month. Polina decided before she left not to behave like a rich daughter who'd made a good marriage in Madrid. No, she would be modest, even humble. She looked forward to giving her parents the money she'd saved; she'd eat their pickled gherkins and drink their homemade vodka; and in reply to all their questions she'd say: People are the same everywhere.

"Everything's just the same as here, *except . . .*" she told them.

The people are just the same as in Ukraine, *except . . .* And then there was no stopping her. *Maybe a little . . . Only slightly . . . but the museums! . . . the colors! Small apartment . . . love it! Safe area . . . great atmosphere! People the same as here . . .*

On that first visit she told people that the huge and total transformation in her life was in fact no more than a superficial, cosmetic change. Only the trimmings and trappings, she said, had changed. Her parents took this to mean that in the West absolutely everything was different.

When they said good-bye their cheeks were wet with tears—not so much of farewell, as of regret that the young woman who was leaving them was no longer their daughter.

∞∞∞

The second summer they had their first proper holiday, in Andalusia. They hired a car and pitched their tent at Torre del Mar. She brought back lots of tropical plants to put on the balcony, and bought cheap wooden frames for the photographs and souvenirs that soon covered the walls. In one picture they stand arm in arm, laughing, as Polina hides a broken-off sprig of geranium behind her back.

She didn't sunbathe on the beach—the Spanish sun was not good for her skin. Next time they'd go somewhere else. To be honest, Torre del Mar was a disappointment.

For as Polina sat on the beach at Torre del Mar gazing at the horizon, while her entire body gradually turned red, and she found herself fighting her disappointment—yes, that's what it was—by repeating over and over: *this is the sea . . . this is the beach . . . it's what I've always wanted, this beauty . . .* , she had to admit she didn't really care for this beach at all. Yes, she was sitting on a beach, but in reality she was still waiting for a beach. Though in fact the kind of beach she'd want to remember, the kind she'd want to come back to, probably didn't exist. If the painters in the Prado, she thought, had felt about this beach the way she did, they could not have loved it the way they did or painted those pictures of it. She was quite sure her memories of Torre del Mar would be different from their memories; she was sure her desire to return to Torre del Mar would be different from theirs. She could not imagine anyone painting with love what she was now experiencing.

She didn't get a tan, but she did get something important from that holiday: the feeling, for the first time, that if it were not for Sam she might be sitting on a different, more beautiful beach, far over the horizon.

One day, looking up from her notebook over the balcony rail as she struggled to recite lists of newly learned words, a poem came to her. She wrote it down on the back of her notebook. Spontaneously, her hand began to describe the state of her soul.

THE TIME WE HAD

was a rolling wave on an endless sea.
Suddenly
the wave reaches the shore.
It stops, as if to leap,
then breaks and rushes back,
and always takes something away.

She decided not to show it to anybody. The poem would remain her secret—not just because it was profound and Polina needed to keep her world simple, but because it would inevitably, and very painfully, *destroy* that simplicity. She would have to give Sam more time.

Da.

Da.

Da.

The Noble School

BY MUHAREM BAZDULJ

(TRANSLATION BY JOHN K. COX)

In the spring of 1989, when the Berlin Wall was still solidly upright, I read John Le Carré for the first time. I was probably too young for such literature, but I loved detective stories; I had read through all the translations of Agatha Christie that were available to me and then someone had recommended Le Carré. I liked his works right away, in that way that first impressions have: the atmosphere was familiar to me from the James Bond movies, but somehow here it seemed more grounded, more intellectual. When you like to read as a twelve-year-old boy, you are already aware that the acrobatics of Secret Agent 007 are closer to fantasy than to reality. But yet: you are drawn to the cloak-and-dagger milieu, to this format in which the individual can influence global politics and history. And it's also appealing when you recognize your own surroundings in the midst of a plot filled with global conflicts. In Agatha Christie's books (let's take *Murder on the Orient Express*, for example), and in the Bond films (for instance, *From Russia with Love*), and in the novels of John Le Carré (*The Little Drummer Girl*, to name just one)—in these works, a major part of the action takes place on the territory of Yugoslavia. In all of the above-named works, Yugoslavia is a kind of transition zone, a "no-man's-land" that the protagonists must traverse on their way from East to West or vice-versa. Yes, Yugoslavia—in the context of the Cold War—was like one of the monsters in a Coleridge poem: East-in-West, or West-in-East. Naturally, as a twelve-year-old you don't think in these categories but you simply revel in the story and in the recognition of toponyms which are familiar to you from your own life and experience. By European standards, Yugoslavia was not a small country, either in terms of area or population; nevertheless, from the vantage point of its inhabitants, it was experienced as small, probably because the country was a federation of small countries that were not aware that the whole is greater than the sum of its parts. And just as denizens of a village or town rejoice when they meet someone from their home region in a metropolis, Yugoslavs were happy whenever foreign authors mentioned their country.

In the Cold War constellation, the Yugoslavs did not perceive themselves as Easterners or Westerners, or perhaps it is more accurate to say that they alternated between feeling themselves to be sometimes Eastern and sometimes Western. Relative to the Hungarians, Romanians, and Bulgarians, who could not travel abroad freely and in whose drab shops there were no cans of Coca-Cola or bars of imported chocolate, we were the West. In comparison to Germany, France, or Great Britain, we were poor and burdened with the imprint of ideology on everyday life—in a word, we were the East. From this position, one did not approach the plots of Cold War-inspired fiction in a partisan manner. With the benefit of hindsight, I would say that this was the source of Le Carré's colossal popularity in the Yugoslavia of the 1980s. The intricate construction of his novels, in which the opposition of East and West was not black-and-white, approximated the prevailing feeling among Yugoslavs. From the Yugoslav standpoint, the Cold War was like a football match in which the team you would usually root for is not playing; at the beginning you are neutral (or, like us, "non-aligned"), but over the course of the match you take joy in the good moves of a player from one or the other team, and your sympathies typically lie with whatever side that is currently the underdog.

From the spring of 1989 on, I was falling in love with Le Carré's books. In the autumn of that year—I remember that I was reading *The Spy Who Came in from the Cold*—the Berlin Wall fell. I was probably too young and I did not think that the destruction of some wall somewhere far away to the west could have any bearing whatsoever on my life. Elementary school would soon be coming to an end, puberty had me all shaken up, and the end of childhood was making itself felt; I was preparing to go off to high school.

In Travnik, my home town, the word *gimnazija*—meaning a "classical or university prep high school, or a *lycée*—has a special ring to it. It is the biggest building in the city, and the oldest one built in the Western style. It was constructed in 1883, only five years after the Habsburg Empire occupied Bosnia-Hercegovina. Chartered as a city in the fifteenth century, in the final decades of the existence of the independent Bosnian state, Travnik took shape as a city over the four hundred years that Bosnia was ruled by the Ottoman Empire. For the major part of those four centuries, Travnik was the capital of the Bosnian *vilayet*, that is, the capital of the province of Bosnia inside the Ottoman Empire. And when, in the first half of the nineteenth century, a group of Bosnian beys and other notables launched a rebellion for greater autonomy within the Empire and, ultimately, for independence, they also proclaimed Travnik their capital. At the outset of the nineteenth century, while Travnik was serving as the Bosnian capital, the French under Napoleon opened a consulate, and the Austrians followed suit. Scarcely twenty years before the coming of Austria-Hungary, the seat of the vizier, who was in essence the governor of the Bosnian *vilayet*, was transferred to Sarajevo. Then the Habsburgs stuck Sarajevo into the role of Bosnia's capital city.

The Society of Jesus came to Bosnia along with the Austro-Hungarian Empire. It was in Travnik—perhaps following in the footsteps of bygone glories—that these Jesuits founded the Archdiocesan Lyceum, which was soon better known as the Travnik high school. Although it was founded under the aegis of the Catholic Church, the school was open from the start to all pupils, with no consideration of their religious affiliation (except for those who happened to be Catholics). That is to say, it was also open to Jews, Muslims, and Orthodox. We might add that Skender Kulenović, one of the finest Bosnian Muslim poets, graduated from there. But although the Nobel laureate Ivo Andrić was born into a Catholic family in Travnik, he did not attend the high school. He moved away from Travnik with his mother while he was still a child, although life and literature both continued to link him to his home town. The best proof of this is the novel—perhaps his most famous—*Travnička hronika*,[1] with its subtitle *The Days of the Consuls*.

---

1. *Travnička hronika*: This title translates literally as "The Chronicle of Travnik," but the novel was first published in English translation by Joseph Hitrec in 1963 as *Bosnian Chronicle*. Another English translation, by Celia Hawkesworth and Bogdan Rakić, was published in 1992 as *The Days of the Consuls*.

This novel has as its subject that very decade from the early 1800s when the French and Austrian consulates were up and running in Travnik.

There was one dimension of Le Carré's novels that I liked from the beginning: the important role played in them by diplomats and diplomatic missions. The manner in which consuls mingle with spies, the way crucial decisions are mixed up with world-altering gambits fashioned behind the thick walls of embassies and official residences—these things were seductive. As with Le Carré, diplomacy was not merely a literary theme in the life of Ivo Andrić. From the time he was twenty-eight years old until he was fifty, a period of time corresponding to the entire interwar era, Andrić was an official in the Ministry of Foreign Affairs of the Kingdom of Yugoslavia; he served in embassies and consulates in the Vatican, Bucharest, Trieste, Graz, Marseilles, and Madrid, and his last diplomatic posting was in Berlin. At the end of the 1930s and the start of the 1940s, Andrić was, to be specific,

Sjemenište Gymnasium

the Yugoslav ambassador to Hitler's Germany. In 1941 his life began to resemble the (at that point obviously unwritten) novels of Le Carré. Behind his back, and in point of fact without his knowledge, Yugoslavia was negotiating accession to the Tripartite Pact. As part of his official duties, however, Andrić did have to attend the signing ceremony. The news about the conclusion of the pact led to a popular uprising in Yugoslavia. On the streets of Belgrade demonstrations began, with the masses shouting "Better war than this pact!" and "We prefer graves to being slaves!" Prince Paul, who had signed the pact, abdicated, and an enraged Hitler attacked the Kingom; it barely took him ten days to overrun it. In the occupied country, the Communist Party, headed by Josip Broz Tito, would call into being a guerrilla movement, and Yugoslavia would emerge from the Second World War as a communist country.

In the years following the end of the war, the position of the Communists towards the religious communities, especially the Catholic Church, was hostile. The Jesuits left Travnik, but the high school remained in their old building. At the time of the fall of the Berlin Wall, it was named for one Antun Mavrak, but everyone still referred to it as the Travnik high school. Incidentally, it was rumored that its name would soon be changed, that it would lose its affiliation with Antun Mavrak. He had been a Communist, and Yugoslavia was rapidly renouncing everything connected to Communism.

Antun Mavrak was born in Travnik in 1899. The Serbian essayist Isidor Sekulić, discussing the Russian writer Alexander Pushkin (who was born a century earlier, in 1799), noted that it is not by chance that Pushkin was born in a year that is "suspended above the summit of a century." Indeed, years such as that hold an exalted place in the world of literature. In the same year that witnessed Mavrak's birth, Jorge Luis Borges and Vladimir Nabokov were also born. Mavrak's life, however, represents a perfect subject for a writer whose poetics put him in the company of Borges and Nabokov: I am thinking here of Danilo Kiš. Karl Georgievich Taube, the hero of Kiš's tale "Magic Card-dealing" (from the collection entitled *A Tomb for Boris Davidovich*) was born in Austria-Hungary in 1899. Taube finished high school in Esztergom, his home town in Hungary; Mavrak graduated from the Archdiocesan Lyceum in Travnik. Both of them longed for the day when they would "see their cities for the last time, from the perspective of a

departing bird in flight, the way people look through a magnifying glass at desiccated and ludicrously yellowed butterflies in an album from high school days—with melancholy and nausea." Both of them left for the West as soon as they could: Taube went to Vienna, Mavrak to Zagreb. Mavrak rose quickly in Communist circles there, and by the middle of the 1920s he had already become secretary of the Regional Committee of the Communist Party for Croatia. His code name was Kerber. In 1926, at the party conference in Križevci, he was introduced to Josip Broz, who in those days was simply a party activist from the provinces. It was only one year later, when Broz, along with his wife and child, was living on the street in Zagreb, without any means of support, that Mavrak placed his apartment at the other man's disposal. In 1929, Mavrak was forced to emigrate to Vienna, and two years later he was exiled to France. In the middle of the 1930s, exactly like Taube in the story by Kiš, Mavrak ended up in Moscow. This was the era of Stalin's purges, and communists from abroad were one of the most frequent targets. Both the fictional Karl Georgevich Taube and the historical Antun Mavrak felt the blows of the purges. Taube, as we learn in the story, survived twenty years on the Golgotha of the Gulag, only to be killed when he was free again, something that was part of the camps' "magical card dealing." Mavrak had most likely already been killed in the late 1930s, on the eve of World War II.

In April, 1941, when the Second World War reached Yugoslavia, Ivo Andrić and the staff of the Yugoslav embassy in Berlin were first forced to go to the city of Konstanz, near the Swiss border. Soon Andrić decided to return to occupied Belgrade. At that time, approaching the fiftieth year of his life, Andrić was almost better known as a diplomat than as a writer, although he did have two or three books of stories under his belt. Then, in the three years of his self-imposed "house arrest" in Belgrade, he wrote three novels: *Travnička hronika*, *Na Drini ćuprija*, and *Gospođica*.[2] Despite invitations from the quisling regime of Milan Nedić, Andrić played no role in public life during the occupation and he even forbade the reprinting of the stories that had appeared earlier. In 1945, as soon as the war was over and Yugoslavia was liberated, Andrić published the three novels mentioned above. The Communists already held all the levers of power, and Andrić was neither respectful of the canonical prescriptions of socialist realism nor on close terms with the new authorities because of his earlier diplomatic work. Yet these three novels were among the very first works published in socialist Yugoslavia. At any rate, Andrić did not leave his house for the first few days after the cessation of hostilities. As part of a propaganda campaign mounted by the Communist authorities, who intended to remind the populace of the collusion of the earlier Yugoslav government with Nazi Germany, enormous documentary photographs were placed along the streets of Belgrade. At Terazije, a square in the center of the city, a billboard was put up with photos of the Yugoslavs signing the Tripartite Pact. On this colossal picture, Ivo Andrić's face could clearly be seen. In the spring of 1945, Andrić could not but interpret this billboard as a "wanted" poster. One day later that spring, however, Milovan Djilas, a high-ranking Communist official and later a prominent dissident—at that time he was actually the heir apparent to Tito—called Andrić on the telephone and asked whether he needed anything. Andrić requested the delivery of some tobacco to his address and—if possible—the removal from Terazije of the photo that included his face. An hour later he got his tobacco, and the photograph was taken down that same night.

Three years later, Djilas was at Tito's side when Tito stood up to Stalin. That famous "NO!" to the Soviet leader echoed around the world, and thanks

A VIEW OF THE GYMNAZIJA IN TRAVNIK (opposite page, credit: Zavicajni Muzej Travnik)

---

2. *Na Drini ćuprija*: Published in English translation by Lovett F. Edwards in 1959 as *The Bridge on the Drina; Gospođica*: Published in English translation by Joseph Hitrec in 1965 as *The Woman from Sarajevo*.

to it Yugoslav socialism took on more humane contours. Over the four subsequent decades the Yugoslavs did not perceive themselves either as Easterners or as Westerners, but rather perhaps as eastern Westerners or western Easterners. If Stalin had lived longer, if the split with the USSR had remained definitive, then perhaps Yugoslavia would have formally become a part of the West by means of the introduction of a multi-party system (which, we should note, none other than Djilas had championed). After Stalin's death in 1953, however, relations with the Soviet Union improved, although they never again returned to a state comparable to that before 1948. Tito utilized his first meeting with Khrushchev to inquire about the fates of 113 Yugoslav Communists whom Stalin had sent to the camps during the purges of the 1930s. Khrushchev promised to investigate, and two days later he told Tito: "*Tochno sto njetu*," or "Precisely one hundred of them are no longer with us." Thirteen of them had been fortunate, but among the hundred who had perished was Antun Mavrak, born in a year ending in the number "99."

Aside from the high school to which they affixed his name, Antun Mavrak also received a monument in Travnik. This monument stands in the heart of the city, and I used to pass by it pretty much every day. A few months after the Berlin Wall was torn down, somebody took a rock and smashed the nose on Mavrak's white, commemorative face. There was nothing at all extraordinary about this in the Yugoslavia of those years; it more or less counted as a harmless incident. All across the country, monuments to Partisans and Communists were being removed or battered or even detonated. The break-up of the country was announced symbolically by the explosives placed beneath the memorials to the creators of socialist Yugoslavia.

The renunciation of the patrimony of socialism, along with the abandonment of the federal government, spread most slowly of all in Bosnia, more slowly than in any of the other six republics. Colloquially Bosnia was known as "Little Yugoslavia" and its coat of arms bore, in contrast to all the other republics, not some historically attested symbol but two factory smokestacks. Even while Yugoslavia was still whole, all the other republics formally dumped the word "socialist" from their names, but Bosnia did not; this same inertia made it possible for a high school to remain named after Antun Mavrak even while, in other regions, streets and institutions named for Communist functionaries were being hastily altered.

In the spring of 1992, two and one-half years after the Wall came down, I read Le Carré's *The Honorable Schoolboy*. I had finished elementary school and was getting ready to take the entrance exam for the *gimnazija*. It wasn't easy to get accepted into Travnik's high school. As much as I tried to occupy myself with the obligations and worries of a typical teenager, the clamor of the outside world was too loud to ignore. There had been military conflicts the previous summer and fall in Slovenia and Croatia; right at New Year's, astride the transition from 1991 to 1992, a cease-fire had been signed. None-theless everybody was saying that fighting would break out in Bosnia, too. I had begun to find something comforting in Le Carré's novels. In them the threat that the Cold War would become a real war was constantly in the air, but it never materialized. One April afternoon, however, as I was walking towards the school to see if the date of the entrance examinations had been announced, the city's outdoor warning sirens went off.

The war began, and in the next few days the school was turned into a refu-gee center. From west-central Bosnia, from Prijedor, Sanski Most, and Ključ, from those areas in which concentration camps had been set up, shocking the viewers of CNN—from there the refugees came every day. Now refugees were sleeping in those spacious classrooms with blackboards on the walls.

Only part of the building, perhaps a fifth, remained for its original pur-pose, and the new school year started in 1993 instead of 1992. Although overflowing with refugees and exposed to almost daily shelling, only a few of the flames of war reached Travnik, especially when you compare it to certain other Bosnian cities. And so we were able, albeit with a year's delay, to start high school. No one really knew what the school's official name was at the moment, or even whether any legitimate decision had been made to "eliminate" the name Antun Mavrak. Although the war did hasten the formal renunciation of our Communist heritage, people still felt a powerful sense of nostalgia for the Communist days: times of peace, the certain avail-ability of jobs, relative prosperity, social equality, and free health care and education. In offices here and there, and in some classrooms, Tito's picture still hung on the wall.

The war in Bosnia lasted four years, my four high school years. It left its mark on the entire final decade of the twentieth century for, after all, the war in Kosovo and the bombing of Serbia by NATO in 1999 were essential parts of this same war. The highly regarded Yugoslav singer-songwriter, Đorđe Balašević, wrote a song about this decade entitled "The '90s." It depicts the 1990s as a terrifying period, the most miserable one imaginable. This song's refrain actually starts with the line: "So go fuck yourselves, Nineties!" On

LETTER SENT BY

BOB DOLE (R-KANSAS)

to prominent dissident

Mihajlo Mihajlov, who was

"public enemy number one"

in Tito's Yugoslavia, and for

whose release from prison

the Senator, and Amnesty

International, had lobbied

hard. June 23, 1978.

(opposite page, credit:

OSA Archivum)

the other hand, foreigners whom I have met since the war have in general spoken of those same years as "the happy '90s." The West perceived that decade as a period of triumph; the East experienced it as a time of connection with the more fortunate part of the world. Left holding the bag were those who did not feel like Easterners or Westerners; the ones who paid were those who swung back and forth between perceiving themselves to be at times Easterners and at other times Westerners. It was Yugoslavia that paid the bill, and above all it was precisely the most Yugoslav part of Yugoslavia that did so: Bosnia.

And now, when we speak of freedom of movement, the situation is completely inverted. The majority of erstwhile Yugoslavs are today held captive by the visa regime, and younger generations are growing up in a kind of isolation comparable to what existed in Romania or Bulgaria over twenty years ago. But now Romania and Bulgaria are members of the European Union, and by that very criterion they are part of the West, without regard for the fact that, geographically speaking, they are situated to the east of Bosnia.

The memory of the era prior to the demolition of the Berlin Wall is, for most Bosnians, bound up with nostalgia. And thinking back to those times reminds me of how we hearken back to our school days: as the saying goes, we only remember the good parts.

In the spring of 2009, twenty years after first reading Le Carré, I was invited to dinner in the Sarajevo residence of an ambassador from one of Europe's constitutional monarchies. I had been asked to similar evening gatherings before; typically there are various diplomats and politicians around, and a lot of discussion of the lingering crisis in Bosnia. The attendance of writers and journalists was likely desired for the sake of diversity of perspective. Whenever I walk into ambassadors' residences, I always think of Le Carré and my childhood awe at the mysteries of that world. I probably think back to my childhood because on those occasions I am ordinarily the youngest of all the people there. This time, though, a blonde woman, twenty-five at the most, stood out among the middle-aged diplomats and politicians. She looked like a young Laura Linney. When we introduced ourselves, she said her name was Sabina. The dinner proceeded as such affairs typically do: hors d'oeuvres, soup, main course, dessert. Wine accompanied each course, along with conversation, in English of course, about local political news and global developments (this time the focus was on Barack Obama and the economic crisis). I did not talk much, and Sabina did not speak up at all, although she did follow the conversation attentively, sometimes nodding her head and smiling politely. After the meal, we all moved to the *salon* for coffee and cognac. There, Sabina and I sat down opposite each other and rapidly switched to nonpolitical subjects. She said that she was twenty-three years old and near the end of her undergraduate studies. The Ministry of Foreign Affairs of her country ran a rolling open competition for junior staff positions in its embassies around the world. She had applied first of all for positions in New York and Vienna; both times she made the short list but was not selected. Then she applied for the embassy in Sarajevo and was accepted. She had

BOB DOLE
KANSAS

United States Senate
WASHINGTON, D.C. 20510

June 23, 1978

SPECIAL COMMITTEES:
AGRICULTURE, NUTRITION, AND FORESTRY
BUDGET
FINANCE

SELECT AND SPECIAL COMMITTEE:
NUTRITION AND HUMAN NEEDS

Mr. Mihaylo Mihaylov
3921 5th Street, N. Apt. 2
Arlington, Virginia 22203

Dear Mr. Mihaylov:

I was delighted to have the opportunity to speak with you and exchange ideas about the Human Rights situation in Yugoslavia and about the Helsinki Agreement. I agree that a great deal more could have been accomplished had the West taken a firmer stand. It is also unfortunate that the situation in Yugoslavia has been largely ignored by the West. I hope your meeting with the staff members at the Helsinki Commission was helpful in rectifying this situation.

I also want to thank you for the copy of your book Underground Notes with your gracious inscription.

Sincerely yours,

BOB DOLE
United States Senate

BD: afm

arrived three weeks ago and liked it here. At that point she halted and said with a smile, "So why aren't we talking in Bosnian?" And the question was delivered in that language, in perfect Bosnian, without a foreign accent of any type. For a moment I thought that she had learned the language in the three weeks since arriving, that in her Ministry she had undergone training of the type that spies in novels by Le Carré go through. She laughed out loud and said: I was born in Bosnia. In Ključ. At that point I was thinking she must have left the country, gone up there to go to school, acquired citizenship, and stayed. But she added, "When the war started, I was six. I barely remember it, but we fled. First to Travnik, where we stayed for several months. Then the whole family—my parents, my two sisters, and I—left for points north. And we stayed."

I'm from Travnik, I stated, overjoyed as if I were meeting someone from my homeland somewhere halfway across the globe. Really? she continued. I barely remember anything about Travnik, but I do recall that they put us up in a school, one of those big old noble ones. We both began laughing when I told her that I had attended that same school. All eyes in the *salon* were upon us; the politicians and the diplomats in their dark suits, with their ties and their white shirts, were looking at us through the lenses of their spectacles, astonished and tense, the way you look when you are trying to see through a curtain.

CONTRIBUTORS

Linda Asher, a former editor of the *New Yorker*, is a translator and a Chevalier of the French government's Order of Arts and Letters. She has translated Victor Hugo, Georges Simenon, Martin Winckler, and Milan Kundera, among others.

Alexei Bayer is a New York-based economist and writer. His literary work has appeared in the *Kenyon Review*, *New England Review* and other journals. A collection of his short stories, *Eurotrash*, was published by OGI, Moscow in 2004.

Muharem Bazdulj (born in Travnik in 1977) is one of the leading writers of the younger generation from the former Yugoslavia. He is the author of ten books of fiction, nonfiction, and poetry, including his award-winning short story collection *The Second Book*, published by Northwestern University Press.

Andrew Bromfield is the translator of the works of Boris Akunin, Vladimir Voinovich, Irina Denezhkina, Victor Pelevin, and Sergei Lukyanenko, among others. Bromfield is also the founding editor of the Russian literature journal *Glas*.

Mircea Cărtărescu is a Romanian poet and novelist. Once a Romanian language teacher, Cărtărescu now teaches Romanian literary history at the University of Bucharest.

Melvyn Clarke was born 1956 in Manchester, England. He graduated in Czech and Slovak at the School of Slavonic and East European Studies (now part of University College London) in 1982. He has been living and working as a teacher and translator in the Prague area since 1990.

John K. Cox, a professor of history at North Dakota State University in Fargo, is the author of historical works on Serbia and Slovenia and has translated novels by Danilo Kiš and Ivan Cankar. He is currently writing a study of the fiction of Ismail Kadaré.

Ellen Elias-Bursać has translated works by several Yugoslavian writers, including David Albahari's *Götz and Meyer*, for which she was awarded the ALTA National Translation Award in 2006. She also received the AATSEEL Award in 1998 for her translation of Albahari's *Words Are Something Else*.

Péter Esterházy, a member of one of Europe's most prominent aristocratic families, was born in Budapest in 1950. His books include *Helping Verbs of the Heart, She Loves Me, A Little Hungarian Pornography, The Book of Hrabal, Celestial Harmonies*, and *Revised Edition*—the last two of which focused on his relationship to his father and his father's family within the framework of Hungary's turbulent twentieth-century history.

In addition to translation, **Jamey Gambrell** works as a writer on Russian art and culture. She has translated many works, including those of Marina Tsvetaeva, Aleksandr Rodchenko, Tatyana Tolstaya, and Vladimir Sorokin.

Keith Gessen was born in Russia and educated at Harvard and Syracuse. He is the founding editor of the magazine *n+1* and author of the novel *All the Sad Young Literary Men*.

Masha Gessen, a Russian author and journalist, was born in 1967. Forced to leave Russia in 1981 due to state-enforced anti-Semitism, in 1994 she returned to Moscow, where she writes for the magazine *Itogi* and the journal *Matador*. She is the author of several works, including *Blood Matters* and *Ester and Ruzya: How My Grandmothers Survived Hiler's War and Stalin's Peace*.

Klara Glowczewska is the Editor in Chief of *Condé Nast Traveler*. She has translated several books by Ryszard Kapuściński, including his final work, *Travels With Herodotus*.

Annett Gröschner, who grew up in the former GDR, is a freelance writer and journalist who lives in Berlin. She has published several books, including the semi-autobiographical novel *Moskauer Eis*. Her latest is the essay collection *Parzelle Paradies*.

Durs Grünbein has been hailed as the most significant and successful poet to emerge from the former East Germany. He won Germany's most coveted literary award, the Georg Büchner Prize, in 1995 when he was only thirty-three. A selection of his poetry was published in an English translation by Michael Hofmann in 2005. Grünbein's haiku collection *Lob des Taifuns* came out in German and Japanese in 2009.

Leigh Hafrey is a professor of ethics at the MIT Sloan School of Management. His essays, reviews, and translations have appeared in several American and European periodicals, including the *New York Times*. In addition to novels by Peter Schneider, he has also translated Marguerite Duras.

Zbigniew Herbert (1924-1998) was a spiritual leader of the anti-communist movement in Poland. His work has been translated into almost every European language, and he won numerous prizes, including the Jerusalem Prize and the T. S. Eliot Prize. His books include

Selected Poems, *Report from the Besieged City and Other Poems*, *Mr. Cogito*, *Still Life with a Bridle*, and *King of the Ants*.

Stefan Heym (1913-2001) was a prolific German novelist and essayist who lived in the United States during the Nazi years and in East Germany after 1952. Some of his most famous works include the novels *The Architects*, *Five Days in June*, and *The King David Report*. An independent-minded socialist, Heym was equally well known as dissident, social critic, and author, and he was elected to the German Bundestag (federal parliament) as a delegate from Berlin in 1994.

Paweł Huelle is a novelist, playwright, and journalist who has lived most of his life in Gdansk. He is the author of several novels, including *Mercedes-Benz*, *The Last Supper*, and *Castorp*, all of which have been translated into English.

Radu Ioanid was born in Bucharest, Romania. He is the author of several books on Romanian history and the Holocaust, including *Sword of the Archangel*, *The Holocaust in Romania*, and *The Ransom of the Jews: The Story of the Extraordinary Secret Bargain Between Romania and Israel*. He works as Director of International Archival Programs Division at the U.S. Holocaust Memorial Museum.

Irakli Iosebashvili was born in Tbilisi, Georgia, grew up in New York City, and now lives in Moscow, where he is an editor at the *Moscow Times*.

Annie Janusch is a German translator and an editor at the Center for the Art of Translation in San Francisco.

Eugen Jebeleanu (1911-1991) was one of Romania's most important twentieth-century poets. He published over twelve collections of poems, received numerous prestigious European literary awards (including the Italian Taormina Prize and the Austrian Herder Prize), and in the 1970s was nominated by the Romanian Academy for the Nobel Prize. The translations in this book are from his final collection, *Secret Weapon: The Late Poems of Eugen Jebeleanu* (Coffee House Press, 2007), and mark the first appearance of his work in English.

Wladimir Kaminer is a Russian-born German short story writer. Though Russian was his first language, Kaminer writes only in German, often about the struggles faced by Russian immigrants to Germany.

Michael Kandel is an author and an editor at the Modern Language Association. In addition to translating the works of Stanisław Lem, he has also translated Jacek Dukaj, Marek Huberath, and Andrzej Sapkowski.

The leading Polish journalist of his time, **Ryszard Kapuściński** (1932-2007) was also a poet, photographer, and author. His best known works are *The Emperor*, *Shah of Shahs*, and *Imperium*, which is about the final days of the Soviet Union.

Stanislav Komárek was born in South Bohemia in 1958, and from 1983 to 1990 he lived in exile in Austria and Germany. He is the author of five books of essays, a book of poems, and three novels. He was awarded the Tom Stoppard Award for Belles Lettres in 2005 and currently teaches Philosophy and the History of Science at Charles University.

Mihály Kornis is a Hungarian writer from Budapest. He has worked in theater, radio, art, film, social work, and politics. He is the winner of the 1987 Book of the Year Award and For the Literature of the Future Prize.

The Franco-Czech novelist **Milan Kundera** was born in Brno, the Czech Republic, and has lived in France, his second homeland, since 1975. He is the author of the novels *The Book of Laughter and Forgetting*, *The Unbearable Lightness of Being*, and *Immortality*, and his several nonfiction works include *The Art of the Novel* and *Testaments Betrayed*.

Christhard Läpple has a Master's degree in journalism, politics, and history at the Free University of Berlin. The editor of *Aspekte*, he has also directed numerous documentaries and written the book *Betrayal Has No Expiration Date*. He has received several awards for his journalism, and he lives with his family in Berlin.

Ingrid Lansford holds a Ph.D in English from the University of Texas at Austin. Her prose translations from Danish, English, and German have appeared in over a dozen journals and anthologies. She received the Leif and Inger Sjöberg Translation Prize from the American-Scandinavian Foundation in 2004 and a grant from Denmark's Kunststyrelsen in 2007.

Oana Sanziana Marian was born in 1979 in Romania and emigrated to the United States as an eight-year-old. She received a Master's degree in poetry from the Johns Hopkins Writing Seminars in 2004, after which she returned to Romania for two years to live and work in the film industry. Her first short film *Sunset* was selected by international film festivals in the U.S. and Europe.

Dorota Masłowska's first novel, *Snow White and Russian Red*, won the Paszport Prize in 2002, and her second, *The Queen's Peacock*, won the Nike Prize, Poland's highest literary honor, in 2006. She is also the author of two critically acclaimed plays.

Benjamin Paloff is a poetry editor at *Boston Review* and is Assistant Professor of Slavic Languages and Literatures and of Comparative Literature at the University of Michigan. His most recent translation is Marek Bieńczyk's *Tworki*.

Victor Pelevin is the author of several novels, including *Omon Ra, The Sacred Book of the Werewolf*, and *Buddha's Little Finger*. In 1992, his collection of short stories, *The Blue Lantern and Other Stories*, was awarded the first annual Russian Little Booker Prize.

Steven Rendall has translated more than fifty books from French and German, two of which have won major translation prizes. He is professor emeritus of Romance Languages at the University of Oregon and editor emeritus of Comparative Literature. He currently lives in France.

After reading modern languages at Cambridge, then at Edinburgh in his native Scotland, **Robert Russell** taught English in Germany and Greece before moving to Prague in 1991, where he now divides his time between teaching at Charles University School of Translation Studies and freelance translating. He is currently working on Miloš Urban's "Prague Gothic novel" *Sedmikosteli*.

Ivan Sanders is an adjunct assistant professor of Slavic languages at Columbia University. He has translated several works including György Konrád's *The City Builder* and Milan Fust's *The Story of My Wife: The Reminiscences of Captain Storr*.

Dmitri Savitski is the author of several books, including *Les Hommes Doubles* and *L'anti Guide de Moscou*, which were written published under the pseudonyms Alexandre Dimov and Dimitri Savitski-Dimov. Savitski has also written several collections of short stories, including *Six Stories* and *From Nowhere with Love*. *Waltz for K* is his first novel to be translated into English.

Liesl Schillinger is a book critic for the *New York Times*, and she writes on the arts for a variety of other publications.

Born in 1940, **Peter Schneider** is a writer and a political activist. During the 1960s he helped organize the Berlin student movement and prepare the Springer-Tribunal, while his 1973 novel *Lenz* became a cult text for the left. His other works include *The Wall Jumper*, *The German Comedy*, and *Eduard's Homecoming*. Schneider has been the Roth Distinguished Writer-in-Residence at Georgetown University since 2001, and he currently lives in Berlin.

Julian Semilian is a translator, poet, novelist, and filmmaker. He has written various works, including *A Spy in Amnesia* and *Osiris with a Trombone Across the Seam of Insubstance*. He has translated works by Paul Celan, Gherasim Luca, and Mircea Cărtărescu.

Kingsley Shorter has worked as an interpreter in Paris, and he also works as a German translator. He translated Dmitri Savitski's *Waltz for K* into English.

Dan Sociu is a member of the younger generation of Romanian poets, the so-called "2000 Generation." His published works include the poetry collections *well-stopped jars, cash for one more week*; *brother louse*; *eXcessive songs*; and the novel *Urbancholia*. In 2003, he was awarded the Mihai Eminescu Prize and the Romanian-Canadian Ronald Gasparic Prize.

Judith Sollosy is senior editor at Corvina Books, Budapest, and university lecturer on literary translation and creative writing. In addition to the work of Péter Esterházy, she is also the translator of Mihály Kornis, György Konrád, István Örkény, and Lajos Parti Nagy.

Vladimir Sorokin is a Russian novelist and playwright. He has written eleven novels, and he is the winner of numerous prizes, including the 2001 Andrei Bely Award for outstanding contributions to Russian literature.

Andrzej Stasiuk is the author of *The Walls of Hebron*, *White Raven*, *Dukla*, *Tales of Galicia*, and *Nine*, among other books. In 2005, he received the Nike Award, one of Poland's highest literary honors.

Uwe Tellkamp is a German writer and physician. Before the fall of communism, he was briefly prohibited from studying medicine and imprisoned when he refused to break up a demonstration in October 1989. In 2008 Tellkamp was awarded the German Book Prize for his novel *Der Turm* (*The Tower*), which describes life in 1980s East Germany.

Born in 1970, **Maxim Trudolubov** edits the opinion and comments page for *Vedomosti*, Russia's leading independent business daily. Trudolubov has a regular column in *Vedomosti* and his pieces focus on culture and history. He also appears on *Echo Moskvy*, an independent radio station. He is the recipient of a 2009 World Fellowship from Yale University.

Dubravka Ugresic is the author of several works of fiction, including *The Museum of Unconditional Surrender* and *The Ministry of Pain*, and several essay collections most recently *Thank You for Not Reading*. In 1991, when war broke out in the former Yugoslavia, Ugresic took a firm anti-nationalistic stand and was proclaimed a "traitor," a "public enemy," and a "witch," and was exposed to harsh and persistent media harassment. As a result, she left Croatia in 1993 and currently lives in Amsterdam.

Alissa Valles is a poet and translator whose work has appeared in the *Antioch Review*, the *Iowa Review*, *Ploughshares*, *Poetry*, *TriQuarterly*, and *Verse*. In addition to the work of Zbigniew Herbert, she has translated Ryszard Krynicki and her translations have appeared in various publications, including the *New Yorker* and the *New York Review of Books*.

Paul Wilson lived in Czechoslovakia from 1967 to 1977, when he was expelled by the Communist regime for his involvement with The Plastic People of the Universe. He has translated work by many major Czech writers, including Václav Havel, Bohumil Hrabal, Ivan Klíma, and Josef Škvorecký, into English. His most recent book is a translation of Havel's presidential memoirs, *To the Castle and Back*.

David Zábranský has worked as a human rights lawyer for numerous NGOs. His first novel, *Slabost pro každou jinou pláž (Any Beach but This)*, was awarded the prestigious Magnesia Litera prize for debut of the year in 2007. He lives in Prague and Southern Bohemia.

Matthew Zapruder is the author of two collections of poetry: *American Linden* and *The Pajamaist*, as well as co-translator from Romanian, along with Radu Ioanid, of *Secret Weapon: Selected Late Poems of Eugen Jebeleanu*. His poems, essays and translations have appeared in many publications, including the *Boston Review*, *Fence*, *Alaska Quarterly Review*, *Open City*, *Bomb*, *Harvard Review*, *Paris Review*, *New Yorker* and *New Republic*. His third book of poems, *Come On All You Ghosts*, is forthcoming from Copper Canyon in 2010. He lives in San Francisco, works as an editor for Wave Books, and teaches in the low residency MFA program at UC Riverside–Palm Desert.

Winfried Hammann (pp. 1, 76, 111, 113, 125, 129).

Brian Rose. Full-color images are available on his website at www.brianrose.com/lostborder.htm (pp. 102, 103, 104, 105, 106, 108).

Bundesbehörde für die Stasi-Unterlagen der ehemaligen DDR (pp. 1, 154, 156, 157, 159).

Oana Sanziana Marian (pp. 1, 107, 169, 170, 173).

From the personal surveillance files of László Péter, renowned literary historian and former professor at the University of Szeged (pp. 139, 140, 141, 143, 144).

From the book *Ivan Martin Jirous: Pravdivy pribeh Plastic People*. With thanks to Publishing house Torst, Prague (pp. 90, 91, 92, 97).

Respekt (pp. 4, 7, 101).

István Orosz (pp. 119, 137).

Zavicajni Muzej Travnik (pp. 225, 226).

Kiddy Citny (p. 79).

Walter Gaudnek (pp. 100).

Lidové noviny, Edice Archy (109).

Words without Borders, founded in 2003, opens doors to international exchange through translation, publication, and promotion of the best international literature. Words without Borders publishes selected prose and poetry in its monthly online magazine, and in print anthologies, develops materials to facilitate the use of foreign literature in high school and college classrooms, and stages events that connect foreign writers to the general public and media.

www.wordswithoutborders.org

∞∞∞

Open Letter—the University of Rochester's nonprofit, literary translation press—is one of only a handful of publishing houses dedicated to increasing access to world literature for English readers. Publishing ten titles in translation each year, Open Letter searches for works that are extraordinary and influential, works that we hope will become the classics of tomorrow.

Making world literature available in English is crucial to opening our cultural borders, and its availability plays a vital role in maintaining a healthy and vibrant book culture. Open Letter strives to cultivate an audience for these works by helping readers discover imaginative, stunning works of fiction and by creating a constellation of international writing that is engaging, stimulating, and enduring.

Current and forthcoming titles from Open Letter include works from Argentina, Catalonia, France, Germany, Iceland, Russia, and numerous other countries.

www.openletterbooks.org